IF I
HAVE
TO BE
HAUNTED

IF I
HAVE
TO BE
HAUNTED

MIRANDA SUN

MAGPIE

To my parents

Magpie Books
An imprint of
HarperCollins*Publishers* Ltd
1 London Bridge Street
London SE1 9GF

www.harpercollins.co.uk

HarperCollins*Publishers*
Macken House
39/40 Mayor Street Upper
Dublin 1
D01 C9W8
Ireland

First published by HarperCollins*Publishers* 2023

1

A catalogue record for this book is available from the British Library

ISBN: 978-0-00-861240-5 (HB)
ISBN: 978-0-00-861241-2 (TPB)

Printed and bound in the UK using 100% renewable electricity
by CPI Group (UK) Ltd

ONE

There was a ghost in the cafeteria again.

Cara stopped dead, shoulders stiffening, fingers tightening on her tray. Her water bottle bounced onto the floor, but she paid it no mind, focused on tracking the silver glow of the specter from the corner of her eye.

Ghosts always got more troublesome this time of year. Last Halloween, a spirit of a teacher from the 1960s, still seething at being fired from Autumn Falls High School, had decided to enact his belated revenge by releasing a horde of rats into the kitchen. Not that Cara had minded the plan itself—when they reopened the cafeteria after a deep clean, the perpetual sour smell of pickles had finally dissipated—it was just the fact that when you saw the dead lurking around, it always meant more trouble for the living.

Milling students shuffled to the side, revealing a man's bleached face, replete with black pipe-cleaner brows.

The heavy backpack slung over Cara's shoulder sank lower in her relief. It was just Mr. Toole, a janitor who'd died a few decades ago from gas buildup in his blocked chimney. She'd found him in an old yearbook after the first time she saw him freshman year. Apparently, carbon monoxide poisoning hadn't stopped him from showing up to work the next day—and for the rest of eternity.

"Cara! Sit down already!" Felicity Qin was twisted around in her seat, waving her arms like one of those people who guide planes to the runways. Across from her, Charlotte Mark waved, too, a tiny tentative movement of her wrist like the flick of a sparrow's wing.

Grinning, Cara scooped up her water bottle. As she sat down next to Felicity at their usual table, her eyes flickered back to Mr. Toole one last time, across the tiles stained with autumn sunlight. Normally he stayed in the south wing, close to the janitor's closet. Why was he sweeping here?

Cara supposed she should just be glad he was the only permanent specter on campus, although another could show up at any time. Her grandmother liked to say that everyone had a ghost waiting inside them, which had been rather scarring to hear as a six-year-old.

Luckily, Mr. Toole had died in a relatively mundane and straightforward manner. He didn't wail for vengeance—mostly just grumbled about *kids these days*. A classic Class B ghost. He was harmless, which made it easy for her to ignore him. It made it easy for her to keep the promise she'd made to her mom at age five: to never let anyone, dead or alive, find out about her ability. The only exception was Cara's grandmother, another ghost speaker.

But then, Laolao was already dead.

Felicity cleared her throat. "So, as I was saying to Charlotte, the French aristocrats' unwillingness to open their bourgeoisie caste to newcomers is today what we call a Bad Move and thus places them firmly at fault for their peasants rising up against them." Felicity dropped her metal spoon like a mic. It landed on top of her blue Jell-O, which rocked at the impact like a choppy ocean.

Cara applauded politely; Felicity bowed her head in acknowledgment.

"I see someone studied last night," Cara said, dipping a languid fry in ketchup. "Meanwhile, I'm not even through the study packet yet."

"Me neither," Charlotte admitted in her soft voice, freckled nose scrunching. Across the table from Felicity, she dragged her fork through her mashed potatoes, rending starchy yellow furrows and setting the mushy peas jittering back and forth in a tiny green earthquake. "I barely understand anything, and half of what I *do* understand is because Felicity just explained it to me now."

Cara smiled. When she was with Felicity and Charlotte, she almost forgot that she wasn't normal. That she didn't just have tests on the French Revolution to worry about but ghosts, too.

The whiff of floor polish and lemon-scented cleaner drifted her way, cold and sharp, and Cara knew without looking that Mr. Toole was close. It was strange, the things death kept. Spirits had no physical bodies, and yet, they often carried the scents of what had surrounded them in life. From how Charlotte and Felicity wrinkled their noses at the smell of bleach whenever the janitor passed by, Cara understood that, even though most people couldn't see ghosts, the dead made their presence known in other ways.

"Seriously, though." Charlotte crossed her arms, leaning forward, curls bouncing. "You guys want to study at the tree house after school?"

Felicity shook her head. "I gotta get some time in with my cello. My recital's coming up, and my parents are making me use all my free time to practice." She pushed up her clear-frame glasses. "Not sure they understand what 'free time' means."

Cara poked Felicity on the arm. "But you just had a recital!"

"Convincing point, although not one I think my parents would respond to. Besides, I made a deal." Felicity's eyes glinted. "If I practice every day this week, they'll let us go to that new haunted house next Friday with Ben and the guys."

"That's the one people are saying really has ghosts, right?" Charlotte asked haltingly.

Oh, no.

Felicity nodded. "Ben and the guys are all making bets on who gets scared the most. And because I know it's illegal to gamble, I only made one small bet—"

"Felicity," Charlotte admonished.

"—that was fifty dollars," Felicity finished.

Charlotte sighed.

"It's not too late to join in on the fun. My bet is Ben won't be able to last twenty minutes—"

"What about our usual Halloween tradition?" Cara tried. "What's wrong with staying inside, watching stupid movies, and eating ten pounds of Reese's Pieces in one night?"

"It's what we've done for forever," Felicity said, chomping down on a carrot stick. It sounded like the crack of a gavel declaring Cara's death sentence. "Not to mention, this is a way better way to celebrate your birthday, don't you think?"

Cara hid a grimace. There was that. Being born on Halloween *and* cursed with the unwanted ability to see ghosts—she couldn't find it more ironic.

"Also," Felicity continued, "I'm going as a woman of science, to prove there aren't any ghosts at this house, because ghosts aren't real."

Here was the problem: unfortunately, ghosts were most certainly real. If there weren't any ghosts at that alleged haunted house, then the worst things that could happen would be that Cara and her friends wasted the five-buck entrance fee and the annual gorging on Reese's Pieces would be slightly postponed. But if there *were* ghosts . . .

They'd be walking right into the specters' domain on the most haunted night of the year.

Halloween was the day the veil between the planes of the living and the dead thinned. The day *all* ghosts, not just the most powerful Class As, possessed the ability to act upon the breathing. Non–ghost speakers still weren't able to see them, but you didn't need to *see* to be scared when a phantom reached into your chest and pulled out your beating heart.

Which, by the way, was *entirely possible* on Halloween.

Laolao, for her part, tried to get the local spirits to behave this time of year, including forbidding them from showing up at haunted house attractions to "show the living how it's really done" in case someone got too suspicious and it ended in people discovering that ghosts were real. But Laolao was just one person, and the dead were many in number—and also bored.

"Please, Cara?" Charlotte said.

"You would think after what happened at the animal shelter last night you'd want to hunker down," Cara said.

"Don't remind me." Charlotte groaned. "That's precisely *why* I need something to take my mind off it."

Charlotte had texted them from where she worked at the animal shelter that the dogs wouldn't stop barking and whining at thin air. At first she'd joked about how they must be haunted—much to Cara's chagrin—until the deer appeared. It was the end of her shift when the dogs went wild again—and when Charlotte glanced out the window, a deer was standing in the parking lot, looking right back at her, dripping in putrid black blood. When she went out to see if she could help it, it had vanished, a pool of dark viscous liquid on the asphalt the only trace of its presence. Even Cara didn't know what to make of that.

"Oh, yes, your *zombie deer*." Felicity said these last two words in a spooky voice, wiggling her fingers at Charlotte. "Maybe we should visit the animal shelter on Halloween instead."

Nope. Absolutely not. Cara had to shut this down. "I'm sorry, guys, but I just don't think I can swing the haunted house."

"Right, the other factor." Felicity snorted. "Is it not on the pre-approved list of places your mom says you can go? We all know it takes five to seven business days to convince your mom to let you do anything that's remotely in the zip code of 'fun.' That's why I'm proposing this now, so you have plenty of time to get your permission slip signed."

"Okay, but—" Cara cut off as she noticed someone storming toward their table. Not a ghost this time. Just Zacharias Coleson, blond-haired and blue-eyed, captain of the swim team, and bane of her existence.

And the bane of her existence looked *pissed*.

"Hey, Tang!" he shouted.

Charlotte, who had abandoned her lunch in favor of drawing Miles Morales surrounded by sunflowers, glanced up from her sketch pad and over her shoulder. She turned to Cara and sighed. "I was hoping we would get a peaceful lunch for once."

"As always, Charlotte, your optimism is endearing but oh so wrong," Felicity said. Taking out a book, she turned to the right, her back to Cara, stretching her lanky legs out across another chair. "Impending nuclear explosion in three . . . two . . . one."

Zach stopped in front of their table, blue eyes iced over and furious.

Cara tilted her head and looked up at him calmly.

"Something wrong, Coleson?"

"Don't act so innocent. Wanna know what I just found in the trash?"

Cara dragged another fry through ketchup. "Oh my God, you finally found yourself!"

Felicity snickered from behind the book she was pretending to read.

"I found this." Zach reached into the pocket of his Arctic-blue windbreaker and slammed a flyer on the table. It was creased and stained from its time in the garbage, but Cara didn't need to read it to know what it said: *Boys Swim Team Tryouts*, with details and whatnot. "All the others were in the trash, too. The hell, Tang?"

People were beginning to look their way, probably intrigued by the prospect of yet another infamous Tang-Coleson fight, but at least the lunch monitor, Mrs. Scanton, hadn't noticed. Thank God.

Cara raised an eyebrow at him.

"So . . . you found all your ads exactly where they belong—the trash—and decided the best course of action was to go dumpster diving in the hallway so that you could then march in here and slam it down on the table, where we're eating?"

A muscle worked in his jaw. "Answer the question."

"Well, Coleson, maybe your papers wouldn't be in the trash if you hadn't put them up over every single freaking flyer for cross-country tryouts, which I know you know I'm the captain of. Yours didn't have time stamps on them, so technically they could be removed without any prior notice."

"AFHS Student Handbook, page twelve, section four point seven," offered Felicity smugly. Without taking her eyes off her book, she raised a palm in Cara's direction. Cara high-fived her.

Zach rolled up his sleeves, baring toned forearms still golden from summer. He leaned forward, hands on the table. Cara stood abruptly, rolling up her own sleeves, chair screeching against the linoleum.

Zach had to jerk back a few degrees to keep their faces apart.

"Here's what you're going to do," he said. "You're going to take all the flyers out of the trash and put them back up. Starting with this one." He shoved the paper at her.

Cara laughed. *Just because his parents are rolling in cash, he thinks he can order anyone around.* "And you think I'm going to listen to you why, exactly?"

"It's not like you've got anything better to do."

"I'm sorry, who was the one who stormed in here and interrupted our conversation? Like, do you ever think about anyone else, or does your ego have a monopoly on all your brain cells up in there?"

"Guys," Charlotte pleaded, but no one paid her any attention.

"Yeah, sure, I bet you all were talking about something super interesting, like your next test."

Cara slammed the flyer onto his chest with a satisfying thud. "You know, refusing to study isn't a personality trait."

Zach yanked the flyer away, making her hand slip away, too. "Neither is staying in all the time and doing nothing but homework."

A collective "*Ooooh*" rose up somewhere to her left, and Cara turned her glare on the perpetrators. A group of theater kids a few tables down had been watching the entire thing with the same interest as if she and Zach were putting on a new production of *Romeo and Juliet*. At Zach's last comment, a few faces from Cara's cross-country team on the other side of the cafeteria tuned in as well. If this escalated any further, the granite-faced lunch monitor was definitely going to notice.

"Okay, keep your voice down," Cara hissed. "You're going to get us in trouble."

"If you're so worried about making a scene, just take the flyer already!" Zach shot back, very much not keeping his voice down.

"Fine!" Cara snatched the flyer off the table, pretending she was surrendering. Then in the blink of an eye, she balled it up, arm swinging to pitch it into the trash.

Just as fast, Zach caught her wrist, sending the throw wide—

Straight into the back of the lunch monitor's head.

The cafeteria quieted. Even Mr. Toole, who had been studiously scrubbing the floor, raised his wizened skull to see what had seized the attention of the living.

Slowly, Mrs. Scanton turned around. Cara swallowed at her stony expression.

"I *told* you," Cara said out of the corner of her mouth, watching Mrs. Scanton approach. The lunch monitor's pace was slow and unhurried, as if she were relishing the anticipation of laying down a punishment. "Oh, my mom's going to kill me." Her grandmother, too. Cara could already hear Laolao's disapproving exhale. The old ghost had had all of life—and death—to perfect that so-disappointed-but-I-won't-say-it-out-loud sigh that made Cara shrink instantly.

"Relax," Zach said, leaning back against the lunch table with his hands in his pockets, completely at ease even as Mrs. Scanton got close enough that the red veins of her eyes were visible. "I'll handle this."

Before the lunch monitor could open her mouth, Zach grinned, broad and winning. "How are you doing today, Mrs. Scanton?"

Mrs. Scanton gaped. "How am I doing today?" she sputtered. "You two threw trash at the back of my head. I should give you detention."

"Over a simple misunderstanding?"

"A simple misunderstanding," Mrs. Scanton said flatly.

"We were playing a game of catch when Tang's throw went wide."

Cara shot him an incredulous look. He was lying through his perfect white teeth, and he was still finding room to blame her.

Ignoring her glower, Zach continued smiling at Mrs. Scanton. "Last time you tried busting us, Principal Olan just let us go. You wouldn't want to waste his time again, would you?"

When Mrs. Scanton was silent, a grudging look on her face, he added, "Your sister's charity auction is next week, right? I'll have to ask my mom if she's still donating that Sargent painting—it was worth half a million dollars the last time she got it valued."

"Oh. Oh, yes." Mrs. Scanton opened her mouth, flapping her hands, then nodded sharply, seeming to come to a decision. "I'll leave you two with a very harsh warning, then. And I'll see your mother's painting next week."

As Mrs. Scanton retreated, Zach turned to Cara with a smug look. "See? No problem."

Unbelievable. "Unfortunately, the problem is *you*." She scowled at him. A six-foot-two-tall problem with messy dark gold hair, unjustifiably impeccable cheekbones, and the unique ability to get under her skin and make her lose her cool like nothing else. "Not everyone can pull out their rich-parents card, Coleson."

So what if Zach's dad was the inheritor of the largest logging company in the region and his mom was the curator of what was allegedly the most prestigious—and pretentious—art gallery in Autumn Falls? So what if their house had been in their possession for generations and was newly renovated and could fit Cara's home in three times over with room to spare? So what if he got a new car for his sixteenth birthday last year and didn't have to rely on car pools to get to practice like some people?

It didn't make him any better than anyone else, despite what he thought.

Zach crossed his arms, leaning closer. "You know, you should be thanking me. I got us both out of trouble."

Cara ground her teeth. She hated his privilege, but she had also benefited from it, however reluctantly. It wasn't like she wanted her mother to know about the weekly arguments with him she somehow got herself into, and she definitely didn't want to be lectured for hours by Laolao. Being a ghost—and Chinese—her grandmother never ran out of breath during a scolding.

"You got yourself *into* trouble by taping your dumb swim team flyers over my cross-country ones."

He smirked, cocking his head toward the bulletin board on the cafeteria wall. "You missed one, by the way."

Indeed, a blue swim team flyer hung between a homeroom bake sale advertisement and a poster about some silent auction. It shouldn't have been possible for a piece of paper to look smug, but because it was Zach's, it managed it.

"Hey, you two."

Startled, Cara looked at Felicity. She'd been so wrapped up in bickering with Zach, she'd almost forgotten they weren't alone. The irritation his presence always inspired tended to narrow her vision.

"If you're quite done arguing for the day," Felicity continued as Cara sat back down, "Charlotte's been trying to ask you a question, Zach."

Zach turned to Charlotte, who, under the sudden spotlight of his gaze, ducked her head, shoulders rounded, cheeks aglow.

"You're still bringing your swim team to the bake sale/adoption day event at the animal shelter this weekend, right?" Charlotte asked shyly.

"Of course. The whole crew," Zach said, in a tone friendlier than he'd ever used with Cara. "I promised I would."

Cara scoffed under her breath, a reply about the worth of Zach's promises forming on her lips, but at that moment, silver flashed through the cafeteria again, and two new ghosts, a man and a woman she'd never seen before, came into focus.

Usually when ghosts stepped into high-traffic areas for the breathing, they drifted about, people-watching. But these ghosts moved with purpose, stopping at each table and peering down, not just people-watching but seeming to observe clinically, conferring with each other before moving on to the next table. Sometimes they would boldly stick their hands into people, making students choke on their food. But whatever they were looking for, they didn't seem to find it, even when they clearly got a reaction: students looking around for whoever or whatever had flung their jacket or pinched their nose shut or knocked their tray onto the floor.

Dread filled her stomach. *They're testing if people can see them.* Table by table, the specters canvassed the cafeteria, slowly making their way toward her.

Should she get up? Could she leave the cafeteria while they were occupied? Or would the pair notice and look at her even more suspiciously?

Zach had the audacity to snap his fingers in her face. "What are you staring at? I'm right here and you're looking at something else?"

In an instant, Cara grabbed his wrist and yanked it away from her face. "Could you be any more obnoxious?"

"Is that a challenge?"

"You just can't stand it when you don't have my attention."

His voice was low and laced with satisfaction. "And you're only too willing to give it to me."

Heat radiated through the sleeve of Zach's windbreaker, his pulse coursing against her fingertips. At the same moment, they both seemed to realize that she was still holding on to him. She dropped his arm with disgust as he yanked it back, crossing his arms over his chest.

"This is useless," a crisp female voice said, and only years of training kept Cara from reacting. "Let's go. God, I hate teenagers."

In her peripheral vision, she could see the two new ghosts were standing in front of her table. Now that she wasn't focused on Zach, goose bumps prickled her skin from their presence.

"Aw, but it's free entertainment," the man said. "Do you think if we throw popcorn at them, they'll fight some more?"

The woman shook her head. "The girl didn't even shiver at our chill. We've got a lot of ground to cover and we don't have much time." She turned on her heel.

"You're no fun," the man groused, but floated after her a moment later.

Heart in her throat, Cara shifted subtly in her seat to watch their backs recede out of the corner of her eye. The ghosts crossed the cafeteria and seemed to ask Mr. Toole questions; what exactly, she couldn't hear. He shook his head no, pointing at the exit. With a nod of thanks, the ghosts floated through, and Cara could breathe again.

"You really are distracted today," Zach said.

Amateur move, she scolded herself. Usually she wasn't so caught up in watching ghosts that other people noticed, but she'd never seen ghosts behave in such a calculated way before. These hadn't been randomly messing with people for fun like poltergeists, and it wasn't the usual pre-Halloween theatrics, either. They'd been after something.

Glowering at Zach, she made a show of wiping the hand that had touched him on her thigh. "Don't you have flyers to put up?"

He smirked. "*Ouch*," he said in exaggerated offense, and shoved away from the table to leave.

Cara scanned the cafeteria again. Even though only Mr. Toole remained, sedate and benign, a shiver ran through her bones. She shook off the cold, tried to ignore it like it was another ghost, but it settled, stayed.

That was the trouble with seeing the dead. They never quite seemed to leave.

TWO

Getting home from school was a feat when you had a single mother who was always working. Cara's mother usually threw her to the mercy of Charlotte's charity and car. But during the lead-up to Halloween when ghosts were more active, roaming about and looking for trouble, Cara's mother insisted on driving her to school and back to make it less likely that Cara accidently revealed her power. It made Cara feel like she was twelve years old and not someone with her own driver's license who was about to turn seventeen. But when Cara had expressed her desire not to be chaperoned from place to place, her mother had said the only other option was for Cara to stay at home for the entire week before Halloween.

And so here she was, sitting cross-legged on a stone bench outside Autumn Falls High School, doing her homework and waiting.

All around her, students streamed from the doors, heading home. Some hung out on benches and under trees, chatting with friends a little while longer. Just close enough that she could overhear, Zach himself was holding court, leaning on the flagpole with a pack of his swim team buddies gathered around him.

One guy, chugging a blue Gatorade at an alarming rate said, "Your parents are out of town this weekend, right?"

Zach scuffed the concrete with his shoe. "Yeah. They leave tonight and they won't be back until after Halloween."

"Oh man, we should totally throw a Halloween party," another friend with bleached-blond hair chimed in. "Shaft, you still have the fog machine you never gave back to your cousin, right?"

When Shaft, the fog-machine-stealing cousin, nodded, the guy with bleached-blond hair fist pumped. "Come on, man, let's do it."

Zach looked around at everyone, making them wait for his answer. Finally he laughed and nodded, upon which his group of friends cheered and whooped loud enough to startle a flock of birds out of a nearby tree.

The Gatorade guy was on his second bottle. "Man, you're so lucky. I love your parents. They're always out of town. Your maids gave out the *biggest* candy bars when we were kids."

The bleached-blond guy patted the Gatorade guy on the back. "Whoa, slow down there, buddy. That's not vodka in there, is it? Because if it is, you're gonna have to share."

The Gatorade guy hunched over his bottle protectively. "For your information, I am getting hydrated. And there's nothing in here but the power of pure electrolytes."

Pencil poised over her math homework, Cara didn't even need to see Zach to know he was smiling and nodding, letting his friends regale him with talk about how sick the party was going to be.

Zach had a reputation for amazing parties. It started with his birthday parties—from ice sculptures to petting zoos; it was a spectacle everyone looked forward to each December when they were younger. Now that she thought of it, Cara couldn't remember Zach's parents at those parties, either—it was always a housekeeper who brought out the cake.

A car horn blared through her thoughts.

Heads whipped in the direction of the sound, then turned to Cara. For the second time that afternoon, all eyes were on her.

"Just when I thought this day couldn't get any worse," she muttered.

From the curbside pickup/drop-off area, the horn blared again. Then a third time.

What had she done to deserve this?

If only luck could save her from the wrath of her mother standing by the open driver's door of their car, one hand ready on the horn, the other waving her over.

Cara refused to run to her execution, but she wasn't above picking up the pace. As she hurried past Zach, he remarked, "Looks like someone's in trouble," in a mocking tone.

Without breaking stride, she raised a middle finger in his general direction. She couldn't see his face, but the ensuing snickers of his buddies were satisfaction enough.

"You didn't have to use the horn," Cara muttered in English as she slid into the passenger seat.

"Why not?" her mother replied, starting the engine and nosing their small red car toward the exit. "It's not as if it could embarrass you more than you've already embarrassed yourself by fighting in the cafeteria again." She spoke in a mixture of English and Chinese.

How had her mother already heard about it? Had to be the Chinese-immigrant parent grapevine. "It wasn't my—"

"Stop. I don't want to hear it." Her mother stared ahead, eyes trained on the road. "We'll discuss this at home."

"But—"

"Do you want us to get into a car accident and die? That's what will happen if you keep talking. I need to concentrate."

Stifling a noise of frustration, Cara fell back into her seat. The power lines zipped by outside. She'd lost count of how many times her mother had said those exact words to her before. Cara's mother treated driving like an extreme sport—one she played only because it was necessary for survival. On the road, there were so many factors her mother couldn't control: the traffic lights, pedestrians, other people's cars. It was like Cara's driving instructor had told their class: *When you're driving, everybody else on the road is stupid.*

And everybody else could get you killed.

Cara didn't know where her mother's obsession with death had come from, whether it was something specific to Chinese people or just her. Once, Cara's mother had seen spirits lurking in the dark, too. But she'd turned her eyes past them in fear, repressing the sight until one day, playing pretend had become real, and she could no longer see the dead.

Cara rolled the window down as far as it would go—which was halfway, because her mother had bought the car used and this window always jammed—and propped her chin in her palm, the wind caressing her face. On either side of the avenue, trees stretched into the crisp blue sky, their crimson leaves so brilliant it was as if they'd been enchanted. Cara's house sat on the outskirts of Autumn Falls, in the shadow of the forest called the Wildwoods. Getting there from school meant navigating the narrow cobblestone streets of downtown, with its boutique shops and restaurants. Courtesy of a shop-local policy, exactly one chain restaurant existed: a Panera.

Cara blinked when their car pulled into a parking space in front of the mom-and-pop grocery store.

"I need to pick up a few groceries," her mother said.

Cara sat up. "I could go in with you," she offered, but her mother gave her a look that said, *No amount of sucking up is going to get you out of this one*, and closed the door.

She watched her mother stop on the way in to talk with a store worker about the squashes outside. The man tipped his ear closer, his eyebrows contorting into that polite *sorry-I-don't-understand-what-you're-saying* expression Cara had learned to recognize when she was five years old. People tended to use it around her mother, even as her English had gotten better and better after she strove to hide the clumsy edges of her speech, to put the correct stresses on the correct syllables, to add *s*'s at the ends of plural words when necessary. To master the kind of speaking prized in the world they lived in.

Cara tensed as her mother went through the motions of explaining again, watching to see if she needed to step in. Once, in third grade, Cara had been summoned to the principal's office because her mother had called about a field trip she wasn't sure Cara should go on, but no one in the office could understand her mother's "dialect." Never mind that "dialect" was the wrong word to use, and if they had bothered to listen a little harder, a little more, they wouldn't have needed an eight-year-old to interpret for a full-grown adult.

But the man's face relaxed, lips splitting into a relieved smile. He nodded, tapping one of the lumpy, orange-and-yellow-striped gourds stacked by the chalkboard sign.

Then a flash of silver past her window distracted her. Cara turned in her seat, watching a spectral woman drift to the cozy coffee shop across the street, the Red Leaf Café. When there weren't cross-country competitions, she worked double shifts there on weekends to earn cash for her dog, Blaze's, necessities, her college fund, and pocket money.

Enough warmth still haunted the late October air that patrons could sit on the patio, enjoying the last of the season's sunshine as they sipped their coffees. One of those patrons was a man tapping his foot beneath the wrought-iron bistro table and checking his watch every two seconds. He would have looked perfectly normal, had he not been outlined in characteristic silver all the way from the little errant strands of his otherwise neatly combed brown hair to his dusty penny loafers. The potted plant sitting behind him was as visible as if his chest were a windowpane.

According to her classification system, he was probably Class B, harmless.

The ghost that had initially caught Cara's attention stopped in front of him, and he looked up, wonder passing over his face, his jaw slack. Then he jumped up, nearly upending the table in his haste to pull out another chair. The woman's back was mostly to Cara, but part of her face was visible, adorned with wrinkles, shining with stronger silver than his—she'd died far more recently. She looked decades older than him, her wispy gray hair bound back into a modest bun, but as they took each other's hands, their eyes fluttering closed, their forms flickered and reversed through time, the teenagers they had once been sliding into existence like old sepia photographs pulled from a yearbook. His brown suit rippling into a blue-and-gold Autumn Falls letterman jacket. Her plain black gown transforming into a flouncy red A-line dress.

When they opened their eyes, their forms settled back, but Cara could still see the high school sweethearts they had been, their past lives glowing inside them like flames inside glass lanterns. They continued holding hands, seemingly content simply to gaze at each other, and Cara wondered how long he had been waiting for her.

When Cara was younger, Laolao had told her about the red string of fate in Chinese culture. So many threads of blood in your body, and one of them became a string that connected your heart to the heart yours was meant to be with, the person whose side you'd eventually end up at. The thread could snarl itself in knots, stretch out over chasms and continents, but it wouldn't break, and one day it would lead you to love, to another hand whose little finger was tied with your string.

The pinkie finger was the more modern version, but the stories first said it was the ankle that was encircled with thread. Cara had giggled, imagining how hard it must have been to walk without tripping. People falling into the arms of their lovers.

Maybe this couple, after all this time, had followed their red strings to the ends to find each other.

A cart rattled up to the car, and Cara's thoughts snapped back to reality. To her mother, who shopped for groceries alone, the wedding ring missing from her finger.

No, red strings weren't a thing at all.

Cara jumped out to help. Silently, they began loading the purchases in the back.

Across the street, another couple sat down at the same table, not seeing that it was technically already occupied. The girl shivered, most likely from the cold the ghosts caused, and rubbed her arms. Smoothly, the guy shrugged off his jacket, draping it over her shoulders.

What did ghosts think of humans? When they witnessed them picnic on graves, laughter spilling from the living's lips like wine, like blood?

She imagined it was a little like standing in the dark outside a house you used to live in, peering through the window as the new inhabitants hosted a dinner party. The familiarity of what was once home at odds with strangers who sat where you'd sat, breathed where you'd breathed. The ache of a welcome mat no longer meant for you, set before a threshold you could cross on the way out but not the way back in. The people that paid you no mind—they couldn't see you, not with the world so bright inside and that terrifying blackness beyond the windowpane, that veil of eternal night, that lack of stars.

To be a ghost speaker was to push that curtain aside. To look into the dark and see something looking back.

For a moment, Cara watched the two sets of couples, one corporeal, the other a figment, thinking the two ghosts would stay there nonetheless, laughing at the living. But then the man shook his head, lips pulling into a rueful smile, and stood, offering his hand. "Come," he said. "It's a bad time to be a ghost in Autumn Falls. Now that you're here we should go elsewhere—until this all blows over."

The woman took his hand. "How long will that be?"

"Until they find the ghost speaker."

The ghost speaker?

Cara startled. Did they mean Laolao? But all the ghosts knew of Laolao. There was only one other ghost speaker in Autumn Falls that Cara knew . . . herself. But they couldn't mean her, could they?

Her blood went cold. Was that why those two new ghosts had been in the cafeteria today, acting odd and trying to get the attention of the living, trying to get them to react? She'd thought they were just messing around, but had they been looking for *her*?

Hand in hand, the couple walked off down the street, their steps stirring fallen autumn leaves. Their joined hands passed through an old woman Laolao's age, whose rose brooch took on a brief bloody glow lit by the specters' skin. She didn't even flinch.

Cara didn't notice that all the groceries were now in the car until her mother impatiently got her attention. She numbly climbed back into the passenger seat, distracted by her thoughts. They were almost home when a woman walked out in front of their car. Head down, her hair swinging in her face, not noticing death barreling toward her.

"Mom!" Cara gasped, jolting in her seat. "There's— Stop the car!"

Her mother slammed the brakes. Tires screeched.

"What, Cara?" Her mother's hands tightened around the steering wheel, bones of her knuckles shining white through the skin.

Behind them, a car honked impatiently.

"There was a—"

Heart thudding, Cara looked back at the walker, almost to the other side of the road now. This time, with the angle of the sun to the side of the woman and not directly behind her, the silver marking her form stood out against the shadows painting the fence along the sidewalk. Clear as moonlight.

"—a ghost," she finished quietly.

Her mother shook her head, accelerating again. It wasn't fast enough for the BMW behind them, who darted out in the adjacent lane, zooming toward the intersection to cross before the light went red.

"What have I told you?" her mother said. "Don't talk to ghosts. Don't think about them. Don't—"

Up ahead, rubber screeched. Cut off. The distinct crunch of metal meeting metal.

They skidded to a halt again, this time in front of the light, with a perfect view of the wreckage.

The driver of the BMW had made it to the other side of the intersection, just not in the way they would have wanted to. A man had stumbled out of the driver's seat, his hand pressed to his bleeding temple. Eyes wide, he turned to his car, then to the brown Kia he'd slammed into. The driver of that car must have continued forward when the light turned green, thinking it was safe.

The female ghost that had initially crossed the street drew closer, staring fixedly at the accident. Other spirits began to arrive: a young girl in a baseball uniform, bat swinging from her left hand, bruises marking her skinny arms; a man with a broken neck, eyeing the scene at an angle; a woman in a long, white, bloodstained gown, bearing a gray-skinned baby in her arms, its wide eyes unblinking.

If her mother had still been able to see ghosts, she would have called these spirits sharks, sensing the blood in the water. Cara liked to think of the gathering spirits as guides, welcoming another home.

This was how she knew, with a sickening certainty that made her stomach hurt, there would be no one stumbling out of the driver's seat of the other car.

No one alive, at least.

Death this loud drew ghosts. The broken glass shattering the air, the keening of sirens, the resounding silence of a stopped heart. The world folding and creating something so terrible nobody could look away, not even the dead.

From the crumpled hatchback emerged a young woman, body framed in silver, chest covered in blood, and the ghosts surged forward to enclose her. Cara curled her hands into fists, digging her nails into her palms. It wasn't fair. The woman—girl, really—had done nothing wrong. Just been in the wrong place at the wrong time. Unlike the other driver, standing there uselessly with only a little blood on his face, when both his hands should be covered in red.

But not everyone who deserved to die did, and not everyone who died deserved it. And you couldn't undo death.

The other aspect of Cara's powers—the one she rarely wanted to acknowledge because it was too big, too daunting—was her ability to help a new spirit pass over. She could do that much, but she couldn't right what was wrong. A ghost was a soul cut loose from the body, and there was no stitch she knew that could tie the two back together.

Cara reached for her mom instinctively, like a little kid. Her mom glanced at her but didn't ask what she'd seen. Instead, hesitantly but firmly, her mom squeezed her hand, holding it as they drove slowly home.

THREE

"It was horrible, Laolao." Cara flung her backpack onto the floor by her desk and sank onto her bed. "I know you always say that everyone has their time, but it didn't have to happen like that."

"Oh, Cara." Her grandmother crossed over the floorboards toward her, stepping daintily around the mess Cara's room always seemed to degrade into—clothes lying forgotten underfoot like leaves, textbooks scattered across the floor as if by autumnal wind, cross-country trophies on her shelf proud under a silver sheen of dust. Laolao could have floated across, but it was a choice she made. Doing human stuff made her feel more human.

Laolao leaned down and hugged her, encircling her in the scent of jasmine hand cream and the incense-like fragrance of the ghost tree Laolao kept alive in the backyard. Cara froze—physical affection from her grandmother was rare. Not to mention that Laolao could touch her—Cara could feel her arms around her—but Cara couldn't return the touch. Trying not to shiver from the chill, Cara hugged her back the best she could, hovering her arms just above Laolao's shoulders. Sticking your hands in a specter and flaunting your corporeality was considered incredibly rude. Death could lay its hands on you, but you couldn't do the same.

This was how it was with a ghost for a grandmother. Cara

sometimes envied Felicity, who had family all over the States, who flew to Beijing every June to see her grandparents. Cara would never have a grandmother who sent her hongbao through WeChat for Chinese New Year, who took her out for dim sum brunch on late Sunday mornings. Cara would never have a grandmother who slipped her chocolate coins in shiny gold foil, who was always willing to eat the orange egg yolk in moon cakes that Cara hated, who pressed unwrapped milky strawberry candies into her palm, little pink lozenges that melted in her mouth, a sweetness she could taste, something *solid* she could hold.

Cara only had this—these fleeting moments when her grandmother wrapped her arms around her, when she could pretend, just for a heartbeat, that Cara was hugging her back.

In moments like these, grief weighed her down. The strange, unexplainable kind of grief her bones had always known, made from mourning someone who had been buried before you were born, someone who had never been anything but lost to you.

Laolao drew away, putting a hand on Cara's shoulder and meeting Cara's ghost-seeing eyes with her own. Both pairs dark brown, so dark they appeared black.

"Don't fret." Laolao patted her reassuringly. Though Laolao was well-versed in English, having briefly lived in the States for a handful of years as a young woman, she preferred speaking Chinese. "I will help her pass on if she wants. I shouldn't have any trouble finding her, if there were so many ghosts there."

Not only did ghosts congregate around death, they liked to gossip about it. It was their favorite topic. Go figure.

Still, the crunch of metal rang in Cara's ears. When Cara looked down, twisting her fingers in her lap, Laolao sighed and sat down next to her, shifting the comforter on the bed not one bit. "We come from death. We cannot change it. We cannot ignore it. But what we can do, xiaogui"—Laolao cupped Cara's face, looking her in the eye— "is decide how we live with it."

Xiaogui. A term of endearment used for children, quite literally meaning *little ghost.* Something Cara's mother had never called her.

Cara gave her grandmother a smile and nodded. She wanted to talk about it more, to have someone else recognize how close she'd been to the scene, to take her shoulder and say, *How scary. I'm glad that wasn't you.* But her mother would only reply, "What more is there to say? I was there. I know what happened."

And death had not scared her grandmother for a long, long time.

When Laolao was six, her entire family had perished in a terrible fire. After that, Laolao had started seeing spirits, the tragedy waking the latent ability in her veins. Her aunt, who had eight children of her own, had taken her in but was resentful of an extra mouth to feed and was especially hard on Laolao, forcing her to "earn her keep" by always giving her interminable lists of chores to do that kept her out past dark when spirits were known to roam. Her cousins ignored her as if she were a stray dog who had wandered in. Lonely down to her bones, Laolao prayed to her ancestors—and they answered. They helped her draw water, told her where the wild quail nested, wove stories to cheer her up and pass down their knowledge. In return, she took care of their graves, brushing away dirt, burning incense, offering food, so that their tombs were always clean even outside of Qingming Jie, the holiday specially dedicated to tomb sweeping.

When Laolao had had no one else, she'd had her ghosts.

Standing in a rush of cold air, Laolao shuffled across the room in her tan bamboo slippers, where she began rearranging the items scattered across Cara's dresser. Her silver glow was far brighter than most, a sign of her power as a Class A specter. Laolao was wearing one of her favorite outfits, a pink-and-purple paisley silk blouse and loose black pants, with her thick, wavy, short gray hair carefully arranged. Plastic amber-framed glasses perched on the end of her nose.

"You know," Laolao began innocently, moving a tiny ceramic yellow-and-white hand-painted horse Charlotte had given Cara, "you could help me help the girl cross over. Use some of that magic I gave you, hmm?"

Cara had known what her grandmother was going to say the second she heard the crafty tone in Laolao's voice, but she waited until Laolao had finished. Though dead herself, Laolao still did her ghost-speaking duties. Helping ghosts move on—another one of those activities normal people didn't do. It wasn't like Cara could add "Volunteered at Phantom Hotline" to her Common App.

"You know I won't. Mom—"

"Yes, your mother does not want you to." Laolao shook her head. Cara's mother and grandmother disagreed on how she should use her powers. Both thought she should follow in their footsteps—learning from her grandmother how to harness her ghost-speaking abilities or copying her mother in pretending they didn't exist at all.

Sometimes it felt like Cara would always be caught between her grandmother and her mother, the dead and the living. Despite being in the same house, Laolao and her mother didn't speak to each other. It wasn't Cara's mother's loss of ghost speaking that stopped them—it had happened long before that and was a loss that ran far deeper, a loss of trust.

Here was the family history Cara had gathered:

Her grandmother had come to the States as a young woman. She'd even found love and married a handsome young Chinese American man, but when a tragedy took him from her soon after, leaving her alone with an infant, she'd returned to China. She would never marry again. Cara's mother would grow up in China, move to America, have Cara. Laolao and Cara's mother would reside on opposite sides of the Pacific Ocean until Laolao showed up as a ghost right after Cara's fifth birthday—and even then, they wouldn't talk.

Cara still didn't know exactly what the rift was between them, but she could put together a skeleton of a guess from the bitter bones her mother and Laolao had dropped over the years. It had to do with ghosts, of course. Laolao paying more attention to the dead than to her own *living* daughter. A final disagreement about the man Cara's mother was determined to marry—a man who she would divorce two years after the wedding.

But whatever harm Laolao had passed down to Cara's mother, Laolao seemed determined not to pass down to Cara. Warmth swelled in Cara's chest at the sight of her grandmother humming an old Chinese song under her breath and sweeping away dust. A bad mother but a good grandmother. A flawed human being but a better ghost.

Still, Cara knew that underneath Laolao's cheerful demeanor, she was disappointed—though she tried hard not to show it—that her granddaughter hadn't fully embraced her abilities. The inheritance of magic, the cursed heirloom that Laolao's descendants didn't want around their necks. *It is our heritage,* Laolao had told her. *It runs in our marrow like a river. Some of ancient China's first stories were ghost stories.*

"Aiya, zhen kexi," Laolao continued with her back to Cara, stacking the books on Cara's dresser into a neat pile. "Leaving your poor old grandmother to take care of all the ghosts in this town." She turned around, and the twinkle in her eye let Cara know that Laolao was poking fun at her. "I have had my hands full helping spirits pass on lately."

Cara sat up, her grandmother's words ringing a bell. "I overheard a couple specters say they needed to get out of town today," she began. "They were looking for the ghost speaker."

"Ah, a lot of dead look for me."

"But wouldn't they already know who you are? It was like they were looking for . . ."

Laolao had gone still, holding tight to a silver frame of an old photo of Cara and her mom. It was as if a great invisible hand had reached out and pressed Pause on her grandmother. There was a beat before she spoke, her voice measured. "For what?"

Cara's door pushed open of its own accord, and she looked up, alarmed, her thoughts darting to spirits, as they always did—but then a shiny black nose appeared.

"Blaze!" Cara exclaimed, forgetting all talk of ghosts for a moment. "Come here, boy."

With a jingle of dog tags, her golden retriever happily flung himself into Cara's arms.

"Oh, what have you been rolling in?" Cara scrunched up her nose. "You need a bath."

Blaze panted and licked her face, not registering a single word she'd said.

Her mother shouted her name from downstairs.

"What?" Cara yelled from her room. No answer. She moved to the railing, Blaze at her heels, and yelled again. A delicious aroma was coming from the kitchen.

Cara groaned in frustration. Why did parents call you just to say nothing when you answered them?

"I think," Laolao said mildly, joining Cara at the railing, "that it might be time for you to go to dinner."

Once they were seated in front of their food, Cara's mother wasted no time getting into everything she'd held back in the car. "What were you thinking today? I don't send you to school for you to make an embarrassment of yourself. You are there to earn good grades and get into a good college.

"And if you get into one more fight with *that boy*"—Cara's mother always referred to Zach as "that boy" with contempt in her voice— "I'll march into school and drag you out of there myself." She shook her head. "It's time to grow up. You are grounded for a week."

Protests stuck in Cara's windpipe, burnt grains of rice, but the tone in her mother's voice brooked no argument. Cara swallowed and nodded. She picked with her chopsticks at the mackerel marinated in soy sauce and sugar. Before eating, she'd need to search the tender flesh for bones. With the way this day was going, she'd probably miss one and choke on it.

But she'd rather do that than ask for help right now.

Her mother cleared her throat. "I'll take out the bones for you."

When Cara hesitated, her mother waved for her to pass her bowl over, impatient. Cara knew picking out the bones herself wouldn't be hard, but having her mother do it was comforting. It reminded her of being younger, when she didn't have to worry about specters haunting the halls at school, when the weight of college and how they'd pay for it didn't loom over her head, when the future didn't seem like some dark road twisted and looped like a noose, going nowhere except around her neck.

Cara's mother excised the bones from the chunks of pan-seared fish with surgical precision. She always got short-tempered around Halloween. In September, she'd glance casually at the calendar on the kitchen wall while cooking, and then she'd glance again, scrutinizing the days left in the month. When it got close enough for decorations, she'd eye the neighbors' jack-o'-lanterns with distrust and draw the curtains shut even during the day. In the week leading up to it, she'd jump at any sound, scold Cara for leaving a window open and making her think the draft was a ghost. Would her mother apologize for any of it? Never.

At least, not out loud.

When Cara's mother took out the bones, she was saying, *I'm sorry, I can't help that it's like this.*

And when Cara took her bowl back, she was saying, *It's okay.*

"I know you don't like hearing it, but it's my job to tell you these things," her mother continued. "Not just about that boy." Her mother reached for another piece of fish. "The world is dangerous. Just look at what happened today on the road. So scary."

That was how it went: Cara messed up, her mother matter-of-factly dealt out the scolding and/or punishment, and then proceeded as if everything was normal. Cara just ate her food, glad this time wasn't worse, as her mother chattered about the good deal she got at the grocery store that the clerk almost cheated her out of: "Always check your receipt, Cara. They double charge you for one item all the time and make you spend more money!"

When her mother told her about a (probably fake) video Ben's mother, Wu Ayi, had sent her, Cara suppressed the urge to tell her mother that you couldn't trust anything you see on the internet. Instead, she nodded along as she always did, mind preoccupied with the ghosts in the cafeteria. Why had Laolao acted so startled to hear they were looking for the ghost speaker?

Cara sighed and glanced out the window at the backyard.

"Did you roll your eyes at me?" her mother said sharply.

"What? No, I was just looking away—"

But her mother wasn't listening. "Butinghua de haizi," she said, clicking her tongue, then pointed her chopsticks at her. "Sit up straight. Who will want to marry you when your back is always hunched?"

Cara adjusted her spine a fraction to be the ninety degrees her mother wanted.

Normally, putting up with her mother's one-sided conversation was fine. It was normal. The unsolicited advice, telling her stories about random people when she didn't care about any of it. Laolao had the ghost community to talk to, the spirits she worked with to help pass over. Cara had her friends. But Cara's mother mostly just had her.

"Ni xiang shenme ne?"

Cara blinked. Her mother was looking at her expectantly.

Like Cara could tell her what she was actually thinking about. "Nothing," Cara said. "I'm listening."

Cara's mother laid down her chopsticks. "Ni meiyou. Are you still thinking about the car crash? This is why you need to always be careful when driving. Don't grab for space, go slow—"

"No, it's not that," Cara said before her mother could launch into another one of her lectures. Before Cara could think better of it, she said, "There were these ghosts in the cafeteria today—I didn't speak to them," she added hurriedly as her mother's fingers tightened around her chopsticks. "But—these ghosts didn't act like they usually do. I think they were looking for me. They wanted a ghost speaker."

"What have I told you? Suppress your powers and leave this ghost nonsense behind."

Cara stifled a sigh. It had been a mistake to tell her mother what she was really thinking. She shouldn't have expected any other response. "And then I would stop seeing Laolao," she returned. Something had lodged in her throat, making it hard to swallow—there must have been a bone in the fish after all. "She actually tries to understand me, to help me. Why can't you support me like she does?"

"Support you? Do you know how I know you were fighting with that Coleson boy again? Because this afternoon, your grandmother left me a passive-aggressive note telling me all about it. Telling me to parent my child better. Apparently, when you behave, you're her granddaughter, but when you don't, you're my daughter." Her mother smirked at Cara's silence. "Those ghosts in the cafeteria you mentioned. They weren't looking for a ghost speaker, they were checking up on you. Must have been sent by your grandmother to do it. Go ahead and defend her. I'll wait."

Underneath the table, Cara dug her nails into her palms until it hurt.

Her mother laughed humorlessly as she continued. "You think your grandmother has your best interests at heart? You don't know her like I do. She wants you to keep your powers for her own selfish reasons."

That's not true, Cara wanted to say, but she kept quiet. What was the use? It wouldn't be worth the breath. Reasoning with her mother was useless—she had her own logic. She heard only what she wanted to hear.

Cara's stomach hurt from swallowing her words.

She wondered, not for the first time, how much different things would be if her parents hadn't divorced when she was just a year old, too young to remember anything of her dad. Maybe he would be on her side, persuading her mother to go easier on her. Maybe he'd side with her mother, shaking his head sternly and presenting a united front but offering her a smile after dinner. She pictured her dad sitting at the table, asking her to pass the hot chili oil or fishing for compliments about the youtiao he'd fried. A little sister, maybe, perpetually annoying, always tattling, fighting with her over the last slice of pizza. A normal family.

Ghosts that never were.

The real world shuttered back in. Her dad was a faceless shadow, and the only things she had of him were the shade of her hair and her last name.

It was just her and her mother, positioned across from each other like chess pieces at their chipped dinner table, silence creeping in like dusk.

Cara's mother sighed. "I don't say these things to hurt you, you know. You have your grandmother's eyes. But you do not have to do what she did. People who say they see ghosts don't go to Harvard. They go to mental institutions."

God, the number of times Cara had heard her mother say that before. She opened her mouth to protest—then shut it. No matter what she said, her mother wouldn't change her mind.

There were so many things stacked against Cara in this world. Child of an immigrant, daughter of a single mom. People looked at her face and expected someone passive, someone who didn't know how to speak English or fight back. Her mother was probably right: she didn't need to add the problems of the dead to her own.

Going to a good college wouldn't merely be an accomplishment anyone would be proud of—it would be a way out. A lit path in the dark woods, leading to a better life than the one her mother had. All her mother wanted was to give it to her.

So Cara stayed quiet.

They ate in silence until her mother finished the last bit of rice in her bowl, then got up and washed the bowl before wordlessly leaving the room.

Alone at the table, Cara set her chopsticks down and closed her eyes. Well, wasn't this a perfect way to cap off the day?

According to Laolao, there were other magical families in Autumn Falls, drawn by the liminal river that flowed hidden in the Wildwoods.

Can they all speak to ghosts, too? Cara had asked Laolao hopefully, six years old and wanting not to be alone.

No, Laolao had told her. *The world has many magics, not all of them like yours.* Some people could summon storms or, with one gesture, grow oaks from saplings. Some could scry the future—albeit a cloudy one—in fragrant tea leaves at the bottoms of bone china cups. And some could heal a bleeding wound in seconds, sealing it up without a scar, as if the skin had never known the knife. With a proud smile, Laolao had said, *You are the only one who can talk to ghosts.*

Cara hadn't learned how to pretend to be happy yet, so she'd ducked her head instead, hiding the disappointment on her face. She'd wanted someone else like her, someone living, someone she could confide in, share her experiences with. Laolao had knelt and brushed Cara's hair out of her eyes, then lifted Cara's chin with corpse-cold fingers, forcing Cara to look at her. *Your sight is your greatest power, xiaogui. The greatest thing I could ever give you. Your mother didn't understand that, but I know you will.*

What would it have been like to grow up in one of those other magical families instead? Cara bet their dinners would never be this lonely.

There was one more piece of mackerel in her bowl, and Cara had been raised to never waste food. But when she lifted it with her chopsticks, the pleasure of the tender fish melting in her mouth was nowhere to be found. The meat sat heavy on her tongue, reminding her that in the end, it was only dead flesh.

FOUR

The next day at school, last night's fight hung over her head. As she sat in her fourth period biology class waiting for her teacher, Mr. Ursan, to arrive, she traced a finger over where she had pressed her nails against the skin of her palm during the argument. The anger stoked in her stomach, righteous and hot.

"If the teacher doesn't come in fifteen minutes, we get to leave!" Kevin Nguyen shouted, and his friends whooped.

Their enthusiasm only soured her more. She propped her chin in her hand, absently scratching at a frowny face another student had determinedly dug into the desk.

At last the door banged open, startling her from her thoughts. Mr. Ursan hurried in, thermos in one hand and leather briefcase in the other. A chorus of disappointed *Aww*'s came from Kevin and his friends.

Mr. Ursan threw a knowing glance over his horn-rimmed glasses. "Happy to see your favorite teacher, are you?" he asked as he busied himself setting down his things. "Well, I just know you'll be equally overjoyed to hear about your next project." He sent a stern look at the projector. "Just as soon as I can get this darn thing to work. I'm telling you, it plots my murder at night."

Cara smiled. Mr. Ursan was old enough to be her grandfather, but surprisingly, he wasn't boring. "Young at heart but not in the rest of my body," he often said with an exaggerated sigh. He gave out Dum-Dums after especially difficult tests, and unlike some teachers, he actually seemed to like kids—which was a low bar, but still.

Ben Forrester leaned over from his desk toward Cara, brown hair flopping into his eyes. "Hey, has Felicity talked to you about the haunted house yet?"

She hid a grimace. "Yeah, but I don't know. Haunted houses aren't really my thing."

His hazel eyes crinkled. "I didn't take you for a scaredy-cat," he teased. "Didn't anybody ever tell you ghosts don't exist?"

Oh, all the time.

She'd become friends with Ben while working at the Wildwood Stables freshman year. Taking care of horses and getting free riding lessons had been fun—until she'd had to quit because the Stables' specter wouldn't stop playing tricks on her.

Cara played with her braid, smoothing out the tangles at the tip. "If ghosts don't exist, then why are we bothering going to a haunted house on Halloween?"

Ben shot her a sly grin. "Because Thomas and Kameron think they do, and we're going to have some fun."

From the front of the room, Mr. Ursan cleared his throat and began passing out papers to the person at the front of each column of seats. "Sorry for the delay, everyone. There was a long line for the coffee machine, and then I had to fight my daily war with the photocopier. Although, you know what? I'll bet my hat you kids are probably glad you had an extra five minutes to goof off."

The class laughed.

"Especially you two, Zach and Eliza." Mr. Ursan angled the laser pointer at Zach, who, with an unabashed grin, turned around from talking to Eliza. Cara narrowed her eyes at him. He thought it was cute to not pay attention in class, didn't he?

"Save the date for after class, will you?"

See? This was why Mr. Ursan was the best.

As the class snickered, Mr. Ursan turned back to the projection screen. "Now, to culminate our unit on cells, you'll be presenting on one of the organelles to the class. You can choose any medium. Slide-show, TED talk, Prezi. Want to do it old-school? Poster paper is in the back. You will be working in twos, and because I am a cruel jester of fate, no, I will not be letting you choose. And now, for the moment you've all been waiting for . . ." The next slide popped up with every-one's partners and organelle assignments.

Cara stared in horror as she registered who she'd been paired with.

She turned to meet Zach's eyes across the room. He was looking back with the same amount of horror.

"Well, that's all for now, folks. You've got two weeks. Any questions? No? Off you go, then." Mr. Ursan sat down, nursing his coffee.

Cara's classmates started to disperse into their groups, finding spots at the lab tables bordering the room to begin their projects.

Cara gathered her stuff, clutching her binder to her chest like it was a shield. "God, I'm so not looking forward to this."

"You could see if Mr. Ursan will let you switch," Ben said, beside her. "I could be your new partner."

"Are you serious? That would be so much better."

"What would be better?"

At Zach's voice, Cara ground her teeth. *Not you, that's for sure.*

Zach glanced dismissively at Ben. "Don't you have a partner to get to, Forrester?"

Cara blinked at the hardness in his voice. Zach was on the swim team with Ben, so she would have thought they'd at least be civil to each other.

Ben didn't react to the coldness rolling off Zach. "Actually, Cara and I were thinking we could be partners instead. Save everyone some fighting, right?"

"And here I was looking forward to it." Zach sauntered toward Mr. Ursan's desk. "Come on, Tang."

Cara sucked in a breath and followed.

Mr. Ursan looked up as they approached. "What's up?"

"Uh, Coleson and I aren't really a good fit for each other, and because this is such an important project, we were wondering if we could get new partners. We're just going to fight all the time, and it would be better for everyone."

Zach nodded along with Cara's words.

Mr. Ursan folded his hands. "Ah, well, that's exactly why I put you two together. I've noticed you have trouble getting along, and I'd like to sort it out early in the school year. Before something breaks in this class, like a test tube."

The test tube he was putting *them* in was definitely going to break.

"Although"—Mr. Ursan smiled—"I'm glad you two have already found something to agree on."

Cara and Zach exchanged frantic looks. Cara stepped forward and said, "Then we've demonstrated what you've asked of us, right? You could give us new partners. Ben is willing—"

"Nice try," Mr. Ursan said. "But you're not getting off the hook that easily. Come on, you two." He steepled his fingers, looking from Zach to Cara. "In the real world, you'll often be forced to work alongside people you dislike, for months or years at a time. Is a group project really too long to be stuck together?"

"Yes," Zach and Cara said in unison, then turned to glare at each other.

I already tried, Cara urged with her eyes. *It's your turn now.*

Zach planted his hands on Mr. Ursan's desk. "My dad—"

"—would be disheartened to know that his son is doing as well in biology as he once did." Mr. Ursan fixed Zach with a pointed glance and sipped his coffee. "Yes, I taught your father. Babysat him once, too, I recall. Please, if you think it will help, do call him. I've been meaning to have a talk with him about your grades."

Zach blanched, drawing back.

Cara turned away to hide her smirk. So Zach's privileged routine didn't work on *everyone*.

"Don't be too thrilled, Tang. This just means you're stuck with me," Zach said pointedly. The smile dropped off her lips. How was he able to tell she was laughing without even seeing her face?

She spun to face him—and jerked back. He was so much closer than she expected, so close she could see the texture of his soft blue hoodie stamped with AUTUMN FALLS H.S. BOYS SWIM TEAM in blocky gold letters. Cologne scented his throat, notes of pine and ice and something that could only be described as *expensive*.

Cara forced herself to address Mr. Ursan. "Thank you anyway," she said, even though internally she was screaming.

Mr. Ursan spread his hands. "You got this. I know you can make a good team when you work together."

Doubtful, but she wasn't going to argue with a teacher. Zach looked like he was going to, though, so she checked him with her shoulder as she moved past.

"Come on. We're already behind." She made eye contact with

Ben, sitting at a lab table with his partner, and mouthed, *Sorry*. Ben shrugged good-naturedly.

At an empty lab table, she pulled out her laptop. Zach slouched on his chair, legs spread so wide one knee grazed hers. She shot him a look of disgust and scooched her seat as far away as she could.

"Okay, so here's how this is going to go," Cara said to Zach. "We're going to get this thing done as soon as possible, preferably in one or two sessions, so that we get a good grade and we don't have to see each other's faces for a minute longer than necessary."

She expected him to protest, but he merely shrugged and said, "Less work for me if you're making all the decisions."

Somehow that annoyed her, just as much as if her words had been met with a sarcastic retort. *Come on, Cara.* She shook herself.

"I'm thinking Google Slides?" she asked, opening the web browser.

He raised his eyebrows, like it was silly for her even to ask him. Zach had somehow gotten a cherry Dum-Dum in the fifteen seconds she'd been preoccupied with her screen. He held it elegantly in his long fingers, as if it were merely a prop for a photo shoot.

"Sure. You're the boss," he said lightly, lifting one shoulder in casual nonchalance, and okay, he was *definitely* doing this on purpose to irritate her.

Cara silently fumed. Their *grades* were at stake here. Their fates in this class were tied together now. She wasn't letting Zach bring her down with him.

Calling him *bendan* under her breath, something Mr. Ursan wouldn't have considered conducive to getting along if he'd overheard it and understood Chinese, she turned back to her laptop. They worked in forced silence until Zach laughed quietly at something on his screen. Then a minute later, again.

Cara looked over to find that he wasn't working on the presentation at all but was flirting with Eliza through text messages. "Are you serious?" she demanded.

He swiveled his laptop away from her glare, practiced as if he'd done it a million times before. "Eyes on your own screen."

"Eyes on your own *group project*," she shot back. "You're supposed to be focused on doing work, not doing— *Eurgh*, would it kill you to be responsible for once in your life?"

Zach cocked his head. "Make me."

"If I could, we wouldn't be having this conversation!" She could hear her voice getting louder, and she took a deep breath. "If you keep wasting time, we'll have to meet more."

"Wouldn't you like that," said Zach, his eyes narrowed.

Cara dropped her voice. *"Go to hell."*

Zach leaned closer. His blue eyes filled her vision, the color of Arctic sea ice, pupils dilated. "I'll see you there."

"How are you two doing?"

Cara nearly fell off her stool. Mr. Ursan had appeared out of nowhere, looking expectantly at them.

"Fine," she said, forcing a smile. "Just fine."

Zach kept his mouth shut, which couldn't have been easy, knowing him, and Mr. Ursan nodded. "Call me if you need anything," he said, and moved on to the next table.

"I need a new partner," Zach muttered the second Mr. Ursan was out of earshot, and the fire flared back into Cara's veins.

She forced herself to calm. "You know what? Our presentation can be in Comic Sans for all I care. As long as my mom doesn't—" She stopped, not wanting to give Zach more ammo to use against her, but it was too late. His eyebrows had raised, his bearing that of a wolf sensing prey.

"What about your mom?"

She gave him a disbelieving look. "As if I'm going to tell you."

"You were about to." Deliberately, Zach closed his laptop and propped his elbow on it. He lounged on the edge of his stool, leaning against the table to face her. He made posing look effortless—but then again, his older sister, Victoria, was a literal model. Thanks to the Dum-Dum, his mouth was redder—wetter—cherry-kissed and sticky with sugar. "Looks like I'm not getting any more work done."

Cara sucked in a breath through her teeth. "All I was going to say was that my mom doesn't want me fighting with you anymore."

Zach let out a laugh. "Why do you care so much about what your mom thinks?"

"You don't?"

He shrugged. "My mom and dad barely pay attention to anything I do." He glanced away. "Only when I get in trouble."

"That explains a lot."

His gaze returned to hers with murderous force. "At least it's better than having a parent raising me to be a suck-up who does exactly what they're told."

Cara's mouth dropped open. *You don't know a thing about me,* she wanted to snap, but she made herself take a long, slow breath and silently counted to ten in Chinese. If she spoke now, there was no chance this disagreement wouldn't ignite and blow up beyond their lab table, exploding in their faces.

But Zach's eyes were hard as flint, just begging for a match, and God, did she want to strike.

Mr. Ursan clapped his hands. "Okay, class, you have five minutes until the bell! This would be a good time to work out when you're meeting with your partner so that you don't have to end up doing it all the night before your presentation, as I know some of you inevitably will."

Man, Mr. Ursan was out for blood today. What was in his coffee?

But Mr. Ursan's friendly voice had defused some of the tension between them, and it didn't seem worth it to Cara to start another fight five minutes before class ended.

"Where do you want to meet?" The undercurrent in her tone said, *I would rather pick off my own nails than see you again.*

"Well, we can't meet at our houses." The undercurrent in his voice said, *If I never have to talk to you again, it would be too soon.*

She nodded. They needed more neutral ground, and the two of them had already gotten banned from most of the coffeehouses in Autumn Falls. "We could go to my tree house."

"What are you, like, twelve?"

She glowered at him. "I seem to recall someone saying it was fine for me to make all the decisions. You know where it is, right?"

He scratched the back of his neck. "Oh, yeah. I remember."

Zach had found their tree house a few years ago, intruding on a hangout between Charlotte, Felicity, and Cara. He hadn't stayed for long, though, because she'd impulsively pitched a pine cone at his head when he showed up, surprising him enough to make him lose his grip on the ladder and tumble to the forest floor. It had been a fall of only eight feet, and only his backbone—and his ego—had been bruised.

"It's hard to forget when *someone* sets your shirt on fire," Zach added testily.

"I did not. I threw a pine cone at you, and your shirt happened to catch on fire all by itself at the same time."

"You know, Tang, I'd have more respect for you if you'd just admit you did it."

Oh, sure. "Except I *didn't*, and maybe you should have worn less AXE body spray in junior high. Would have made you less flammable." Cara paused, then added, "You probably just caught on fire from thinking you were so hot all the time."

Zach opened his mouth to retort—then shut it, apparently not able to think of a response fast enough.

Which meant she had won.

Glowering, he glanced out the window at the sky, which had turned darker and darker from the start of class. "And what if it rains?"

"There's an amazing invention the tree house has called a roof. I've got cross-country tryouts to watch after school," she informed him. "I won't be there until five." She paused. "Don't be late."

As Cara was packing up, the air shifted suddenly, as if the room had sucked in a breath and held it, bracing for something to happen. A strange shiver slid between her shoulders, and Cara turned to the windows lining one side of the classroom—just in time to see every single one of them shatter in a spray of shards as a heaving black mass swarmed into the room.

Bats, Cara realized with horror, picking out leathery wings, tiny terrified black eyes, and open mouths full of sharp white teeth. Hundreds of them, squeaking and jostling. Students screamed and ducked under desks; others swatted at the creatures midair with textbooks and binders. The bats writhed, dodging the attacks, tangling with each other, as panicked as the students were. Cara snapped out of her trance when she felt claws twisting in her hair. A small furred body brushed past her cheek, membranous wing dragging over her eyes, and she stumbled; for a heartbeat, she couldn't see anything, only darkness filling the room, clawing and frantic.

"Everyone stay calm!" Mr. Ursan shouted as he dove behind his big desk. "They don't want to hurt you; they're more scared of you than you're scared of them! Just keep your heads low."

A hand grabbed hers and pulled her down.

Disoriented, Cara caught her breath and realized it was Zach who had tugged her to safety beneath a lab bench. It was not an ideal hiding spot, too cramped for one person, let alone two, which meant that in the process of tucking herself under the table, she'd somehow ended up in Zach's arms, her back pressed to his chest.

Zach seemed to realize this at the same time as her. He quickly disentangled his arms from around her waist.

"What are you doing?" Cara yelped.

"Trying to protect you from a horde of bats?" Zach's voice was irate, but his words were slightly muffled against her hair. "It's not my fault there's no room under here—"

"There's no room under here because your ridiculously long legs take up all the real estate." Cara tried to wriggle forward, away from him, but there simply wasn't enough space.

A few feet away, one of their classmates had tucked herself into a tiny ball under one side of the lab bench. Her partner was half in, half out from under the table on his hands and knees, trying to capture a grounded bat with a beaker. But the container was just shy of being big enough—as he brought it down, it came down on one splayed, delicate wing.

"Don't hurt it!"

For a second, Cara was confused. She knew those words had come out of her mouth—but she'd also heard them by her ear, reverberating against her back.

She twisted to meet Zach's eyes.

Jinx, she thought, but didn't say it, still annoyed at his closeness and now at the fact they'd had the same thought, too.

As if Zach had read her mind, he raised his eyebrows and said, "You owe me a soda."

Cara gave an incredulous snort. "When the apocalypse is over," she said dryly. The bat had latched onto the boy's sweatshirt sleeve with a tiny black claw. When he noticed, he yelped, jumping up with the bat clinging to his arm. It used the momentum to take off, flying back into the frenzy.

From where Cara huddled—pressed as far away from Zach as she could manage, thank you—she could see papers and binders and pencils scattered across the tiles, knocked over by frantic bats or students as they ducked for cover. Shards of glass glittered. Quite a few of the small creatures had plunged to the floor, where they either lay blinking in the harsh fluorescent light or feebly dragged themselves across the linoleum in a dead man's crawl.

What had made this mad flash mob of bats fly high-speed through the windows—in the middle of the day, no less? A freak impulse of nature? She remembered the deer, the ghosts. . . . Maybe it was something more sinister?

One of the creatures crashed to the ground near her hiding spot. Cara flinched, then noticed something strange on the bat's fur. She was out from under the table before she had even thought to move, keeping low and staying off her hands to avoid the broken glass. Hunched over the bat, she didn't touch it, but bent as close as she dared.

The fur on its back was raised in a peculiar shape: the most perfect circle she'd ever seen in her life. She couldn't say why, but at the too-flawless shape of it, unnatural against the creature's matted sable fur, uneasiness crawled across her skin with tiny claws. Cara glanced at another grounded bat, then the next, then the next.

Circles upon circles met her eyes, each impossibly perfect.

"What are you looking at?" Zach asked.

"There's a weird marking on this bat."

Zach scooted over to where she was looking. "I don't see anything."

Annoyance flared in her, but then, she looked back down, and the frustration turned to foreboding: all the circles had suddenly vanished from the bats, as if they'd never been there at all.

"Is everyone all right?" Mr. Ursan called, clapping his hands. The bats had settled on the ground. He popped his head up from behind his desk. A gash had sliced through the wrinkles on his forehead, and he dabbed at the blood with his pink-and-white-striped tie. "Does anyone need to go to the nurse's office?"

"Tang." Zach was looking at her oddly. "You're bleeding. Are you . . . ?" He hesitated. "Okay?"

Warm liquid was indeed clinging to her cheek. When she tentatively touched it, though, she found unbroken skin underneath. "It's not mine, I think. A bat brushed against me. It must have been bleeding from the glass."

By now the security guard Mr. Ursan had called had entered the room and was on the phone, gesturing at the window with a *Why did this have to happen on my shift?* expression. Students for the next class were gathered outside the doorway, peering in with shocked, questioning eyes.

Mr. Ursan cleared his throat. "Everyone, you may go if you're unhurt," he announced. "Bats can carry rabies, so check to make sure you haven't been bitten and that you don't have any winged passengers clinging to your bags or clothing. If you need the nurse, come here and let me write you a note. Line up nicely, please, and also watch the bats underfoot. I don't need anyone or anything crushed in the excitement of getting out of your next class. For those of you who are outside waiting for your next class, I believe Mrs. Tanager will be taking you to another open classroom while we figure out what exactly happened here today. What a scare we were given, right? Although I think the poor bats were more scared. Animal control is on its way."

Cara wiped the blood off her face and quickly packed her bag. The week before Halloween was always filled with strange occurrences, yes, but usually the town was only bothered by ghosts. Not bats. But the strange markings and odd behavior lingered in her mind.

Was it Halloween or was there something even bigger coming?

Cara shook herself. She had to hurry to economics. "See you after school," she reminded Zach.

"I'm serious about that soda, you know," he said as she swung open the door.

Rolling her eyes, Cara called back, "Don't hold your breath."

FIVE

Where was he?

Cara fired off another text—*If you want to show up sometime within the next century, that would be great*—and then, in a fit of frustration, threw her phone across the tree house, where it landed perfectly in the snack basket. She inhaled, filling her lungs with the smell of wood and fresh air. The smell of home.

Breathing deep only calmed her nerves a little. 5:20 p.m. and not a word from Zach. Slumping back into her beanbag, she picked at the faded fabric, tracing her finger over one of the many miscellaneous stains that had appeared over the years. These beanbags had been in the tree house so long the beans inside had started to pack together, the colors fading as the seasons turned, though Cara could still make out the original colors: hers was red, Felicity's was blue, and Charlotte's was yellow.

Fall light fed through the dusty windowpane, warming the denim on her thighs, and wind rustled the rusted leaves outside. Her gaze drifted to the old bookcase, where the entire Magic Tree House series—give or take a few installments—sat in all its dog-eared, water-stained glory. The books had inspired the girls to build a tree house in the Wildwoods—with their parents' help. Their houses all bordered the forest, so they could come and go whenever they wanted.

Her phone buzzed, and she dove for it.

Unfortunately, it wasn't Zach apologizing, but it was the group chat, which was the next best thing.

E=FC^2 SQUAD:

Felicity: when will my motivation return from the war

Charlotte: I believe in you!! You got this.

Cara smiled. Oh, yeah, and they'd hooked up a hotspot to their tree house a few years ago. Wi-Fi in the woods? *That* was magic.

Cara: Aren't you supposed to be practicing for your recital?

Felicity: uh-huh

Felicity: but

Felicity: am i practicing?

Charlotte: Yes??

Felicity: no i am not

Felicity: that'll be Self-Destructive Tendencies for 500, thank u very much

Charlotte: Alsdjflskdjflkdsf

Charlotte: I trusted you!!

Felicity: & that's UR mistake. u can't trust anyone in this cold, harsh world

Charlotte: Yeah you can!! Everyone's got some nice parts.

Cara: Not Coleson, who's currently standing me up for our group project meeting

Charlotte: Come on, Cara, he's bringing his whole swim team to the bake sale/adoption day this weekend

Cara: That doesn't mean he's a good person; he could be doing it just to look good and altruistic. I can see the headlines already: youngest Coleson son donates to local animal shelter. Photo op for the month: checked

Charlotte: If that means that at the end of the day, all the shelter pets get adopted into forever homes with loving families, then does it really matter if he just did it to look good??

Cara: Et tu, Brute?

Charlotte: I'm just saying!!

Cara: Well plan for him to be half an hour late to the shelter as well

Felicity: you should just ditch him

Felicity: also thinking of just throwing my cello out the window tbh

Cara: Sounds expensive

Cara: and heavy

Felicity: shit u right

Charlotte: Language!!

Felicity: ok captain america

Charlotte: Oh!! Are we still doing our Marvel movie marathon after the haunted house??

Felicity: yeah, but we gotta extract cara from her house

Felicity: your mom can't jail you on halloween *and* your birthday, that's like, a violation of the geneva conventions

Cara began to tap out a reply, then stopped and deleted the meaningless words she'd written. She'd figure out what to do later. Right now, she was heading home before it got too dark to see. In autumn, each sunset came earlier than the last. Zach was never going to arrive. She really was going to have to do this project all by herself, wasn't she?

Jumping off the last rung of the tree house ladder, she began walking—fine, *stomping*—toward the trail leading out of the forest.

Some people in town were afraid of the Wildwoods; they whispered that specters lurked within the trees. Cara knew better. She could say with more certainty than anyone else that this place didn't have ghosts. That was one reason she loved it so much.

There were dead things here, but this decay didn't have a face. It didn't speak, only rotted.

Even in her anger, she could appreciate how the Wildwoods rose around her like an oil painting, a palette of ground-level browns and greens and, up above, ruby and sulfur and amber. Leaves crackled in her wake, the crisp bones of fall splintering under her soles. A late October zephyr suffused her lungs with what could only be described as *autumn*: the aroma of loam, sun-dried, sun-warmed earth; cider, somehow; cedar and pine; and underneath it all, the bite—the cold, coming.

But it wouldn't snow until December. Autumn Falls saved its frost for the winter, the days still relatively warm long into November, as if the snow was stored in the clouds until the time was just right. They had a White Christmas nearly every year.

As if to remind her of that fact, thunder rumbled from above. Cara glanced up, frowning. The heavens had darkened beyond that of a normal dusk. Out of nowhere, iron-colored clouds had materialized, a cavalry heavy and ready with rain. A gale hurtled past her face, ferrying with it the smell of ozone.

She peered ahead, trying to see how close to home she was, only to realize that wherever she was going, it wasn't the direction she wanted.

Cara took a step back. Branches snapped under her shoes. Shaking her head, she looked around for a familiar marker. There, the oak she'd passed countless times in her childhood. That would get her home, hopefully *before* the clouds broke.

And then, not five minutes later, she passed the oak again.

She stopped dead.

Her heart thudded in the cage of her chest, and she closed her eyes, taking deep breaths. She hadn't gotten lost in the Wildwoods since she was a little kid.

But it would be okay. She was just a little turned around; she could find her way out.

Cara studied the woods again, and this time she noticed a trail of crushed leaves leading farther into the forest.

Growing storm forgotten, she squinted at the tracks. Did they belong to Zach? No one else she knew would have recently been here. Except for Charlotte and Felicity, the neighbors all avoided the Wildwoods like it would eat their children.

So maybe that's why Zach was late, he'd gotten lost. Squaring her shoulders, she followed the tracks. She'd find him, yell at him, and then they could go back home and leave this awful project for another day. Her resolve calmed the pulse ringing in her ears, although the hair on the back of her neck still tingled, a result of the electricity in the air from the gathering storm.

But the farther she went, the less certain she became. She hadn't explored all of the Wildwoods, but these trees didn't seem like they were even part of the same forest. They grew stunted and thin, and most of their leaves had already fallen off, crumbling in piles that choked the dying autumn grass.

And then she came to the clearing.

Here, the sky was noticeably lighter than the one she'd just been under, the landscape was different, too. What was this place? Colossal oak trees, their scarred trunks that spoke of centuries, ringed the entire clearing. Long emerald grass grew along their tangled roots. On the near side of the clearing glimmered a small pool, fed by a creek that threaded its way through the undergrowth and disappeared north into the forest beyond.

The only familiar thing was the boy sleeping under the largest oak, a twisted column growing on the western side of the clearing, to her left. Even though he was slumped, his face hidden in the shadows, Cara recognized him immediately.

"Oh, you can't be serious," Cara muttered, striding over to where he lay. Zach had decided to take a nap? She was definitely going to enjoy waking him up.

Right before her fingers grazed his shoulder, a voice rang out from behind her.

"What are you doing?"

Startled, Cara spun around. "I was just trying to wake—"

She came face-to-face with familiar blue eyes, and her words died in her throat.

Zacharias Coleson stood in front of her, arms crossed in what was clearly meant to be a threatening gesture, though it didn't match his expression. He looked as shocked to see her as she him. But the thing was, she was solid.

He was not.

Cara looked from him to the identical figure under the tree. In one fluid movement she dropped to her knees beside him and leaned close. This time her fingers went to his neck, feeling for a pulse.

There was none.

Above, the first raindrop fell.

SIX

Her blood thundered in her ears, as loud as the storm burgeoning above.

This cannot be happening.

Cara's hand dropped uselessly to the forest floor, and she dug her nails into the dirt, grounding herself. Her palm sank deep into the mud. Wet earth, cool and slick, pressed against her pulse.

Okay. Damage control.

She'd seen the silver kissing his shoulders. Felt the lack of an answering heart in his throat. Responded instinctively, stupidly, to the sound of his voice, so alive and familiar.

Still, maybe he hadn't noticed. She could get out of here, leave his ghost behind. Call the police, let them take it out of her hands. She took a few deep breaths, then stood up.

"Tang?"

But of course, Zach never made anything easy for her.

Eyes fixed straight ahead, she walked past him.

"Where are you going? You saw my body, right? You saw me. Hey."

His presence swept up to her side like a blizzard, chilling the air around her, making her already wet skin frigid. She was almost out of the clearing, but Zach waved a hand in her face.

"You heard my voice. You *reacted*. I know you can see me—"

Cara sucked in a tiny breath, a mere reflex to his annoyingness, but apparently, it was all Zach needed.

He yanked on her arm, dragging her to a stop and spinning her to face him. "You *do* see me," he said triumphantly. "You did that thing you always do when you're annoyed with me."

Cara stared at him, at a loss for words. She had a tell?

She pulled away from him, hard, and took a step back. Now that she'd been caught, she met his eyes with a glare. Of course Zach would be the one to find out her secret, and he'd do it solely by frustrating her. She was used to ignoring ghosts. She just wasn't used to ignoring *Zach*.

He wasn't solid—couldn't be—yet the rain didn't fall through him so much as it slid around him, falling over his silver edges to the ground. Like his presence was unnatural. Like him standing there, blue eyes challenging hers, bent physics. Warped the very laws of the world.

But it was just Zach. A boy she'd known since kindergarten. He broke crayons and girls' hearts, not storms, and he walked through life as though nothing could touch him, because nothing could. He was invincible. He was infuriating.

And now he was dead.

It sounded so wrong. How could Zacharias Coleson be *dead*?

The wrongness of it turned her stomach, filling it like lead, mixing with the frustration and the fear.

She glanced at his body again, but seeing it only made the uneasiness rise, choking her throat and making her eyes burn. She swallowed hard, clapping her hands over her mouth and breathing deep, trying to keep her emotions at bay. He looked as though he were sleeping.

How Cara wished he were sleeping. Then the only decision she'd have to make would be how much she was going to yell at him once he was awake. She wouldn't be staring at his ghost in a clearing she'd never seen before as rain fell harder and harder around them.

"What happened?" she asked.

Just as he blurted, "Why are you the only one who can see me?"

"I asked you first."

"I asked you second."

They glared at each other, before Zach let out a groan and ran a hand through his hair.

"I got lost trying to meet up with you, and this snake bit me on the ankle, so I tried to get help, I stumbled out of this clearing and somehow back out of the forest. I tried waving down cars, but no one noticed me, not even when I stood right in the middle of the road. I didn't know what to do, so I came back, and that's when I saw you. But when I said something, you looked up. So I'll ask again: why are you the only one who can see me?"

There was no easy way to say this, so she might as well get it over with. "Because you're dead."

He snorted. The amusement on his face faded when she looked at him, completely serious.

"Hold on. I'm not—I'm not actually dead, am I?"

Great. He was one of those ghosts who refused to believe in their own death. "Take a wild guess," Cara said, flinging an arm toward his corpse.

"No, this is some weird prank. I can't actually be— I'm dreaming."

Unbidden, a spark of sympathy manifested inside her. "You're not," Cara said.

Maybe he heard how her voice had softened, because he pressed again. "So then what is it? Why can you see me?"

His ice-blue eyes were piercing, compelling an answer to the surface.

Her next sentence snagged on her tongue.

Her mother's words floated in her head, words that had controlled her every decision since learning as a child she could see ghosts: *Promise me you'll never tell anyone. Not your friends. Not your classmates. No one.*

And her answer, a child's, innocent and obedient: *I promise.*

"What is it?" He cocked his head, eyes curious. A raindrop reeled down from his temple, crested his cheek, traced the sharp swoop of his jaw—and then just stopped there, lingering. As though he, too, could hear her childhood words, he said, "I promise not to tell. And a Coleson never breaks a promise."

He'd already discovered she could see him. Sure as the storm soaking the back of her neck, she had revealed her secret in every way but name. Whether she meant to or not—whether her mother knew it or not—she *had* broken her promise.

Might as well finish it off.

Cara took a deep breath, bracing herself.

"The reason why I'm the only one who can see you is because you're a ghost, and I'm a ghost speaker."

There was a pause. Zach stared at her, brow furrowing as he tried to process the information.

"You're a what?"

Okay, so she was going to have to spell this out for him.

"That means I can see and talk to ghosts. I can amplify them. I can help them move on. If I'm powerful enough . . . I can even control them."

She'd never said those words to anyone before, and she instantly wanted to take them back, and she also wanted to keep saying them. They didn't fall through the air and disappear into the ground like rain. They stayed, suspended like a storm.

And then Zach laughed.

It was disbelieving, deriding, sharp and wrong. "You've gotta be kidding me. *You talk to dead people?*"

Her cheeks burned. She should have known better than to expect anything else from him.

All sympathy she had went up in smoke. Anger presented itself out of the emotions tangled in her chest, a weapon and defense, an easy knife—and Cara took it gladly. She leveled a scorching glare.

"Well, now you're one of them. I wouldn't be laughing if I were you."

His jaw clenched. She'd hit a wound. She'd known she would.

They brought out the worst in each other.

He threw up his hands. "This has gotta be some kind of punishment. You're telling me that I'm dead, and it turns out that *you*"—he spat the word as if it were poison—"are the only one who can see me?"

"I'm not having a lot of fun here, either. If this is what someone up there devised as your punishment, I wish they'd left me out of it. You're not alive anymore and I'm *still* forced to look at your face!"

"Excuse you, you should be grateful that you get to look at this." He gestured grandly to himself.

Cara rolled her eyes to the heavens. "How are you literally dead and still this *insufferable*?"

"You're suffering?" His smirk was vicious. *"Good."*

She growled before she could stop herself. Turning her back on him, she began pacing around the clearing. The long grass strangled the sound of her furious footfalls. "My mom made me promise never to tell anyone, and I was doing just fine before you died! Do you even know how hard I've worked to keep this secret? To make sure no one found out? Why do you always have to ruin everything?"

"Hey, it's not like I died on purpose! You think I want to be here, arguing with you?"

Cara stopped by the stream's bank. She sent him a glare that could have turned all the water to steam. "Well, I just remembered that *I* don't have to be here. I'm calling the police and reporting your corpse, and then I'm going home and forgetting you exist."

"Wait," he said, a sudden note of panic in his voice. Cara was pleased to hear it. She folded her arms and looked at him expectantly. "Sorry you got mad because I didn't take you seeing dead people seriously."

"That's not an apology."

He grimaced. "You expect me to actually apologize?"

Unbelievable. Zach was a Class A ghost, all right. A for *Asshole.*

"Look, you're a . . . ghost speaker or whatever. You see dead people. I'm"—his voice faltered, and it softened the angry set of her shoulders, just a bit—"dead, which has got to be some kind of mistake. You have to help me figure this out."

She laughed, stalking back toward him. "I don't have to help you with anything. I came here to do a group project. This"—she gestured at him in a mocking mirror of the way he had gestured to himself—"is not a group project."

"I'll haunt you for the rest of your life."

"You wouldn't dare."

The blue of his eyes turned to ice. "Try me. You thought I was annoying when I was alive? I'll top that."

So he really thought he could force her into doing what he wanted.

It was the swim team flyers all over again. "Okay, then! I'll ask my grandmother if she knows how to do exorcisms! Have fun getting banished to the demon realm *where you belong.*"

She was bluffing, but it was kind of entertaining to watch the color leave his face.

Speaking of which, how did he look exactly like he did when he was alive? He hadn't faded one bit. If anything, his skin actually glowed *more.* She only knew he was a ghost because of his corpse on the ground at their feet and the silver gracing this form.

Maybe she would have cared if he hadn't been so arrogant. But he was every degree as demanding as he'd always been.

Not my ghost, not my funeral.

"You wouldn't," he said, but the hesitation in his voice betrayed his uncertainty.

Cara tilted her head and smiled, going in for the kill. "Guess what, Coleson? Being rich doesn't make you immortal. You still die, like everyone else, and you just have to live with it. Or I guess you don't." She shrugged. "Sorry to break it to you, but you're not the first person who's ever kicked the bucket and turned into a ghost. And unfortunately for you, I don't care enough about you to stick around and enjoy the show." She turned, but a hand grabbed her wrist.

"Please," he whispered. "Don't make me beg."

Cara whirled around, yanking her arm from his grasp and moving to push him away before remembering that her hands would go right through—

But they didn't.

He stumbled back, and they stared at each other, her breathing hard from shock.

Her wrist tingled where he'd touched it. The sensation traveled up her arm to her brain, where it hummed, sending shivers down her spine.

Slowly, she said, "I shouldn't have been able to touch you. Why was I able to touch you?"

His eyes didn't leave hers. More humming, all across her skin now. "What are you saying?" he asked.

She was going to regret this. But the storm pushed her forward, curiosity crackling in her mind, the lightning driving logic out of her limbs as she looked back at the boy she'd known all his life and now the beginning of his death, a boy untouchable by rain even as water drowned her hair into an ocean.

"I'm saying I might take you home after all."

SEVEN

Cara had forgotten about the ghost-repelling charms around her house until Zach slammed into an invisible wall and swore.

"The hell?"

Cara looked at him trapped outside the gate. It was tempting to leave him there and forget anything had happened.

And yet, raindrops pattering onto her shoulders, she knelt by the fence and brushed aside dead leaves until she found a rectangular box made of peach wood, a raised skull on its surface. Nestled inside were three miniature bones, slender as rays of moonlight, bundled with three willow twigs.

Cara didn't know much about ghost speaking; that had been her choice. But Laolao had insisted she learn to maintain and break specter-repelling charms. Considering Laolao was a ghost and Cara's mother refused to have anything to do with the dead, it was Cara's responsibility to ward their family against bad spirits.

Modifying the barrier to let Zach in as well as Laolao was relatively easy. Quick enough that she barely had time to digest the twinge of unease as she unlocked the front door. If it came to it, she supposed she *could* ask Laolao how to do an exorcism, but for now, she had to contend with the ramifications of letting Zach into her home.

Blaze greeted them excitedly in a jingle of dog tags and tapping of claws against walnut floorboards. He barked at Zach, feathery tail whipping about. Cara shushed him, but the house was dark and quiet and remained so; her mother must still be at work.

Cara left Blaze to guard Zach in the foyer while she ran upstairs to take the world's fastest shower. When she returned, feeling slightly better now that she was in dry clothes, she found Zach waiting in the living room, Blaze sitting calmly at his feet.

Zach didn't look as uncomfortable or out of place in her house as she might have expected. Then again, Zacharias Coleson was always most at ease when he was annoying the hell out of her.

Zach was examining their red leather couch still covered in the same plastic from the day her mother had bought it two years ago. Her mother had been so excited, so proud. Finally, they had a brand-new couch of their own, not a used one a neighbor had abandoned.

Now, as she looked at him looking at it, a boy whose house sprawled over acres of land, with enough room for a thousand couches and no need to wrap them in plastic, she felt shame crawl up her cheeks.

Before he could comment on the couch or anything about her house, Cara cleared her throat and gestured for him to follow her up to the attic, commanding Blaze to stay downstairs. The attic was the one place her grandmother got any peace and quiet to herself in a world full of ghosts demanding her attention, and Cara felt a bit of guilt to be interrupting it.

She pushed open the door. It creaked, a shout in the silence of the house, and Cara coughed from the dust. "Laolao?" she called hesitantly. "We have a visitor."

Laolao was sitting in her rocking chair, perusing a newspaper covered in Chinese characters. Cara could read enough to know that it was today's edition: Friday, October 24.

Laolao looked up, and lightning arced behind the window, washing the room in white. Cara squeezed her eyes shut. The afterimage burned bright against her lids: the attic's eaves crouched over their heads.

When Cara blinked, Laolao stood right in front of them, peering at Zach. Cara hadn't heard her move.

She watched as her grandmother took in how Zach's figure glowed silver.

And then Laolao turned to her, face deadly serious.

"What," she said, "have you done?"

After Cara had protested her innocence, she made the necessary introductions.

"Laolao, this is Zacharias Coleson, from school. Coleson, this is my grandmother. You can call her Laolao."

Cara eyed him, wary that he'd declare that he was going to call her something "easier to say," but he only stepped forward and held out his hand, his upbringing taking over. "I'm Zach. I'm sure you've heard of me."

She rolled her eyes. Conceited, yeah, but he wasn't wrong. Cara had lost track of how many times she'd come home from school and thrown her backpack on the floor before stomping up to the attic to complain about Zach.

Laolao shook his hand gingerly.

"I found him in the Wildwoods after school," Cara continued. "Laolao, I can touch him. He's not exactly solid, but he's more solid than any ghost should be."

Sure, there was no way one could brush against him and mistake the cold for something alive. But he was more . . . *there*. Condensed moonlight spun into a form one could feel.

Laolao put a hand on Cara's arm, but whether it was to comfort Cara or steady herself was unclear. "You know that should be impossible." Then she hesitated, a new thought crossing her features. "Your promise—does this mean you have chosen ghost speaking?"

"I broke it accidentally." Cara hated to see the disappointment in her grandmother's eyes, but she forged on. "Mom doesn't know."

Laolao nodded, then turned back to Zach, scrutinizing the opaqueness of his form. First and foremost a ghost speaker.

"Why don't you sit down and tell me what happened, dear?" she suggested, guiding him to the armchair.

But a grandmother at heart.

It was at this moment that Cara realized she, too, was interested in the answer. She'd been too shocked about the fact that Zach *was* dead to wonder about the *how*.

Zach sank warily into the seat. "I went to meet Tang after school in the woods, but I kinda got lost. I ended up in a clearing, and this weird-looking snake came out of nowhere and bit me on the ankle." Laolao stiffened. "Then everything went dark, and when I woke up, I was . . ." He choked on the words as if they were a rotten apple. "Dead."

Cara paced the perimeter of the room as Zach talked. Wind battered the branches against the glass of the round attic window. The sooner they figured out what was wrong, the sooner they could help him pass over.

Laolao was nodding, asking questions, and as Zach hesitated, she reached forward and placed a comforting hand on his shoulder as if he needed it.

But maybe he did.

Cara turned away, facing the bookshelves.

"Xiaogui, could you join us, please?" Laolao was rummaging through a cluttered table. She pulled out a piece of paper and pen, then cleared off the surface. "Zacharias is going to show us what the snake looked like."

Cara reluctantly did so, giving Zach a wide berth as he bent over to draw.

After a few minutes, Zach straightened and slid the paper over. "It looked like that."

Laolao touched the sheet with trembling fingers. Her face had gone as pale as the paper. "This is what you saw?"

Cara leaned forward, expecting to see the snake equivalent of a human stick figure, but the image Zach had drawn pinned her in place with its eyes. A serpent lay coiled on the page, glaring up at her with slashed pupils. Scales armored its whiplike body, gleaming along its taut neck, braced for a lunge. Most heart-stopping were its fangs, so sharp it was a wonder they hadn't pierced the page. Dripping with venom.

Laolao set the drawing down and hurried to the shelves. Cara traced a finger over one fang.

"Since when can you draw?" Cara said, her surprise sharpening the question into an accusation.

Shoving his hands into his pockets, he shrugged. "My mom's an artist."

Laolao returned to the table, muttering to herself in rapid-fire Chinese, too fast for Cara to catch. She held a heavy brown tome in her see-through arms, her manner as serious as if she were digging up a grave. Laolao dropped the book on the table, spine first. It landed with a foreboding thud, sending up a cloud of dust and making Cara erupt in a flurry of sneezes, and falling open to a page near the end of the book. A page with a snake on it. A snake Zach had drawn almost perfectly moments earlier.

Laolao adjusted her glasses and read, "'The Signet Snake. A serpent the color of bone, its hisses sound strangely close to words. What it lacks in size it more than makes up for in speed. Hard to spot despite its blinding white scales, it has a venom that is fatal and fast-acting.

"'Though accounts are few and far between, spanning centuries and generally conflicting in location, circumstance, and details, what is clear is that this is no ordinary serpent, but an intelligent agent of chaos, leaving death in its wake. It is believed that all sightings are of the same being—one snake behind everything. Every time the Signet Snake appears, destruction occurs in due course. Some liken it to Jörmungandr, the Midgard Serpent in Norse mythology prophesied to catalyze Ragnarok, the end of the world; only this ophidian restlessly stirs up trouble on land rather than waiting patiently within the sea.

"'Cleopatra, queen of Egypt, famously took her own life with an asp bite after the death of her lover, Mark Antony. However, it is likely she used the Signet Snake instead, as Cleopatra died too quickly for an asp's venom, and it would have been difficult to smuggle a serpent as large as an asp into her mausoleum.

"'The Snake was seen throughout the ages—from the final days of the Roman Empire to the battlefields of World War I—but never in the same place twice. It was seen by a Parisian with the name of Severin Proulx, the day before his friend was bitten in the spring of 1603. It was Proulx who reportedly discovered that oddly, upon being bitten by the Snake, the victim is turned into a ghost and has seven days to find the antidote before he or she cannot be resurrected. But one would need a ghost speaker, for obvious reasons, and as such persons are incredibly rare, it would be a fool's shot in the dark. *(For more information on ghost speakers, turn to page 268.)*

"'A flower called the analyx has been thought to be significant to the victims as a potential antidote, but reports are not conclusive.

"'There are also rumors that whoever is bitten gains enhanced powers. But no one has ever returned from the dead to confirm this.'"

Silence hung in the air, thick as dust.

Zach looked up at Laolao. "This is for real?"

Laolao nodded. "I have read a bit more than what is in this book and can confirm from my research that the Signet Snake does not merely kill but turns the victim into a ghost, their essence cut loose from their body by the venom. The victim has seven days from the exact moment of their death to be retethered before they fade away completely. A loophole, if you will—one open for exploitation and chaos."

Cara shook her head. "Wait, this—I thought there was no way you could come back from the dead, and I've never heard of the Snake." Her world was careening on its axis, the laws of life abruptly amended. "How come I never knew about this? How come you do?"

Laolao shut the book. "You have never asked, like how you have never asked about any magic. And ah—I suppose you could say the Signet Snake is a personal interest of mine."

"So there's a chance?" Zach interrupted. He spoke carefully, as if he questioned it too closely, too brazenly, the miracle would dissolve on his tongue. "I don't have to stay dead?"

Laolao's reply was equally measured in caution. "*If* you find the antidote and a willing ghost speaker within the next week."

He opened his mouth, but she answered before he could ask.

"Not me, I'm afraid." She smiled, as if to soften the blow. "I am a ghost speaker, but you need somebody alive. Someone who can anchor your essence to their own and bring you back to the side of the living."

They both turned to Cara.

Zach stepped toward her, blue eyes deadly serious. He was so close he could have reached out and touched her again.

Startled, she returned his gaze, fighting the urge to back away. It was not an easy thing. He was looking at her in a way that he never had before, in life or death.

"You're the only one who can help me," he said. "I'm completely at your mercy. Isn't that what you always wanted, Tang?"

A hand at her wrist, a shiver up her spine. Her skin hummed at the memory.

Don't make me beg.

She tipped her chin, arms crossed against her hammering heart. "I think what I want is to never be bothered by you again."

"You wouldn't let me die, would you?"

Cara scoffed, finally turning her head away from the force of his regard, the celestial pull of his attention. "Let you die? I didn't even know until now that you could be brought back."

He had gone and gotten himself killed. But if she let him fade away now, then it would be her fault. She would be letting him die twice.

Laolao was watching her, an inscrutable look on her face. *Does this mean you have chosen ghost speaking?* her grandmother had asked her.

If Cara brought Zach back, she didn't necessarily need to give up her secret. She could return to pretending she couldn't see ghosts; it wouldn't need to leave this room. It never needed to come out she'd broken her promise to her mother.

But then again, why *should* she keep her promise? Her whole life, Cara had done everything to please her mother, but there was always more, some way in which she was lacking. It would never be enough, so why keep trying? To her mother's eyes, Cara had failed her the moment she'd been born, ghost-speaking abilities slumbering in her veins.

The storm rumbled outside in time with the rush of thunder in her ears.

At least it's better than having a parent that raised me to be a suck-up who does exactly what they're told, Zach had said earlier today.

Cara knew exactly what her mother would tell her to do right now. But she was done listening.

Cara was allowed to make the decisions she wanted, and Cara was allowed to use her power the way she wanted. She wasn't a child who needed to be kept safe from herself.

Here was her chance to make good on what she'd told her mother at dinner. Here was her chance to become her own person, not just her mother's daughter.

Before Cara could say anything, Zach blurted. "All right, fine," he said. "I'll pay you to help me." When she gaped at him, he added, "Am I wrong in guessing that's what you want?"

She hated the insinuation, but his offer sweetened her decision. She hesitated. Money would make going behind her mother's back well worth it. What good was studying to get into an Ivy League if she ended up not having enough money to go? She and Zach both had futures to consider. She couldn't be blamed her for that.

"Okay," she said. "I'll help you. Do whatever is required as a ghost speaker." She met his eyes. "For five thousand dollars."

"Cara," said Laolao pointedly.

"Right," Cara said. "Ten thousand dollars."

"Are you serious?" Zach said. "You really want ten K—"

"Eleven thousand." Cara smirked at him. She was starting to enjoy this. "Every time you complain, I'll raise it another thousand. Until we have an agreement."

Despite being rich enough to show up at school with a new pair of expensive sneakers every week, Zach seemed to have trouble agreeing. Typical.

"What? You can't just help me out of the goodness of your heart and your moral superiority that you like to hold over my head—?"

"Twelve thousand dollars. *And* a letter of recommendation from your dad to the dean of whatever school I want."

Zach shut his mouth. Closed his eyes. Breathed.

She supposed the motion of it helped him, because he certainly didn't need to breathe to live anymore.

"Something wrong, Coleson?" she said, smiling up at him. "You want to go ask the ghost speaker next door?"

"Fine," he ground out, opening his eyes. "Twelve thousand dollars and a letter of recommendation—but only if you bring me back to life. You get all or nothing. Are we good?"

He held out his hand.

For a heartbeat, she let herself wonder what it would be like if Zacharias Coleson stayed dead.

There would be monotonous days without arguments to break them up. There would be new space in the air when a teacher took attendance. A pause tripping on a tongue. An empty seat.

A new grave with his name on it.

The storm's gunmetal-gray shadows drew across the paneled wooden walls, painting this future in cold, washed-out light. She could see it. She had only to step back and it would happen, without her having to lift a finger. She hefted the weight of his life in her hands, as heavy as an urn, turning it over in her mind. Holding it was power, plain and simple. Mesmerizing and terrifying. Her own heart beating harder knowing she could silence his for good.

And just when the confidence in his blue eyes fractured into fear, Cara clasped his hand.

The cold of his palm, his touch, traveled up her arm in a shock, but she didn't let it show on her face. "We're good."

She dropped his hand quickly and looked to Laolao for approval. Laolao nodded, though there was a gravity to her expression that looked a lot like worry or apprehension.

"No going back, then," Zach said. "You won't give up if it gets too hard? You'll see it through to the end?"

He had the nerve to imply she was a quitter. She should have taken it further. Brought him to his knees.

"You know what, Coleson? *I promise you.*"

Lightning splintered the sky. Thunder, loud and low.

Even in the flashing darkness, Cara didn't miss how his shoulders dropped in relief. He grinned, and he reached for her then, his fingers grazing her arm for one electric second before he drew back, seeming to remember they were enemies. He rewarded her with a smile instead. A true one, without hidden malice or smirking triumph, the first of its kind he'd ever given her.

It was the kind of smile that had the power to blind her to all else. The kind of smile that built bridges, forged political alliances, unfurled the sails of ships. Lethal in its charm.

Bridges could break. Alliances could cannibalize. Ships could sink.

But she'd be lying to herself if she said it didn't have the intended effect. When he was like this, it was hard to hate him. When he was like this, he was at his most dangerous.

When he was like this, she just might do anything he asked.

Zach turned his grin on her grandmother, the sole witness to a miracle. Cara rubbed her wrist and watched as he practically lit up the attic.

He didn't look like a ghost.

He looked like a god.

Cara swallowed, very aware of her spiraling mind.

AXE body spray, she thought frantically. *AXE. BODY. SPRAY.*

Luckily, Laolao spoke up.

"Well then, it is decided. Come on, you two. We will take a trip to the Wildwoods. And bring an umbrella."

Cara gaped. "We're going *back* outside?"

The downpour seemed to be on its way out, but the sky was still a furious, mournful mass of wind and darkness.

Her grandmother's eyes crinkled, like she was letting Cara in on a secret. In that moment, she seemed so much younger. As if Cara was seeing Laolao like Laolao truly saw herself.

"We have to hide the body, don't we?"

EIGHT

By the time they made it out of the house and into the Wildwoods, the sky had blanked into gray. Cara had brushed her drying hair into her typical braid and opted for a burgundy windbreaker instead of an umbrella. With the hood on, her black hair spilled out onto her shoulder like the severed head of a snake.

Although the rain had stopped, everything was still drip, drip, dripping. Occasionally, water slipped from a branch onto her skull. It was as if they were walking in a great sink of cedar and silt and someone had turned off the faucet but not quite tight enough. Depressions in the forest floor had birthed infant puddles, feathery crimson leaves floating at the bottoms like wet fire. Iridescent beetles scuttled out of the wood chips; and hidden from sight, birds called to each other, replacing the storm's song with their own. The smell of pine rose from the needle-strewn soil, saturating her senses with a dizzying scent. Petrichor.

For the forest, the worst was over.

But for her, it had only just begun.

Laolao had asked Cara to lead them back to the clearing, a tall order considering Cara had found it by accident. Sweat trickled down Cara's back. Her shoes sank into the muddy, storm-softened ground. Behind her, Laolao and Zach walked effortlessly over what she could not. Her grandmother simply *glided*, like the air was passing through her instead of the other way around.

And Zach—Zach had always moved with an easy, reckless grace, but as a ghost, the effortlessness of his existence was even more so: elegance magnified in the seamless lines of his form. Leave it to Zach to look even better in death than in life.

Cara had never been so aware of how her hot, heavy breaths sounded. How dull the plodding thuds of her feet were as they struck the ground, like a heartbeat marking the earth again and again.

The steps of the dead made no sound when they walked; neither did their hearts.

She was the loudest thing in the woods.

"Do you even know where you're going?" Zach asked.

Correction: she *had* been the loudest thing in the woods.

She swung her head back to glare at him. "Of course," she fired back, even though, truthfully, she wasn't sure. They were following the same path they'd taken from the clearing to the house, but it was possible the forest could have changed it on them, like it had when she'd first tried to go home from the tree house but found herself walking in circles. "I know the way if the Wildwoods doesn't change it," she amended. "I didn't even know this clearing existed until the forest forced me here."

Laolao stopped dead. "The clearing wasn't here before?"

Cara's heart quickened at Laolao's expression. "I've been in this area before many times and never saw it. Which means this is . . . Yeah. This is new." She didn't like the idea that this place had always been here, in her favorite forest, unseen and lurking in the shadows, a trap designed to lure Zach to his death. "What does it mean?" Cara asked.

Laolao only shook her head, eyes trained on the path ahead.

The clearing opened up in front of them, like a hand had taken a knife to the body of the landscape and made an incision, leaking a green reveal of trees and grass.

Cara arched an eyebrow at Zach in a silent *See, I knew where we were going* before filing in. Laolao made a beeline to the slumped shape at the base of the biggest oak and set about examining the area, musing to herself in Chinese, finalizing the spells she was casting.

Zach stood stock-still, staring at his body.

"At least I make a handsome corpse."

Cara turned her phone's flashlight on the body and wished she hadn't. He'd fallen at the foot of the greatest oak, roots snaking around his limbs. The rain had polished the leaves into jewels, every ruby facet glittering.

Her mind pulled up the memory of him in life, golden and arrogant.

He had been destined for greatness. Trophies with his name on them lined up in glass cases. A spot in an Ivy League, guaranteed by legacy and athletic achievement. Invitations to charity balls, sweeping the room in a suit and tie with a pale beauty on his arm and an effervescent flute of champagne in his hand, his dark blond hair shining under the chandeliers, a winning smile at the ready.

He wasn't supposed to die before he was old.

This figure at her feet was an empty shell in comparison, and Cara didn't want to look at it a second longer.

Only one letter between body and boy. She tipped her head back, closing her eyes and inhaling.

Her shoulders relaxed as the familiar scents of the Wildwoods filled her lungs: loam, things growing, the clean scent of rain overlaying everything like a colorless shade of paint. She breathed deeply, in and out—

"What," said Zach's derisive voice, "are you doing?"

Her calm shattered. Her eyes snapped open. Irritation made her answer quick and jagged. "Uh, *breathing*? Did you already forget what that is?"

Instantly, his face darkened. She pressed her lips tight.

After fighting their entire lives, they knew exactly where each other's weaknesses were. They pressed their fingers into each other's wounds to win. But now that Zach had crossed the line between life and death, it seemed she was getting closer to breaching a line herself. He was dead, and she was the only one who could see him. She was a ghost speaker, and he was the only one outside her family who knew. The rules had changed, the stakes had been raised—and they were still holding on to old knives, seeing how much they could make the other bleed.

"I just really like how the forest smells after it rains, okay?" she said. "Is that a problem?"

"It doesn't smell like anything—"

Realization crashed down upon them at the same time.

The loam, the growing, the whole rain-shaded air—Zach couldn't smell any of it. And because of that, he couldn't feel any of the joy from it. How it felt to throw your head back and revel in the life around you. Not anymore.

He was dead.

Cara imagined a gray cloth of death draped over her face, muffling her senses, filling her nostrils with nothingness—

Suddenly, she couldn't breathe.

"Xiaogui?" her grandmother called, and Cara loosed a shaky

breath. Laolao was waving her over to the oak. "Could I have a hand?"

She smiled at her grandmother, glad to do something useful. "Of course," she said, and offered her palm.

Laolao took it. She closed her eyes and stood still for several heartbeats, drawing in strength. The gray of her form shimmered *more* silver, gained more dimension, as if it were being traced over and over with a sharp colored pencil.

"What are you guys doing?" Zach asked, brow creased in confusion. He had followed, watching them.

Letting go of Cara's hand, Laolao opened her eyes, which gleamed with renewed power. "Cara was kind enough to lend me a bit of her strength for the upcoming spells. As a ghost speaker, she can act as an amplifier for us."

"What's an amplifier?"

"Someone who has the ability to intensify the magical powers of others," Cara answered. "Super rare, very sought after. But like Laolao said, I just amplify the dead. I make them more . . . *there.*"

Zach looked skeptical. "It doesn't suck your own life force?"

"Only if you take too much. And Laolao would never do anything to hurt me." After amplifying, her breathing became a little more difficult, but with every shuddering heave of her lungs, renewed strength welled up in her body like groundwater.

Laolao waved a hand. "All right, you two, enough with the questions. Let me concentrate."

Cara nodded and backed up, giving her grandmother space. Laolao raised her arms over Zach's body.

"Moqiu dakai," she said.

A bubble of air, ringed in silvery flame, appeared right above the body's chest. It hovered for a second, as if uncertain, and then began to expand, its radius widening until it enclosed the corpse, part of the sphere arcing back and disappearing into the tree.

"Moqiu guanbi," Laolao commanded.

The transparent sphere spun, a flash of silver, then tightened, an explosion in reverse. And when it closed, it took the corpse with it.

"Whoa," Zach said.

Cara grinned. *Yeah, that's right, Coleson. My grandma is awesome.*

Laolao relaxed. Her thin shoulders were transparent again. It had taken something out of her, even with Cara's help. "Your body is still there—but hidden. We would not want someone else finding you during the week."

Cara turned her eyes to the grass. Where the barrier met the blades of green, a few bent, pressed down by magic. Noticeable if you knew what you were looking for.

"The tree's leaves protected your body from the rain, which was good. But I also set up preservation spells. Precautionary ones. Make sure you do not come back to decay."

"Thank you," said Zach, eerily polite, his eyebrows raised. He looked like he couldn't decide whether to be impressed or horrified.

"Now, Cara," Laolao said. "When it comes time to administer the antidote, you need to be able to remove the barrier. I am going to give you the words to do so."

She hesitated. "I can do that? Take down the barrier?"

"Of course you can. Now, clear your mind and ready yourself."

Cara nodded.

Laolao focused her eyes on her and said, "Gei ni—"

Cara replied, "Shou dao—"

The moment trembled. Waiting.

Laolao said, "Moqiu xianxian—moqiu zi hui."

Knowledge shimmered silver in her mind.

Cara opened her mouth, but her grandmother put out a hand.

"Don't say it now," she cautioned. "The barrier is primed and waiting to break whenever you speak the spell. Only do it when you're ready to use the antidote."

Cara focused on holding the words in her mind, running her attention over each shining sound until she was sure she had it. She nodded at her grandmother.

Laolao smiled. "I'm proud of you, xiaogui."

Her chest warmed at the praise. She didn't miss the irony that it was something she rarely heard from her mother, least of all when it came to her ghost-speaking ability.

In fact, if her mother knew about what she'd just done, she wouldn't congratulate her. She'd probably confine her to the house for the rest of eternity.

Especially if she found out Cara had broken her promise.

"Let us return to the house, shall we?" Laolao said, unaware of the tiny crisis that was going on in Cara's head. "Xiaogui?"

With a sinking dread Cara hoped her mother wouldn't already be home, or she could add violation of her grounding to her list of grievances.

On her way out of the clearing, her eyes snagged on something bright blue.

"Wait a second," she said to Zach. "Your stuff." His cobalt backpack was lying in the grass by the pool of water on the nearside of the clearing, his phone on the ground next to it. He must have dropped it after he'd gotten bitten, before he staggered over to the tree.

Cara stooped to retrieve the items, passing through a patch of shimmering air to reach them. Up close she realized what she had thought was a small pond of water was more like a hole in the ground from which the creek flowed: spurting water rather than holding it, like a wound in the earth, bleeding. If she followed it, where would it lead?

"Did you tell your parents where you were going?" she asked, standing back up.

Something strange passed over Zach's face. "No."

Cara shoved his phone at him. "Okay, then make sure you turn your phone's location off. We can keep your stuff in my room for now."

Back on the forest path, Cara was relieved to see that the Wild-woods hadn't changed again, and they were able to walk home without getting lost. Up ahead, Zach and her grandmother were holding an amicable conversation, which was, frankly, alarming.

"The existence of the clearing might not be cause for concern," Laolao was telling Zach, her tone grandmotherly and reassuring. She looked back at Cara to let her know she was talking to her, too, before turning back to Zach. "The Wildwoods is steeped in magic, with a mind of its own. It has a habit of shifting its paths with the seasons. Who knows why it decides to act as such?"

"It's a *magical forest*?"

"All forests are," Laolao said matter-of-factly. "But some more so than others."

The wind whispered at their heels.

Cara frowned. She'd known the Wildwoods was magic since she was little, but she'd never seen it behave like this.

"How are you holding up?" Laolao asked Zach.

Cara half expected Zach to give a sarcastic nonresponse, but he answered honestly, if wryly. "I didn't think ghosts were real until I woke up as one, so that's something I'm getting used to."

"You seem to be taking this well, given the circumstances."

His broad shoulders rose and fell in a shrug. "It takes a lot to faze me," he said, and wow, was he seriously bragging about how well he had handled dying?

Cara stepped over a young sapling sprawled over the path—it must have snapped during the storm.

"How did you learn to do whatever it is you did back there?" Zach asked. "Is that the same as ghost speaking?"

"It's magic but not the same." Laolao paused, gathering her words. "I learned those spells from a book. Anyone who already has some magical ability can learn them and practice."

Silence. Cara could feel the words as though they were stones thrown at her. Guilt only a grandmother could induce settled at the bottom of her stomach.

After a moment, Zach asked, "So if ghosts exist, do werewolves and vampires and all that stuff you see in movies exist, too?"

Laolao laughed but not unkindly. "No, no. The world we live in may make monsters and beasts but not out of men. The only thing humans turn into are ghosts."

"What about zombies?"

"If a powerful enough ghost speaker put their mind to it, then per-haps they could create zombies. They could not bring the dead back to life entirely, though—the reason there is a chance to bring you back is because of the unique circumstances of the Signet Snake—so the bodies they resurrected would move solely at their master's com-mand. Mindless beings. Not very smart."

"Could *you* do it?"

"When I was alive, yes. But *could* and *should* are two very different things. I would not risk messing with the balance of the world in such a way. And I imagine controlling an army of zombies would be painstaking work. Too much trouble for an old woman like me."

They chuckled together. The sound of Zach's laugh, bright as sunlight beside her grandmother's easy joy, chilled Cara's blood. They'd just met and already her grandmother was treating him as if she'd known him for years. No fraught family history hung between them like Cara's with Laolao.

And now here he was even charming the living daylights out of Laolao, being handsome and cordial and completely undermining everything Cara had told her about him. If he kept this up, he was going to get on Laolao's good side and turn her own grandmother against her.

Cara had seen this side of Zach show up whenever it was favorable for him. He knew how to conduct himself around adults. How to speak to them like he was their equal—or when it was useful, their superior. He had the breeding and the upbringing and the confidence that came with them. He walked into every room knowing he could turn any situation, any person, to his advantage with his good looks and honeyed mouth—or if it came down to it, money and power. Cara, on the other hand, had second guesses but no second chances: the carefulness cultivated from knowing she didn't have room for mistakes.

Privilege haunted his steps like a ghost, even if he didn't see it. Dead or alive, Zacharias Coleson had always been able to move through the world more easily than she could.

It occurred to her that if she didn't bring him back, he'd become a saint. Pretty much everyone—except for her—liked him. Even her own friends, Charlotte and Felicity, the traitors. He was captain of the high school swim team, son of one of the most prominent families in town, and annoyingly good-looking. He was the golden boy of Autumn Falls. And if he died, she'd never hear the end of it.

She couldn't hate him in public after that, either, because what heartless person would hold a grudge against a saint?

Another reason to make sure he didn't become one.

As if Zach sensed her thoughts, he half turned, caught her eye, swung a shining smile her way. Like a friendly knife.

Cara sent daggers back.

Stay away from my grandmother, asshole.

Zach and Laolao halted, and for a second Cara feared she'd accidentally said that out loud. But no, they'd reached the edge of the Wildwoods. Across the street, home beckoned—with darkened windows, thankfully.

"Will you be going home?" Laolao asked Zach.

Zach stiffened, and Cara knew why.

If he went home, he'd go home to a place he used to be alive in. Unable to talk to his brother or sister, who wouldn't even believe it was his ghost if they saw him with their own eyes. Alone in a house filled with people who might not have even realized yet that tonight Zach wasn't coming home.

Was a house still empty if the only thing in it was a ghost? Or did a ghost make it emptier?

"Don't look at me like that," Zach's voice demanded, and she realized that she'd been staring at him, and now *he* was staring at her, blue eyes cold and furious.

Cara lifted her chin. "Like what?"

"You were looking at me with pity or—or *something*." He snapped his mouth shut, seeming to arrive at the conclusion that, while he might be right, this wasn't the point he wanted to make.

Zach had his arms crossed in front of him, and she crossed her arms, too, mirroring him.

As uncomfortable as it was for her to feel pity for him, it had to feel far worse to be on the receiving end.

Laolao broke the stalemate. "You know what? How about you stay with us tonight, Zacharias?"

Shock sparked through her. "But, Laolao, he can't—"

"He can because I say so."

Her grandmother was using her commanding voice, the one that brooked no argument. Did her mother know she sounded just like Laolao when she gave out orders?

Zach smirked at her, certain that at least one thing hadn't changed. Another adult had taken his side. Again.

"I knew your grandfather," Laolao said to Zach, surprising him enough that the smirk disappeared. "He did something for me once, and I owe him a debt. You are welcome to stay for the remainder—for as long as you need."

"You knew his grandfather?" Cara said. "Why didn't you ever tell me that? What did he do for you? What kind of debt do you owe him that means I have to deal with Coleson staying—"

"*Cara*," Laolao warned.

You weren't supposed to argue in front of people who weren't family.

Laolao must have seen that Cara intended to do it anyway, because she cleared her throat and said, "Zacharias, would you mind giving us a moment alone?"

Cara glared at him for the length of the time it took him to cross the road and phase into her house.

"Why do you really know so much about the Signet Snake?" Cara blurted out when Zach was gone. "You knew what it was immediately."

Laolao sighed, turning away. "It is a personal interest, as I said."

Cara pressed on, speaking to Laolao's back. She wasn't supposed to question authority, either, but ghosts weren't supposed to be solid. Dead boys shouldn't have been possible to resurrect. "Why is it a personal interest?"

"If you must know, I had a friend once who was bitten by the Signet Snake."

Cara stopped in her tracks. Shadows the shade of rot stretched their fingers across the grass like a blight. Laolao glowed faintly in the darkness; silver silhouetted her frail shoulders. The headlights of occasional cars shone right through her. The drivers must be wondering what Cara was doing, standing on the side of the road by the mouth of the Wildwoods as the sun set, deep in conversation with no one at all.

"It was a long time ago," Laolao continued before Cara could say anything. "But I spent days trying to find answers. I learned that whenever the Signet Snake shows up, trouble comes. All the examples of the Snake appearing through history . . . what did you notice about them?"

"Death and destruction."

Laolao nodded. Her hands were clasped behind her back, head bent under the weight of her words, eyes shadowed behind her amber glasses. "It makes me wonder why the Snake chose Zacharias. I said that the clearing appearing out of nowhere might not be cause for concern, but . . . it does not bode well, I am afraid. Not for him or anyone else near him. It makes me worry for you. What do you do when an apple grows mold? You throw it out, before it can spread to everything else."

"Hold on." Cara's brow furrowed. The implication in Laolao's words— "You don't mean just letting Coleson fade?" It was a dark thing to imagine. Laolao couldn't possibly mean it.

"No, no, I do not think that would be kind. But I want you to temper your expectations, xiaogui. Do not get too invested. Whatever is at work here is far beyond just you."

Cara made a disbelieving noise. Her grandmother sounded so sure, so *pessimistic*. Laolao had wanted her to use her ghost-speaking abilities from the moment she got them, and now that Cara was, however unwillingly, even if it was solely for this week, Laolao was apprehensive and concerned?

"So that's it? He's doomed?" Cara swept a glance at her house. "I made a *promise* to him."

"I know you did, xiaogui." Laolao patted her on the head. Cara jerked back. For once, her grandmother's touch didn't comfort; instead, it brought chills. "But oaths mean nothing to death."

NINE

An obnoxious sound blared through Cara's dreams.

She jolted upright like she was Frankenstein's monster awakening. Blaze, who'd been curled up at the foot of her bed, leaped to the floor, barking, ready to face the intruder.

Zach stood by her door, grinning and holding an air horn.

"*What the heck?*" she shrieked, grabbing a pillow and throwing it at him.

It sailed wide by a solid foot and hit the wall behind him.

Zach started laughing. There was a reason Cara hadn't tried out for softball.

"Screw you! Why are you in my room? Get out!"

"Your grandma told me to wake you—*but* she didn't specify how." Mouth curled into a smirk, he paused, eyes lingering on her torso. "Nice shirt. Isn't that from eighth grade?"

Heat bloomed on her cheeks. Not only was the shirt a ratty piece from junior high, she was also wearing nothing beneath it.

"Piss off," she told him, fighting the urge to cross her arms over her chest. She opted to grab a comb off her nightstand instead, yanking it through her hair. She didn't care what he thought of her appearance; it was for her own dignity. "It's too early for your crap." 10:02, to be exact. Which, on a Saturday morning, was practically 6 a.m. "Fun fact, *some of us* still need sleep to live."

Zach ignored her, dropping the air horn—where had he even gotten it from?—on her dresser and crossing to the window. Cara continued untangling her hair and tried to listen for footsteps. Thankfully, it seemed her mother hadn't heard the blare.

"Holy shit," Zach said a moment later. "It's snowing."

"It is not snowing. You don't have to lie to get me out of bed."

He looked over, mouth crooked into a grin. "Would I ever lie to you?"

"Sixth grade, May," she said at once. "You announced your family owned every tree in Autumn Falls and I owed a fee for every time I'd even touched one."

"Not my fault you believed it. And, in case you forgot, it was to get back at you for ruining Christmas the year before."

Cara tugged at a stubborn snarl at the back of her neck. "I'm sorry, what fifth grader still believes in Santa Claus? I was doing you a favor."

"Narc," he said.

"Dunce," she shot back.

The comb gave up, snapping at the end and leaving two ivory teeth nested in her hair. Cara flung them into the trash can with twin perfect *pings*.

See? My aim's not completely *terrible*.

She dragged herself out of her blankets into the chill of the room.

"This better be good," she said, but just as she got to the window, he opened it.

A blast of freezing air hit her, so cold it tore a gasp from her throat. She shoved at him. He staggered sideways, laughing.

But he hadn't been lying. It *was* snowing.

It was Saturday, October 25, six days away from Halloween, six days away from her seventeenth birthday, six days away from Zach's final death—and it was snowing.

Stars of frost spiraled past the gaping window frame. Cara placed her hands on the sill, cold to the touch, and leaned closer, as if proximity would make the vision realer. White blanketed the ground in their backyard. The ghost tree by the back fence wore cuffs of snow on its boughs.

It doesn't normally snow until December.

Zach's laughter had died down to snickers. She turned to spit another remark at him, but it faltered on her lips.

Zach always looked like he'd just rolled out of bed—dark blond hair effortlessly messy, soft mouth two seconds away from a sarcastic yawn that said he could be anywhere else but here so weren't you lucky he was gracing you with his presence?

And Zach's presence came with ice storms. Crushed pine needles. Expensive cologne, like he'd stepped right out of the pages of a fashion magazine.

When she looked at him, it was like getting caught in a winter wind: exhilaration thrilling in her veins, the force so strong she could barely breathe.

If Cara hadn't been awake before, she was now.

Cara shook herself and planted her hands firmly on the windowsill, grounding herself in the chill. Was it climate change making the weather out of whack?

I learned that whenever the Signet Snake shows up, trouble comes. Laolao's voice echoed in Cara's mind. This was more than a freak storm. It was an omen.

After breakfast, Cara settled into an armchair in the attic with a book. Zach had told her that Laolao had left early that morning to ask some ghosts around town about the Signet Snake. Meanwhile, they were supposed to look through Laolao's disorganized library for any more clues about the antidote.

Cara's conversation with Laolao last night hadn't left her mind. She'd never seen her grandmother so uneasy. Almost . . . afraid. It didn't make sense because her grandmother was never afraid. She was the strongest ghost speaker ever. Whatever was coming must be truly terrible to upset her like that.

Laolao was no stranger to peril. When she was a little older than Cara, she defeated a guy who was basically a supervillain. An ambitious ghost speaker named Ambrose, who hadn't been satisfied with his magic, who had wanted more, more, *more*. He was the only one who ever came close to rivaling Laolao's powers, but with his fiancée at his side, an amplifier who could augment his abilities, he was nearly unstoppable. He'd set out to build an army of zombies. To control not only the dead but the living.

But Laolao had stopped him. With the help of a few other magical families, Laolao had taken care of the amplifier, had saved the day, had saved everyone. Ambrose had vanished, never to be seen again.

Cara had loved that story. As a kid, she'd made Laolao recount it again and again, spending hours sitting on her grandmother's lap as Laolao rocked back and forth in her creaking chair, telling her scary ghost stories—made scarier by the fact that they were real.

But now Cara was in a story of her own, she didn't like it one bit.

Normally, she would be at the Red Leaf Café by now. But she'd texted her manager last night that she'd come down with a bad cold. Cara didn't know what she'd do for all her other responsibilities this week: captain of the girls cross-country team, secretary for student council, animal shelter volunteer. She'd cross those bridges when she came to them.

Blaze whined inquisitively from his place at Cara's feet as she read, never taking his eyes from Zach who was pulling books off Laolao's bookshelf. The golden retriever had followed them to the attic, excited about a new ghost in the house.

Cara flipped through a red book whose title, *The History of Autumn Falls*, was printed in gold letters. Stale air riffled off the pages. Nothing useful, so she put it on the floor. Five minutes later, *The History of Autumn Falls* was joined by a smaller but equally useless book.

The next twenty minutes yielded as much as the previous books had.

Frustrated, Cara turned to the piles of paper scattered across the tables. She riffled through sheets and sheets of Chinese, fingers passing over characters she couldn't read.

A faded orange flyer fluttered to the floor.

26th Annual Fall Festival! it announced in exuberant curving script. *Saturday, October 12, 2–5 p.m., St. Athanasius School's Church-yard! Scary storytelling! Live music! Antiques market! Food, fire, fun for the whole family!* A clip-art jack-o'-lantern grinned up from the page.

This particular Fall Festival had been, what, four years ago? Cara didn't remember it specifically, but knew she would have attended it with Felicity and Charlotte. Either Felicity's or Charlotte's parents would have taken them because *her* mother thought it was a waste of time.

Now in high school, they attended a celebration of their own with the rest of their classmates every November. Their bonfire night involved a lot less pumpkin pie—and a lot more booze. They even had their own tradition: you wrote the name of the person you liked on a slip of paper and tossed it in the flames. It was a wish you made that your crush would turn into something more. Some people called it the *bone*fire, since if you put a name in, it was because you wanted to, well . . .

"I feel really sorry for the guy whose name you're planning to set on fire this year," Zach said from beside her.

He'd wandered over, a blue tome in his hands, and was reading the flyer over her shoulder.

Cara slammed the flyer on top of the pile with unnecessary force. "And I pity whatever poor girl you try to ask out next. She's probably going to wish she immolated herself in the bonfire along with your piece of paper."

Zach's brow furrowed, and Cara could tell he was trying really hard not to ask what *immolated* meant.

She paused, planting a hand on the stack and turning to face him. "But it's nice to know you're thinking about whose name I put in the bonfire."

Zach scoffed. "Don't flatter yourself." He busied himself with flipping through his book at light speed.

There was no way he was reading that fast. She opened her mouth to tell him so, but Zach made a noise of interest under his breath. He'd reached the end of his book.

"What?" she said.

"There's something under here. Feels like the last page's been glued down. . . ." To Cara's horror, he began picking at the inside of the back cover.

"Have you lost your mind? You can't do that to my grandma's book. To any book—"

"Got it." Tongue between his teeth, Zach pulled out a rectangular piece of paper. "Huh, looks like I was right."

"What is it?" Cara snatched at his hand, but he pushed her away easily and swung the arm with the paper high into the air. She cursed the several inches of height he'd gained on her over the past few years.

He took in the find, his eyebrows rising. "Well, this is interesting."

Cara clawed at his arm like a cat. "Okay, okay," he said, and handed the picture over.

A grainy, faded photograph showed an ordinary flower with eight delicate petals the color of fresh blood. Ordinary except for the fact that it seemed to be sprouting out from a stone, pushing the rock apart with the sheer force of blooming.

On the back of the photograph was a date in thin, elegant handwriting: *Midnight's Peak, 11/5/61.*

"Midnight's Peak," Cara breathed. "That's the cave behind the Falls."

"You think that's the flower—what's it called, the analyx?"

"It might be. It's not like any flower I've ever seen."

"That settles it. We go to Midnight's Peak, and boom, we'll find what we're looking for. See?" Zach said smugly. "And *you* didn't want me to rip up one of your grandma's books."

"That is *not* the takeaway here." Cara glanced back at the photograph, the unnatural bloom. "It can't be that simple—"

Blaze lifted his head, ears pricked at something she couldn't hear. Then:

"Cara?" Her mother's footsteps, coming up the attic stairs.

"*Crap.*" Cara looked to the door, then the window. She pushed

Zach toward it.

"Hey, what—?"

"Phase through the wall *now* and don't come back in until I say so."

"But—"

She shoved him outside, flung open the window—a bitter draft rushed in—and spun, thrusting the picture back inside the book just as her mother opened the door.

"I thought I heard you up here," her mother said, making her way over with a frown. "Don't you have work?"

"I, um, couldn't go today. I feel a little sick."

"Oh. I can make you pugongying tang."

Dandelion tea? Cara wasn't drinking the bitter brew unless she had to. "I'm okay," she said quickly. "It's just a little tickle in my throat. I'm sure it'll go away soon. But thank you."

Her mother's eyes scrutinized her, then flashed to the open window. She reached over, shut it with a bang. "This is why you're sick. You open the window in this kind of weather."

Cara smiled weakly. "I wanted some fresh air while I read."

"If you feel well enough to be up here reading and opening windows, then you are well enough to help me with the jiucai. Come to the kitchen."

"But I have to—"

Her mother, already halfway to the stairs, turned back around. "You have to what?"

"Nothing." Cara was aware of the hidden picture in her hands. "I'll be there in five minutes."

Satisfied, Cara's mother nodded and disappeared down the steps.

"Did you have to push me out the window?" Zach complained

from behind her. "It's not like she could see me."

"I didn't say come—" Cara hissed, but he was already phasing back inside.

She stared as an arm and leg came through the wall, then the rest of him. It was moments like this that she recalled with an unwelcome jolt—like a nightmare tapping on the glass of a dream—that Zach was a ghost. Not that she had ever fully forgotten, of course, but it was easy to let it slide to the back of her mind when he looked the same as before, save the silver touch of death.

"Yes, I had to," she said. "My mom may not be able to see you, but she could have still figured out you were here. I opened the window to mask the real reason the attic's freezing."

"You could have said it was cold because your grandma's here."

"I didn't want to risk it. Besides, you have different smells."

"Different what?"

Time to exit this conversation. Putting the photo in her pocket, Cara turned toward the door.

"Don't leave me hanging." Zach followed, Blaze on his heels. "What do I smell like?"

Cara whirled, planting her hands on either side of the doorway. "I have to go help my mom," she said. "Wait here until I'm done, and we'll make the trek to Midnight's Peak together. If you go *anywhere*, I'll kill you—" She paused, hearing what she'd just said. "Well, just don't move."

"Sure, take as long as you need. It's only my life on the line."

But it would be *her* life on the line if her mother found out what she was doing, Cara thought, and slammed the door.

TEN

Cara's mother kept her busy until dinner. And after that, when Cara retreated to her room, preparing to sneak out, her mother showed up with a bowl of pugongying tang and forced her into bed, saying that she needed to rest (never mind that she had made her do chores all day).

Finally, once her mother was asleep, she found Zach in the attic and the two of them snuck out together.

Laolao was still gone, but that was nothing to worry about. When Zach asked why her grandmother wasn't back yet, Cara shrugged and told him that Laolao kept to her own schedule.

She and Zach walked through the trees, darkness settling over their heads. It was still snowing and chilly. She shoved one gloved hand deeper into the pockets of the scarlet winter coat she'd dug out of storage, her other hand holding her phone with its flashlight on. The climb to the top of the Autumn Falls, their town's namesake, was long and torturous. Cara had picked the easiest path she could remember, one leading to the top of the Falls. Nonetheless, sweat trickled down her back.

Stars glinted like hundreds of watchful eyes. The Wildwoods was silent, toned in silver and black. Snow drifted from the sky.

An owl called: hushed, haunting.

By the time they reached the top of the Falls, Cara's legs were lit matchsticks. She stood by the water for a few minutes, simply sucking in breaths. Her lungs burned for oxygen in the winter-sharp air. Flowing too fast to freeze fully, the Autumn Falls River rushed past to plunge over the rocks.

The Wildwoods fell away at her feet, trees ringing the pool the waterfall cascaded into. Beyond, her town slumbered, stitched in squares of ivory and silence.

"I'm gonna check out the cliff face," Zach said. "See if I can find the cave." She nodded, and he disappeared over the edge.

Crossing her arms, Cara rocked back on her heels, angling her head to loosen the sore muscles in her neck. Slowly, she took her first deep breath alone that night. And then she let it go.

"Found it," Zach said, landing beside her. His hair fell into his eyes, and he brushed it away. "You can't get to it on foot. It's behind the waterfall."

Had Zach been alive, his face would have been shadowed, but his ghostly features were clear. Lucent.

"Okay, so you'll take me," she said. She wasn't missing out on a waterfall cave.

Zach's brows raised slightly. "You sure? I'd have to carry you."

"As long as you don't drop me."

The corner of his mouth lifted. "I'd be stupid to," he said, and walked toward her.

Being carried bridal style by Zach was exactly as uncomfortable for Cara as she'd thought it would be, especially because looping her arms around his neck for an increased sense of safety—as false as it may have been—put their faces closer together.

Her stomach swooped every time he suddenly dipped, her heart speeding. The rush reminded her of playing on the swings as a kid, vision blurring as she rushed toward the ground, fear and excitement tingling through her body.

The Falls tumbled past. Water skated over clenched fists of ice, gripped in the throes of a strange winter. The ice was opaque, milky blue, with twigs or bits of leaves trapped like fossils from a sunnier time.

As they descended, the cliff face swayed away from the Falls, where erosion had broken down the rock with sheer power. She'd learned in geography that the Autumn Falls were created from the last ice age, the river carved out by glacier melt. The water crashing above their heads was at least ten thousand years old, forever running until it froze, dried, or diverted.

Droplets stung her face as Zach maneuvered behind the Falls, landing on a ledge before Midnight's Peak.

He set her down carefully, one hand lingering at the small of her back a second longer after he'd let her go.

As they ducked under the low overhang, moonlight illumined the first runners of frost dripping down the limestone walls.

Inside, the ceiling curved upward; stalactites grasped for them from above. The walls yawned around them, fangs of frost beautiful in a breakable way. Everything shone with eerie blue iridescence, like fingers had smeared paint over the cave walls some centuries ago.

"It's beautiful," Cara said, reaching out to touch the ice.

"Yeah," Zach grudgingly agreed, and Cara had to keep herself from staring at the air where his breath should have bloomed. In the cavelight, Zach's eyes were the dark blue of Arctic waters.

They moved forward, her footsteps echoing around them.

Columns of ice bounded their path. In them, she saw snatches of herself: fractured, shattered, infinite. At every turn, her face was unrecognizable, no matter how hard she looked: her eyes two gouged-out shadows; mouth, a dark, warped line; expression, a stranger's.

And she was alone.

Zach wasn't beside her in the images. In this silent world of ice and stone, there was only her.

Her eyes sought his shape to reassure herself, his form familiar, lines she could trace in the dark: his cheekbones, his jaw, his limbs, as striking and sculpted as ice. Frozen in time.

The back of the cave was thick with frost. How could flowers grow here? No red blooms crawled out from granite cracks. Cara hugged her arms to her chest.

"S-see anything?" Cara said, teeth chattering.

Wind howled into the cave, whistling past the stalactites and raising an eerie song, and she shivered violently. The gust made something flutter.

"What's that?" she said, pointing to something peeking out from under a rock.

Kneeling, Zach tugged out a folded, yellowed sheet of paper brittle with age.

"Wait, I think there's something on there," he said.

Cara stepped closer to Zach to get a better look at the paper.

From words in elegant ink, she read out loud:

To Ambrose,

I am writing this because you will never read it, love. You never did like letters much. Or heights.

Time is running out. In less than seven days, I will be nothing more than flowers, bones, and dust. Unless you find the antidote.

But I know you won't.

Cara glanced at Zach, who met her wide eyes with his own.

Dying feels both like an eternity and like nothing at all. At least oblivion promises to be short. I can feel the end eating away at me with each passing hour, spinning my spirit into the dark.

I know you are trying. I just wish you were trying for me.

You were in such a rage when dawn rose on my corpse. You would not believe there was nothing that could save me, that you would have to watch me fade away before your eyes.

When you found out the analyx might bring me back to life, your eyes sparked like gun steel and your chest swelled. It drove you, having something tangible to hunt. You ordered men into the wild after a wisp of a solution.

It's easy to chase after ghosts.

It's harder to live with them.

Even as I write this, you are searching still. You do not know what I've discovered: that the analyx is not the cure.

I don't think you'll ever find the antidote. You would have gone to the ends of the earth to get what you wanted. But my love, you would not have risked your own skin. And to save me, you would have had to risk everything.

Oh, you would have killed for me—but you would not have died for me. No, you are far too important for that. Your ambitions have never involved oblivion. I know you had big plans for us. And she wrecked every single one of them. Didn't she?

Maybe, once upon a time, you were different.

But as I am now, that other you is dead.

Perhaps someone who needs this will read it and figure out a way to finally defeat you. I cannot save you from what you have become. I cannot—will not—help you. Not anymore.

My love, my love, my love.

You will never find me.

Yours till death,

R

Later, Cara would blame the letter for the reason she did not hear the hiss sooner.

ELEVEN

Just several steps behind her, a white serpent was blocking the exit of the cave, staring at her. A forked tongue flickered out, tasting the air. Cara could swear the serpent was smiling.

Iridescent light gleamed off its scales, which themselves were the color of bone, of snow-white corpses, as it uncoiled the sinuous rope of its body, perhaps six to eight feet long. It bared its fangs: two scythes. Forget flesh—these fangs looked like they could cleave through steel.

She could not run. It would be no use, like fleeing a plague, like fleeing death. Blood rushed hot in her ears as she met its eyes, pitiless slashes of pupil. In its vision, she was only a scared animal in the woods, winter waiting for her body.

It reared back—

And suddenly Zach was in front of her, brandishing a stalactite like a sword. "Like *hell* you're touching her," he said, voice low and dangerous.

And tremoring. Just the tiniest bit.

Zach?

"Coleson—"

"Stay behind me," he ordered. "If it wants you, it's gonna have to go through me first."

Laughter cut through the cave.

The snake was lengthening, form oozing as it morphed into the shape of a man. Stumps became limbs; scales melded together into smooth, colorless flesh. Fangs warped into a cruel white smile.

She caught a glimpse of the man in his whole form—a sleek silver suit, slitted eyes above mirrored sunglasses resting on his crooked nose, dark hair, and lithe, lethal limbs—before he *struck*, moving so fast he was a blur.

In one heartbeat, he was behind her, a hand clamped over her mouth, something sharp and cold angled between her ribs. His flesh burned like a brand, the heat given off by something decomposing, the fever of an infected wound. Her heart thudded so loud she was sure the cave echoed with it.

Cara couldn't see his face, but she could hear the cruelty in his tone as he spoke to Zach, "You went and found yourself a ghost speaker. I have to say, I'm impressed. That rarely happens." Silence. She imagined those slitted eyes narrowing. "Such a shame I'm going to kill her in front of you."

Zach had gone very, very still. His jaw had been clenched, face tight, but at this, something broke. Slid out of place and shattered.

Zach was worried—for *her*—which meant this situation had officially exceeded all known danger levels. Cara's breath went shallow.

Thoughts flashed through her head. The Snake—the Snake that had bitten and killed Zach—could also turn into a human, somehow, and now it was set on killing her as well. She writhed in his grip, but her struggles may as well have been the movements of a mouse. The Snake clamped down harder, his ring cutting into her lip. The knife he held pressed into her skin a degree farther, slicing through the fabric of her clothes. She froze, and the Snake chuckled, his voice a worm in her ear. "That's right, girl. Best just to stay quiet and don't move."

Fury and fear flared in her chest, but she obeyed.

"Let her go," Zach said.

"Not a chance," said the Snake delightedly. "That letter you just read? I killed the writer in this very cave. Same spot where you stand, in fact. Oh, how she *screamed*. I expect this one will as well. I can hear her pathetic heart quaking in her chest. Doesn't this make you wish you'd gotten more done in life, human?"

"You don't know me," Zach growled.

"Know you? I've killed you. Countless times, over countless centuries. Boys who believed themselves men, gods—something more than mortal—because of earthly powers like money, looks. You all thought you were special. That you would never die." The Snake's laugh hissed out in coils. "Guess where they are now."

Zach's hands tightened around the stalactite.

"I'm older than your pitiful brain can possibly fathom, boy. I'm an Ouroboros. They called me Kingsbane when the world was young. I toppled thrones with a single bite. I brought death everywhere I went. I set cities *aflame*."

"So what do you want with her?" Zach said. "She's nothing."

Nothing. It hurt more than she thought it should.

"Nothing?" the Snake echoed. "She's a *ghost speaker*, and you need her to resurrect you. She can undo the death I laid down. I can't have that, can I? Someone unstitching all my hard work? All of my beautiful terror and pain?" The Snake gestured broadly, sweeping grandly with the hand that had covered Cara's mouth. His voice raised. "I thought of biting her, too, but I wanted something slower. Something *sweeter*. You see, I was made to tear the world apart. I'm destruction." He moved his hand back toward her mouth, his raving reaching a fever pitch. "I'm *hell incarnate*—"

Seizing her chance, Cara bit down on his hand with all she had.

Bone cracked between her jaws. Blood rushed her mouth. The pressure of the knife eased. She wrenched herself from the Snake's grip. As she did so, her teeth caught on the ring on his hand, sending it spinning onto the cave floor. He dove for it, but faltered as though something inside him was preventing him from moving. He collapsed to his knees.

Cara swallowed. Iron scorched her throat, burned all the way down to her belly. "No," she said. "You're just a bully."

The Snake howled, an inhuman noise, terrifying and indistinct. The sound stabbed through her head, and she bent over, clutching her ears. Stalactites shivered and shattered. *"My ring—"* he hissed, gripping his bleeding, mangled hand, before falling to all fours, scales sprouting along his skin like disease.

And then the serpent began to grow.

Within seconds, he had doubled his length, even larger than before. When he reared up, his diamond-shaped head scraped the ceiling, knocking aside stalactites. Giant icicles hit the ground and fractured. *"You'll pay,"* he hissed, his eyes glowing.

A hand grabbed Cara's. "Time to go," Zach said.

The ring glinted even in the rising dust. For a simple piece of jewelry, the Snake seemed awfully attached. "One second," Cara said, bending to grab it before they took off toward the mouth of the cave.

The Snake thundered after them, bulldozing through columns of ice as if they were paper. The ground shook under their feet with the Snake's pure rage. Cara lost her balance, but Zach pulled her back up. They hurtled down the tunnel and shot out into the moonlight.

Cara skidded to a stop right before the edge. The Falls roared overhead. She and Zach turned to face the Snake as he rushed after them. Behind the serpent, the cave rumbled, rocks falling to fill its mouth, sealing it shut.

There was nowhere to go.

"You," hissed the Snake, "have something I want."

"Funny." Cara tilted her head. "So do you."

"I could knock you off this puny ledge with one swipe."

"And I'd catch her." Zach's fingers tightened around her own.

"And," Cara started, heart hammering in her throat, "you'd lose the ring. This is what you want, isn't it?"

She held it up. It was a simple gold band, nothing more, but the inside of it was carved with an inscription in some ancient language, and the moonlight seemed to bow around it, the darkness more pronounced next to it.

"Something about this makes it valuable to you. I can't imagine it's the metal itself—as an assassin of kings, you'd have been paid ships of gold. As old as you are, you might not even care for material wealth at all. No, it's something else." She locked eyes with the Snake. "It's magic, isn't it? This is what makes you human."

And she couldn't imagine why, out of all the things he could be, he would ever choose to be human—but the Snake had gone rigid, so still he could have been a statue, so she knew she was right.

"Let's make a trade," she said, hoping her voice didn't shake. She took a deep breath, finalizing her terms. "This ring in exchange for information. What's the antidote? The letter said it wasn't the analyx."

For a moment, the Snake didn't speak. Then he said, hateful and slow, "Of course the analyx isn't the antidote. That little flower only grows where my victims fall. Its existence derives from their deaths; it can't *possibly* bring them back."

He had a lot of condescension considering none of his information was something she could just Google. Cara gritted her teeth. "So what's the antidote, then? Where do we find it?"

"Where do you find *her*," the Snake corrected.

"What?" Zach said.

Something in the Snake's voice had changed. "My other half. My antithesis. Her venom is the antidote."

The world shifted on its axis again. A puzzle piece slotted into space. A satisfying click.

There is a second Snake.

"She resides at the end of the ancient river, the first river. The water that connects the lands of the liminal world."

"Where do we find that?"

"You already have." The Snake twisted its head. At this size, its fangs alone were longer than Cara's body.

Understanding glimmered in her mind. The clearing. The creek spurting water like a wound. How the air itself shimmered, like a tear in the fabric of the world.

"We've been there, yes," Cara said. "But nothing happened."

"Nothing happened," the Snake said, "because you are not an Ouroboros, and if you are not an Ouroboros, you need a mark from one." It surged forward, and Zach stepped forward as well, brandishing his weapon of ice. *"Now give me the ring."*

Cara gulped. The Snake was so close she could see herself reflected in the glassy white of its eye, so fragile and small against the backdrop of the night.

"Okay," she said. "I'll give you the ring—*if* you give me a mark to travel through this liminal world. And promise you'll leave us alone after this and do us no harm."

The Snake hissed. "You ask for too much."

Steadying her shaky fingers, Cara held the ring above the drop. The waterfall thundered past her hand, the kinetic force of it almost magnetic. It would take the ring in a second if she let it. She looked back at the Snake.

"Those are my terms," she said. "Something valuable for something valuable. I think you'll find it a fair bargain."

A long, shuddering moment.

And at last, the Snake said, every word dripping in venom, "Fine. I agree."

Cara tossed the ring forward. The second it touched the Snake's scales, the serpent changed back. The man stood in front of them, mirrored sunglasses slung low enough on his nose to show his slit-pupiled eyes burning with rage, twisting the ring into place on his finger with practiced nonchalance.

Without warning, he lunged forward, grabbing her wrist. His nails bit into the soft flesh. Her skin began to burn, and a gasp of pain tore from her lips.

"*You're hurting her,*" Zach said, but the Snake scoffed.

"If I could hurt her, I wouldn't settle for this. I'd take her apart, limb by limb, and I'd make you watch. *This* is the mark she so desperately wants."

Right as the pain concentrated on her wrist reached a head-splitting level, the Snake lifted his hand, and it dissipated. Where his fingers had been curled was a small circular shape: a snake eating its own tail. An Ouroboros.

"My venom isn't the only thing that's dangerous," he said. "Every part of me is poison, especially my blood. You don't know the fate you've bought." His eyes cut to where Zach's and Cara's hands were joined. "Enjoy that while you can, ghost. You're going to stray further and further from being human. Becoming incorporeal. Unable to touch what you desire most. At the end, you'll be begging for pain, just to feel something."

He paused, and his voice softened, the way a cadaver does days after death, a hint of nostalgia creeping in like rot. "Say you actually make it there. That you don't die, as you most likely will. Tell her I sent you, would you? I haven't seen her in so long." His lips stretched into a smile, wider than humanly possible, with too many teeth. *"Tell her it's not over."*

Before Zach or Cara could react, the Snake was shifting again, the serpent a flash of bone as he slithered through a crevice in the cave-in and vanished.

In unison, they dropped each other's hands. Inhaling deeply, Cara hugged her arms to herself, more out of emotion than cold. Warmth continued to crawl along her skin, adrenaline running hot in her veins.

"What an asshole," Zach said.

She mustered up the energy for a snarky reply. "Takes one to know one."

"I'm not anything like him," Zach protested.

She shook her head. Walking to the mouth of the cave, she stopped in front of the blockade of rocks. "Did that feel too simple to you?" When she laid a finger on the mark on her wrist, she could feel her own pulse thumping beneath, almost as if the serpent symbol were alive.

"You're never satisfied, Tang. We got what we needed. I told you we would."

"I don't know. We don't know much about the Signet Snake, but from what we do know, I have a feeling he wouldn't let us go that easily."

Maybe he hadn't.

It does not bode well, I am afraid. Not for him or anyone else near him. It makes me worry for you. . . . Do not get too invested.

Laolao's words echoed.

Zach snorted. "You wouldn't be happy if we hadn't found out what the antidote was, but you're not happy that we found it out, either. No matter what that mark means, we need it for the liminal world—whatever the hell that is—so we're already ahead. Not everything has to be hard all the time."

She scoffed, turning to face him. "Easy for *you* to say, dumbass—"

Her retort died in her throat.

Zach had gone transparent. Standing with his back to the sky, the heavens filled his form; stars threaded his silhouette. Polaris winked at his temple, and Andromeda wound her fingers through his hair. Only his eyes had stayed the same—and then he blinked, and Cara was seeing stars.

"What?" Zach said, the night sky cutting his cheekbones.

Cara caught her breath. *It's just him*, she reminded herself. "It's happening. What the Snake said. You've gone incorporeal." She hesitated, and continued, quietly though she didn't know why, quietly as though it were a confession, "I can see the stars in you."

He looked down at his arms, turning them over. "Holy shit," he said, and held his hands to the heavens. Novas ringed his knuckles, suffusing his palms in godly light.

Zach took a step, diaphanous. New constellations shifted to kiss his skin.

He was a star that had already died, but the last of his light was still reaching her eyes. Maybe in this way all ghosts were faraway stars, and she was only seeing them as they had been in a younger universe, before death and darkness caught up.

Cara felt his gaze on her but forced herself to stare pointedly past him, at a section of the night sky he did not hold. She couldn't look at him. Not like this.

Then Zach said, "You have blood on your mouth," and raised a hand toward her face, and for some reason, she didn't immediately step away.

It was only when his thumb grazed the corner of her mouth, ever so gently, that she jolted back from him, as she should have from the start.

"Thanks, but I'm good," she said, raising her arm and dragging her sleeve across her mouth—rough enough that it burned—both to get rid of the blood and the sensation of his fingers on her skin. But even after she turned her head and spit, the iron taste of the Snake's blood lingered on her tongue, sour and hot. The Snake's last words echoed in her head. *Every part of me is poison.* Cara raised her chin, meeting Zach's gaze. "Did I get all of it?"

She didn't know why he was looking at her like that. If scarlet still stained her teeth—well, it wasn't as if he hadn't seen her like this before.

"You didn't have to protect me," she said carefully.

For someone who rarely had to, Zach wore terror well, like one would a tie or a three-piece suit. And now that the occasion for it was over, he had slipped it off, swapped it for something more becoming, ironed out the tension from his expression.

He shrugged. "I had to, didn't I? It's like the Snake said: you're my ghost speaker, and I need you to bring me back."

Something inside her went tight. Of course. The appearance of the gesture had been new, but the reasoning behind it was the same as always.

He wouldn't have let his one chance at life be taken away. He had stepped in front of her, yes, but he had done it for himself.

That was the Zach she knew.

In some way, she was grateful for the loathing that rose inside her, spilling through her veins like snowmelt from mountains in spring—natural, familiar.

Some people didn't change, not even in death.

red sleeping bag out of the closet, Blaze latched on to it, forcing her to tug it out of his teeth. He flopped his fluffy rump down in defeat and whined.

Cara sat down, too, taking Blaze's face into her hands. "Oh, you poor baby. I'll be back. I'm just going away for a little while, okay?" She ruffled the fur on top of Blaze's head. Gazing up at her with plaintive eyes, he thumped his tail once.

Well, now that she'd lied to her dog, it was time to lie to her friends.

E=FC^2 SQUAD:

Cara: Hey guys—so I'm still grounded, but I actually won't be at school this week either

She paused, thinking over her words, then quickly tapped out another text.

Cara: Super unplanned, but I'm catching a flight to China today. I probably won't be able to text until I get back

Felicity: huh

Felicity: doesn't sound like ur grounded

Cara: ??

Felicity: you're gonna be on an airplane

Felicity: so you'll be

Felicity: flighted

Charlotte: Wow!! That was terrible!!

Cara: Change of plans. Instead of going to China, I'm now driving over to your house to murder you for that godawful pun

Charlotte: I call shotgun!!

Felicity: none of u appreciate my GENIUS and one day you shall all regret it

Felicity: so why are u suddenly taking a trip to zhongguo

Cara frowned at her phone. She didn't want to lie to her friends any

TWELVE

They left at first light.

Now that they knew what the antidote was and where it was, the only thing left to do was to go after it. When they'd returned from Midnight's Peak the night before, it had been too late to go trekking through the woods again, and Cara had needed sleep, exhausted from climbing up to the Falls and back. She'd also wanted to tell Laolao about everything they'd discovered—

But upon Cara waking, Laolao still wasn't home.

So at 6 a.m.—before her mom got up—Cara sent Zach to the kitchen to pack food for the rest of the week, then wait for her in the Wildwoods while she got ready to go. She'd been running hot since waking. At first, she'd thought maybe she'd caught a cold from being outside all night, but her forehead was free of fever. This felt different, anyway. It was warmth filling her body like blood. Pooling in the palms of her hands, the pit of her belly, the hollows of her skull.

If she didn't know better, Cara would almost call it magic.

Blaze was very distressed about her leaving. The golden retriever ran circles around her legs, nearly tripping her as she packed the barest essentials. Clothes, toothbrush, hairbrush. Winter boots and her regular red Converse, in case the weather was out of whack in the liminal world. A towel. Some cash, just in case. When she dug her old more than she had to. Pretending she couldn't see ghosts—yeah, she was used to that. Simply lying by omission was one thing. Straight-up telling them falsehoods was another.

But what if they asked her mother? Or said some offhand comment, years later? She had to keep the story straight.

Cara: My great-aunt is sick

She sighed.

Felicity: well now i feel like trash

Felicity: even more than i usually do that is

Felicity: that sucks i'm sorry

Charlotte: That's awful . . . I'm so sorry :(((

Cara: It's okay, guys. Seriously. But could you get my assignments for me from school?

Charlotte: I'm gonna be optimistic here . . .

Felicity: when are u NOT

Charlotte: But I don't think missed homework will be a problem!!

Cara: ?????

Felicity: oh cara

Felicity: my sweet summer child

Felicity: have u looked outside a window lately

Felicity: it's gonna be SNOWMAGEDDON, BABEY

Charlotte: I bet we're definitely getting tomorrow off!!

Felicity: i bet we're getting the whole week off

Felicity: twenty dollars

Charlotte: I'm not betting with you anymore!! Not after last time!!

Felicity: it's not MY fault that i'm very, very good at winning

Charlotte: I lost sixty dollars.

Felicity: that's showbiz, baby

Cara was smiling so hard her whole face hurt. She was going to miss them.

Cara: Hey guys, we're about to board. Talk to you when I get back

Charlotte: Bye!! Sending love!! <3

Felicity: do i hear thirty dollars

Cara: Do not bring me into your illegal gambling ring, Felicitous

Felicity: whaaaaaaa it's v legal

Felicity: but in all seriousness

Felicity: pls know that i

Felicity: and my thirty dollars

Felicity: are always here for u

Cara notified everybody else—her manager, her cross-country team coach, student council, the animal shelter—giving them the same excuse. She left a letter under her mother's door and a letter in the attic for Laolao, explaining what she was setting out to do. The deal she'd made with Zach, securing his future in exchange for hers. It wasn't like Laolao to be away from home for so long, but maybe she had gotten caught up in asking about the antidote around town, not knowing that Cara and Zach had already figured it out.

Gray dawn light filtered in through the curtains drawn over the living room windows, reflecting off the shiny plastic of their red leather couch. Her stomach ached, but Cara forced herself to turn away, toward the front door. Her pack weighed heavy on her shoulders. With each step, however, the leaving seemed easier: pure momentum moving her feet.

She was almost out the door when she heard a quiet voice.

"Cara."

She whirled around, caught between the screen door and the main door.

Her mother was standing in the living room, Cara's note in her fist.

Like a lion on the hunt, her mother moved toward her, and Cara stumbled outside, letting the screen door bang shut.

Her mother's eyes found hers through the wire mesh. "Come inside."

Of course. Wouldn't want to risk losing face by letting the neighbors glimpse their fight.

Cara hesitated, then shook her head.

Thin-lipped, her mother came outside, closing the front door. She was dressed in day clothes, but her black hair still tangled around her face, as if she'd wanted to chase after Cara as soon as she got the note but had to stop and look presentable. To her mother, appearances were everything.

But she would have been scary even wearing a nightgown. The look in her eyes sent a shiver down Cara's spine.

She shook the note. "What," she said, "is this?"

In the harsh regard of her mother's gaze, Cara's spiteful decision to chase after the antidote seemed not only foolish but reckless. Cara stared down at the doorstep covered in snow that had continued to fall during the night. "This is for my future." Her voice turned pleading, like a child's. "It's all explained in the note. I left one for Laolao, too—"

A laugh erupted from her mother's lips. "I knew it. This is all your grandmother's doing, isn't it? *She* put you up to this." Her mouth twisted. "She still isn't satisfied. As if she hasn't done enough for one lifetime."

Her mother's words were a steel blade striking against the flint of Cara's heart.

Something inside her sparked.

Laolao wasn't the one venturing into a liminal world. *Laolao* wasn't the one who intended to raise the dead. *Laolao* wasn't the one who had made a promise to a desperate boy in a desperate storm, in an attic lit by lightning.

"No," Cara said. "Laolao has nothing to do with this. She isn't even here." *In fact, she warned me not to get too invested.* "This is my choice and mine alone."

Her mother didn't look satisfied with her answer. Again, she stepped forward, this time gently touching Cara's hair.

With a *tsk,* she said, "You don't want to do this." A lion coaxing a cub back to the den. "Did you even brush your hair when you woke up? Come back in. Let me do your braid."

Cara had grown up sitting at her mother's knee on mornings like this, dove-gray light the only decoration on her mother's bedroom walls, letting her mother brush her hair into a perfect braid for school until Cara was old enough to do it herself. Braiding Cara's hair was a way for her mother to show she loved her without saying it.

It was also a way for her mother to exercise control, to brush the errant parts of Cara back into something fit to be seen.

The two reasons were braided together so tightly, so inseparably, that over the years, they had become a knot that not even time's fingers could untangle. At least that Cara could see.

But it had never been quite enough for her mother, had it?

Cara tugged out of her mother's grasp. She shot a quick look at the woods. The silver of Zach's form glowed in between the trees, waiting.

When she turned to face her again, her mother's gaze darted to the trees, then settled back on Cara. Her lips tightened—she'd discerned there was a ghost somewhere in the forest.

Which would her mother find worse: running off with a ghost or with a boy?

Ghost boy, Cara decided. *That* was the worst.

"So that's it?" her mother said flatly. "You're choosing your grand-mother?"

"I'm choosing *myself*." *Whatever that entails—I'm going to find out.* "I'm tired of being fought over and used as a pawn in your war with Laolao."

It was never about what Cara wanted, even if she stopped refusing to pick a side and finally came to a choice. Even then, at the moment of Cara finally deciding to do what she wanted, Laolao and her mother would twist it for their own satisfaction to use it against each other.

"I'll ground you for the rest of high school," her mother said calmly, as if she hadn't brought out a grenade and was standing there ready to pull the pin. "For however long it takes."

And how long would that be? Weeks? Months? Until Cara was old enough to live by herself? Old enough to become a ghost?

In some ways, Cara had been grounded her whole life.

She took a deep breath, threw her shoulders back, and locked eyes with her mother. "I'm doing this," she said. "I've made my arrange-ments, and I'm going. And you can't stop me."

Her mother could have dragged her back into the house. She could have gone nuclear, pulling out more threats, launching tests to gauge the grade of her daughter's resolve, what punishment Cara might eventually fold under. She could have told Cara to never come back, that she'd never speak to Cara again.

She did none of those things.

Everyone said Cara looked like her mother, that they had the same eyes, but she'd never known if that was just something they said to be polite, especially when they didn't have her father to compare to. Try as she might, Cara had never been able to see the similarity. Even Laolao said Cara had her mother's eyes—but Cara's mother said Cara had Laolao's eyes.

And yet, as Cara stared into her mother's eyes, the same shade of dark brown, so dark it gleamed black, so dark it seemed to assimilate all light, she had to wonder if maybe it wasn't the shape or the shade after all that connected them—it was the stubbornness that burned in their irises.

When her mother spoke, her voice was neither wraith nor smoke but venom.

"Maybe your grandmother isn't making you do this, but she sure played a part in your decision. You have your grandmother's eyes, and every time I look at you, I see her. Which is funny, you know, because when your grandmother looked at me, she saw nothing at all. Like the only things she could see were ghosts.

"You are your grandmother's, selfishness and all. *She* didn't keep her promises, either."

And then her mother turned and went back into the house, easing the door shut behind her as gently as one might the lid of a coffin.

Cara stood there for a moment. She had gone cold inside. Her mother's words hung in the air like ashes.

She reached for the door—then stopped. The metal of the doorknob bit into her fingers, but she held on to the solidness of it; the cold was something tangible, even if it was cruel.

She could open the door. Go into the warmth, the golden light of the kitchen. She could take it all back.

But even if she went in, that didn't mean she'd be home.

Her mother had asked her to make a choice on this doorstep, this threshold. And Cara had made it. She'd chosen her own path. She might be able to open this door, but she'd closed the one that mattered.

And there was no opening it now.

Cara whirled around like a wildfire, aimed in a new direction by wind.

Zach pushed off the tree he was leaning on when she arrived in front of him. "About time—" he said, then stopped when he saw the look on Cara's face. His eyebrows went up, but he said nothing, only held out a pack of food that Cara snatched as she stormed past him.

Anger choked her throat like smoke, and only a lifetime of politeness being hammered into her every fiber allowed her to bite out, "Thanks."

Snow crunched under her boots. Her decision smoldered inside her. She swiped at her eyes. *You don't know what I've done for you*, she thought at Zach, and then, a quiet voice said to herself: *Do you even know what you've done?*

The hard part was, she knew her mother loved her. It was the little things, the ones you kept in a jar like fireflies and would take out to see that they were still glowing. But they also got caught under your nails like dried blood, built up in your throat until they became a choked sob that you didn't know how or when to let go.

I'll take out the bones for you.

But if love meant controlling every single aspect of the other person, she wanted no part of it.

She reached for her hair tie. She tore out her braid as she moved forward, fingers clawing at the carefully woven strands, sending her hair fanning out over her shoulders like flame. For a moment, she considered leaving it down—but no. That was too wild. She swept it up in a ponytail instead.

They were almost to the clearing when Zach said, "Hey, Tang."

She looked up. Zach had apparently decided to take on the risk of approaching her.

"Are you okay?" he said.

Oh, no. She wasn't doing this. She'd already had enough of lying to the people she loved. She didn't have enough energy to start with the ones she hated.

"Why do you care?" she said, poison coiled in her voice.

"I don't," he said, shoving his hands into his pockets, and that would have been the end of it if he hadn't continued to keep pace with her. After a minute, he said, "So what's a liminal river? What does 'liminal' even mean anyway?"

She eyed him, but his questions were innocent enough. "Liminality concerns thresholds. Boundaries. It's where things transition from one state to another. Where things *change*. You've been in liminal spaces before. Haven't you ever been at school after everyone's gone home and the halls are quiet and the lights are dim and flickering?"

"Yeah, for swim meets. It's always a little creepy."

"Liminal spaces do that to you. They affect your mind, your emotions, your decisions. They unsettle you because they're not permanent, and you're not meant to stay there. Airports are liminal spaces. So are IKEAs. But there are also more ancient kinds, those the liminal river runs through. Laolao first told me about it when I was a kid. She said, 'It's where all the magic in the world flows from, seeping from its waters into the soil. An ancient river that stretches around the whole globe, in hidden channels and the tiniest tributaries and underground streams.'" Cara ended the quotation from the book Laolao had read her. "Apparently, part of it's in Autumn Falls."

"What's the liminal world, then?"

"Laolao didn't tell me much about it. It's hard to explain. Do you remember when we learned about the Greek underworld freshman year? When we read *The Odyssey* in English class?" He nodded, and she went on. "In those days, the world was vast and unexplored, and it was easy for people to imagine a physical place for where you went when you died. They had a place for where the gods lived, too. And seas full of monsters." She was beginning to sweat under her coat, even with the snow, and she tugged the zipper down, took off her gloves. "But now pretty much every part of the globe has been charted— except for the depths of the oceans—and there are no places for gods to hide. There are pockets of land, though, where the soil takes up a little more magic, where strange things grow. Crossroads. Where it's easy to slide from life to death, or vice versa.

"Liminal spaces are stitches. They may look separate—but like a needle threading the fabric of the world, the liminal river connects them all."

Zach's mouth quirked. "Hey, remember all those times you told me to go to hell?" he said. "Bet you didn't think you'd be coming with me."

"It's not hell!" Cara protested. "It's still the real world. Did you not hear a single thing I said—?"

But he was laughing, stepping into the clearing. "Okay, Annabeth."

It surprised her enough that she stopped at the clearing's edge. One, he remembered a character from the Percy Jackson books their

English teacher had read to them? And two—she wasn't angry anymore.

Whether Zach had done it on purpose or not, he'd distracted her from her fight with her mother.

Zach bent by the place where his body was hidden, staring at the scarlet-spotted snow. She made her way over to him and knelt, too. All around the cloaked corpse bloomed small crimson flowers. They almost looked like poppies: innocent symbols of eternal sleep.

"The analyx," Zach said in a low voice.

Stretching out a hand, Cara snapped one of the stems, plucking an analyx from its garden of damasked death. If she didn't know why they were growing, she might have thought them beautiful.

"Whoa, look."

In the spot she'd just picked, a duplicate welled up out of the snow like blood.

Slowly, the teardrop-shaped petals, wet and wrinkled, unfurled themselves, like butterfly wings from a chrysalis.

That little flower only grows where my victims fall. Its existence derives from their deaths.

It seemed the analyx were immortal as long as Zach was dead.

Standing, Cara turned toward the shimmering patch of air she now knew to be the opening to the liminal world. Strange—the stream, despite being shallow and sluggish in comparison to the Autumn Falls River, wasn't frozen over, spurting steadily from the spring. When she dipped a finger in, she gasped.

The water burned.

Like she'd dipped her hand in a gash in the earth, in an open vein, in blood still warm from the kill.

Unsettled, she stood and turned to where Zach was waiting. The threshold shimmered in the air like a veil of heat on a summer's day, the world warping within it. Maybe the Snake had given her a mark that didn't work, only hurt. Or maybe he'd stayed true to his word, and there was nothing keeping them from leaping over the precipice. She couldn't see what lay beyond the plunge. There was nothing else to do but move forward.

A thought occurred to her. "Oh," she said, looking up at Zach. "If only beings with this mark can travel through the liminal world, then maybe we should hold hands when we walk through."

Zach shrugged. "Whatever you say."

She hated the way his fingers fit so perfectly when he slid his hand into hers. She didn't even mind the cold of his touch anymore—somehow, she'd gotten used to it.

Cara cleared her throat. "Okay," she said. "I think we're ready." She searched his face, his blue eyes. "Into the dark?"

At that, he smiled.

"Into the dark," he echoed, and together, they stepped forward.

The world settled in a blink.

The forest seemed to have been cleared away, the trees set back from the river, and the river widened like someone had taken a really big spatula and flattened out its banks. The air was warmer. Unlike the sudden cold back home, autumn was still in full swing here, winter waiting its turn by the wall like it should.

In the distance, perhaps fifty feet or so away from the bank, sat a red-and-white wooden building that looked like a general store. Cara glanced behind them—nothing to see besides countryside meadow grass. The threshold they'd come through had vanished.

Cara tugged her phone out of her pocket. She had no service, but the time hadn't frozen. That made sense: this was still the real world, just a different part of it.

Zach seemed to realize at the same time she did that their hands were still joined, and they jumped apart. She shrugged off her heavy winter coat, hoping it would help with the heat rising in her face.

"The threshold worked," she said.

Zach nodded at the building, whose front read, "Mortmanger's Emporium," in blocky white letters. An Open sign hung in the door window.

"Wanna go see what's inside? Maybe we can find someone who can tell us where we are."

The wooden steps creaked as they ascended the front porch. When Cara opened the door, its rusted hinges protested.

"Hello?" she called as she entered, Zach on her heels.

White fluorescent panels lit a variety of products on shelves. Yellowed bone and yawning sets of animal fangs—"Try putting your hand in and see what happens!" a small sign suggested cheerily. Silver serpent statues coiled and copper kettles glinted. A display showcased metal signs emblazoned with catchy phrases like *Mortal Crossing* and *If You Can't Beat 'Em, Eat 'Em.*

No one appeared as they walked deeper. One section seemed to be hunting and camping equipment: canvas tents that were "elderbeast-proof guaranteed or your money back to your closest surviving relative" and lanterns that alleged to "ward off even the brightest will-o'-the-wisp."

Cara surveyed two types of ropes hanging from hooks. A hiss emanated from the viciously green-colored one, making her jump back. The other one was a normal tan, as harmless as a garden snake. It wiggled, almost seeming *friendly*, for lack of a better word.

Without seeing a single customer or salesperson, she and Zach made their way back to the food section. Giant gummy garden gnomes paraded in front of monster granola bars. Cara squinted at a rack of packaged meat called "Werewolf Jerky."

Zach paused by a five-foot-tall pyramid of brightly colored drinks. "'Devil water,'" he read off the sign. "'Four ninety-nine for four . . . A good way to slake your thirst, straight from the carbonated pits of Hell.' That doesn't make sense," he said to Cara, swiping the can that comprised the point of the pyramid and turning it over. "This is just LaCroix."

Cara snickered. "Same thing."

They reached the register at the far end of the store. The seat behind the counter was empty. There was only an open book left lying cover up and a silver service bell, which rang pitifully when Cara pressed it.

"All right," Zach said after a few minutes. "I'm gonna go find the manager."

Cara looked around at all the abnormal items they'd seen. A tendril of unease crawled into her mind. "You know, maybe we should just go—"

Zach cleared the counter with an easy leap and sauntered through the open door of the dark back room.

Of course. Because when did he ever listen to her?

She leaned against the counter to shout after him. "If you don't come back, I'm leaving you!"

No response from the shadows beyond the doorway, but she could *feel* him ignoring her.

Cara raised her voice. "You listening, Coleson? I will straight up leave your ghost here!"

Still no answer. She sighed in exasperation, crossing her arms on the counter and letting her gaze drift over the book cover.

She stared at the title.

Ducking around the counter, Cara barreled into the back room, words tumbling from her mouth. "Hey, we have to leave right now—"

Zach turned, eyebrows raised, and she just barely stopped herself from running into him in the darkness. A bare bulb flickered to life above their heads.

"What?" he asked in irritation, taking a small step back.

From under his shoe, there came a click, then rustling—

And the world turned upside down.

"This is all your fault. If you hadn't decided to stride in here like you owned the whole place, then—"

"Oh, yeah? And who followed me?"

Cara growled in annoyance. It was the best she could do, because all her limbs were tangled up in the net Zach had summoned when he'd stepped back on some kind of trigger mechanism. They were now hanging over the ground, suspended by heavy black nylon. She'd ended up beneath him, ponytail pressed into the net, Zach on all fours in an effort to keep apart in the impossibly small confines. Still, he was directly on top of her, his legs straddling hers, his ice-and-pine scent engulfing her senses, and amidst her aggravation, all she could think was that his mouth was way too close to hers. "Because I was trying to warn you! Did you see that book on the counter?"

"Why would I have willingly looked at a book?"

Diamonds of nylon dug into her back. "The title of that book was *The Ethics of Cannibalism: It's Only Human*! Whoever works here eats people!"

Zach rolled his eyes, trying to push away from her. He only suc-
ceeded in making the net shake, rattling her heart rate. "Or maybe
they're just reading a book and you shouldn't be judgmental all the
time, but sure, okay. It's all my fault. Just like everything else."

"Say that last part again but more sincerely, and I do believe you
could have your first inkling of self-awareness."

Zach glared down at her. Cara pushed up on her elbows to glare
right back, even though it put her face even closer to his. His hands
were unbearably close to her ribs.

"Just phase through this thing and find a way to cut it down, will
you?"

With a frustrated noise, he closed his eyes, brow creasing in concentration.

Footsteps. Unsteady ones, with an accompanying *tap-tap*,
approached. Cara twisted in the direction of the noise, trying to see
who it was, but only the shadowy, indistinct shapes of the storeroom's
contents met her frantic gaze.

"Hurry up, someone's coming!"

"I'm *trying*! Could you stop distracting me?"

The footsteps grew louder. Then stopped. She heard the sound of a
switch being flicked, and light consumed the room, briefly blinding.

"Why, what a delicious surprise," said a reedy voice.

Pressing her cheek into the square mesh, Cara blinked away the
last of the brightness and craned her neck to see a decrepit old man
hunched in the doorway, leaning heavily on his metal cane. The
name tag pinned to his stained, beige-plaid button-up shirt said Mr.
Mortmanger, and he had rumpled brown trousers pulled up almost
to his armpits. At the sight, she couldn't help but relax.

Cara cracked a strained smile. "Uh, hello, sir," she began, but the elderly store owner held up a knobby finger.

"Let me just put on my glasses to get a better look at you. My sight's not quite what it used to be." He fished a pair of wire-rim frames from his shirt pocket and put them on his nose. "Oh, would you look at that."

"Sir, if you could—" Cara started, but again, the old man waggled his finger.

"Ah ah ah." He put a hand to his ear, fiddling with a hearing aid. "*Much* better," he said, and though his hair was silver, his voice was steel. "I can hear *everything* much better now."

"Hey, Tang," Zach said in an undertone. "I can't phase through."

Try harder, she thought, because with the old man right there, she could hardly talk to empty air.

Mr. Mortmanger's face wrinkled into a gap-toothed smile as he began to hobble in a circle beneath the net. Cara tried to follow him with her eyes.

"Um—would you be able to let me down from here, sir?" She kept her voice polite and steady, despite the unease snaking around every limb and screaming for her to claw her way out of this net and run. "I'm sure you had good reasons for having a trap like this, catching thieves or whatever, but—"

"Hrmm, very good, very good," Mr. Mortmanger was saying to himself, not paying any attention to Cara.

"Excuse me, sir?" she tried again. He was just an old man; he had to be harmless. "Maybe you need to turn up your hearing aid a bit, because you didn't exactly answer—"

"Oh, no," said Mr. Mortmanger, and ground to a stop, staring up at her with clear yellow eyes. Suddenly, he looked less like a confused old pigeon and more like a raptor surveying its prey. "My hearing's just dandy."

Her stomach lurched. It lurched again as Mr. Mortmanger pulled a set of levers she hadn't noticed on the wall by the door. And it lurched one more time as their net was sent flying toward a large cage in the corner. The net jerked to a stop, the top of the cage opened, and they were dumped in.

The top clanged shut.

Ow. Elbows and butt smarting from landing on cold steel, Cara sat up, flinging the net off her and trying to discreetly untangle her legs from Zach's. The old man puttered toward them, his creaky laugh filling the space like sawdust.

His giddy grin congealed into a rigid smile, and his entire bony frame stilled as he appeared to—but no, that couldn't be possible—stare at Zach.

"And my eyesight is good enough, too," the old man said to Cara, a liver-colored tongue darting out to lick at his lips. "Good enough to see *you aren't alone.*"

THIRTEEN

Cara stared in shock. He could see ghosts? He was like her?

Zach had frozen, as if by not moving, he'd be invisible.

"What do we do?" he whispered out of the corner of his mouth.

"I don't know, I've never been in this situation before." *And I was right, this is cannibal central*, she wanted to say, but now was not the time.

The old man's face split ear to ear in a sickening grin, like a moldering jack-o'-lantern. "Oh, what a delight! A ghost speaker and a ghost. So close to Halloween, too—a seasonal surprise."

Dread curled through Cara's stomach, unsteadying her even as the solid metal of the cage floor enclosed around her. Her skin crawled; she could swear she'd felt something pass over them when they were dumped into the cage.

Mr. Mortmanger tapped closer until his face was right in front of the bars. "You may think you're special, ghost speaker, but you'll taste just like any other human in a stew."

"You're going to eat her?" Zach shouted.

The old man jabbed his cane through the bars, forcing Zach to jump back. "Don't speak unless you're spoken to, son! But, yes. After I eat you."

"Sir, you can't—you can't eat us," Cara said, gripping the bars. A lifetime of being raised to respect her elders had her compulsively calling him "sir." Fear flared inside of her, her heartbeat kicking up and her fists growing hot. For a weird moment, she thought she might melt the metal out of sheer panic. "There are *laws* against that."

"Well, I suppose they must not be enforced very well, because I've been doing this for years." Mr. Mortmanger threw back his head and laughed. "No, I'm afraid you won't be getting away." He paused to slide in a pristine set of dentures. "Do you know, I once dined on this woman—tasted beautiful with roasted russet potatoes and a sprig of mint—and when she returned as a ghost, I ate her again? It was marvelous."

"This guy cannot be serious," Zach muttered.

On the other side of the room was a kitchenette complete with a little round table; one rickety, metal folding chair; a small beige, old-looking fridge; and an oven and stovetop. Whistling a meaningless tune, Mr. Mortmanger set to work.

"I'm so excited for this, you know," he said, pulling pots and pans out of the cabinets. It took Cara a moment to realize he wasn't talking to himself. He was talking to them—chatting up his victims before he killed and ate them was probably the only social interaction this deranged old man ever got. "I haven't had a treat like this in so long."

"Really?" Cara said sarcastically. "What do you normally eat, sir, when you can't get wild-caught children from the store?"

"Prunes, kale, and fish, mostly." Mr. Mortmanger set a canister of sea salt on the counter. "I consider myself a select pescatarian. But over the years, I've developed a taste for human flesh—I prefer adolescents; adults are too tough on my jaws—and ghosts, when I can get them." He tied a dirty white apron around his waist that read, *Eat the Cook*. It was covered with miscellaneous red splatters that definitely weren't tomato sauce. "Keeps me healthy. Everybody always says to me, 'Bob, how do you look so young? What's your secret?' And I always say, 'The blood of children, with caramelized onions,' and they always laugh for some reason, but"—he shook his head in consternation—"I'm never joking."

"I'm sorry, sir, *what*?" Cara said. "You can't just gum on grapefruit and oatmeal like a normal old man?"

He glared balefully at her. "I'm going to pretend I didn't hear that, you disrespectful little morsel, if only because I'll be eating you soon. You'd better not give me indigestion."

"Oh, she definitely will," said Zach.

The old man pointed a spatula in Zach's direction. "I know *you* won't, son. See, I'm going to boil you down nice and slow, get a good specter stock out of you. Many people think ectoplasm is inedible, that once you've killed something you can't kill it again—but pah! What do they know? Necessity is the mother of invention, and *I* have discovered, through my many years of wisdom and experimenting, that if you turn the heat high enough in a specially-made metal pot, you, too, can cook a ghost."

With a grunt, the old man fetched a fat yellowed book from the top of the fridge, thunking it onto the table. Licking his wormy lips, he fanned through the pages with the expectant relish of a diner browsing through the menu.

"And *you*, my dear," he said to Cara, "I'll put in the oven. It gets the skin so nice and crispy, it practically crackles when you put it in your mouth!" Closing his eyes, he leaned on his cane and let out a sigh of satisfaction. "I've never had the pleasure of trying a real live ghost speaker before. Oh, the things I'm going to make out of you!"

Fear seared through Cara's body, along with a healthy helping of disbelief. This could not be happening. It was their first day in this liminal world, and they'd already gotten caught by a monstrous geriatric who had his personal cookbook for turning human beings—and ghosts—into four-course meals.

"Don't look so distressed," the old man chided. "You'll feel much better soon—the magic metal in the cage is designed to calm you down and make you more agreeable."

Cara backed away from the bars. Not like that would do her any good.

Mr. Mortmanger set the oven to preheat, then slapped a palm to his forehead. "Shucks, I've forgotten a few things from the front. Silly me." Humming cheerfully to himself, he puttered out of the room, leaving them to stew.

The second he was gone, Cara started pacing, looking for a way out. A suspicious patch of rust encrusted a large part of the floor, which she avoided. Their prison was a cage big enough to house a tiger, with a heavy padlock on the door. When she stood, she was barely able to push against the top of the cage, which didn't move an inch.

She dropped her head against the wall in defeat. "A cannibalistic old man is going to eat us, and the only seasoning he's going to use is *salt*."

Zach was slouched on the floor on the other side of the cage, one arm propped up in front of him on his knee. "Hey, don't make assumptions. Maybe, if you're really lucky, he'll also add a sprig of mint."

She rattled the bars in frustration. "If you had simply listened to me, we wouldn't even be in this position."

Zach flung up his hands. "How was I supposed to know we'd

wandered into a store owned by a psychopath? We *both* agreed to go in."

"Is your only line of defense that it's both our faults? Because then you're still admitting that a large part of this is on you!"

Zach threw his head back to glare at the cage ceiling, muttering, "Of all the ways I could have imagined getting trapped in a tight space with you, this is definitely not in my top ten."

Cara glanced over. "You have a *list*?" she said, but Zach didn't seem to hear her.

"Anyway, we're only in trouble because the guy happens to be a *ghost speaker* who uses his power to eat ghosts like me!"

She sent a scorching look his way. "Do *not* associate me with him." The thought made her sick to her stomach. The fact that there was someone out there, someone like her, someone who had the same power, was also someone who killed and ate people . . . What this old man was using his sight for—Laolao would have been furious. Had her mother known people like this existed? Was this one reason she didn't want Cara messing around with ghosts or magic? "I bet you haven't even thought of phasing through this stupid cage yet."

"Actually, I have, because contrary to popular belief, I *do* use my brain. And guess what?" He reached up and knocked a fist against the bars. "Didn't work."

Cara stared at the ordinary-looking metal. "It must contain something that makes it impervious to phasing. Or it's spelled to be a spirit barrier, like the one around my house. The net, too." Bones and blooms baked into the steel.

"Damn, if only we had some *useful* magic to help us get out." Zach waved his hands around when he said *magic* as if he were approximating the grand gestures of a wizard.

"Oh, screw you." Though she had to admit—what good was seeing ghosts if the only thing she could do with it was get mocked by one? "We don't even need magic to get out. If you had used your brain a little more, you might have noticed that there's a good old-fashioned lock. Too bad the old man didn't drop his keys."

At that, Zach abruptly stood and walked over to the door. Cara watched, surprised, while he reached an arm through the cage bars to fiddle with the lock.

He made a satisfied noise under his breath—something that sounded like, *Gotcha, old man*—and looked at her. "Bobby pin."

"What?"

"For the lock," he said. "Bobby pin. Don't all girls like to carry around those little bobby pins and then complain about losing them?"

Cara shoved her hands into her jacket pockets. "I don't even use—" Her fingers met a distinct shape, and she stopped. With a sigh, Cara fished out the hairpin. It was sunflower yellow, one of Charlotte's, and Cara couldn't even remember when she'd gotten it or why she'd borrowed it, but she was glad for her friend's hairpin now. She held it out by one end.

Smirking triumphantly, he took it by the other end, fingers careful not to touch hers.

"Just be quiet and pick the lock."

"Didn't say anything," he said, the smirk still in his voice, blond head bent in front of the bars.

Cara huffed and crossed her arms. "Since when can you pick a lock, anyway?"

The corner of his mouth curled. "There's a lot of things you don't know about me, Tang."

"I know you got us into this mess."

"And now I'm getting us out of it."

"I'll save my applause until the end."

Cara slid her gaze over the shelves of the room, past jars of eyeballs labeled, "Snacks," cans of condensed she-didn't-want-to-know-what, gloves and knives and rolls of receipt paper.

She glanced back at Zach, who looked slightly less confident than he had five minutes ago.

"Any day now," Cara said.

"Shut up," he muttered, brow furrowed. "It's been a while since I've picked any locks."

Having cataloged everything in the room, she turned to study him while he worked. He'd rolled up his sleeves, as if that would help him better break out of the cage. Even dead, humans had their habits. Thin blue veins ran under his skin like rivers of ice.

"I'm beginning to think you don't even know how to—"

Something clicked. The shackle slid loose. Zach smirked at her.

"You were saying?"

When Cara didn't deign to answer, he swung the door open and gestured grandly, the paragon of chivalry.

"Ladies first."

Zach had just stepped out of the cage when she heard humming steadily increasing in volume.

"The door," Cara said instantly, and they each took up a position on opposite sides of the entryway.

Tap-tap-tap.

"Here's the plan," she whispered, back pressed against the wall. "When he comes into the room, you tackle him, and then we both drag him into the cage and lock him up."

"I don't like your plan."

"Do you have any better ideas?"

"Yeah. We bowl one of those eyeball jars toward him, trip him, and then shove him into the oven."

"I said *better.*"

"It's not a bad idea!"

"It's worse."

Tap-tap-tap.

"We're doing my plan," Cara shot back, right before the old man entered the room.

Mr. Mortmanger made it a few paces, then paused, eyes narrowing on the empty cage.

"What in the—?" he muttered.

"Now!" Cara yelled.

True to plan, Zach launched himself from his hiding place and tackled Mr. Mortmanger.

But the old man had faster reflexes than expected. He rolled with the tackle, sending both Zach and himself into a shelf of canned fingers. Preserved digits rained down.

Mr. Mortmanger was up first, face a rictus of fury. Holding his cane in the air, he twisted the handle—a sound like a gun reloading—and steel claws emerged from the other end. He drove it into Zach's chest. Zach shouted in pain.

The plan had shattered in a matter of seconds. Cara hesitated by the door—then turned and ran from the room.

"*Tang!*" she heard Zach yell after her.

Aisles and items blurred. LaCroix. Jerky. Granola bars. Animal bones. Where was it? *Where was it?*

There. The camping aisle. Rows of ropes.

Grabbing a brown one, she wheeled and hurtled back toward the storeroom, hoping she wasn't too late.

She rounded the corner and skidded to a stop.

Mr. Mortmanger and Zach were wrestling in front of the checkout counter. The old man flung out a hand and grabbed his cane from where it had landed on top of the register. Rearing back, he planted the claws in Zach's chest again, eliciting another shout of pain. Zach grabbed the cane, trying to push it away from himself, but Mr. Mortmanger dug the claws in deeper, and Zach visibly winced.

"You're a special one, aren't you, boy? Almost"—Mr. Mortmanger jabbed the cane in harder—"*solid*. And the most disrespectful ghost I've ever had the grace to meet. I don't see anything stopping me from eating you right here and now."

Keeping one hand on the cane, he removed his dentures, replacing them with a set of sharp ivory teeth. Cara, staring at the way the saliva dripped down the fangs, almost didn't register the rope wriggling in her hands of its own accord.

"Actually, sir, there is." Cara spoke casually, although she was freaking out internally. The old man, inches away from Zach's jugular, went stock-still. "I mean, yes, he's annoying and deserves to be eaten but think of how irritated your stomach lining will be."

Mr. Mortmanger straightened, vertebra by vertebra, turning his head like an animatronic skeleton at a Halloween store. "Come to rescue your boyfriend from becoming entrée number one?"

Cara advanced slowly, rope looped and ready in her hand like she was aiming to take down a mad bull. "I'm tying you up just for that."

Mr. Mortmanger sprang at her, a snarl hungering at his mouth.

She flung out her rope—

And it curled and twisted in midair, wrapping around the old man's body. Mr. Mortmanger fell to the floor with a grunt, trussed up tighter than a prize hog.

Zach was up on his feet. "Throw me a chair."

"On it." Cara turned to a stack of Four Horsemen of the Apocalypse–themed lawn chairs and, using both hands, flung a Famine one at Zach.

He easily caught a chair leg in one hand and brought it to the ground. Together, Zach and Cara wrestled the old man into Famine—the chair, that is.

She snapped her fingers, and the rope obliged, unwinding to tie the old man's wrists and ankles in place.

"Nice work, Tang," Zach said, and she turned to find him grinning at her.

"Not so bad yourself, Coleson," she replied, grinning back at him—wait, was she actually smiling at him of her own accord? The adrenaline must be getting to her.

But, for the first time that she could ever remember, they had actually worked together. As a—what was the word?—*team*.

Zach crouched to look the old man in the face. "Oh, how the tables have turned."

"I thought you two weren't cannibals," Mr. Mortmanger said gleefully.

Cara sighed. "He means that you're the one captured now, sir."

The old man's face crumpled. "I was only hungry! I'm sorry that you felt so strongly about being eaten."

"Tough luck, old man," Zach said. "How does it feel being the one trapped now?"

"So bad, so bad," Mr. Mortmanger wailed, teeth glinting. "Please, let me go. I can't hope to run my store if I am tied up like this! How will I feed my grandchildren?"

"I almost pity him," Cara said as the old man rocked back and forth, mumbling about his precious meat pies who were always so hungry. "I mean, he's an old man. He probably has arthritis."

"You *should* have pity!" Mr. Mortmanger snapped, his self-pitying state suddenly vanishing. "Now untie me; my wrists are starting to cramp up!"

"No way," Zach told him, eyes wide. "You literally tried to kill us."

"Sir, what I want to know is . . ." Cara approached the old man warily. "Why you, a ghost speaker, would eat ghosts."

Mr. Mortmanger threw his head back and laughed. "Me? *A ghost speaker?* Pah! No, girlie, I'm not one of *you* people."

"Then how can you—" Cara stared, seeing the old man's glasses and hearing aids in a new light. He'd adjusted them several times upon first entering the back room. "You can't speak to ghosts on your own," she realized. "You've got magical devices."

The old man cackled so hard Cara thought he was about to cough up a lung. The glasses slid down his nose, and he leered over them at her. "Indeed! You're not so special if someone like me, a harmless old guy, can just manufacture stuff to see what you see."

Cara took a few steps back, disgust bubbling up inside her. What Mr. Mortmanger was doing was antithetical to all the lessons Laolao had imparted on her over the years. "That's not what ghost speaking is about," Cara said, anger rising like lava, her voice obsidian sharp with an edge she didn't know she had. "You're supposed to respect the dead. Make their afterlives better. Not *eat* them."

To be fair, she didn't make a habit of helping the dead with her power, either, but at least she wasn't going around picking them off like they were items on a menu.

"We'll take those." Zach swiped the glasses and hearing device off

Mr. Mortmanger's head. "Try seeing me now, you old geezer."

"You insolent specter! Do you know how long it took me to make those?" the store manager griped. His neck bulged as he strained forward as far as the rope would allow, glaring daggers in Zach's general direction. He was off by about two inches.

Zach's mouth curled in a way that indicated he couldn't take this seriously. "Do *you* know how many people you ate?"

There was a pause, since Mr. Mortmanger couldn't hear ghosts anymore.

"Ask him," Zach said.

Cara rolled her eyes and repeated the question.

"Am I counting their ghosts separately?" the old man asked, and Zach threw up his hands.

"And that's why we're taking these," he said. He attempted to pocket them before realizing his pockets didn't really work anymore and held them out at Cara.

Glaring at Mr. Mortmanger, Cara put the devices in her bag. The old man's eyes tracked the movement, as if he were calculating whether or not he could take a chunk out of her arm from this distance.

"While we have your attention, sir," she began sarcastically, earning a snort from Zach, "I have some questions. We're hoping to find a creature called the Signet Snake by following the river through this liminal world. You're clearly at home here. What can you tell us?"

"Find the Snake?" Mr. Mortmanger guffawed. "You don't know what you've signed up for."

The first Snake's words echoed in her mind: *You don't know the fate you've bought.* She shook them away.

"This liminal world does stuff to you. Gets in your head. Creeps under your skin. Changes you."

"Changes you in a bad way?" Cara asked.

The store manager chuckled. "You'll find out." He settled back with a sniff. "There are many doorways in this world, and you can't control which ones the river will take you through. You could always walk out, back into the real *real* world, which would be the best option for you, missy—the living don't live here long. Now him"—Mr. Mortmanger nodded his head, presumably at Zach, although the old man was looking in an entirely different direction—"he'll be all right. Ghosts are liminal beings."

"Why aren't you dead, then?"

"Eating ghosts keeps me alive." Mr. Mortmanger smiled, the darkness between his jaws as black as the underworld. "Sometimes I think I can still feel them, jostling around in my stomach, trying to get out."

Cara cleared her throat. "Do you know how long it'll take to reach the Snake from here?"

"Take a look-see at the brochure."

Next to the register was a plastic brochure holder. Zach slid one out, and Cara moved next to him, reading over his arm.

"The Liminal World," the first page proclaimed in curling gray letters. Printed below was a glossy photo of a cornfield under a bright blue, cloud-brushed sky, stalks waving in an invisible wind. It could have been any cornfield in any Midwestern state, endless and indistinguishable, except for the bloodred liquid that ran down each stalk from burst kernels. *So fun you'll want to stay forever and ever . . . and you just might!*

The brochure expanded to showcase more images and descriptions. Zach flipped it over to reveal a map.

At one end was a small icon of a country store, "You Are Here," in a red circle printed above it. At the other end was a midnight-black serpent curved into a circle, eating its own tail. Cara glanced at her wrist. The mark matched perfectly.

Between the depictions of the country store and the Snake lay a bare, green expanse, filled with hazy veils. Liminal spaces connected to each other. A world built of thresholds.

"Why is the map blank?" Cara asked, holding it in front of Mr. Mortmanger.

"Travel more and it won't be," he said mysteriously, then leaned closer to the page. "Ah . . . with that number of threshold crossings, it looks like you'll reach your destination by nightfall on October thirtieth. If nothing goes wrong." The implication hung in the air for a few seconds before Mr. Mortmanger added, "Now untie me this instant! I've helped you enough."

"Absolutely not," Cara replied, folding the brochure into her pocket.

"So what are we going to do with him?" Zach asked her.

Just then, there came a beep from the back room. The oven had finished preheating.

Zach raised his eyebrows.

"*No*," she said. Although it would be wonderfully satisfying to give the old man a taste of his own medicine.

She considered Mr. Mortmanger, his bald head drooping pitifully like a turtle's. Deceptively harmless in his beige-plaid button-up shirt, apron, and wrinkled, armpit-high trousers. Anyone entering the store might be naive enough to take pity on the old guy and untie him. "We'll write a note and call the police."

Cara dialed 911 using the store landline while Zach found a paper and a writing utensil. Despite being in a liminal place, they were still somewhere in the real world, so hopefully it would work. Mr. Mortmanger wouldn't stay tied up forever.

After speaking with an officer, who promised to send a car to check out the store, she glanced over Zach's sign: Warning: Cannibal. WILL eat you. Untie at your own risk.

The old man spat. "Pah! Children these days"—he shook his head—"they have no respect. Ungrateful tiny snacks."

Zach took a step away from him. "Come on. Let's get out of here."

"Wait, I gotta grab some things." Cara dashed off into the aisles. She scooped up a canvas tent and all the monster-sized granola bars her backpack could carry. This stuff was one way Mr. Mortmanger could make it up to them for trying to eat them. For a second, a weird dizziness spun through her, stopping her in her tracks, but then it was gone from her body and her mind. On her way back, she passed the pyramid devil water and paused.

"This one's for you, Coleson," she called, waiting until she had both Zach's and Mr. Mortmanger's attention. And then she slowly, deliberately, pulled a can from the center of the bottommost layer.

The entire pyramid instantly crumbled in glorious, carbonated cacophony. She made pointed eye contact with the horrified store manager the whole time.

Cara grinned. "*Now* we can go." She didn't miss the impressed look on Zach's face as she passed him, tossing the can of LaCroix at his chest.

Mr. Mortmanger wailed, "You have no idea how long that took me to set up, you impudent, mouthwatering little upstart! *You should have let me eat you—*"

The door swung closed behind them with a cheerful tinkle, cutting off the rest of Mr. Mortmanger's tirade, leaving them standing on the stoop overlooking a peaceful, blue river.

FOURTEEN

The second Cara stepped with Zach through the next threshold, hot, muggy air settled onto her like a second skin. Sunlight poured down, golden and thick as honey, and strange plants loomed all around them. Ferns taller than she was unfurled in front of her; purple orchids larger than her head sprouted everywhere in an affliction of violet; fuzzy balls of pollen floated through the air like embers.

She guessed they were in some sort of swamp—the river had to be nearby, judging by the humidity clinging to the back of her neck.

Fighting the old man had been oddly cathartic in a way. Cara had been raised to respect her elders, no matter what, but she'd found that sometimes, certain adults simply didn't *deserve* her respect.

Especially when they tried to eat her.

"You look pleased with yourself," Zach said, dropping her hand.

For once, she didn't feel inclined to snap at him for breaking her train of thought.

"Well, we did just defeat a cannibalistic old man." *Take that, river.* Whatever other challenges it decided to throw at them, they could handle.

Zach tossed his can of LaCroix in the air, throwing it and catching it with one hand. "I'm surprised."

"Surprised that we won?"

"Surprised that you had the guts to fight him. I guess you're not such a pushover after all."

Good God, it was impossible to be happy with him around.

She watched him fling the can into the air again. As he caught it, he winced, and she remembered how Mr. Mortmanger had sunk the cane into his chest and how Zach had cried out in pain, even though he shouldn't have been able to feel that, not anymore.

It wasn't just the Signet Snake Laolao hadn't taught her about. She'd also never taught her about things that could hurt ghosts. Cara was deeper in a magical world than she'd ever imagined, and she had no idea how the cane had been able to hurt Zach. To wonder if Zach was hurting more than he was letting on.

A voice whispered in her head: *You could ask, though.*

Yes, she *could* ask, but that didn't mean she *would*. They weren't friends.

But he'd distracted her when she was angry about her mother. He didn't have to do that.

She pressed her tongue against the roof of her mouth, hesitating, then swallowed and said, "Does it hurt?"

Zach glanced over at her, raising his brows. She could tell he was surprised, because it took him a beat to reply. "Does *what* hurt?"

Her shoes weren't built for this rough terrain, and she stumbled. "Mr. Mortmanger. He, um, had that cane with the claws, and when he used it on you, it sounded like it hurt."

A grin spread over his face, and she began to regret her decision. "I'm fine," he said, so easily she wondered if he was lying. "But if you're so worried about me—"

"I'm not."

"You can help by carrying this." Sunlight glinted off the LaCroix as Zach held it out.

Was he serious?

"No way. Do you see all the other stuff I'm already carrying? Just leave it."

Zach looked offended. "I'm saving this until I can drink it."

"You're going to save it until—" Cara pinched her brow and sighed.

"It doesn't expire until next year."

"The answer is no."

He shrugged. "I guess I'll carry this around, then. I mean, we could bump into someone who might get suspicious that there's a can floating in midair, which you'll probably find hard to explain away. Which I'm cool with, you know, because I don't care, but it would probably go against your 'no one can know I see ghosts' policy."

Cara sucked in a breath. With a smirk, Zach handed over his can, and she stuffed it into her pack. This was what she got for being nice.

After pausing for a quick lunch atop a large flat rock, they resumed walking. Wings hummed over her head, and Cara instinctively ducked.

She looked up to see a gigantic dragonfly zip through the sapphire-tinged air. Bars of blue striped its belly, and buzzing filled the sky, as loud as the engine of an airplane. *For the love of God, please don't be carnivorous*, she prayed, squinting up at it. But it seemed disinterested in them and hummed off into the sunlit distance.

Eventually, the plants spaced out a little farther, and Cara no longer had to force her way through, although she still had to focus on not tripping on the uneven terrain. The hot, fetid smell of things decaying mixed with the verdant scent of growing flora.

Despite the dragonfly sighting, the swamp was almost peaceful. She'd never seen plants like this: spotted ones that emitted the smell of rotting flesh; ones whose innumerable curling vines grew every which way; enormous cup-shaped ones, their vibrant lipsticked mouths pursed toward the sun.

She heard humming again. The striped dragonfly from before had returned and was maneuvering through a cluster of cup-shaped plants. It hovered in front of one, wings a blur as it seemed to decide whether to land—

The plant lunged, lips closing around the insect's body, making its decision for it. It struggled, tail sticking out of the plant's mouth, then slowly stilled.

"What the hell?" Zach recoiled.

As if on cue, another plant lunged at Cara, missing her by an inch, crunching down on the air right before her shoes. "Run!" she screamed, although it probably didn't need to be said.

They took off as the other plants, which had been stationary mere moments ago—like plants *were supposed to be*—sprang to life.

If the landscape had been an obstacle course before, it was a death trap now. Everywhere she turned, there was a plant lunging out of the greenery to meet her, hungry and gaping. How could she have known it wasn't the giant bug she should have been concerned about but the *plants*?

"*Why* do the *plants* have *teeth*?" she heard Zach shout from somewhere behind her.

Up ahead, she spied more greenery, this time trees—but no more cup-shaped plants. Cara dodged another one as it lunged at her, nearly twisting her ankle in the process, and made a break for the forest ahead.

The landscape buckled and swelled into a hill as they dashed into the woods. Cara didn't think, just pressed on until she reached the top, where there were no more carnivorous plants. The air was drier, cooler against her skin, and around them loomed giant sequoias, their peaks spearing the sky.

Bracing her palms on her knees, she bent over, trying to catch her breath. *Goddamn.* As captain of the girls cross-country team, she was athletic enough, but she hadn't ever trained with murderous meat-eating flora, having to dodge death left and right. A look behind her showed the cup-shaped plants settling back down, seeming to sense their prey was gone. Within seconds, they were motionless, moving only with the wind.

Sweat dripped into her eyes as she glanced around. The hill was small, not tall enough to give her a peek at the upcoming land. Any second, one of these trees could come to life and try to kill them. She narrowed her eyes at a suspicious-looking sapling.

Zach raked a hand through his hair, as if the run could have possibly messed it up. He wasn't out of breath, but of course, he had none to give. "Why do things keep trying to eat us?"

Cara wiped her forehead. "At least they can't chase us—"

The ground underneath her swayed.

For a second, she thought her legs were giving out from exhaustion. But then the ground swayed again, and a roar echoed through the air. A roar that reverberated through her soles.

And the hill *moved.*

It rose, breaching the tree line. Struck off balance, Cara pitched to the side, tumbling off the hill into empty air. Green blurred in her vision as she fell—

Strong arms caught her right before she hit the forest floor. She opened her eyes—she hadn't even realized she'd closed them. Zach's wide eyes met her own, like he'd moved instinctively and was equally surprised as she was that she hadn't gone *splat,* that she was in his arms. Her heart rate jumped right back up again.

Another roar sundered the air, and still in his arms, she craned to see over his shoulder.

Behind them, the hill climbed to its feet.

What she'd taken for a hill was in reality a four-legged creature with long matted grass covering its back. Mushrooms sprouted along its skin. It had no neck, and its head—barely distinguishable from the rest of its massive overgrown body—was shaped sort of like a tortoise's, studded with two shiny black stones. A gray film swept over them like mold, then withdrew. It was blinking, Cara realized. Those black stones were its eyes.

The hill-beast shook its head from side to side, then focused its stare on them and let out another roar, exposing huge jagged rocks lining its beaked maw like teeth. Now at ground level, the sound traveled over them in a putrid wave. Bits of moist earth sprayed through the air.

"It's kinda ugly," Zach said, as if remarking on a new art piece in his mother's gallery.

The monster bellowed but began moving backward. Relief relaxed Cara's shoulders as it took one step back, then another, leaving massive footprints at least three feet deep in its retreat. Each impact shook the earth like a quake. Trees as tall as power lines wavered and broke as the hill-beast scraped backward.

But then, with its shiny black eyes still fixed on their faces, the monster stopped in its tracks. Its expression, if she could call it that, was oddly intent.

It wasn't running away after all. It was getting ready to run *toward* them.

The monster bent its head and charged.

"Run!" Cara screamed, hooking her arms around Zach's neck for necessity. He'd be faster in the air than she'd be on foot.

For once, Zach did exactly as he was told without snark or argument. He took off, the trees blurring as he shot forward, passing just over the forest floor. The wind whistled in Cara's ears.

"What's the plan?" he shouted.

"The plan is to get away!" she shouted back. "A threshold—we need a threshold!"

"I don't see a threshold!"

"Then keep going!"

Zach's jaw tensed.

"I can't believe you had to insult it," Cara muttered.

"How was I supposed to know it was such a big baby—?"

His hold on her disappeared, and she plummeted toward the ground.

Only years of training at the Stables saved her. Instinctively, she curled into a ball, protecting her head. She hit the ground and rolled before coming to a stop on her hands and knees. One of the most important things you learned in horseback riding was how to fall. Of course, the technique worked best when you were falling from something horse high. Thank God Zach hadn't been very high when he'd *lost his grip on her.*

Head down, Cara heaved a breath. Her vision settled. She took stock of the situation. Every inch of skin that had contacted the ground stung with scrapes. The knees of her jeans had torn open. Underneath the denim, blood trickled down her calf, as hot as the liminal stream in the Wildwoods had been. Sheer indignation propelled her to her feet.

She spit out a mouthful of dirt.

"You dropped me!"

Zach, too, had landed on the ground. His eyes found hers, his expression almost concerned, but when he saw she was okay, his face settled back into annoyance.

"It's not like I did it on purpose!" He held out his hands, and that was when she realized they had gone translucent.

Oh, *crap.*

Panic hammered hot through her chest. "This is a really bad time to go incorporeal!"

"No kidding!"

A roar rocked the forest, and Cara staggered, nearly losing her balance again. Cracks echoed as the monster pushed its massive bulk through the trees, which delayed its momentum somewhat but not enough.

"Just find a threshold and tell me which way to run!" Cara screamed, and took off. Until she knew where to cross, she was running in the next best direction—away from the monster.

Panting, she leaped over logs, swerved around pines. Heat coursed through her blood like fire.

Something green shot past her head and hit a trunk. *Thwack.*

Thwip. Another followed a second later, this time ricocheting to a stop right in Cara's path. She cleared it, realizing what it was a second later.

The hill-beast was sending vines after her.

She looked back to see another one unfurling from the monster's enormous maw, snaking past rows of stone teeth to lunge at her head. One vine grazed her side, slicing a gash into her shirt.

Twhip, thwip, thwip. A volley of vines shot toward her. One wrapped around her calf, and she crashed to a halt, eating another mouthful of dirt.

Its grip tightened, and it began to pull. She clawed at the ground. *No, no, no!*

Suddenly, the vine's stranglehold slackened, then loosened completely. Still on her stomach in the dirt, Cara looked over her shoulder.

Zach sailed through the air with a sharp rock, the broken ends of the vine falling to the earth. He turned to meet her gaze, blue eyes glowing with triumph. Her pulse sang in her ears. Cara shot up. A running start her coach would have scolded her for, one her hamstrings protested at. She heard the vines hit the spot where she'd just been—*thwack, thwack, thwack.*

There. A break in the trees. She couldn't see what it was, but it was something that wasn't green, something that wasn't more forest, and that was enough. She made for it—

And found herself in a grassy space enclosed by rock.

Cara looked up. And up. And up. Above loomed the scarred, gray face of a mountain. An unclimbable, impenetrable wall of stone.

Wood splintered behind her. The deep roars continued.

Cara backed against the mountain, facing the monster as it thundered closer and closer. Its vines reeled back into its mouth, like the hill-beast had decided it didn't need them now that it had her trapped.

Zach broke through the tree line, form still transparent. She saw the instant he registered the mountain and what it meant.

Rock slammed into her back, and she came to a stop. The monster continued to barrel toward her. Despair blazed through her body. Terror sparked along every limb like warning flares.

But this kind of flare was worthless, not when she couldn't do anything in response. Not when there was nowhere to turn, nowhere to run. She could see the end in sight as clearly as a flame against the dark.

As the monster closed in, she threw up her arms, squeezing her eyes shut—*because what else could she do?*—hands up, palms open. Hoping it would be quick.

The hill-beast's hot breath fanned over her face like air from a bonfire.

But no vines sliced through her skin. No jaws ripped her arms from their sockets. No teeth tore open her chest, cracking her rib cage to dust. She was still whole.

Cara opened her eyes.

No. She was something more than whole.

Fire radiated from her outstretched hands. Scarlet flames, bold and sure as the sun. And although the heat that emanated off her palms was intense, it did not burn her. It did not hurt.

The monster stared back at her, and reflected in its large glistening black eyes, she saw herself.

A girl, trembling, face streaked with dirt and fear.

A flame.

FIFTEEN

The monster blinked at her, wet gray film sliding over its eyes. It opened its mouth—her heart nearly burst—but it let out only a gentle *huff*, a breath that swept over Cara's face and hair, smelling of damp moss and dirt, making the flames in her hands waver.

A small disbelieving voice in her head noted: *there were* flames *in my* hands.

With a sound like rocks grinding against each other, the hill-beast slowly lowered its head. Again, it blinked, appearing to be waiting for something.

This close, Cara noticed the gray, cracked patches of dirt on the creature's face, spreading across its body like a disease, encroaching on the beast's grassy pelt. Even the areas where its grass fur grew long and tangled, the ends were thin and browning.

Another slow, mildewed breath swept over her, guttering her flames, bringing with it a realization.

The monster was dying.

Hesitantly, moving without conscious thought or decision, she reached out a hand, knowing it was right without really understanding why. Her palm came to rest on its face, and as flames leaped across the creature's skin, it let out a joyful rumble—one that tremored all the way through her body—and it closed its eyes for the last time.

The fire in her palms extinguished. Her arms dropped to her sides. She watched the monster go up in smoke quicker than something that size should burn, a forest catching during fire season. She remembered, dimly, Felicity telling her once that some trees needed fire to germinate. It was how the species made sure its lineage continued.

The smoke cleared, and in the flattened grass where the monster had stood lay a tiny acorn, glowing in the sunlight.

Cara stooped to pick it up. It was warm like a still-beating heart, and when her fingers closed around it, it thrummed, pulsed. Gave one final quiver before the glow faded. She tucked it in her pocket.

At that moment, her legs finally gave out, and she stumbled back, sliding down the rock face to the ground. Her heart was shuddering inside her chest; her chest was a room full of panic and smoke. When she squeezed her eyes shut, she saw flames, burning against the darkness of her lids.

Opening her eyes again, she drew her knees to her chest and held her hands in front of her, turning them over and over. They looked the same. The long lifelines on her palms that Laolao nodded at approvingly; the slender half-moons on her nails; the bee-sting scar she'd gotten on the first knuckle of her right ring finger the summer Felicity, Charlotte, and she had spent entirely in the Wildwoods. Didn't her hands look the same? Only the motes of ash drifting through the air like pollen and the acorn digging into her hip indicated this wasn't some detailed hallucination.

No. It *had* to be a hallucination. The sure sense of who she was, the sense she'd carried with her like a torch her whole life, had sputtered out like it had been doused with water. She dug her nails into her palms, hard, and tried to gather the faint embers of words that glowed in her mind, lighting up what she was still sure about.

I'm Cara Tang. I can see ghosts, like my grandmother can. I made a promise to my mom to keep it a secret.

I broke that promise.

I can make fire—

She shook her head. No. *No.*

Someone was calling her name.

"Hey, Tang. Are you there?" A hand waved in front of her face. Zach was corporeal again. "Can you hear me?"

She snapped her eyes up to glare at him. "I wish I couldn't."

Her stomach was tight, and she was *this* close to freaking out. And of course Zach was the one here. He would love to see her lose it.

Zach exhaled—out of habit, she supposed—and sat back. He'd fetched her pack from the forest. "Oh, thank God. You actually had me worried for a second."

"I'm so sorry I worried you," Cara said, every word dripping with venom. She ignored the way his eyebrows shot up. Her many cuts throbbed as one, and she took a deep breath, tracing a finger over her knee where the skin had scraped open, angry and raw. Bruises were already beginning to bloom like roses. First things first. She'd disinfect the cuts, and then she would get up, and she wouldn't think about how she now had *yet another secret to keep*—

Another secret that Zach knew about her.

She reached for the first aid kit, but it was already being offered to her. She took it from him with a curt, "Thanks."

Cara sucked in a breath as she poured alcohol over her scrapes. It burned like fire—but that wasn't true, was it? Not when the fire that erupted from her hands didn't hurt her at all.

She could feel Zach's eyes on her skin like live coals. The question of what had happened hung in the space between them, like smoke.

"Could you stop staring at me?" She concentrated on smoothing one Band-Aid, then the next, over each abrasion.

"You've got dirt on your face."

"And whose fault is that?" She lifted a hand to her cheek. Bringing her thumb to her mouth, she licked it and used the saliva to clean her face, the way her mother had when Cara was younger.

Nide lian, her mother would say, bending down to examine the object of her disapproval more closely. *You look like you've been running around in the woods all day.*

That's because I was! Cara would protest.

And then, despite how Cara complained, despite how she would try to wriggle out of her mother's grasp, her mother would use her own spit to carefully clean her daughter's face, leaving her with a kiss on the forehead before finally letting her go.

Her mother didn't do that anymore.

Cara wondered what her mother would make of this new development, these fire powers. How disappointed she'd be.

She shook her head. *Get it together,* she told herself, and stood up, to which her bruised body took great offense.

"Did you find a threshold?" she asked.

Zach pointed back into the forest.

"Great." She stalked past him, refusing to acknowledge him with a look.

There was nowhere to look, really. Hadn't been since Zach had appeared as a ghost in the Wildwoods. Hadn't been since she was five years old, playing in the front yard, when she'd blinked and seen her grandmother waving outside the gate, a woman who had died before she was born.

Her eyes had never been her own.

They had belonged to the dead, to those that refused to move on, to the countless times she'd stared at the ground so that ghosts would not find out she could see them. And they belonged to Laolao, to her legacy.

You have your grandmother's eyes.

Now her hands weren't hers, either. They acted of their own accord, burning with flames to ward off beasts.

Her *life* wasn't hers. Here she was, tromping through a strange, swamp-like land with a ghost boy on her heels, risking hers to save his.

The adrenaline had drained away, but the heat had stayed, crawling over her arms, under the back of her shirt, inside her. She was putting the pieces together about why she'd felt so overheated, and she wondered if it would ever go away or if she'd always run a few degrees too hot.

Not for the first time, she wished Laolao were here. Laolao would know what to do. Laolao would tell her that it was okay.

But right now, Laolao was far away, and Cara had only Zach.

With that thought, Cara broke out of the forest and found herself on the edge of a wide marshy swamp. The river belched and gurgled, bubbles of methane popping through the green, algae-slick surface. Twenty feet away, a threshold hovered at the edge of the water.

She closed her eyes and took a breath—then regretted it, because the stench was really something. She was wood, calm and impassive. She would not burn.

But if she was wood, then Zach was a woodpecker.

"So do you wanna tell me what's going on, or are you just gonna leave me in the dark?"

She whirled around. The dangerous look in her eyes must not have been enough, because he didn't stop.

Zach swung an arm back toward the trees. "That thing ran you down and almost *killed* you, but then you set it on fire? With your hands? Since when can you—?"

"Since just now, apparently!"

"But how—"

"I don't want to talk about it." The only reason he was privy to her ghost-speaking powers in the first place was pure coincidence, and she wasn't letting him in any further.

"You don't want to talk about the fact that you can shoot *fire* out of your fingers? I don't know about you, but *I* kinda thought that was something that doesn't happen! Is that, like, supposed to be normal in your family, or—?"

"I don't know. It doesn't come from my mother or Laolao, and I never knew my dad!" She bit her tongue, chest rising and falling rapidly; it was more than she'd meant to share. "But," she continued, "it doesn't matter. I don't plan to use it." It was just another thing she had to hide, another thing that would complicate her life in the real world.

He caught her hand, holding on when she tried to pull away. "You're just going to ignore it? I never thought I'd be the one saying this to you, Tang, but that's really stupid."

But what else could she do? Embrace it? She nearly laughed at the thought. She imagined what her mother would say, the look on her face, and Cara's chest instantly constricted.

It was bad enough that she'd accidentally broken her promise not to see ghosts for Zach's sake, that he knew something about her that not even Charlotte or Felicity knew. And now she had another thing that would separate her more from the ones she loved? Another part of herself that she had to control, that she had to keep secret.

What was worse was that Zach, of all people, was witnessing this: her breakdown, her fear, her careful exterior scraped open like the skin on her knees.

Cara squeezed her eyes shut, quelling the emotions threatening to overtake her. Opening her eyes, she said, "We're not friends. We don't even like each other. My magic is *none of your business*."

Something passed over Zach's face. "Fine," he bit out.

Cara gave him a tight-lipped smile that she could feel didn't reach her eyes. "Glad we're on the same page," she said, and stalked toward the threshold, pulling him along, touching his skin just long enough to step through the doorway into another place.

Wind whipped around her, and she dropped his hand, bringing up her own to shield her face.

For a second, she thought she was home. They stood in a sparsely populated copse of trees, the trunks glittering with ice and snow. Icicles longer and thicker than her arm hung from branches.

But no, this wasn't the Wildwoods. These trees grew stunted, their bare branches sun-starved and twisted, aching for light. Cara squinted against the snow, tiny shards of glass that nipped at her skin. They melted upon contact, trickling down her neck. The sky was a spiderweb of white light, and she could just make out the river's frozen surface creeping through the trees far off to her left. The sun would set soon.

And yet, despite the wind, her core blazed with warmth. She could register that it was freezing, that there was a vast difference in temperature between her body and the world, but she didn't *feel* cold.

"Let's find a place to stop for the night," she said, marching forward.

Zach followed without a word.

The path led them to the rocky edge of an escarpment, with a steep drop of at least two hundred feet. Below lay more snow and trees.

They continued on in silence, passing mounds of stones, caves lurking within. Scattered across the ground were curious bluish-white, spear-shaped things as long as Cara's forearm. Cara picked one up to study it. They weren't icicles, and they were pliable, springy, making a sound like a tuning fork when she bent them. Maybe these trees dropped them like pine needles.

By the time Cara found a clearing to pitch camp in, dusk had arrived, darkness eating away at the light with its vast shadowed mouth.

Cara tried and failed to set up her emporium tent for forty-five minutes—the instructions were in a language she'd never seen—before Zach stepped in, wordlessly setting it up in a third of the time. When she tried and failed to start a campfire with flint and carbon steel, refusing to use her fire powers, he stepped in, too, starting a fire almost instantly but not saying anything about it, without even a smirk.

This is fine, she thought, eating dinner in silence while they ignored each other. *This is totally, completely fine.*

Only when she'd washed her plate and silverware in the river and returned to camp to find Zach had taken up residence right in front of her tent did the quiet break.

"What are you doing?" she said, surprise making the words leap out of her mouth.

He glanced up at her, then away. "Guarding you," he muttered.

Blaze curled up at the foot of her bed like this, determined to protect her from intruders every night. The ice in her chest melted a little, and she had to fight to put the necessary edge in her voice when she spoke. "Could you guard me from a little farther away, please?"

Looking disgruntled that she didn't appreciate his efforts, he moved farther away from the entrance to her tent.

Inside, Cara undressed and changed into her sleep clothes, back prickling with awareness that Zach was only a few feet away on the other side of the canvas tent. Yet exhaustion pressed down on her mind, and her muscles ached as she slid into her sleeping bag, her several cuts still stinging. She missed Laolao. She missed her friends. She missed her *dog*. What she wouldn't give to have Blaze by her side, wagging his tail and pressing his wet nose into her hand for more pats.

And she missed her mother.

Did her mother miss her back? She wasn't so sure.

Maybe this hadn't been the right choice after all. Day one and already she'd nearly been eaten multiple times. And a strange new power was running through her veins, one she knew nothing about.

Restless, she checked the map. Icons had popped up marking the plant threshold and the winter landscape threshold, and from the blank expanse, she could tell they still had a long way to go.

Suddenly, the map blurred before her eyes. Dizziness swept through her, so strong it was like she could feel the world spinning off-kilter on its axis beneath her.

Her eyes flashed open. Heart thudding, she stared up at the tent fabric, confirmed the world wasn't suddenly moving again. *I'm just tired*, she told herself. *Exhausted from my new fire powers.*

Still, it took her a long while to fall asleep.

SIXTEEN

The next morning, the third threshold took them to another forest, unlike the previous frozen woodland in almost every way. Here, the air moved like molasses, thick and slow, buzzing with cicada song. Skinny longleaf pines shot up all around them. Bouquets of ferns sprouted at the base of every tree.

The river—or bayou, rather—didn't seem in a hurry to get any-where. It meandered, the sun glinting off its greenish-brown back like the scales of a fat trout. Rocks cropped up throughout the shallow water.

Something beeped.

Cara startled. That wasn't a sound she was expecting. When she looked up, she was even more surprised to find a girl on the opposite side of the river, staring in their direction. Her black baseball cap shaded smooth brown skin, and she clutched a black, rectangular device in one hand, which beeped again.

"Who the hell is that?" Zach asked, as if Cara would know.

Cara turned to him, pretending she was looking behind her.

"Don't talk," she whispered. "Let me handle this."

"Why can't I talk?" Zach complained. "She can't even hear me."

"Yes, but I can, so shut up."

The girl took off toward them, bounding across the boulders, the bulging pack on her shoulders apparently weighing nothing. She dashed from slick rock to rock, lanky brown arms outstretched for balance, her many braids bouncing with each leap. She should have slipped, what with her scuffed Doc Martens that didn't look like they gave her any purchase, but she didn't falter once.

The girl landed on the riverbank, and before Cara could react, she was drawing a knife from the sheath on her thigh.

"State your name and business, specter," the girl demanded, leveling her knife at Cara. She looked about Cara's age, although she stood about half a head taller. Her accent sounded Southern; Cara didn't know enough to be more specific. "I thought we made it clear you spirits were to leave this forest well alone."

"I'm not a ghost," Cara said, confusion mixing with her alarm. "What are you—?"

"Oh, I wasn't speaking to you, ghost talker." The girl's dark brown eyes, a circle of gray around each pupil, settled over Cara's shoulder, to where Zach was standing. "I was speaking to *him*."

Thoughts flew through Cara's head: Ghost *talker*? Was that the same as ghost *speaker*? And wait, this girl could see Zach? Then: the girl wanted to hurt Zach?

Cara's palms heated.

"Okay, how about you state *your* business?" she said.

The girl yanked down on her black baseball cap, which was emblazoned with a grinning silver skull. "I'm Brittany Livingston," she said. "I'm a ghost hunter. And I take down ghosts like him."

She moved forward, toward Zach, whose eyes widened. Instantly, Cara moved as well, putting her body between Zach's and the knife.

"He's my ghost. You're not touching him," she said, voice dangerous. Without thought, her hands blazed with fire. This time, she allowed them to burn. The protectiveness that had ignited inside surprised her, but she leaned into it, let it fan her flames higher.

Brittany's eyes flicked to Cara's hands, completely unfazed by her magic. "You think a little fire scares me?" she said. "I've hunted down the dead in the West Quarter on All Hallows' Eve. Level three hundred spirits. I could—" Her eyes fixed on Cara's wrist. "Is that an Ouroboros mark?"

How did this girl know so much?

"What about it?" Cara challenged.

Brittany lowered her knife, reconsidering the two of them. "I'm trying to find one of the Snakes," she said. "I thought my best bet would be Destruction, because to find Creation, you need passage through the liminal world, and you can't do that without a mark, which you can't get without tracking down one of the Snakes . . . but *you can take me there.*"

"I—what?" Cara said. The other girl's eyes were alight with fervor, and it was a little unnerving. "I don't even know you—"

Brittany was pacing back and forth, knife waving alarmingly in the air as she gestured. The tiny skull beads in her braids clacked against one another each time she turned. "This is just like Gran talked about," she muttered. "Ghost talker . . . ghost . . . ghost hunter. A cycle."

Zach bumped Cara's shoulder. "Is it me, or is she not making any sense?"

"Nope. Let's get out of here while she's distracted."

While Brittany may have stumbled upon the same liminal space that the river had brought Zach and Cara to, she couldn't follow them through another threshold and deeper into the liminal world without the Ouroboros mark.

The ghost hunter whirled toward them. "The thresholds," she said. "Do you see one—?"

A shadow fell over them as an enormous vulturelike creature swooped overhead. It slowed, wings stalling in the air, then turned around to dive at them, talons outstretched.

Brittany's eyes flashed. "This way if you want to live!" she yelled, and bolted, not even looking back to see if they were following her.

Cara hesitated—follow a girl she didn't trust at all or stay and see what this bird-creature wanted? But this was Brittany's forest, not Cara's.

So she ran.

"Please do stop your running, Britannica," came the voice of an irritated English professor. Cara looked up to find the old vulture-creature regarding them with intelligent yolk-yellow eyes, and she nearly tripped over a log in her shock. "Your mother is furious and requires you to return home this very instant!"

"What the hell is happening?" muttered Zach next to Cara.

"Do you ever get tired of being a snitch, Harold?" Brittany yelled. She swung her pack from her shoulders and dug around in it as she ran. "And before you say it, a 'snitch' is *not* a good thing!"

Even from thirty feet below, Cara could hear Harold sigh. "Running away from home? Stealing the bag of winds, a family heirloom? I cannot even fully express how dismayed I am! I'm aghast! For flight's sake, your mother—"

Brittany produced a sphere from her pack and threw it at the bird. Midair, it turned into a net.

Captured, Harold thudded to the ground, yet he never broke his lecture.

"That is hardly the way to deal with your problems, Britannica," the elderly vulture admonished through his nest of rope. "I am very disappointed in you."

A threshold glimmered through the trees. Tugging on Zach's hand, Cara pulled him toward it.

"Sorry, Harold! You know deep, deep, deep down I love you!" Brittany called. "Wait, guys! Wait up—"

Cara and Zach stumbled into the reaches of a wide river valley. Viridian grass rolled in an unbroken swath before them, cut only by the cerulean ribbon of river that snaked far off to their right. Trees dotted the landscape here and there, as if some painter had placed them strategically. In either direction, mountains sloped gently into the air, like the ground was too comfortable and they couldn't be bothered to rise farther. Cloud cover hung low over their peaks, and fog drifted in the distance, formless, nearly blending in with the colorless sky.

"Shit, it's cold," said a voice behind Cara.

Her jaw dropped. Brittany was here? But Cara hadn't been in contact with her when they'd crossed—

Maybe you didn't need to physically touch someone with a mark when you crossed. You just needed to be *nearby*.

"We held hands for nothing?" she said to Zach.

He rubbed the back of his neck. "Guess so," he muttered.

Cara turned on the ghost hunter.

"Hey. Britannica," she said. "You want to explain what the heck you're doing here?"

Brittany had been fiddling with her backpack straps, but her whole body stiffened at Cara's voice. "Okay, first of all," she said with a glare, "never call me that again, unless you're looking for some new holes in your face. And second of all, I already told you. I need to find one of the Snakes."

Cara stepped toward her. "Well, you can go find it somewhere else, because this isn't your quest."

Brittany's hand went to her knife. "Don't tell me what to do."

Flame lit Cara's palms. She had sacrificed so much to be standing here, and this random girl thought she could just hijack her quest because she wanted to?

"Whoa, chill," said Zach, moving between them, though he'd gone incorporeal again. "How about we put away the dangerous objects?" To Cara, he said, "Listen. We can't send her back."

"*Thank you*," said Brittany. "I'm glad someone here is reasonable."

Utter disbelief snuffed Cara's flame.

He shrugged. "The threshold we came through disappeared, right?" He gestured to where it once was, nothing but landscape stretching out around them now.

"Whose side are you even on?" Cara growled.

"I'm just pointing out the obvious—"

Brittany sighed dramatically. "It's fine. I can tell when I'm not wanted." She waved her knife in the air like it was a gavel. "I'll walk off into the mountains, then, and leave you two in peace. Sorry for hijacking your weird quest-slash-date-thing—"

Cara nearly choked on her spit. *"Excuse me?"*

Brittany eyed them with renewed interest. "You mean you're not together?"

"We're not—" Cara said.

Zach said, "That would never, ever, ever—"

"I'm sorry, but you're incredibly wrong."

"Strictly business," Zach added.

Brittany raised an eyebrow. "Soooo . . . I can join you?"

"No," Cara said immediately just as Zach said, "Why not?"

She waved an arm at him. "Are you just going to invite anyone on the quest? We should have invited Mr. Mortmanger, I guess!"

"Look, Tang," he said. "She has knives. She's clearly good at fighting, and since you refuse to use your fire . . ."

Cara gritted her teeth, but what did it matter? They were on a tight time line, and she didn't have time to argue with Zach over expanding their merry little band of travelers.

"Whatever," Cara muttered, turning away and walking deeper into the valley. "Let's find a threshold."

Cara stalked into the grassland. The fog drifted closer in dense, thick swaths, little tendrils curling toward her.

What, was he going to pay Brittany to help him as well? How much money was he willing to give up? He was really going to let this stranger distract from their goal—

A laugh from behind broke her train of thought. Despite the fact that Brittany had literally threatened him with a knife less than twenty minutes ago, Zach was chatting with her. From the snippets of conversation that drifted toward Cara, Zach was filling Brittany in on everything: why they were here, what they were doing.

Cara had a right to be mad. Didn't she? Here was yet another person who found out she could see ghosts. Cara had done a very good job of keeping her promise to her mother her whole life, and in just a matter of days, she'd blown it to multiple people. Besides, this wasn't even Brittany's quest. It was just supposed to be Zach and her, and Brittany had hijacked it.

Cara frowned. Wait. Zach and her quest? That didn't sound right. It wasn't like she had any personal claim to Zach's company besides pure necessity for getting the antidote and resurrecting him.

Fingers of gray crept toward Cara, beckoning, welcoming, gaining in speed. White as a shroud.

And then the fog rushed toward her and swallowed her up.

SEVENTEEN

Gray-white flooded her senses. Cara blinked, hard, but that did nothing to clear her vision. She couldn't see anything—it was like she'd been engulfed by a cloud. Her chest tightened.

"Coleson? Brittany?" she called, but there wasn't an answer.

Where had they gone? Hadn't they been just behind her?

But the fog was so thick that they could have been standing a few feet away, and she wouldn't have known.

Tentatively, she took a step. She called again, but the fog seemed to swallow her words. It was like dropping pebbles into a vacuum. All sound was dulled; the far-off burble of the river had been sucked away completely into an eerie emptiness. Even her own voice sounded muted to her ears.

She tilted her gaze up. Nothing but fog, billowing over her head, blocking out any light. A feeling of claustrophobia crept into her veins, and she drew a shaky breath, feeling as if she were inhaling nothing but fog. There was no sign of life. Or afterlife, either.

Then: in the distance, a figure.

She squinted.

The gray curled back to reveal a ghost standing by himself, the silver kissing his skin almost blending in with the fog, his blue eyes oh so familiar.

Cara wasn't ready for the relief that rushed through her body and roared in her ears in contrast to everything else in this strange, silent space. She found herself running. "Coleson!"

He turned around, and she was gratified at the relief that flashed across his face. Maybe he'd been worried about her. Not that it mattered to her whether he'd been worried, she reminded herself. "You're okay," he said, sounding as if a weight had been lifted off his shoulders.

She pulled up. "Am I imagining things, or do you actually look happy to see me?" she teased, but the uncharacteristic concern didn't leave his features.

He took her hand, and startled, she let him. "I am," he said. "I was worried I'd lost you."

Cara's eyes flitted to their intertwined fingers. "Yeah, well, let's not get separated again—"

But Zach interrupted her. "And I'm not saying I was worried just because I'd be in trouble if I lost the only ghost speaker I know. I—I can't stop thinking about how little time we have left together. I gotta tell you something. Now, before it's too late. When we fought the white Snake and I said I needed you, I meant it." Zach closed his eyes, then opened them again. "I need *you*, Tang."

Her mouth had gone dry. Cara licked her lips, trying to form words. "What—what are you saying?"

His eyes were bright and blue and burning. She couldn't look away.

"I think," he said, "you know exactly what I'm saying."

"Coleson, I—" she started, but he pulled her forward so hard and so fast her arm protested. She opened her mouth, but he laid a finger on her lips. His hand moved from her wrist to her waist. It skimmed the bare skin under her shirt, and her mind went instantly, completely blank.

Zach slid his other hand away from her lips to cup the curve of her face. In a low, suddenly husky tone, he said, "Do you know how long I've wanted to do *this*?"

Heat erupted along every inch of her skin. She didn't move as he leaned down, slowly closing the chasm between them. Cara was having difficulty coming up with rational, coherent thought with Zach this near. But why had she ever bothered to form thought at all, when she could have had him—

Flames erupted from her hands, an automatic response to her emotions, and he stopped, his mouth hovering just above her own.

"Do you think you could put that thing out?" he murmured, his voice soft, so soft.

"What?" she said, blinking dazedly.

Zach pulled back a little, gestured to the flame burning in her palms, his perfect mouth twisting in disgust. "The fire. Obviously. Do you think you could get rid of it for me?"

Cara glanced at the fire, the scarlet flames burning hotter from his proximity. Each part of her was lit up with sensation, waiting. He made it sound like such a simple request.

But the Zach she knew wouldn't have made the request at all.

Cara stared at her hand, the brightness of the flame burning off the gray haze that had infiltrated her mind, then turned that stare on him. "No," she said. "I don't think I will."

Planting both hands firmly on his chest, she shoved him back.

The thing—because it was not Zach, which she should have realized from the start—teetered away, charismatic smile turning ghastly as it slowly reached a hand up to its torso where her handprints were burning away to reveal more fog behind it. "You hurt me," it said, sounding surprised, sounding so like him, she almost stepped forward. "You . . ."

And then it began to dissolve. Cara went cold as all the color leached from the figure. Its eyes turned white, blue bleeding from its irises. Fog snaked from its eye sockets, and then from the rest of its body, losing form and hue to return to the gray.

While she'd been preoccupied, the fog had crept up all around her. Only the space surrounding her palmfuls of fire was clear. Her heart beat frantically, and her fire roared higher, her anger and disgust and fear fueling it.

With a shriek, the fog recoiled.

Fire. The fog didn't like fire.

Cara examined her hands, then clenched them into fists of flame. Fine. She'd use her fire magic, but only to get out of here. Only because it was necessary. She didn't want to get used to using it. And she certainly wouldn't use it in the real world. But this wasn't the real world.

She gathered herself and pushed forward, the gray hastily parting like she was a ship pushing her prow through the water.

I should have known, she thought angrily. *I should have stopped it immediately.*

But she'd been so relieved to see him again. She'd run to him, for God's sake. Clearly, her guard had been down.

And the rest of it . . . She shuddered to think of that *thing* putting its hands on her. The fog must have some kind of mind-altering substance, some intoxicant, because there was no other way she would have let herself be fooled like that, with something that looked like Zach, no less. And nearly ki— She broke off that thought.

The blood in her veins felt more sluggish. Like when she'd been trapped in the fog's thrall, it had been slowly draining her of her energy.

A familiar voice called her name, and she turned before she could think better of it.

"Laolao?"

The fog parted to reveal her grandmother, the beam on her face an expression Cara would recognize anywhere. Despite her shock, Cara automatically smiled back, like a good granddaughter would. Something felt off—but how could anything feel off when her grandmother was here?

Eyes bright, Laolao drew closer, laying a hand on Cara's arm. Any unpleasant feelings vanished at her grandmother's touch, like a candle being snuffed.

"Come, xiaogui. There is so much I have to tell you about your mother," Laolao said, tugging on Cara's arm to lead her forward.

Cara blinked, falling into step at Laolao's side. "You mean you're finally going to tell me why you guys never talk?" Her nerves overtook her tongue. "It can't be because she can't see you—you guys are smart enough to overcome that. You could use my phone to WeChat her! Or use a notepad and take turns writing. Not just to leave each other passive-aggressive notes, I mean. To actually have a conversation. I could even help you guys talk, if you want—"

Laolao waved her hand, and Cara fell silent.

"So many questions." Laolao smiled, tightening her grip on Cara's wrist. "You have always been so curious. It is your mom's fault, you know. Why you no longer want to learn about magic. Her bitterness toward it has poisoned you, as well."

"And is that why you refuse to talk to her? Or is there more?"

"You are a sensible child. You must be, because I raised you. Why don't you use that big head of yours to figure it out?"

"But Laolao, you said—" Something cracked underneath her foot, and Cara glanced down, but her grandmother tugged her onward before she could get a good look.

Cara increased the fire in her free hand, trying to see more in front of her. "Where are you taking me?"

"You will see." Laolao smiled, but something about it was less genuine than before, and Cara slowed as she felt yet another object crunch under her shoe. This time, Laolao didn't tow her forward fast enough.

Cara stopped dead. The pieces were hard to make out, small as they were, nestled in the grass, but she knew at once what they had to be—pieces that might have been in someone's hand, or foot, now splintered into disarticulated white shards.

She had stepped on bone.

Laolao stopped, too. Expression the picture of grandmotherly concern, Laolao reached her hands toward Cara's face. "What is the matter, xiaogui?"

Palms full of fire, Cara caught the thing's wrists and squeezed.

It shrieked in fury and tried to wrest free, but Cara clamped down until what looked like its hands burned to stumps, and the figure hobbled back, flames racing up its arms, outrage swirling in its now cold gray eyes as the color seeped from its skin.

"I almost had you," it said in a creaking voice, before the fire ate through its face and it disintegrated.

Cara stumbled, exhaustion pounding her temples. She refueled her fire, which at the moment seemed like a godsend, forcing the gray back once more. She shook the clutches of the fog from her mind.

Touch. She couldn't let it touch her, even if she'd never needed a hug from her grandmother so badly before. That was how it drained her energy. Sucked the life out of her.

Somehow, the fog had access to her memories. It showed her what she wanted, or at least what it thought she wanted.

It wasn't just messing with her body; it was also messing with her mind.

But its weakness was that it had no mind of its own. It couldn't invent something entirely new. She'd wanted to know why Laolao and her mother had given each other the cold shoulder for nearly twelve years, and so the gray had promised exactly that. It had said it would let Cara in on all the secrets she wanted, but it couldn't, because what Cara wanted was precisely what she didn't know. And because Cara didn't know, the fog didn't, either.

She gritted her teeth and stalked forward, anger blazing a path. She had to find Zach and Brittany and get the heck out of here.

She'd made it five steps before a voice said, "Cara?"

Cara stopped short, squeezing her eyes shut. *No.* Zach had been expected, her grandmother surprising yet plausible, but this . . .

The fog seemed to solidify, roiling up before her. It wanted her to turn around. She lashed out with her hands, and the fog billowed back but did not retreat.

"Cara." The voice, firm and authoritative as ever. "Are you really going to ignore me?"

She couldn't.

She turned around.

Her mother smiled at her. "There we are. Now, let me get a good look at you. Have you been eating, baobei? You look skinnier." She reached her arms out, and Cara backpedaled so fast the fog at her back hissed as it made contact with her flames.

The smile froze, dropped, shifted into a frown. "Is something wrong, Cara?"

"Yes," she said to the fog, walking toward the image with fists of fire. "What's wrong is that you messed up."

"What do you mean?" asked the fog. It sounded so much like her mother—the confusion painfully genuine, the lilt of her mother's words, the sound of home, it threatened to rend her heart in two. "I was just trying to do my best. To do the best for you. I regretted my last words to you almost immediately. I've been following you all this time. I want you to come home."

Home.

Cara's arms shook as she held them in front of her, the fire as high as she could push it. She swallowed hard, tried to blink back the moisture gathering in her eyes. "That's a lie and you know it," she said. She never would have talked to her mother like this—but this wasn't her mother. "You've been following me? Really? Is that the best you could come up with?"

In the corner of her vision, she saw a tendril of fog snaking toward her, aiming under her arm at her unprotected rib cage. She drove it back with her fire, the gray hissing with displeasure.

"But baobei, it's true. I—" Her mother's hands waved helplessly in the air. She switched from Chinese to English, then back, trying to find the words. "I'm so sorry I doubted you. You've been so brave. I shouldn't try to control you anymore. I see that now."

Anger twisted inside her, fury at the fog for thinking it could trick her like this, fury at herself for wanting to be tricked.

None of this is real. None of this is true.

"What about my fire?" Cara asked, her voice thick. Traitorous tears slid down her cheeks, distracting signs of weakness. She didn't dare lift a hand to wipe them away.

The image wavered the slightest degree. "Oh, Cara. Nothing you do could hurt me. I'm your mom, aren't I? That means I love you unconditionally, no matter what."

You have your grandmother's eyes, and every time I look at you, I see her. Which is funny, you know, because when your grandmother looked at me, she saw nothing at all. Like the only things she could see were ghosts.

"No matter what," Cara echoed.

She kept hearing the sound of her real mother's voice in her head. The resolution in it, like her mother had made a choice, and it hadn't been her. The click of the door as it shut, leaving her in the cold.

The image smiled and held out her arms.

"Put out your fire, baobei. Come home. Let me hold you."

She could barely see her mother through her tears.

All the choices Cara had made since finding Zach's body in the Wildwoods, all the compromises, all the promises. Each one had led her further from what her mom wanted her to be. A daughter who didn't see ghosts. A daughter who didn't use magic.

A daughter who was her mother's definition of good.

"What about the promise you had me make?" Cara asked so quietly she could barely hear herself.

But the fog heard her, because the fog *was* her, made of her fears and hopes and dreams. Her mother edged closer.

"I don't care about any of that, baobei," she said. "I just want my daughter."

But Cara's mom had cared so hard she'd forced her to leave.

Not this one, though. Standing in front of her with the same build, the same hair, the same eyes.

Cara swallowed, but the tears kept coming. Slowly, she let the fire die. She walked forward. And because she had to, she reached for her mom.

Eyes gleaming, her mother opened her arms for an embrace—

And at the very last second, Cara lit up her hand and tore the thing in half.

She watched her mother fall apart.

The fog screeched in frustration. "You see?" the thing hissed as it disintegrated. "This is why your mother doesn't love you."

Cara stood in the emptiness, breathing hard.

Her tears dripped down, and the fog took even those, billowing up around her feet to lap up her pain.

The anger simmering in her chest boiled over. With a shout, she threw out her arms, sending fire through the air in both directions.

With a ghastly shriek, the fog vanished. Not shrinking back but simply evaporating as Cara's fury caught up with the gray and devoured it before it could devour her.

The area surrounding her cleared, and only then did she raise an arm and wipe her tears away.

Yeah, she'd wanted a hug—of course she did, when touching her on the shoulder was the most her real mom ever did—but that would have meant letting the fog win. And she couldn't have let that happen when she still had to save Zach.

All of that was made-up. Things that will never happen.

"Tang! Brittany!" a voice yelled. "Where the hell are you guys?"

Cara groaned. "You tried this one already!" she shouted at the fog, and wheeled, hands at the ready.

Zach raced into view. When he saw her, he pulled up short, looking at her hesitantly. "Your fire," he said in wonder. "You're using it."

Cara dropped her arms for a second, uncertain. It looked so much like him, corporeal once more: the messy blond hair, the bright blue eyes, the sun-kissed skin limned with silver light.

But then, so had the first one.

And she was not going to make that mistake again.

"I hate you so much," she told him. "Don't even *think* of touching me, you pretender."

"Hey, hey." Zach held up his hands. "I'm real!"

Yeah, that's what the fog would say, stupid. "If you're real, then prove it."

"I could say the same thing to you!" He sounded so genuinely offended that it nearly did it for her—but maybe the fog had stepped up its game. It knew she was onto it, and it would say anything to lure her in.

She couldn't listen to what he said. She had to watch what he did.

Cara knelt, placing one hand on the ground, and focused. It took her a few tries, but eventually, a path of fire, at least three feet high, blazed across the earth from her to him. Crackling and hissing.

She stood. Jutting out her chin, she met his eyes, smiled, and said, "I said, prove it. Come to me."

If he were fog, he would burn. But if it was truly him, then she'd know, because ghosts couldn't be touched by flame. By anything.

"I'm not going to walk through fire just because you say so—"

"Walk." She fixed him with a stare. "Or I'll bring the fire to you."

He let out a groan that was so very Zach, her heart leaped. And then he began to walk.

Holding her gaze, he moved toward her, step by step through an inferno. Her breath caught as the flames reached for him, but he never paused, never flinched. His eyes never left her face.

When he reached her, he stopped, almost close enough to touch. Head cocked, he smirked down at her, dark blond hair falling across his temples.

In a low voice, he said, "That good enough for you, Tang?"

Yes.

She exhaled. How reassuring it was, simply to know that what you were seeing was real, was safe. She stepped toward him, but he leaned away, a grin tugging at the corner of his mouth.

"Hold on," he teased. "How do I know *you're* real?"

"I told you I hated you, Coleson."

"That doesn't completely rule it out," he said, voice suddenly strangled.

"Fine." Cara swallowed. There was still a lump in her throat from everything the fog had shown her, and the relief that Zach was real hadn't taken it away, just added to all the emotions she was struggling to keep down.

Zach paused, eyes searching her face. When he spoke again, the previous playfulness was gone. "Are you crying?"

Crap. She swiped at her eyes, but that made more tears come, borne of frustration. She always ended up crying when she got mad, and she hated that he was seeing her like this.

"No, I'm not *crying*, I just got a little fog in my eye." She scrubbed harder. How was there more?

There was a careful hand on her jaw, tipping up her chin, and worried blue eyes.

"Hey, hey," he said, panicked. "What happened?"

She faltered, her hands dropping away uselessly. "What—what are you doing?"

His thumb swept across her cheek, gentle, like a lover's touch, like he wasn't standing in the flames of someone who could end him, who held his fate in her shaking hands.

"Trying to distract you from crying. Don't get the wrong idea," he warned.

She laughed, but it came out choked. "And what's the right idea?"

"That I'm still an asshole. I already figured out it was you when I walked toward you. I just wanted to mess with you a little. And, well, the fog shows you what you desperately want to see. Trust me, I don't actually love the sight of you crying." He smiled like it was an inside joke.

Cara put her hand on top of his, tears forgotten. His fingers stilled under hers. "Wait? You were *sure*?"

Zach shrugged. "Seventy percent sure. That's a passing grade, you know."

"You came to me when you weren't even certain I was real? No, *that* was one hundred percent idiotic."

With his other hand, he brushed a tangled strand of hair back from her eyes, tucking it behind her ear. "Was it?"

She stared at him, tongue suddenly useless. Normally, she would have no problem replying. But normally, he would have said it like a challenge. He would have said it with a smirk.

She didn't know how to respond when he said it like this: with his cool fingers on her skin, dangerously close to her hammering pulse. With a knowing smile curving his lips. With a kind of softness in his voice that she hadn't heard before, the kind of softness that she wouldn't, couldn't trust.

But right now, right here, in this fog of false visions and voices, Zach was the one thing that was familiar. The one thing that wouldn't hurt her.

A scream tore through the spell, and they broke apart.

"That was Brittany." Cara glanced around. Through all this fog, she couldn't tell where they were, let alone where the scream had come from. Did she really want to go searching for a girl whose way of saying hello involved pointing a large knife at people's faces?

No, she didn't, but they couldn't leave her.

The scream came again, louder, and now that Cara was listening for it, she was able to pinpoint the vague direction. Or at least where she thought it was. She would need to burn their way there.

Cara reached for Zach's hand and found that he was already reaching for hers. When had it become like instinct to turn to him?

"Hold on," she commanded. "I don't want to have to find you again."

His fingers interlocked with hers. "Are you kidding? You're the one with fire. I'm not letting you go."

And they took off running, Cara stretching out her free hand to blaze a path of flame, the fog a gray fury around them.

EIGHTEEN

As they ran, Cara called Brittany's name, but no answer came. She stepped on more bones, each crunch a stark reminder of the fog's past victims.

"What was that?" Zach asked at the sound.

"Bone," she said grimly.

"*Bone?*" he repeated, but she tugged him on.

At last they found Brittany in a gap in the fog—the gray writhing in consuming spirals around the struggling ghost hunter. She moved her knives so fast they shredded the fog, but it re-formed moments later. She was attempting to stay out of reach of a fog-formed old woman—Brittany's grandmother, Cara would guess.

Cara dropped Zach's hand and shot flames through the center of the gray figure. A hole formed where the fire struck, and the fog screeched. A section gathered itself, darkening, and redirected itself, speeding straight toward Cara. Only a few more hasty blasts of flame kept it from hitting her in the face.

Cara sent more fire into the fog surrounding Brittany. The gray billowed back, hissing with each punch of flame. It retreated enough for Zach and Cara to race into the gap and take up positions at Brittany's back, forming an outward facing triangle.

Cara knelt. Concentrating, she drew a line of fire in front of her.

Flame sprang up, protecting the lower half of her body. It scared and exhilarated her, seeing her fire spark so readily to life.

"Okay, rotate," she said to Zach and Brittany. "I'm making a circle of fire."

"Sweet," Brittany said, panting.

"Shuffle to your right," Cara ordered. "On three."

She completed the circle and stood up, wiping her forehead.

The fog circled them like a panther, considering its prey. Cara tried to grow the flames higher, to form a wall around them, but whether it was something mental or physical inside her, she couldn't force the flames any higher. Seizing its chance, the fog regathered, bunched up like it was tensing, and pounced at Cara's face. She flung up fresh fire from her hands, slicing the fog into pieces. The tendrils twitched in the air, then turned and moved toward her as one. She swept her arm in a wave of flame, dissipating them.

But there were still more, and more.

This wasn't working. It had been hard enough to destroy the illusions targeted toward her, but now the fog was angrier, more desperate. She only had two hands, and the fog could splinter itself into a thousand tiny pieces that could worm onto her skin, wriggle under her defenses.

"Cara, if you come home, you'll be safe," her mother's voice said, hands reaching through the gray, and Cara's heart shuddered.

"Step forward," Laolao said next. "Didn't you say you wanted to know? Wouldn't you do anything for the truth?"

Before fog Zach could fully form, she dispelled him, too.

Her energy flagged, but the fog didn't seem to grow tired. It was wearing her down like a cat taking jabs at a trapped mouse. Cara could feel the sweat dripping down the back of her shirt and her breathing was becoming more labored by the minute. She was play-ing straight into the fog's soul-sucking arms.

She needed to end this once and for all.

Zach glanced over at her. "What's the plan?"

Cara shot another pulse of fire. "What?"

"I know that look in your eye. You're cooking up a plan in that brain of yours."

In her surprise, her next pulse of flame misfired. The beginnings of a plan *had* begun to swirl in her mind like mist, but her thoughts hadn't even coalesced enough for her to realize it—at least until now.

A nasty tendril of fog lunged for her face. She dispatched it.

She'd always thought she could read Zach, but it was disconcert-ing to realize that maybe he could read her just as easily.

He sliced apart one of the fog's arms. "And now you look annoyed, which is definitely my fault. Just tell me what you want me to do."

Do you know how long I've wanted to do this?

Unexpectedly, her cheeks burned with heat.

"Actually," she said, "I don't think I need you at all. Brittany!"

The other girl inclined her head in her direction. "Yeah?"

"Harold mentioned a bag of winds. Any chance you could use it?"

"I could." Brittany moved back, tightening the triangle. She dis-pelled a flank of fog. "I was kinda saving it for an emergency, though."

Cara sputtered. "This doesn't qualify as an emergency?"

Brittany shrugged. "In my book? Nah. Not until something's about to blow up."

Cara stepped back, too, taking a deep breath. "Well, I've got an idea. On the count of three, I need you to open your bag of winds into the fog, just as I shoot out my fire. Got it?"

Brittany held up the bag, grinning. "Clear as day, ghost talker.

Although I guess not this day. . . ."

Cara drew back her shoulders. Gritted her teeth. Aimed her palms at the ground. "On my mark. Three . . . two . . . *one.*"

She shot out a wave of flame at the earth, turning as she did so. Within seconds, a widening circle of fire raced outward, away from their group. As the flames went, they gained height, piercing more and more into the underbelly of the fog.

At the same time, Brittany unleashed her bag of winds. The zephyrs blew back the uppermost reaches of gray, the ones the fire couldn't reach, caught sparks and carried them farther.

In the face of wind and fire too fast to retreat from, the fog was either scorched or dissipated. It unleashed one last screech before the sound, too, vanished.

The sky was clear. Still gray—but clear.

Brittany whooped, her joy ringing extra loud without the fog to stifle it. She held out a fist to Cara, who blinked at it in fatigue for a second before extinguishing her palms and completing the fist bump.

Panting, Cara let the rest of the fire vanish. Twin flames of exhaustion and exhilaration swept through her. But it was the good kind of exhaustion, the kind that left you clearheaded, if swaying in its wake. The pent-up anger, the fear that had taken up residence in her rib cage ever since gaining her fire powers, had disappeared. Gone up in smoke.

Igniting had made her feel tired, but her exhaustion hadn't spread along with the rest of the fire. So maybe it cost energy to ignite a flame and to hold it, but not once she gave it something external to consume. If she wasn't careful, she could burn herself out.

Good thing I'm not going to use my fire after this.

She looked out across the expanse of land, and her mouth went dry. Bones littered the earth like the remains of a banquet of giants. Scattered in the grass were everything from fully intact femurs to parts of rib cages to the most fragile shards of ivory that wouldn't make a whisper as they crumbled underfoot. Skeletons picked clean by intangible teeth.

That could have been us.

Cara looked at her hand, turning it over. Leftover heat shimmered near it, her own kind of liminal place. Without her fire, she might have joined all these bones.

I am not my hands. I am not my eyes.

I am something more.

A wave of nausea rolled through her, so strong she doubled over.

At once, a freezing hand was on her back, steadying her. "You okay?" a worried voice asked.

When I said I needed you, I meant it.

She pushed down the nausea and scrambled away from him, almost stumbling. "No. I mean, yeah! Of course. Why wouldn't I be?"

"Because you just evaporated all that fog in like twenty seconds flat?" He folded his arms, Brittany's knife still in one hand. "Which, I gotta give it to you, was pretty cool. No wonder you didn't need me."

I need you, Tang.

Tilting her head, she mustered up a smile. "Don't worry. I'm sure I'll find some use for you the next time we're in life-threatening danger."

"I'm counting on it." Zach grinned at her, and Cara's stomach flipped. The adrenaline of almost dying had wiped away her previous anger. Somehow, it had become normal for him to smile at her like that, as normal as the silver silhouetting his arms. What once was a sure sign of trouble had become a strange source of reassurance, which itself was so confusing that her stomach was twisting into knots at the sight.

Cara waited for it. For the smirk, the smugness in his voice as he pointed out how he'd been right about using her power, how *she'd* been wrong.

So she was ready when his eyes fell to her hands, his expression darkening as he stepped toward her. She braced for his blade, another argument.

And then he dropped his knife, letting it fall to the ground, and took her hand.

"The fog hurt you."

His voice had gone hard as ice. Startled, Cara glanced down— and for the first time, fully saw her wounds. Slashes on her palm she hadn't examined, lines of red on the forearm she'd used to shield herself. A gash running parallel to her collarbone, blood trickling down her chest. One at the top of her thigh, close to her hip bone. Clothes ripped, skin licked open by the fog. As soon as she noticed the wounds, sensations began to pour in from her brain, none of them pleasant.

She grimaced. These were going to be a pain to patch up.

"It even got your back," Zach said from behind her, his voice still taut with that emotion she couldn't name. When she finally placed it, her confusion deepened.

It was anger.

He circled back around, his jaw clenched as he glared at the distance where the gray had come from. At his sides, his fists clenched, knuckles shining silver-white. "I wish fog was punchable."

Cara had never seen Zach like this. What would he have gotten angry about in life, when he got everything he wanted? And she'd certainly never seen him like this on her behalf. Most of the time, Zach was angry *because* of her, not for her. But now he looked furious enough to do something with the blade lying on the earth, to set something on fire himself.

"Hey, ghost talker," Brittany interrupted, sidling up to Cara. "I, uh, don't think you and I got off on the right foot, so . . . reintroduction? I'm Brittany Livingston. Third-generation ghost hunter." She held out a hand, brown eyes hesitant like she wasn't sure Cara was going to take it. "That was some good work with your fire."

Cara shook it using the palm that wasn't cut up. "Cara. Nice job with your bag of winds. And . . . thanks."

"You've got cuts, too," Zach noted to Brittany.

"Stupid-ass fog. Not as bad as her, though." Brittany nodded at Cara. "Need help patching those up?"

"I'll do it," Zach cut in.

"I can do it myself," Cara said automatically, heartbeat picking up.

"No, you can't. How the hell are you going to wrap your injured hand? Or reach your back?"

"I think I'll manage." Inside, she was kicking herself. Why? Why did she always say stupid stuff around him?

"Yeah, but it'll hurt like *hell*—"

"You know what?" Brittany said, gaze switching between Cara and Zach. "I'm gonna go over there and do an inventory on my stuff, make sure I'm not missing anything, pour some alcohol over these cuts. Can I have my knife back, ghost boy?"

Without taking his eyes off Cara's face, Zach picked up the knife and held it out to Brittany.

As Brittany left, Zach crossed his arms, cocked his head, and gave Cara a look. "Do you really not want my help, or are you just refusing because you like to disagree with everything I say?"

"I don't disagree with everything you—"

Cara pressed her lips together.

To his credit—and to her surprise—he didn't rub it in. "Come on," he said. "If I mess it up, you can insult me."

She wavered. "I would have done that anyway," she informed him, and sat, shrugging off her pack. Instant relief at being off her feet flooded her body, the tension bleeding away. It didn't matter if the fog came back; she refused to get up again for the time being.

Zach sat across from her. Rolling up his sleeves, he took out the first aid kit. Then, with a gentle touch, he removed her Band-Aids from the day before, revealing cuts that hadn't even healed yet, then deftly popped the cap off the rubbing alcohol.

Cara reluctantly held her hand out, palm up. He wrapped his fingers around her wrist, more gently than she'd expected, sending shivers all the way up her arm.

The alcohol stung, but she bit back a hiss, not wanting to show weakness in front of him.

"What, did you get tired of watching me patch myself up the first time?"

Zach didn't look up, his eyes focused on her skin as he wrapped bandages around her left hand. "Something like that," he said.

Silence settled.

Against all reason, her heart was kicking up a fuss in its cage. This past week, she'd been in physical proximity to him more times than she had in her entire life. But they'd always been more focused on other things, like searching for the cave behind the Falls. Right now, there was nothing else to focus on except for *him*: his head bent in front of her, irritatingly long lashes standing out against his tanned skin, bottom lip drawn between his teeth in concentration—

"Where'd you learn first aid, anyway?" she asked abruptly.

Zach's eyes flicked up to hers as he moved on to her right hand. "My dad. Once I turned thirteen, he dragged Luke and me out into the forest preserve every other weekend."

Huh. Now that Zach mentioned it, she remembered him complaining about that a few times in homeroom. Loudly.

"He also taught me, in spite of my trying my best not to learn anything, how to pitch a tent and start a fire. Said I'd need them someday." He pressed down another Band-Aid. "Guess he was right."

"Did he teach you how to pick a lock, too?"

He snorted. "No, that I did all by myself. One summer—sixth grade, probably—Luke got it in his head that we were going to break into the liquor cabinet in Dad's study. Which meant Luke forcing me to learn how to pick a lock."

"What was Luke's role?"

"Lookout." He scoffed. "I spent three whole weeks practicing. By the end, I could have picked the locks on everyone's lockers. I was a pro, okay? We had it all planned out. The big day comes. Our parents are away on a business trip. Luke and I are in the study psyching ourselves up. Then Vic walks in and asks what we're doing."

"Your older sister, right?"

"Yeah."

Zach finished with Cara's hands and slid his fingers up her wrist to the cuts on her forearm. She fought back a shiver even as fire built in her belly. The evocation of the fog Zach floated in her mind, disorienting and strange.

"Well," Zach continued, "we try lying, but somehow she's not fooled, even with our awesome deception skills. She threatens to call

Mom and Dad about our trespassing right then and there, so we tell her. We think she's gonna rat us out, but instead, she busts a gut. Falls to the floor and everything. She laughs so hard there are literal tears in her eyes. Luke and I are like, *What the hell, Vic?* When she finally stops laughing, she fishes a key out of this random vase next to the liquor cabinet.

"And then she opens it.

"Our jaws *drop*. Luke and I must have looked like a couple of goldfish. All that work when we didn't have to do shit."

Cara imagined it. A giggle bubbled to the surface.

"Yeah, yeah, laugh all you want. But who's laughing now? Not Mr. Mortmanger." Zach grinned.

Forearm finished, Zach edged closer. "Is it okay if I do the one on your collarbone, too?"

Her pulse beat in the column of her throat. When would this be over?

"Yeah," she said lightly. She might die inside, but sure, it was okay. "I can't do it myself, so you kinda have to, right?"

"Right."

She gritted her teeth as he pressed an alcohol-soaked cotton pad to her skin. The sharp smell burned her nose but was overshadowed by ice and pine.

He reached for more gauze, and Cara's eyes caught on the long slender scar that reached from his elbow to halfway up the underside of his forearm. It was from the summer before eighth grade, when they were thirteen and old enough to know better. He'd challenged her to a race to determine who could climb the fastest up a chainlink fence and down the other side—and when that didn't work, he'd double-dog dared her.

So of course she'd agreed.

Technically, Zach had won, but only because he slipped halfway down, slicing his arm open on a stray wire in the mesh, and fell the rest of the way to the ground. Cara wasn't the one who'd spent the night getting stitched up in the ER, so really, who had been the real winner there?

Zach's thumb grazed her hip bone, and her breath caught in her chest.

While she'd been lost in the memory, he'd moved down from her collarbone, was now touching her waist the way his fog version had, an unsettling echo of phantom sensation.

Cara swallowed. Cleared her throat and said, hoping she didn't sound as unmoored as she felt, "You're close with your siblings, then?"

Thankfully, Zach was focused on pressing a bandage to the top of her thigh, so he probably hadn't noticed the point when both of them weren't breathing. At her question, he gave a little scoff, a wry twist of his lips. "I wish."

She'd said something wrong. She waited, because she also didn't know what else to say.

Zach moved behind her. Her awareness of the gash on her back, the slice between her shoulder blades, heightened in response. His fingers brushed her hair out of the way; the lightest touch, a touch that stung with its carefulness.

Then Zach said quietly, "That was one of the last times we were all in a room together laughing and having fun. The next summer Luke turned eighteen and left for college, and Vic the year after that. She's four years older than me. Luke is five."

Cara did the math. Vic was twenty, and Luke was twenty-one. Light-years away.

"But even after that—when they came back for summers, when they moved home to help with the family business—they never seemed to notice me, not even when we were in the same room. They're grown up, and they still see me as just the kid brother."

Cara turned his words over in her mind like stones, looking for the things underneath, the buried emotions he wasn't saying. "Your parents?" she asked hesitantly.

"They're busy, too. Always running around taking care of the family business, putting out fires. . . . Sometimes, I'll walk into a room and all four of them will look up from their conversation and go silent." His voice constricted. "But most of the time, they won't notice I'm there at all."

Cara had learned to live with the hollowness in her house. A mother who asked if she'd studied yet instead of saying hello, a ghost of a grandmother who was there, sure, but who she could never quite hug. No dad, no siblings. She'd always thought if she had those missing pieces, maybe they'd fit together to make a house filled with warmth, the windows glowing with golden light, the rooms ringing with laughter.

But maybe you could have all those things and still build a house that wasn't a home.

Cara gave him a wry smile. "So it sounds like your problem is that your parents are never there and your family members don't pay you any mind, and my problem is that my mom and grandmother are *always* there. Telling me what I should do, hovering over me, weighing me down with their expectations."

"I'd offer to trade, but somehow I don't think you'd go for it."

Too much love or not enough. Which was worse?

But they weren't trying to outdo each other here. Simply sharing, and listening.

And then, so softly she thought she'd imagined it, Zach said, "I don't think they'll miss me if I don't make it back." ·

"What?" Cara twisted to look at him, which the cut on her back promptly punished her for. She didn't care. She'd already caught a glimpse of the hard line of his mouth, his blue eyes shadowed. "That's ridiculous. For one thing, you're not staying dead, so they won't get the chance to miss you."

He came back around to pack up the kit. He shrugged, eyes cast on the ground, and said nothing.

Without thinking, she said, "*I'll* miss you."

His gaze jerked up to hers.

Crap. Why had she said that?

Before Zach could ask what she'd meant, Cara grabbed his arm, hoping to change the subject. "That scar," she said quickly. "Do you remember when you got that?"

His mouth tugged up at the corner, a half-smile. "Yeah. You totally freaked out, saying that we needed to call 911."

"Because we *did*. But you just looked up at me, nonchalant as could be even with your blood running down your arm, and said—"

"'*Calm down, it's not like I'm dying,*'" they said together.

Chills swept through her. Something passed between them, a trembling thread of memory they both held the ends to, wrapped around their fingers. Tying them together.

She didn't know what possessed her, but before she could stop herself, she was tracing a finger along his scar, the line of it softened by ghostliness, only the memory of a memory of a wound. When she looked up, she thought she saw Zach shiver.

As if a ghost could feel the cold.

She drew her hand back hastily, crossing her arms over her chest. "You were right, by the way," she said. "Freaking out and deciding to ignore my new fire powers wasn't the best course of action."

Cara kept her eyes on her bandaged hands, not wanting to see the smirk that must be on his face, no matter how much he tried to hide it.

"And yes, being able to set things on fire made it much easier to defeat the fog," she continued. "So there you go. I was wrong. You can go ahead and congratulate yourself now."

"Just so you know, I wasn't being obnoxious about it because I wanted to be right," Zach said after a moment, and she looked up. "Fine, maybe a little. But I was *mostly* being obnoxious about it because you've always been one of the smartest people I've ever had to put up with, but your plan to deal with your new fire powers made no sense to me, and I wanted to give you the chance to talk about why you didn't want to use them."

Cara stared at him, but he was focusing extremely hard on moving around the items in the first aid kit. "Did you just admit you think I'm one of the smartest people you know?"

"I— It wasn't a compliment or anything," he muttered, voice rough. Underneath the silver glow, his ears were turning pink. Was— was he *blushing*? "Don't let it go to your head, Tang."

He put away the first aid kit, then stood and offered a hand. With a light grip on her elbow, he pulled her to her feet. When he took his hand away, a feeling almost like disappointment flashed through her. For some illogical reason, she could still feel the touch of his fingers lingering on her skin like whorls of frost. *Zach only patched up your wounds because he needs you to bring him back to life*, she reminded herself. *He's only interested in your powers for what they can do for him.*

"So, with this new change of heart . . . got anything to say about laughing at me when I told you I could see ghosts?"

Zach winced. "I'd just woken up to find out I was dead and you were the only one who could see me. *Not* that that excuses it, or anything," he added hastily at the look on her face.

"Besides," he continued. "Your powers have come in handy. So yeah, it wasn't real cool of me to do that."

Cara arched an eyebrow at him.

He sighed. "By which I mean, I'm . . ." He stuffed his hands in his pockets. ". . . sorry."

Zacharias Coleson, for the first time in his life—for the first time in his *unlife*—had *actually* apologized. Of his own free will.

Cara smirked. "Wow. And here I was laboring under the impression that the word *sorry* wasn't in your vocabulary. If I'd known getting injured by a bloodthirsty, disembodied fog would get an apology out of you, I'd have tried to get injured sooner."

Zach was saying something, a pained look on his face, but blood roared through her ears, drowning out all other sound. Black spots spun before her eyes, bringing her to her knees.

"Tang!" His hands were on her shoulders, holding her. "What the hell just happened?"

She pushed him away, still dizzy. "I'm fine."

"No, you're not." The edge in his tone was back, that strange almost-protectiveness. Like he cared about her. "Tell me what's wrong."

"There's *nothing* wrong—"

"I *know* that's not true."

"I'm *fine*," Cara bit out in a voice that dared him to say otherwise.

Clambering up onto traitorously shaky legs, she marched off to where Brittany was sitting on a rock polishing her knives.

Zach chased after her, reaching her and Brittany in seconds with his long legs. "If you're fine, then what was that back there?"

"I'm just exhausted from all the fire," Cara said, pushing back stray strands of hair. She had to be. "I've never used it willingly before." Zach opened his mouth, but she wheeled on him fully, putting a shushing finger to his lips. "Drop it, Coleson."

"Oh, fun, you guys are arguing again." Brittany looked up at the two of them with distaste. "I left and you were fighting, now you're back and you're still fighting. . . . Do you have any hobbies or—?"

Brittany's eyes flashed, and she shot to her feet, shifting into a hunter's stance with a readiness that sent a chill down Cara's spine. "Hands off, *now*."

Zach jerked back from where he was hovering his hand over Brittany's knife set.

"Good choice." Brittany's serious demeanor dropped as she chuckled to herself. "Touch that and your buns are toast."

"I was just looking. I touched the knife you gave me in battle and I was fine," Zach grumbled.

Brittany moved toward Zach. "That's because that was *normal* metal, ghost boy. But these are ghoststeel." She slid out a blade from her set and turned it nimbly in her hands. "Braced with Ouroboros blood. Made for hurting ghosts and ghosts only." Brittany stuck out her arm and brought down the knife—Cara flinched—but the metal went through as if Brittany was the one who was incorporeal. "Which is why . . . hands off."

"Maybe that's what Mr. Mortmanger's cane was made of," Cara wondered.

"If it hurt the ghost, then ghoststeel, definitely." Brittany slid her knife back in and rolled the canvas case shut, securing it with three exterior buckles. "We use it to kill ghosts. It shreds any attachments they have to this dimension—or at least makes them think twice about tormenting the new inhabitants of an apartment."

"You said it has Ouroboros blood in it?" Zach asked. "How did you make weapons with it?"

Brittany regarded him. "My gran traveled this world once, with a ghost and a ghost talker. They were looking for the Creation Ouroboros, too. She ingested blood from the Destruction Ouroboros, briefly giving her the power to see spirits. When she came back home, it was her inspiration to start ghost hunting as a family business.

"My gramps was a blacksmith. He was the first one to forge blades made with Ouroboros blood. As long as the ghoststeel is in contact with our skin, we can see ghosts." Brittany lifted a slender silver chain from underneath the neck of her shirt. A ghoststeel pendant dangled in the shape of a snake biting its own tail. "Every ghost hunter wears this. Can't wear it for too long, though, because— Ohhh, *shit*."

Brittany's eyes had caught on a patch fifty feet away where a few shreds of gray were swirling like a miniature tornado. As Cara stared, another scrap condensed out of the air to join the others, hovering over the lifeless brown dirt.

Zach swore. "Not again."

Leave it to the fog to ruin a good moment. Cara looked at Zach and Brittany. "All in favor of running and hoping the river takes us away?"

"Typically, I would say *fight*, but Harold is always telling me to pick my battles, and I think this is what he means." Brittany shouldered her pack. "Let's head out."

NINETEEN

The world was so, so green.

Trees rose from the earth, their trunks pillars holding up the sky. Enormous roots sprawled over thick, lush grass.

The sky curved above their heads, the exact shade of a robin's egg. Cara took a deep breath, filling her chest with pure oxygen, head going light. The air tasted so clear it was almost sweet. Everything glazed with honeyed light.

And the trees *sang*. Some wordless chorus, more ancient than anything she'd ever heard, a polyphony that had played ages before humans ever uttered a word. Zephyrs whirled through the branches, spinning the leaves into dance. A million miniature movements. A remembering.

"Whoa," Brittany said, summing up all their thoughts with one word.

Out of the blue, a kaleidoscope of butterflies whirled around them.

One alighted on Cara's wrist. Its delicate wings opened and closed, symmetrical windows framed with the tan brown of wood, pale fragile blue unfurling from both sides of its body across the panes of its wings like frost.

And then the kaleidoscope of butterflies rose as one, color spinning away into the cageless air.

Cara imagined how the three of them must look, so small and earthbound, from a composition of a thousand insect eyes.

They walked forward. The soft, springy grass around their legs thrummed with insects, and Cara trod as carefully as she could, not wanting to crush them. She already felt she was disturbing this place merely by existing: dirty and clumsy and oh so human.

Indeed, despite the clean air and beautiful surroundings, she felt very much like the flawed human vessel she was. She held her aching arms away from her sides. Her shirt stuck to her back, cold and damp from evaporated sweat, and hair plastered the back of her neck, her ponytail pretty much undone. Cara glanced at Brittany, who was subtly wiping sweat from the back of her neck, clearly feeling the exhaustion from the battle, too.

Meanwhile, Zach looked perfect as he strode on, tireless. He was always effortlessly composed but even more so as a ghost, when he didn't fatigue and his appearance didn't change. She scowled at his back, at how the gold hair at the nape of his neck curled just so against his skin.

They reached the hill's crest. Below, the river flowed by: a sweet, wide, meandering thing shining in the summer-tinged air. The grass sloped down to the bank like an invitation.

Brittany elbowed her. "Are you thinking what I'm thinking?"

Cara lifted the neck of her shirt away from her skin. "Probably."

Brittany flashed a grin at Zach. "Better make your exit, then." Her grin deepened. "Unless you want to stay."

Uncharacteristically, Zach flushed. "I—I'm going," he muttered. Avoiding Cara's eyes, he turned and walked off in a random direction.

Brittany ran down the slope, whooping all the way. She

cannonballed in, but there wasn't much of an impact since the land slid right into the water. She surfaced, waved at Cara. "Come on!"

Cara set a towel and a fresh change of clothes on a reed-shaded rock by the bank, then stepped into the shallows. She figured she could clean the clothes she had on as well as herself.

The water washed over her skin like a balm, soothing her nerves and her muscles. It was murky, but not in a creepy, *something's-going-to-bite-your-toes-off* way; more in a *this-river-has-secrets* way. Moss softened the sharpness of rocks, and curtains of reeds swayed in the breeze. Giant lily pads, large enough to sit on, decorated the river's surface, interspersed with white and pink water lilies emanating a subtle floral scent. Damselflies clipped past, their long slender bodies brushstrokes of red-orange that painted slivers of sunset wherever they hovered. The water was exactly the right temperature.

Closing her eyes, Cara treaded and took a deep breath. She could feel her energy returning, something healing sinking into her skin and bones, into her very cells. It was as if the river knew they needed a rest after the fog and had brought them to a place that would not only give them a breather but allow them to actively recharge. She was a little suspicious of its intentions, but might as well enjoy it while it lasted—at least until another monster appeared.

See? she told herself. The dizziness from before was completely gone. She'd just been depleted, and now that she was relaxing, it was all fine.

She was content to float in the water, but then something brushed her leg. "What the heck was that?" she shouted. It had felt almost smooth—not entirely the sleekness of a dolphin, but far from the bumpy snout of a crocodile. She drew her legs up and, holding her breath, went underwater.

Through the drifting, golden plant matter, she made out the shape of a rotund creature, its paddle-shaped flippers churning. A manatee—or some strange cousin—peered back at her with dark, dewy eyes like tapioca pearls before swimming away into the murk.

Cara resurfaced to a susurration of wings blocking out the sun. A cloud of birds whirled overhead, and when the flock dipped closer, Cara caught the dusty blue-gray of their feathers, the red-brown patch staining each neck and belly like rust.

"Passenger pigeons," Brittany said, eyes cast skyward.

"Wait," Cara said. "Aren't passenger pigeons . . . extinct?"

Brittany nodded. Still fixed on the heavens, her profile could have been that of a statue, submerged neck-deep in an old river, time and moss yet to claim her. "Harold never stops lecturing me about the foolishness of humans and how we've destroyed the Earth, including some of his relatives."

If the birds above were extinct, then everything else here most likely was, too. The manatee, the butterflies, the other insects hovering around the water. Congregating in this meadow, this sanctuary, kept them alive, when normally, they'd have disappeared from the world entirely. Animals didn't become ghosts. Especially when humans were the ones who'd killed them in the first place.

The liminal world at work again, its magic evolving the impossible into existence.

Cara spoke. "So why do you need Snake blood now?"

"A week ago," Brittany began, "someone broke into our armory and our house. Stole nearly every piece of ghoststeel we had. I may have been outside at the time, breaking curfew and hunting ghosts when I wasn't supposed to, so unlike everybody else, I still have my knives. But if we don't get Ouroboros blood to forge more ghoststeel, we can't hunt. We won't have enough weapons to pass on to the next generation, nothing to train them with. My gran's legacy will fall to ruins."

The passage of wings continued overhead, so endless, so infinite, it could not be possible that, everywhere else but here, these creatures did not exist.

"That's why I was so eager to join y'all," Brittany continued. "Sorry again for jumping on your quest, by the way. I just . . . saw a ghost and a ghost talker and got excited, because I thought it was a sign. That I was on the right path to upholding my gran's legacy by doing what she did."

"That ghost was bitten by the white Snake, too?"

Brittany nodded.

Cara shifted in the river, cool murk slipping between her fingers. Had he tried to kill that ghost speaker as well? "Why was Harold chasing you? And trying to stop you from pursuing your legacy?"

Brittany sighed. "I'm my mom's baby—I have a sister and brother who are much older and got a head start on making a reputation for themselves. Not to mention all my cousins who also do cool things and have found their own niches and ways to help the family with their unique skills.

"Just because I lost my first necklace on a ghost hunting mission and let the ghost get away, they took it as confirmation that I was too hasty and inexperienced. My gran was the only one who didn't look differently at me after that. Who didn't lose faith in me.

"I'm doing this all for her now. I just want to make her proud. To see her smile again."

Making her grandmother proud and proving herself to her family. Cara could relate to that.

"She's been sad ever since my grandfather passed away last year. This necklace?" Brittany lifted the chain from her neck. "It's hers. The very first Livingston necklace that was ever forged. She gave it to me right before I left. I tried to refuse it, but she said she didn't need it anymore. That the only ghost she wanted to see was my grandfather."

"If it's your family legacy at stake, why are you the only one here?" Cara asked. "Or did you all decide you'd have a greater chance if you split up?"

"Divide and conquer? No. Unless it's ourselves. My family is still arguing with each other about who could have taken all our ghost-steel, whose fault it is. One of my cousins even had the gall to blame me, saying that I somehow sabotaged our family because I'm jealous no one lets me hunt." Brittany drew in a breath through her nostrils, attempting a façade of calm, but Cara could tell she was nettled. "When I suggested finding a way into the liminal world and getting more blood from the Signet Snake, they looked at me as if I had gone bananas. So I'm soloing it."

"Not anymore," Cara said.

Brittany brightened. "You're right, ghost talker. Not anymore."

"And you know what obstacles we're going to face, right?" Cara said. "If your gran has been through this world before."

Brittany shook her head, long braids dragging through the water. "'No man ever steps in the same river twice.'" Upon Cara's puzzled stare, she elaborated. "Heraclitus of Ephesus. Ancient Greek philosopher dude. He was a huge fan of the unity of opposites concept—death can't exist without life and vice versa—and that the one constant in the universe is change—life becomes death, everything is circular, all that jazz. You can swim in a river one day and come back the next, but the water is new; the water from before is long gone. Yet if the river didn't perpetually flow in flux, then it wouldn't be a river. It'd dry up or become a lake or something. Kinda the same idea here. Just because we're in what we call the liminal world doesn't mean we're gonna see the same things my gran did. The currents shift, and we can't control them. We can only hope they'll take us where we wanna go."

Cara raised her eyebrows. "That's deep."

Brittany gave a self-conscious sigh. "My pa's a professor of ethics at the local university and also a giant nerd."

Cara snorted. "You said this was a . . . family business?"

"Yup." Brittany swam to a lily pad, resting her arms on it. Cara took up a spot on the other side. "My ma and pa, my aunts and uncles, my nieces and nephews, my cousins . . . you get the gist. The only one who isn't interested is my big sis, but that's because she has a stick up her ass anyway." She rolled her eyes.

"What do you guys all do?"

"Well, one of my cousins is in grad school and has a job at some big fancy lab in the city. But on the side, she helps us cook up better ways to fight ghosts. She updated the metal-magic alloy in our knives so they're even more effective than before." A greenish-yellow frog the size of an emerald jumped on the lily pad, then into the water, disappearing with a *ploop*. "And another cuz is just thirteen, but he's got brains. I swear on my steel, he's gonna be running his own company someday. Right now, though, he sits at the kitchen table after school and designs posters for our business—"

Cara broke in, shock making her rude. "You guys advertise your abilities?"

"It's a family business," Brittany said. "Kinda gotta to keep it going."

"But . . . you don't hide the fact that you can see ghosts?"

"Nope," Brittany said, popping the *p*. She shot Cara a quizzical look. "That would be kinda silly—it's the whole foundation of what we do."

As Brittany continued on about her ghost hunting business, Cara thought of her own family. Her grandmother, who would be interested to learn that there was a whole group of people out there dedicated to taking down spirits gone rogue. Her mother, who'd likely scoff at the whole thing.

If her mother and grandmother weren't at odds, maybe Cara would have grown up in a house full of ghosts, doing her homework at the kitchen table with at least three nosy specters each trying to tell her how to do it based on how *they'd* been taught math when they were in school. And despite the dead—or because of it—her home would have been filled with life.

"How did your parents meet?"

Brittany's face cracked into a wide grin. "It's kind of a funny story. The best, actually. They take turns telling it at every anniversary, so I pretty much have it memorized already.

"First off, you need to know that as the youngest out of my gran's eight children, my mom had a lot to prove. Like, major chip on her shoulder. Maaajor. She was looking for her big break, ghost-wise. So one day she hears about this case. This man's neighbors report strange paranormal activity and naturally she was like, *'Here's my chance. I can prove myself to my family, and get rid of a ghost.'*

"She scopes out the place. Hears the noises for herself. Feels how the place seems to be both empty and occupied at the same time. On the third day, she hears wailing at one in the morning, she assumes it's her ghost.

"My mom damn near breaks down his door. But when she busts in, she doesn't find a ghost. Just a man in a sweater vest crying because he just spilled two-day-old coffee all over the only set of notes he has for his thesis.

"So my mom says, 'Your neighbors have reported strange noises at odd hours of the night, thuds and moans and a disembodied voice groaning about how he'll never fulfill his purpose on this Earth.'

"And my dad goes, 'Ma'am, that's just me. I'm working on my dissertation.'"

Cara snorted. Brittany's eyes were alight as she talked about her parents. And Cara couldn't help but wonder if she sounded like that when she spoke about her family. Or if she just sounded sad.

Something shifted in Brittany's expression, and the humor faded from her eyes. "Knowing that story, I don't know why my mom doesn't understand why I need to prove myself, too."

"Sounds like your relationship with your mom is complicated," Cara said.

"You could say that."

"I could. Mine is, too."

Proving herself on this journey was what Cara was doing, too, only she had no idea how to do it.

"Can I ask you a question?" Cara said. "You're so confident about ghost hunting. You don't seem to care what other people think. How do you . . . do that?"

Brittany answered without missing a beat. "It's my heritage," she said. "It's my ma's. My gran's. I'm the latest link in this chain, and I'm not about to break it."

Cara nodded. If ghost speaking in her family were a chain, too, then hers was already broken.

Cara could ignore the chain, shove it into a drawer in the back of her mind and live out the rest of her life pretending she still didn't see it every time she closed her eyes. . . .

Or she could fix it. Hearing the pride in Brittany's voice made her want to. But she didn't even know where to start.

Or maybe she already had. She'd decided to help Zach with her abilities. And she'd used her flames to defend him, to defend herself. Perhaps the way to repair the chain was to embrace herself for who she was and what she could do. And to stick with the people who helped her do that.

TWENTY

Her hair was still wet.

As Cara devoured her packed lunch on the riverbank, so fast she barely tasted any of the food, she considered, once more, using her fire power to dry her hair. And then, once more, she dismissed it. She had a long way to go with her magic. Burning off all her hair would be a terrible way to start.

When wet, her hair was a dark, tangled mane streaming past her shoulders. She pushed it behind her ears, but a strand escaped and then another and then another.

If I do burn all of it off, at least I won't have to deal with this.

Brittany was still in the water; she'd elected to stay in when Cara's stomach made it clear it was time to eat. The ghost hunter was doing backstrokes, as carefree as could be, a contrast to the steel she'd showed in their fight with the fog.

Cara stuffed her trash into a pocket of her backpack, then shrugged it on and stood.

When she ascended the hill, it took her a heartbeat to spot Zach. He was lying in the ring of trees, cushioned on the thick, lush grass between the wide sprawling roots of the largest oak. His arms were tucked behind his head.

And he was shrouded in butterflies.

Of course he was.

At her footsteps, the shroud took flight. In moments, all but one had vanished into the sky. Zach's eyes were closed; the last butterfly had alighted on his left brow, frost-blue wings fanning his skin.

As she neared, he cracked open his right eye.

"You scared them off," he remarked.

"Not all of them," Cara said, but as if to spite her, the last butterfly chose that very second to take off. She glared at it as it flew away.

Zach sat up, making room for her among the roots. She hesitated—should she sit? Did he want her to sit?—but inertia won out, and she gingerly sank into the grass beside him. Every inch of skin on the side close to his tingled with awareness, but she could get no farther away; though the oak was the most colossal one she'd ever seen, towering above their heads, its roots still only grew so wide.

"Where's Brittany?" he asked.

"Still in the river. Said she wanted to relax as much as possible before things started trying to kill us again."

Zach's lips curled into a half-grin. "Can't blame her. Never thought I'd say this, but I *almost* miss school. At least then, I only had to worry about people wanting to metaphorically kill me."

His eyes traced the hair around her face and lingered.

"You let your hair down," he said.

Cara shrugged, reaching up to push it behind her shoulders again.

"Only until it dries," she said. "I thought of speeding it up with fire, but I don't trust myself that much yet."

He gently tugged a strand out of place, and Cara stilled, the sensation of his fingers tucking her hair behind her ear rising in her mind once more. Water trickled down the back of her neck and under her shirt, one droplet tracing the bare curve of her spine.

"I like it like this," he said, and let it slip from his fingers.

She scoffed, leaning back against the trunk and savoring the feel of the bark, how solid it was. "Like you wouldn't have enjoyed seeing me burn all my hair off."

"Hey, you're the reason I had no hair for a significant part of first grade."

She smirked up at him. "And I enjoyed seeing *that* very much."

Zach gave a little *hmph* and lay back down, reaching up to cross his arms behind his head again. As he did so, his elbow grazed the side of her thigh, nearly as high as her hip. The hem of his sweatshirt rode up, exposing a slice of toned, sun-gold skin.

He was incorporeal again, though not so much she didn't notice how unfairly long his lashes were, pale gold and almost invisible in the summer light and his ghostliness.

They were so long that when he blinked at her, slow and sweet, they kissed the tops of his cheeks.

She tore her gaze away from him and turned to the sky, to the sun that would not blind her nearly as much.

Above, the branches and leaves of each oak created a dome— but strangely enough, the leaves of different trees didn't touch. The canopies followed each other's shape exactly, mirroring each curve like puzzle pieces that would click together if only they were daring enough to come closer, the barest but surest splinters of air separating them from each other. Rivulets of blue sky ran between the canopies of individual trees, like tributaries of a river, and through these lanced light.

Crown shyness. She'd read about this once upon a time.

To only grow so far and no farther. To sense without seeing how close you were to another, close enough to touch, and yet stop.

It was impossible, all of this: a magic river leading them to a place where there were extinct mammals in the water, disappeared birds brushing wings through the cerulean sky, oaks so giant they could have been seedlings in the Cretaceous.

And him, in the grass, hair gold as the sunlight that slipped past the canopy to knife right through him. The sun. A body. A boy.

Like he was another one of these creatures, something that should have been dead but did not act like it, something that was alive because it didn't know how not to be. Like if she blinked, he'd disappear, like he had never existed.

Death usually took the soft things first, decomposed them into dust and rot. The hard things were left: bone gleaming like a smile in the forest dirt.

But ghosthood had done the opposite to Zach. He was more vulnerable than she'd ever seen him, his arrogance stripped back, his ego eroded. Underbelly exposed.

He was nicer to her these past few days than he'd been in years, but when she brought him back, would she bring back all of who he had been before? The cruelness and rudeness, too? Or would she resurrect something more evolved, a kinder iteration?

Cara didn't realize she was staring until Zach turned and caught her.

She scrambled to say something before he could, something to divert his attention.

"What did you see in the fog?"

For a long moment, Zach didn't speak, simply looked at her until her heartbeat quickened under the sheer force of his gaze. The air between them trembled with that thing she'd felt earlier when he'd bandaged her wounds. *That's not good*, she thought. It wasn't like she'd never felt anything between them before—shoulders brushing as they both tried to look at the same thing, a scorching look across a classroom—but those sensations had always burned bright with anger and faded just as quickly. They'd never wrapped around her skin and *stayed*.

And then he said, his voice soft and serious:

"I saw you."

Before her skin could even begin to heat, he turned his face away and added, "And a bunch of other girls, all telling me they loved me. They wanted me to choose one of them, which was probably more nightmarish than the fog was looking for. I mean, how am I supposed to pick? You can't expect me to—"

Cara picked a rock off the ground and threw it at him.

It bounced through his torso, over a root, and out of sight.

"Ow," he said even though there was literally no way it could have hurt—he didn't have nerve endings anymore, the asshole—and gave her a smirk.

"God, I hate you," she said.

His smirk widened, but she felt herself flash back to the fog, where he'd told her in a strangled voice that her saying she hated him didn't "completely rule it out" that she was or wasn't real.

"Too late to turn back now, Tang." His voice brought her back to reality.

She scowled. "I know."

He'd shifted nearer, but she reminded herself it meant nothing. Heat was what all ghosts wanted, even without knowing they wanted it.

She was a living human, a ghost speaker who could amplify him, a girl who could call up flame with a thought. To a ghost, that was the best they could get, besides resurrection.

"So, how did *you* know the fog wasn't real?" he asked.

A memory seared her skin, just under her shirt.

I gotta tell you something. Now, before it's too late.

She cleared her throat. "It didn't like my fire. What—what about you?"

"Because they could see me."

A wind whirled through the branches, song cascading from the leaves.

"It also helped that I was already dead, and I didn't have a body it could drain," he added smugly.

"All right, smartass." Cara swept an arm toward the sky. "How do we know any of *this* is real? Maybe the fog got us after all. Maybe this is a dream."

"Depends. Do you usually dream about me?"

Crap, walked right into that one.

"Oh, shut up."

He ran a hand through his hair. "Well, I think it's real. I wouldn't have before—hell, I didn't believe in ghosts before, and now look at me. I didn't believe in magic, either. But this—" He looked up at her. "I believe in this."

It was a good answer, considering she'd been expecting none at all.

But this week, Zach was making surprising her a habit. "So, how'd you deal with finding out ghosts were real? And that you weren't just losing it?"

She didn't have to answer. None of this mattered, after all. In four days, by sunset on Friday, she would bring him back, and then everything would return to normal.

Which was maybe why she drew her knees to her chest and said,

"I was five the first time I saw a ghost. Mr. Porter, an old guy who lived next door, whose funeral my mom had dragged me to the week before." As a specter, even the rims of her neighbor's circular glasses, the ones that always made him look like a surprised owl, glowed silver. "Everything's possible at that age, so I wouldn't have known until much later that seeing ghosts was supposed to be impossible, if not for my mom, who made that very clear. She also made it clear that I wasn't going crazy, but I think she might have actually preferred that to having a ghost speaker for a daughter. I'd never seen her look so disappointed. Years later, I realized she hadn't just been disappointed in me—she'd been disappointed in herself, for passing down to her own daughter a trait she hated." She swallowed. "And then Laolao showed up. My grandma was the explanation for how I could see ghosts, and she told me that while most people believed ghosts didn't exist, that didn't mean that what I saw wasn't real."

"Wouldn't seeing a ghost make it real?"

She shook her head.

"You know how people won't believe something, even if they see it, until they feel it? Like, even though the sign says *Wet Paint*, at least one person is going to sit down? How people pinch their cheeks in case they're dreaming? It's all about what we perceive. What we get back when we check our perceptions against those of other humans. If this is a dream and none of this is real, well—at least we're stuck here together."

Cara paused, waiting for the judgment to arrive on Zach's face, for him to laugh and call her a nerd for taking his question so seriously. She'd never said anything like this to anyone, not even Laolao, and it was oddly freeing, even though nothing would come of it, even though this moment was temporary. Perhaps that's what made it so freeing. He stayed quiet, waiting for her to go on, and so she finished softly.

"But ghosts are intangible. You can't hold death in your hands."

Zach half sat up, leaning back on his elbows. "What about me?"

"You're an annoying exception," she told him, but her irritated tone didn't keep his mouth from curving into that familiar, easy smirk of his.

"And how are you sure you're not imagining me right now?"

He grinned up at her, open and golden and whole, and for a moment he was only a boy: a boy who had not yet learned what it meant to die.

She hesitated. It was a simple question, but it sounded like a dangerous one, and she wasn't sure why. He was so close. A wild, dizzying feeling unfolded itself within her, rising like a flight of butterflies, and though she waited for it to fade, it did not, but amplified until her heart was fluttering like so many wings.

"I don't know," she replied. "Maybe I am."

He paused, then dragged himself up all the way, meeting her eye to eye. So close his breath would have fanned her face, if he'd had breath, if he were still alive.

"So touch me," he said. "Make me real."

The world had gone silent. She knew, somewhere in the back of her mind, that the trees hadn't ceased singing, that the river was still flowing, that the earth hadn't stopped spinning on its axis.

But right now? Right now there was nothing else but the way he was looking at her, her pulse crescendoing in her ears, and *him*, something in his eyes rooting her to the spot like the tree they lay against.

Nothing but breath between them.

Then footsteps pounded into the clearing, and Cara jolted back like she'd been shot. She looked up to see Brittany standing at the edge of the ring of trees and panting.

When Brittany spoke, her voice was urgent. "There's something you've gotta see."

TWENTY-ONE

Brittany refused to tell them what it was beforehand, insisting that they had to see it for themselves.

As Cara followed the ghost hunter, she combed her hair, snuck another look at Zach striding beside her.

He never used to be this confusing. She yanked her brush through a knot more aggressively than needed. Last week, she'd known where they stood with each other. Her default response to him was irritation. But now?

What would have happened if they hadn't been interrupted?

Cara recalled his smirk after he told her what he'd seen in the fog. Gritted her teeth as she pulled her hair back into a ponytail. Right. Based on previous evidence, he'd been playing with her, and it would have ended in her getting annoyed and stalking off.

This meadow might have been real, but nothing he said was.

She twisted her hair tie around one last time, then tightened her ponytail, satisfied that she'd gotten her head in order.

Brittany led them to a spot between the bank and trees. Here, the river ran so shallow in some places that the bed of muddy silt was clear beneath the surface. Beyond the ring of great oaks rose a forest, no doubt hiding even more creatures.

"Take a look at this." Brittany tapped a sign by the bank. It was wide and set at an angle, like the interpretive kind used in zoo exhibits or nature trails.

"'Extinction Meadow,'" Cara read. "'Haven for vanished things. If you would not exist elsewhere, you will exist here. You will remain alive. Death will not touch you as long as you stay in this place.'"

She looked at the others. "This explains the extinct animals. This place . . . preserves them. Saves them."

"I'm thinking it saves ghost boy, too." Brittany nodded at Zach. "If you stay here, you'll be able to live. Kinda. I mean, you won't have any Netflix or Wi-Fi, but you'll exist. You just won't be able to leave."

This place could change their whole quest.

Zach was leaning on the sign with both hands, staring down at it. For a long moment, he didn't say anything.

Then he said to Cara, "What do you think?"

"Why are you asking me?"

"Because"—he ran a hand through his hair—"we made a deal. If I stay here, that's upended. You'll lose out on twelve K." He hesitated, eyes searching her face. "You cool with that?"

Cara bit her lip. Upon realizing Zach could either remain in the meadow and have some form of an existence or take his chances by continuing on, a wild hybrid of trepidation and hope had instantly taken root in her stomach. Without even having to think about it, she knew what she wanted him to do.

To stay—not in this meadow but at her side.

And there was no way she was admitting that.

"I mean, if you want to stay here, be my guest," she lied, faking a casual shrug. "Or be the meadow's guest, rather. Mind you, I will be pissed that I wasted all this time traveling and got nothing out of it, but I'll live. What you decide makes absolutely no difference to me."

There. She'd sounded *cool with that*, right?

Zach didn't look satisfied with her answer. He rubbed the back of his neck, glancing over the sign, then muttered, "I need to think about this," and walked off toward the river.

Arms crossed, Cara watched him go.

Brittany let out a snort.

Cara frowned at her. "What's so funny?"

"Oh, nothing." Flopping on the ground, Brittany took out a Nutri-Grain bar from her pack. "I'm just appreciating the wonders around me, including some of the worst lying I've heard, ever."

Cara gaped, sitting down. "I wasn't lying."

Brittany swallowed a bite and mimicked, "'What you decide makes absolutely no difference to me.' *Bullshit.* The miracle is, ghost boy actually seemed to believe it."

That was good, at least. Cara wanted him to believe it. *She* wanted to believe it.

"Y'all are ridiculous," Brittany continued, idly ripping out blades of grass. "Not on a quest-slash-date. *Sure.*"

Cara felt her eyes go wide. "There's nothing going on. We told you." She took a breath. "Strictly business."

Brittany snorted again. "The one inch of space between you and Casper the *Very* Friendly Ghost when he was doing your bandages didn't look like *business*. No way there was enough room for Jesus in there."

Heat rushed to Cara's face. "I—" she sputtered, but Brittany shushed her, holding up a finger.

Grass rustled. A few feet away appeared a dodo, regarding the two of them with friendly, inquisitive eyes.

"Hiiiii," Brittany cooed to the dodo in a tone Cara had never heard her use but recognized nonetheless. It was the baby voice strangers used on Blaze when they saw Cara taking him for a walk. "Who's a good bird? Do you want some Nutri-Grain?"

The dodo crept closer, nudging Brittany's fingers with its curved beak. While it was busy eating a bit of crumbly apple breakfast bar, Brittany scratched its fuzzy brownish-gray head.

"It was necessary that Zach be so close to me," Cara insisted, having finally organized her thoughts into coherence. Despite her embarrassment, this wasn't so bad. It reminded her of talking with Felicity and Charlotte about crushes at sleepovers. Something normal in this strange liminal world. "How else would he have put the bandages on? I couldn't even reach the cut on my back."

"If you say so. Anyway, I'm not about to argue with a lost cause. Like Gran says, you have to see the light on your own. I'll just leave you with this. Wanna know how I knew Zach was there today?"

"Didn't you have your ghost detector?"

"Sure, but even without it, I'd have figured it out eventually." Brittany looked at Cara and said, "You'd have given it away. The little glances, your facial expressions. Your whole body was turned toward him."

"Oh."

Brittany grinned. "And ghost boy was the exact same way."

Oh.

The dodo emitted a loud, displeased half grunt, half squawk. It had finished all the Nutri-Grain in Brittany's palm.

Brittany fished another bar out of her pack for the dodo.

"You're adorable," she crooned, petting it. "Aren't you, you fluffy little bowling ball?"

The bird squawked in affirmation and flapped its wings.

The air cooled, and Cara looked up to find Zach had returned.

"I've made my decision."

When he paused, Brittany made an exaggerated, *well-go-on-then* gesture.

"Is that a . . . dodo in your lap?" Zach asked.

"His name's Duncan."

"You *named* it?" he said, but his voice died as Duncan swung his wide head to lay a death-stare on him that only an animal with eyes on both sides of its skull could. "He doesn't seem to like me. Which makes my decision easier." His gaze found Cara. "I'm gonna risk it. Let's keep going for the antidote."

Cara was on her feet. "You're not staying?"

Brittany rose, too.

"I want to get back to Autumn Falls." His voice went quiet. "See my family again."

Warmth spread through her chest. He wasn't going to remain here.

He was going to go with her.

"Those are good reasons," Cara said lightly.

"Well, Brittany made a point about the no Wi-Fi. Kind of a deal breaker in the afterlife." He grinned, and Cara caught herself grinning back.

Duncan, angry that Brittany had stopped petting him, marched up to Zach and bit him on the ankle.

"*Ow!*" Zach yelped, leaping back as Cara burst into laughter.

"Good boy," Brittany praised, motioning the dodo back to her side and feeding him more Nutri-Grain.

"Why does it hurt?" Zach groaned.

Cara pressed a hand to her mouth as the last of the mirth left her and considered. "Well, maybe it's because you exist on the same plane. If the dodo were alive, he wouldn't be able to bite you. Then again, if he were alive, we'd have much more to be concerned about."

It was then the ground began to tremble under their feet. "Did you feel that?" Cara asked.

"Yeah," Zach griped, rubbing his ankle.

Brittany straightened, her shoulders settling into the stance of a hunter's. "Something's coming."

Brittany gave Duncan one last bit of Nutri-Grain, then nudged him on the rump with her Doc Marten. "Off you go, Duncan," she said. "Find a friend, won't you?"

The dodo craned his neck up at her and squawked mournfully but relented when she gave him a kiss on the top of his feathery head. With one last baleful look at Zach, the extinct bird waddled off, just as the first of the creatures came into view.

It was a massive snow-white deer, emerging from the woods, antlers soaring into the sky. Cresting the low hill in front of them, it cantered across the river.

Then came another, then two, then five, like snowflakes, like a blizzard. An avalanche of hooves upon hooves upon hooves, shaking the earth. An exodus. An earthquake.

The herd poured past and around them, vast and largely oblivious to their small human presence, although several individuals acknowledged them in various ways. An ear twitching in their direction, an eye rolling to the side, their flanks shying away if they ran too close.

Minutes could have passed, or mere seconds, but the river moved on.

At last the herd thinned to only stragglers, small calves and old deer. Then finally, three healthy-looking stags, muscles rippling under their pure white coats, slowed and completely stopped before the three of them.

Maybe the meadow had heard Zach make his decision. It was giving him a send-off.

"I think they want us to go with them," Cara said.

"*I* think that if the past few days are anything to go by, they want to eat us. Specifically me," Zach replied, but his sardonic tone was belied by the wonder in his eyes.

One of the stags fixed his eyes on Cara. He looked in the direction that the herd had gone, then back at her, dark eyes shining.

With a glance at Zach and Brittany, she approached the beast carefully. The stag stood so tall she didn't even reach his shoulder hump.

He lowered his heavy head, antlers dipping to the trampled earth. Then he sank to the ground.

The other two stags bowed and knelt as well.

Cara climbed onto the great stag's back, grasping handfuls of his thick white fur, soft as freshly fallen snow. When he stood, it was so fluid that she only noticed because the surroundings briefly blurred; she gasped at how small everything had become at this height, the river so far away. He took one step, then two, building up steam, then sailing forward like a ship, the grass softening into waves of emerald. Or maybe she wasn't moving, but the world was.

Behind her, Brittany let out a whoop.

Cara drew a deep breath; the wind whipped her hair out of her face. Her head had never felt clearer, her body never lighter. It was like she was astride a dream.

What was a group of gone beasts called? A stillness. An extinction.

Onward and onward their mounts moved, galloping beside the river, stride never slowing. Time went forward. Relentlessly. Things died; the Earth still spun. Relentlessly. Her heart was a machine firing as fast as it could just to stay where it was, just to keep her alive.

A threshold took them, relentlessly.

TWENTY-TWO

Cara found herself at the end of a run, inertia hurtling her forward, before she stumbled to a stop.

Beside her, Zach and Brittany were also slowing to a standstill.

The stags were gone. In their place lay a desert, dust and more dust.

Cara twisted to check for the threshold they'd passed through—but it had vanished behind them, like she'd known it would. Dullness throbbed in her rib cage, so intense it almost felt sharp. She missed the viridian of the trees, the cerulean of the sky. Her breath caught in her throat—she would never see those animals again. Not without the help of a book, a museum, flat black-and-white photos.

A yawning loss mummified inside her, one she couldn't articulate. When she saw a literal tumbleweed bounce past, she wanted to laugh, and then she wanted to cry. Emotion welled in her chest as if from some cut, some invisible blade of memory.

And nausea swirled in her stomach. She gagged, coughing on a dry throat, but she didn't throw up. It was blood she found when she took her fingers away from her mouth, bright crimson beads spotting her palm like analyx had sprouted in her hands.

"Tang?" Zach was staring at her with horror. "What's going on?"

Even if she had had the energy to reply, she wouldn't have known what to say. Dizziness swirled through her mind, and then her knees were buckling, dry desert dirt scraping her palms raw.

Zach knelt at her side immediately. "Talk to me."

"Let her breathe, Casper."

Zach turned on Brittany with a snarl, who jerked back.

"Hey, watch it!"

The sound of Zach and Brittany arguing was muffled by the buzzing in Cara's ears. The taste of blood sickened her and was becoming all too familiar—the last time she'd tasted blood had been just recently and was the Snake's.

The Snake.

My venom isn't the only thing that's dangerous. Every part of me is poison, especially my blood. You don't know the fate you've bought.

She'd thought he'd been bluffing, but . . .

Cara straightened suddenly, fingers curling against the denim of her jeans even as she thought, *No, no, no.* But her body knew it before her brain did.

"Hey, Brittany," she said, eyes on the ground. "Right before we ran from the fog a second time, you were saying something about . . . not being able to wear your ghoststeel pendant against your skin? What did you mean by that?"

Brittany crouched. She studied Cara's face, her lips pressed tight before answering. "Because the power—and problem—with Ouroboros blood is that even one drop is potent. It awakens magic. My family first tried to use the blood in pills, but if they took too many pills within a period of time, there were serious side effects: dizziness, nausea, lethargy . . . even death. It was too great a risk. The good thing with ghoststeel is, as soon as we realize it's been contacting our skin for too long, we can simply take it off." Brittany's words rang in

Cara's head.

Ouroboros blood awakens magic. Was that why she had fire powers? Had they lain in her veins all along, inherited from her dad but not activated until now?

Dizziness. Nausea.

Was lethargy next? Was *death*?

Cara licked her lips. "I think," she said weakly, "I might have ingested some Ouroboros blood."

Zach's eyes went wide. "No."

Brittany sucked in a breath through her teeth. "Okay. That's not great to hear. Walk me through it. How long ago was it?"

"Two days," Cara said. Her words sounded methodical, dull, even to her own ears, reciting the facts as if they belonged to another body, one that didn't have poisonous blood consuming it from the inside out.

"What do we do?" Zach asked.

Brittany pursed her lips, sliding her knife from its sheath at her hip and spinning it in her hands. "Honestly, guys, I'm not sure. I've never dealt with anyone who ingested straight-up Ouroboros blood. I do know that it takes a minute for the symptoms to show, but when they do, they start ratcheting up, faster and faster."

"There *has* to be something," Zach said in a low tone that dared anyone to disagree, and Cara glanced at him. From the way Brittany raised her eyebrows, she'd heard it, too. That determination that didn't take no for an answer, even when it came to death. That self-assuredness that looked at the card fate dealt, and said, *Yeah, I don't think so,* and bought a way out.

Brittany stood up, flipping her knife in the air and catching it. She looked at it, then back at them. "There *is* something . . . but I don't know if it will work."

"Try it," Zach said, standing as well.

Brittany nodded. "Then we need the river."

It wasn't easy to find in this liminal space, but finally they spotted it: a brown shriveled thing, too sickly to even reflect the sun. Brittany crouched over the nearly dry riverbed. Sliced her palm open and let the blood sink into the water that was left, muttering something as the sluggish current struggled to carry her offering away.

"When my gran traveled this world with a ghost speaker and a ghost, they met a group of magic healers. Some mystic temple. Again, I don't know if this'll work"—she fixed Zach with a firm look—"but water has a memory. Blood, too. The river may lead us there, if it chooses. But it's gonna take time."

Time. Cara sank her own bloodied fingers into the creek, cleaning them. All the while she'd thought Zach was the one running out of time, when she was the one who needed it more than anyone.

The sweat on her palms made it difficult to hold on to the map, and the headache battering her temples made it difficult to read.

Cara leaned against one of the monoliths peppering the landscape and gripped the paper harder, ordering herself to focus, even as the midday sun arced down. In the trail of icons representing the thresholds they'd crossed—plants, fog, meadow—that had popped up, she was interested only in the little temple that had appeared after Brittany dropped her blood in the river. The magic healers. The temple shone in the middle of the expanse, farther up, near the border of the map. In the opposite direction of the Snake.

But with her worsening symptoms, it was a necessary detour. If they didn't go there, it wouldn't matter if they made it to the Snake at all.

Ever since arriving in the desert the night before, she hadn't been able to keep anything down. Not her dinner last night or the one bite of apple she'd swallowed in a sorry attempt at breakfast before the nausea had surged again. Now that they were stopped for a lunch break, she hadn't even bothered, just put her head in her hands.

Looking at this map didn't make her feel better, either. They'd crossed several liminal spaces this morning—stopped to rest in another desert—and their row of icons was leading closer to the temple, but they weren't moving fast enough. Her stomach seized. She pressed her hand to her mouth, but there was nothing left to throw up.

Cara kept replaying her encounter with the white Snake, thinking about what she could have done better, cursing herself for biting him, which is when she must have swallowed his blood. Regret coated her tongue, bitter and heavy.

Of course, her past self had done the best she'd could to escape the Snake's deadly grip then. She hadn't known she'd only be pushing back her fate.

And wasn't that what they were all doing? Whenever you put on a seat belt or wore a helmet, you were delaying the inevitable, hitting snooze on a clock that continued to count down. Pulling the blanket over your head and telling Death, *Just five more minutes, please.*

Even if she resurrected Zach, she wouldn't be saving him forever, only adding more seconds to an account that would always run out.

A hand tugged the map from her grasp, and she glared at Zach. He'd taken the pack from her last night, insisting that he carry it, and now he didn't even think she was strong enough to hold a piece of paper?

Throwing an arm against the monolith to support herself, she pushed up, suppressing the waves of dizziness that threatened to pull her back down. Zach hovered at her elbow. He opened his mouth, then closed it. She ignored the concerned glances he and Brittany exchanged.

"Let's move," Brittany said. "We're losing time."

Moving was easier said than done. Lethargy swathed her limbs like the shroud of a corpse, making her steps clumsy, dragging her feet against the ground. Zach and Brittany easily outpaced her, no matter how much she pressed herself forward. Their heads bent together in conversation, and every so often, one of them would flash a look backward, as if to check she hadn't collapsed yet.

She curled her hands into fists but found she didn't have the strength to dig her nails into her palms anymore. Weakness had snuck into every cell, making her feel heavy and untethered at the same time.

Her heart fluttered in her throat, fast and frantic, trying to leave its dying body.

It was worse, though, when it slowed, and she was aware of each and every beat, the seconds between them, how she could feel the fist of her heart clenching in her chest.

The next threshold flung them into the dark.

Cara lit her hand, despite the way even a second of flame drained her already low energy reserves, despite the way Zach's eyebrows immediately knit in concern. The flame showed they were in a low cavern, the walls pressing in as if they were in the stomach of some great beast. In the distance, she could hear a thin trickle of water over stone, and a strange sort of rhythmic wind, air being inhaled and exhaled.

There were a few sticks on the ground, though, and Cara picked these up, passing on makeshift torches to Zach and Brittany so she could use the wood to sustain the fire instead of herself.

In unspoken agreement, they moved forward in silence.

Brittany was the first to see it.

A monster slumbered in front of them, bulk taking up most of the passageway. The floor vibrated with each of its breaths, the spectral-white light dangling from its forehead reminiscent of an anglerfish's. The shaking of the ground threatened to unbalance Cara, and she leaned against the wall even more heavily, pulse flickering wildly in her chest as they scooted past the beast, trying not to touch it.

They hadn't made it far when another monster approached. This one was a hulking thing, lit up and shaped like a Christmas tree, with red and green spots blinking on and off. As it lumbered past, Zach yanked her behind a rock. She watched the two tiny milky-white eyes that sat near the tip of its head where a tinsel star would have been propped.

They tiptoed through the connected caverns, trying not to wake the monsters, which seemed to all be sleeping except the Christmas one. The sound of the creatures' breaths enfolded them; Cara listened hard for a change in the pattern, any indication that another monster had roused. Torchlight played over the stone walls. Her heart jumped at each shadow that had a little too much life to it, curling forward like the claws of a beast. The swaying of the darkness magnified her dizziness. Every so often, she heard the strange, mournful cries of unseen things. Water trickling.

Cara had no idea how long they'd been down there by the time they found a monster with hundreds of glowing green limbs sprawled out all across the passageway like tangled tree roots. It shuddered in its sleep. Its eyes were invisible when closed, or maybe it didn't have any at all.

One by one, they picked their way over the maze of limbs: Brittany in the front, Zach bringing up the rear, and Cara lagging in between. Cara had almost reached safety, Brittany bouncing with anxiety on the balls of her feet by the exit of the cavern, when the monster moved in its sleep.

A limb swept against Cara's ankle.

She hit the ground. Hard.

Pain jolted through her body. Lethargy had claimed her so entirely she could do nothing but lie there, looking back over her shoulder. The monster didn't seem to have stirred—

And then it opened eyes all over its body and *screeched*.

Its center was all mouth, like a horrific thousand-armed starfish. Teeth upon teeth upon teeth.

The breathing in the air changed. The ground rumbled. Clearly, all around them, the monsters were waking up. And with Cara's luck, they were coming after her.

The starfish monster spasmed, legs wriggling in controlled chaos as it flipped over onto its stomach-mouth. It reached for her, but Zach grabbed her arm and pulled her up.

They hurtled through the darkness, their panting breaths joining the monsters in a horrible symphony. A creature with oozing red skin slurped across the ground toward them, but Brittany sidestepped it, dragging her knife down as she went so that the creature split in two, its gelatinous halves wobbling to either side with a repulsive, undulating scream.

Their torches illuminated an end to the passageway, but upon bolting through, an abyss stretched before them.

Awful crooning sounds swayed up from the pitch black, so loud Cara could barely think. A narrow, unstable-looking stone bridge linked their precipice to the other side, where a threshold glimmered, its faint light almost blinding in the dark, a hope so close yet so far.

Brittany kicked a rock over the edge. It didn't make a sound.

Behind them, screeches echoed off the stone, louder and louder.

"You ready?" Brittany said.

A hand on Cara's elbow. "Let me carry you," Zach said. "I promise I won't drop you this time." When she hesitated, he said softly, "*Please*."

She supposed she didn't have a choice.

A strange sense of calm took hold when he lifted her into his arms. It was wrong to feel this safe in Zach's embrace, of all people's, in a cave full of monsters. But maybe that was how far gone she was, poisoned with Snake blood.

As the sounds ascended, they reached the threshold. A monster tongue reached out from the darkness behind them and wrapped around her arm, slick and slimy.

The world exploded into light.

The monster came through with them. A boneless, slimy yellow blob around the size of a hubcap with one long pink tongue, which it was currently using to pull itself closer to Cara's skin.

It was a good thing the monster was less used to light than they were because they recovered their vision faster.

Brittany dispatched it with a few swipes of her knife. Its tongue released Cara's arm.

Cara blinked in the sunshine, watching as the monster shuddered and grew still, its innards seeping out into the grass like sunny-side up yolk.

Cara found her voice. The adrenaline was draining away, leaving her a husk. Her words sounded less like a demand and more like a plea as she said, "Put me down."

"You actually—" Zach sighed. "Fine. I'll put you down—if you look me in the eyes and tell me, *without lying*, that you can walk on your own."

She couldn't do that. He'd see through her in an instant.

Her fingers curled against his chest. "I don't want you to think I'm weak," she whispered.

"I would never." His voice was completely serious.

Pain from her fall, pain from the Snake's blood slowly killing her, had seeped into every part of her. She couldn't keep her eyes open. Her resolve to stay awake, was fighting with the fatigue bleeding through her bones.

God, she was tired of fighting.

She buried her face in his neck and said nothing.

Zach brushed his knuckles across her cheek, so gently it could have been a kiss, then said, voice angled at Brittany, "She's not arguing with me anymore. That's a bad sign."

Cara heard Brittany walk closer. A hand, cool but not ghost-cold, touched her forehead for a second—then Brittany swore, fingers lifting.

"Her skin's burning like metal in summer."

Paper rustled—the map.

"Good news: that was the last threshold," Brittany said. "This place"—Cara imagined her gesturing with her knife but didn't have the strength to open her eyes to see their new surroundings—"holds the temple somewhere."

Cara lost track of time after that. Hours could have passed, or minutes, as she let Zach carry her. She was burning up, and pressing her face to his cold chest felt so good.

Once, she roused to Zach gently shaking her and calling her name, mounting desperation in his voice.

"Stop that," she mumbled, not bothering to open her eyes.

He released an aggrieved sigh as he adjusted his grip, nestling her closer to him. "Just checking."

"Still kicking."

"Good. You're not allowed to die."

"Don't tell me what to do," she muttered into his chest.

Later, she was wrenched from her drowse when her heart contracted so violently a whimper escaped her lips.

"What is it?" Zach asked softly.

She gathered her breath, waiting for the pain to pass. "It hurts," she whispered, eyes closed. "In my chest . . . Everywhere." Her voice came out pitiful. She hated how weak she sounded.

Zach didn't say anything for a moment. Then his arms tightened around her. "I'm gonna kill him," Zach muttered, low and furious. "I'm gonna find him and rip the scales from his face." Another pause, and then he whispered, "This can't be worth the money, Tang," but Cara didn't have anything to say to that.

Cara didn't register when they arrived at the temple; she was barely awake. The outside world, so far away from her body, came to her in snatches of sound, movement stirring the air over her skin.

A flurry of voices, feminine-sounding, one asking, "What's wrong with her?"

"You *have* to help her."

"There will be a price—"

"You don't know who I am, do you? Whatever it is, I'll pay it."

Something pressing into her lips, voices encouraging her to drink, cool liquid washing down her throat, bitter and tasting of herbs.

And finally, darkness.

TWENTY-THREE

It was nearly dark when Cara woke.

She was in bed, but she didn't remember getting in bed. For a heartbeat, she stared at the ceiling, the cracks spiderwebbed against the white plaster.

And then a thought:

I'm not dead.

She sat up, checking her arms.

No silver. She wasn't a ghost, either. She sighed, and was overwhelmed with relief: it didn't hurt to breathe anymore.

Someone had changed her bandages. She was in new clothes, too, oatmeal-colored linen that scratched at her skin.

The room was empty and small, about the same size as a hospital room. But the décor wasn't the bleached-white palette of hospitals; no fluorescent lights cast an eerie glow. A chair sat at her bedside, and though Cara couldn't say why, when she looked at it, her heart skipped a beat, expecting to see Zach there.

Her eyes adjusted to the darkness, taking in the remainder of the space. Oddly enough, scorch marks decorated the entire room: the walls, the bed frame, even the floor. Except for the blackened marks, the furniture was the shade of pages of old books. Through the open window, the remaining rays of sunset shone. Wind lifted the cream curtains in a waltz; several fire-singed holes gleamed in the cloth. Violet intertwined with pink glowed in the sky, the faintest line of yellow glinting on the horizon above the tree line like a lost relic.

A woman bustled in with a basket propped on her hip. "Oh, good, you're awake," she said pleasantly, lighting the lantern on the wall. Her white hair was pulled back into a strict bun. Pouring a glass of water from the carafe on the bedside table, she shoved it into Cara's hands. "Drink. You must be parched."

She was. Cara gulped the entire glass without pausing to breathe. "How long have I been asleep?"

The woman didn't answer immediately, focused on folding the clothes from the basket—Cara's clothes—into a pile on the bed. Her light brown hands moved with methodical precision; Cara could tell she'd done this task so many times it was muscle memory. She didn't need to pause folding as she met Cara's gaze with eyes of amber, infinitely old despite the smooth skin around them.

"Two days."

Time stuttered to a halt. *"Two days?"* That meant—Thursday. It was now Thursday, the day before Zach's life ran out. How were they supposed to get to the Snake on time?

"Yes. Frankly, that's a miracle, considering how much Ouroboros blood you consumed and how long you waited to get help. You were knocking on Death's door by the time you showed up here. Consider yourself lucky you're not sleeping for eternity."

Cara wrapped her arms around herself. Drinking the water had reminded her stomach how empty it was; hunger was a hollow ache in her belly. She was starved for information, too. "Who are you?" she asked. "How did you heal me?"

"We're the Memory Keepers, dear." The woman's ancient eyes

held hers as a cold wind whipped into the room, carrying the scent of the surrounding trees, night settling in. "We store memories in the library inside our temple. Safeguard them, for if memory fails, so does the world. We were created after the Library of Alexandria burned, so that forgetting on that scale could never happen again. As for healing you, we simply helped your body remember what it was like to be free of Snake blood."

"The Library of Alexandria? How—? You're not a ghost."

"No, my dear." The woman smiled. "I'm simply very old."

"What happened there?" Cara asked, nodding at the various scorch marks.

The woman moved to the window, closing it. "You did." She laughed at Cara's shocked expression. "We had to replace your pillows and blankets, your bedside table. The only things you didn't burn were your own clothes—you seemed to consider them a part of you. No, those weren't the only thing. Your young man couldn't be burned, either. He was the only one you let get close. Your other traveling companion was wise enough to hang back entirely and 'let the professionals handle it,' as she put it." The woman drew the curtains closed, considering the holes with miffed, snow-white eyebrows. Another person who could see ghosts, another person who knew Cara was a ghost speaker. That was nothing new at this point. "We don't normally allow outsiders into the infirmary, but we had to let him in because no one else was able to calm your fire. Also"—her lips puckered into a frown—"he has not a single ounce of regard for the rules and would have come in anyway."

"He's not"—Cara swallowed, clutching the blankets to her—"'my young man.'"

The woman's eyebrows raised in interest. She turned a knowing expression on Cara. "Well, he held your hand through the night. Didn't leave your side once. And he sacrificed a memory for you."

The last of the light left, warm gold melting into air.

"He did *what*?"

"It was the price for healing you." The woman's tone was level, unfazed by Cara's reaction. "A joyful memory. It's in our permanent collection now."

Cara fisted her hands in her blankets; she was strong enough to clench her fingers again, the fabric shaking in her grip. "How is it even possible to take a memory?"

"You should know the answer to this one, my dear. A ghost is all memory." The woman tilted her head, seemingly listening to something Cara couldn't hear. "Ah. I think I hear him now."

In a blast of wintry air, Zach phased through the door. He nodded at the woman. "Mnemosyne," he said in greeting.

Zach. Locking her eyes on him, Cara swung her legs out of bed. But although the pain was gone, her body was still weak, and her knees gave out instantly.

"I've got her," Zach said, lifting her back into bed. With a shake of his head, he waved Mnemosyne out of the room, who promised to bring the night's meal soon.

Cara gripped his arm and said, "We need to *talk*."

He didn't respond, tugging the covers up to her waist, hands on either side of her hips. The ice of his touch seared her skin even through the blankets, her clothes; all of that might as well have been paper poised to go up in flame.

If he was going to treat her like a child, then she was going to act like one. She immediately flung the blankets off, glaring at him where he sat on the side of her bed, a distance too intimate, too close.

"What did you do, Coleson?"

"So Mnemosyne already told you." At her unchanged, furious expression, he gritted his teeth and elaborated. "I gave up a memory. That's all."

"That's *all*? Do you remember what it was?"

A muscle jumped in his jaw. "No."

Cara shook her head, blowing out a short, angry breath. "I can't believe this. You shouldn't have done that. You don't have much more of yourself to give up. Losing that memory could have endangered the tether to you have to this Earth. You could fade faster, and then this entire journey would have been for nothing. *Ghosts are all memory*, Coleson."

"And that's *my* risk to take." He sat back, away from her. "I can't believe the way you're acting."

A laugh sputtered from her. Wild, indescribable emotion had welled up in her the moment Mnemosyne had told her what Zach had done, and now it was all coming out as anger. Coming out wrong. "How did you want me to act? Oh, yes, here: my endless gratitude for not letting me die! You didn't have a choice—you need me to bring you back to life. What do you expect, *a thank-you card*?"

"I don't know what I expected." Zach stood. "Why do *you* even care? You didn't have to give anything up. It wasn't your memory."

"And it's not yours now, either." Cara gestured wildly. "This isn't part of our *strictly business* agreement. You can't get that memory back. Even when I resurrect you, it'll still be gone."

"I *know* that. I'm not as stupid as you think I am."

They stared at each other. The air between them tightened, all the strings snapping taut.

This wasn't like the fights they normally had—petty ones, over stuff that didn't matter. The argument they'd had about flyers last week seemed centuries away, the concerns of another world. She didn't know how to win this one.

And in some terrible way, it felt like she'd already lost.

"Forget it," he said. Turning around, he headed for the door.

The words burst from her mouth.

"I don't want to be in your debt."

Zach stopped. His back was to her as he said in a low voice, "How do you think I feel?"

She didn't say anything. Didn't know what to say.

Zach took hold of the doorknob. Paused. Head down, he said, "My—*the* memory isn't important. Finding the Snake's antivenom is and so is keeping you alive." He looked at her then, and the emotion in his eyes pierced her through, the same shade as ice and just as sharp. "You were dying," he said softly. "I would have given up any-thing."

The door clicked behind him, and she was left alone in an empty room, staring at the space where he had been.

TWENTY-FOUR

After a quick meal at the Memory Keepers' temple, Cara, Zach, and Brittany left. According to the map, they had a few more threshold crossings before they reached the Snake, but Cara didn't know how long those would take. They were up against their last hours—last minutes, most likely.

Two thresholds passed without incident: an abandoned playground trapped in perpetual sunset, empty swings swaying on rusted chains; a desolate highway with a gas station whose neon lights flickered like trapped ghosts. Spirits were low, and Cara wasn't speaking to Zach. She'd been lagging behind him and Brittany—slow not because she was dying but because she was recovering from almost dying.

In the third threshold, stars scattered across the heavens like flecks of gold in a prospector's pan. The moon gleamed, as round and silver as the bottom of a miner's tin cup hung on a hook to dry.

Below lay a deserted town of dust.

"Welcome to Fool's Gold," a sun-bleached, wood sign said in Old West–style letters. *"Est. 1849. Population:"* And here someone had painted over the number with thick red paint. One of the chains attaching the placard to the frame had broken, leaving it to knock about in gusts of wind that whistled hollow and thin as if it had lost one of its teeth.

Fool's Gold was a ghost town. And they were the ghosts.

They'd agreed after leaving the temple that they wouldn't stop, they'd continue walking through the night, but now, as they started down toward the abandoned town, Cara's hamstring burned. She pressed a hand to the back of her thigh, trying to massage the muscle into working, but the pain didn't leave.

"Something up?" asked Brittany.

"It's my hamstring," Cara said. "I don't think my legs are fully up to speed after not using them for two days."

Zach raked a hand through his hair. In the darkness she couldn't help noticing how much he'd faded over the last days. The streets shone through his form, his body disappearing against the landscape. Without looking at her, he said, "We'll stop for the night, then," and spun toward the buildings.

"No!" Cara straightened and made to run after him, but her hamstring protested. "Fine. Just for an hour."

Stop doing selfless things, she pleaded with him silently.

They needed to reach the Snake before he faded, and she was slowing them down again, but it wasn't as if she could keep walking.

Worry reared its ugly head. *What if we don't get there tomorrow—?*

They'd cross that bridge when they came to it.

The nearest two buildings were boarded-up stores, but the door to the third gaped open, darkness inviting them in.

"Wait here," Zach said. "I'll see if it's safe."

He reappeared a few minutes later with a shrug.

"Nothing alive in there, at least."

After the sweep of Brittany's ghost detector turned up nothing, too, Brittany relaxed her hold on her knife by the tiniest degree, and Cara pushed open the door.

The room held its breath. Starlight stained the warped floorboards like dried blood. Crumbling shelves lined two of the walls. Dust suffocated everything. A broken clock hung on the wall, its cracked face forever showing that it was 2:49.

When Cara stepped on a loose plank, the pressure sent a can rolling toward her shoe. She picked it up, then shuddered and dropped it. Canned asparagus.

She continued toward the staircase, her shoe going through a rotted step halfway up, but Brittany hauled her on to the next, more intact, one.

The second floor was one open space. The roof's eaves leaned low above their heads, slanting toward each other as if for one last kiss. Tucked into the corner opposite the staircase was an upright piano, its smooth wood the same brown as a coffin lid, its lacquered surface dulled with dust.

Cara put her stuff down near the corner farthest from the staircase while Brittany and Zach settled closer to the center of the room. Cara started a fire in the grate, and the glow lit up their bleak surroundings, making up for the fragile moonlight that crawled through the one square window and revealing a ladder propped against the wall, leading to a hatch in the roof.

Cara rolled out her sleeping bag so she could have somewhere to sit while she practiced her fire magic, trying to calm her anxiousness. She forced herself to do sets, seeing how far she could send a gout of flame. Her chest felt less tight, her breathing more relaxed, when she thought of her fire ability as a muscle, something she could exercise in drills and tone up. She'd never been able to do that with ghost speaking because she couldn't turn it off, couldn't *stop* seeing ghosts if she wanted to.

Now sitting by the back wall, Brittany idly produced what looked like a lighter. A little snick of sound, and light flared into existence. But the light was an ethereal, commercialized blue, drifting around with tiny high notes like sound effects in a video game. It spun into different shapes: a crescent moon, a horse, a ballerina that pirouetted in place.

Zach flopped down next to her. "Can I try?"

Brittany sighed. "Wish I could let you, but its mundane appearance masks a hellish weapon. The moment you touch it, your ectoplasm will peel away and you'll melt out of existence in utter agony."

His face fell.

"I'm kidding," she said, and tossed it to him, laughing when he caught it and his eyes relit.

How could he be so at ease with his death so close to being permanent? Was she more worried about him than he was? That was ridiculous. He always coasted through things unscathed, but she never thought he'd have the same attitude about death.

The next burst of flame tore a hole in the wall.

"Yo, ghost talker, try not to burn down the place while we're *in* it," Brittany called.

This was where Zach should have joined in, ribbing her.

But he stayed silent, eyes focused on the lighter.

Cara prepared for another blast. It was good she'd blown a hole in the wall. Now she had a target to aim for. If she could narrow her focus enough, maybe she could shoot the fire through the hole and send her blasts even farther.

In the corner of her eye, she could feel Brittany looking back and forth between her and Zach. Cara tried not to sigh audibly when Brittany got up and then dropped next to her.

"Trouble in paradise?"

"Brittany, you are about two seconds away from a burn-induced scar."

Brittany eyed her but huffed. "Fine. Wanna talk about something else?"

Giving up on the plan to practice her fire powers in peace, Cara thought for a moment. "What is that thing?" She nodded at the not-lighter in Zach's hands.

Brittany scratched her temple. "*Technically*, it's a toy meant to occupy little kids. Gen—my big sis—gave it to me when I was six and upset about not being old enough to go on ghost hunts with the others. I think some might call it a bribe, but hey, it worked. To this day I don't know where she got the lighter from, but it's magic: you can imagine the light into anything. She told me to pull it out whenever I felt down or missed her." Brittany shrugged. "It's silly, but even after aging into the hunt, I still take it everywhere."

"Do you miss her now?"

"Hell no," Brittany said immediately. She chewed her lip. "But between you and me, off the record . . . a little. Even though I know if Gen were here right now, she'd be nitpicking every single thing I do. She used to be actually kind of cool, but now she never talks to me except to tell me off. 'Brittany, don't scare your five-year-old cousins by telling them stories about Headless Bertha!' 'No, Brittany, you're not allowed to hunt poltergeists without backup, and that's final!' 'Brittany, put down that ghost grenade before you blow your hand off!'" Huffing, Brittany propped her face in her hands and her elbows on her knees. "Like I'd be unprofessional enough to blow my hand off. That's an amateur move. The most I'd lose is two fingers, tops."

Cara snorted.

"She thinks she's in charge of me or something." Brittany rolled her eyes. "One time, I broke curfew getting back at two a.m. after a date with my first girlfriend. My mom was out of town chasing ghosts and my dad is a heavy sleeper—the man would probably doze right through the zombie apocalypse—so I should have been home free. But there my dear old sis was, waiting at the top of the stairs with her arms crossed. Loomed out of the dark and scared the shit out of me. She scolded me so loud I'm pretty sure she woke the whole damn house."

Cara winced in sympathy. "Two in the morning, though? My mom would kill me."

"Yeah, well." Brittany grinned. "It was worth it." She leaned back on her hands. "Other than that, though, Gen's not, like, the *absolute* worst. Do you have any siblings?"

"No. It's just my mom, my grandma, and me." Unbidden, a flame flickered to life in Cara's palms. It was the color of butterscotch: warm, golden, and sweet. She looked down, watching it waver and sway in the shelter of her hands. "But I always wanted a sister."

"You can borrow mine. Gen will gladly boss you around even if you're not related. So you're an only child? Your house must be so peaceful."

Cara closed her hand into a fist, and the flame went out. "I guess you could say that. But you could also say lonely."

They were quiet for a moment, the building creaking around them.

"Families," Brittany said finally. "Too bad you can't choose 'em, huh?"

How different things might be if you could. "What made your family decide to start hunting ghosts, anyway? It's not exactly the most lucrative business."

"'Cause we had to. The white ghost hunters? They weren't worth shit. They refused to deal with the ghosts in our neighborhoods, just let them terrorize our block. Said it wasn't 'their problem.' And if they did get rid of one of our ghosts, the way they dealt with them was . . . awful. So my gran stepped up." She sighed. "It's still bad, but it's better. We're getting there."

"You're saving your city," Cara realized. "You're following your grandmother's legacy."

And what was *she* doing? Ignoring her power and those it could help, and hoping no ghosts noticed her.

Would she one day live to regret it?

Brittany unsheathed a knife and began to carve a circle into the floorboards. "America likes to pretend its ghosts don't exist. That its sins are safely buried in the ground. But pretending something isn't there doesn't make it go away. It just makes you less prepared for when the time finally comes to reckon with your own haunting." She smiled grimly, blue lights bobbing in her eyes. "We take care of our own," she said. "In more ways than one."

Laolao had told Cara stories about how she'd struggled to feel at home in America. It wasn't just the language or the food—the dead were different, too. The West didn't see the spirit world and the "real world" as constantly interacting, but separate, a delineation rigid as a corpse in rigor mortis. It was jarring to Laolao, who mingled with the dead on the daily. But she hadn't told Cara much more, because her grandmother didn't like talking about the past, especially the bad parts.

"Much better to focus on the present," Laolao liked to say whenever Cara pressed. "For example, we have air-conditioning now. No use thinking about the sweat from six decades ago."

But then, after Cara nodded in agreement, when Laolao no longer thought Cara was looking, her grandmother would stare out the attic window, her gaze as far away as if she were still watching the smoke billow up from her house, once again a girl witnessing her own orphaning.

The crackle of flames accompanied Cara's words. "My grandmother had a hard time adjusting to America when she first moved, especially its ghosts. White ghosts would leer at her or call her names or else ignore her entirely. She was never sure which was worst."

Cara crossed her arms, shoulders hunching, and continued, "She tried to help them, too, but they laughed at her English, asked if she needed help finding her way to Chinatown. They didn't want her help, but—"

"—they were A-OK with assuming she needed theirs," Brittany finished. Understanding glowed in the other girl's gaze.

A recollection surfaced in Cara's mind: the time she'd gone to a summer art street festival with Charlotte and Felicity. When she'd heard almost incomprehensible muttering, she'd glanced at the speaker—then immediately glanced away. It had been a raving spectral old man with his face nearly radish red. He didn't seem to like the look of Felicity or Cara, but the way his expression twisted when he fixed his eyes on Charlotte, who took after her Black mom more than her white dad in appearance—Cara had instantly pretended she'd had too much sun and convinced Charlotte and Felicity to catch a nice, air-conditioned movie in the old-fashioned theater instead. She'd spent the entire film keeping watch out of the corner of her eye. Thankfully, he hadn't followed them. She hadn't thought about it in the longest time—she hadn't wanted to—but recalling it sent chills down her spine.

People did the ugliest things when they thought no one else was watching.

But she'd also been glad he didn't know she could see him—who knows how it might have set him off when he knew he could get a reaction out of her.

Snapping back to the present, Cara admitted, "With experiences like that, I sometimes don't quite understand why my grandmother loves ghost speaking so much. It seems like all it does is cause more trouble."

"Well, it can be useful, right?" Brittany toyed with her knife thoughtfully. "Besides being able to see ghosts without ghoststeel, which everybody in my family wishes they could do"—Cara shrank a little inside—"the amplification can be useful, too."

"Isn't that the opposite of what you'd want when ghost hunting? Amplification makes ghosts what they were. It makes them more alive."

"Correctomundo. Usually, we want ghosts weak, we want to banish them from this dimension. But sometimes, if you meet a mindless wraith and you want to find out why it's terrorizing a certain area, amplification might get you your answer. It doesn't just make ghosts stronger—"

"It makes them remember what they were," Cara recalled. "I see your point."

"And if you're a ghost talker, you can also help ghosts pass over, which is one way to get rid of an angry specter that won't let civilians live in peace. Now us ghost hunters have to cut their ties to this plane with knives, which is a tad less peaceful, but they all end up at the same place anyway, right? I've always wondered—how does it feel to do that? What if the ghost doesn't wanna go, but it's too lost to listen to reason?"

"I wouldn't know," Cara admitted. "My grandma's a pro, but I've never done it."

Brittany stared at her for a moment, then nodded to herself, tapping the handle of her knife on her chin. "According to my gran, it's a wonder to watch. The ghost talker she met could compel specters to pass over with just a word. It was like witnessing a miracle."

Cara should be able to do that. But she'd never learned, never bothered to, even though her grandmother had offered at every turn.

If—when—she got out of here, Cara promised herself, she was going to ask her grandmother for help understanding and practicing her powers.

It was, after all, her legacy.

TWENTY-FIVE

Cara must have accidentally fallen asleep, because the next thing she knew, Brittany's ghost detector was beeping its head off like an alarm clock from hell, and Cara was opening her eyes to find two ghosts leering down at her.

She startled back against the wall.

"Well, how about that?" one ghost said, his tumbleweed-brown eyebrows rising under his prospector's hat. "She can see us." And he spat a slur that made the heat in her blood hike.

Then he slashed his knife toward her.

She leaped up, turning toward the staircase, but more ghosts blocked her way, plunging the temperature in the room to that of a walk-in freezer. All of them glowed an intense silver—strong enough to touch the living—and looked to have been prospectors in a past life, with timeworn faces, hats, and dirty bandannas wrapped around their necks. Most held knives, but a few carried pickaxes, and one even had a shallow mining pan, like he'd forgotten his blade but still wanted to join the fun. Dawn light glinted off the weapons—real ones, not ghost ones.

It was Halloween, and the dead had shown up to party.

"Brittany? Coleson?" she yelled.

"I'm on the roof!" came Brittany's voice. "We've got a little problem!"

"Yeah, I can see that!"

"I *told* my cousin there's no point in updating the ghost detector unless it can detect a three-hundred-mile range, but did she listen? *No*—back the *hell* up, mister!" Brittany's complaint broke off with a shout, presumably as she was drawn into a spectral sparring match.

Cara's fear flared up, and so did her fire, spreading along her arms to light up the room like a second sun. Her eyes flickered from each silver-burnished face. Perhaps seven miners faced her, cutting off her escape.

And where was Zach?

The lead miner, the one that had tried to stab her, chuckled at her fire. "You think that's going to do anything, little girl?"

No. It wouldn't. Fire couldn't kill a ghost. Nothing could—except ghoststeel.

She whirled for Brittany's equipment beside her sleeping bag, but another prospector snatched it out of her reach, dangling it off one dirt-smudged finger.

"Looking for this?" With a sneer, he tossed it out the window with a smash of shattering glass.

Cara clenched her fists. Her fire magic could not shield her, and her ghost speaking—well. If she'd listened to Laolao, if she'd tried to learn, maybe she could be like that ghost speaker Brittany had talked about, able to cut a ghost's ties to the mortal plane with a single word. To banish them back to dust and decaying memories.

But she refused to die like this, murdered by hateful ghosts in a dilapidated room, far from home with the scent of rot the last thing in her lungs.

Cara had to try. She stepped forward, holding out a hand, reaching deep inside herself for the threads of magic that enabled a ghost to pass over. The lead miner's eyes flickered warily. He backpedaled a little as Cara planted a palm on his chest.

Laolao had told her, once, what it was like to help ghosts cross over. That it was harder than dying. It was a battle of wills. The body wanted to give up.

The soul, less so.

Some ghosts would never leave, because the thing keeping them there wasn't a wish to see their widowed spouse get married again or to see their forgotten paintings brought to light; it was the experience of the haunt itself.

And these were the ghosts you had to help along a little bit more.

Cara drew in a breath. She locked eyes with the miner. "*Leave*," she intoned.

Wind whirled in from the hole in the wall, dust rising—

And then the miner laughed. Grabbed her by the arm. Flung her into the remains of last night's fire, scattering ash everywhere. With a heavy boot that hurt no less in ghosthood, he kicked her in the stomach when she tried to get back up.

Cara gasped for air. She lay on the ground, one arm clutching her torso as the miner advanced.

He grabbed her chin, his hand rough as sand.

"You reckoned you could make me leave, eh, little girl? This town is *mine*. And I ain't leavin'."

The temperature plunged.

"*Get away from her*," snarled a voice.

Zach.

She hadn't seen him appear, but here he was, his broad, intangible shoulders taut with anger, in the midst of the circle of ghosts.

The lead miner straightened but didn't step away. The prospectors exchanged glances of surprise and apprehension. None of them moved.

"Maybe you didn't hear me the first time," Zach said, and again there was that cold edge to his voice, dangerous as an avalanche. He strode toward the lead miner. A hefty prospector with a red beard moved to block his path, and Zach lashed out, faster than Cara thought possible.

The ghost fell soundlessly, clutching his side. Cries of shock and outrage flew up from the other miners as the one Zach had attacked began to dissolve, silver silhouette peeling away out of existence like he was another fog creature faced with fire.

Her gaze flew to Zach's hand.

In his fingers glinted ghoststeel.

Cara's heart sank, right through the floorboards. *No, you idiot.* He held the hilt, but if one of the miners took hold of the knife and turned it back on him—

"Let's make one thing clear. I don't care what you want," said Zach to the other ghosts. "I don't care about who you are. I don't care about whatever the hell keeps you on Earth. I only care about protecting her."

He whirled on a second spirit.

"But you're one of us," the miner said, half in confusion, half in disbelief.

"No, I'm not," he said, and drove the blade into the other ghost's chest.

She didn't recognize this Zach, Cara thought as she inched toward the staircase, planning to find one of the ghoststeel knives outside and rejoin the fray. Perhaps dying had halved him, darkened him. Or maybe it was the memory he'd given up, something he didn't realize was valuable to his true self. But Zach advanced on another miner, sending him to oblivion as the specter's pan clattered to the floor-boards in a cloud of dust, and she had to revise her statement.

Arrogance shone in the powerful lines of his shoulders as he moved, cockiness in the set of his jaw as he rounded on the remaining spirits, armed with a weapon that could end him just as well.

This was the Zach who had put himself in front of her when the Snake showed up. This was the Zach who'd looked ready to fight a disembodied fog when he saw the wounds it had given her. This was a Zach incandescent with power, cold fury in his ice-blue eyes, venom coiled in his voice.

This was a Zach who had something to protect.

And he was protecting her.

No, she corrected herself. He was protecting his chance at resur-rection.

Something cold and sharp and undeniable pressed into her throat, and Cara froze, her foot on the top step of the stairs. She'd turned her back on the fight. Now, with a knife at her throat, she was paying for it.

"Good," said the satisfied voice of the prospector behind her. He dug the blade in harder; Cara instinctively flinched backward, clammy cold pervading her body as she passed through the prospec-tor's see-through form.

She tried to run, but the knife bit once more under her chin, pressing her back against the panels. She managed to turn her head to the side; the hand that was holding the knife led to an arm that disappeared back into the wall. The miner must have been almost completely outside the building—he was using his ability to go through objects against her solid flesh, using her as a shield to protect himself from Zach's wrath, killing her at the same time.

"*Coleson,*" she whispered.

He turned, the second-to-last miner dissolving. Now there was only one left—and he was out of Zach's reach.

The color fled Zach's face, and he stared at her, stricken.

"*Tang,*" he said, her name like a breath, like something he needed to live.

He moved, seemingly without thought, but the miner only sank the blade deeper into her throat. Zach stopped.

"That's more like it." Cara couldn't see the prospector's face, but a sneer emanated from his voice. Terror rolled off her skin in waves of heat, her heart a fearful furnace. The blade was no longer cold, but that was a small comfort; the miner pressed it tight enough to crush her windpipe. "Who's in control now, boy?"

Zach held up his hands, the ghoststeel still in his grip. "Let her go, and I swear—"

Laughter slithered behind her. "There ain't nothin' you can give me. Nothin' that I would want. You see, it gets lonely out here, and I haven't had fresh company in so very long. And I'm going to need it even more now, since you've gone and slaughtered all my friends." She could sense the specter grinning. "I'm going to kill your sweetheart, boy. I'm going to make her into a ghost, and *there ain't nothin' you can do about it.*"

Zach looked like the miner had reached into his chest and taken out his heart. "*No,*" he breathed.

Cara's heart pulsed hotter, quicker, against its cage.

Maybe there's something I can do.

Cara closed her eyes, letting her body sag against the wall, and drew in breath after breath, shallow as they were with the knife cutting off most of her air supply. She'd need to focus all her energy toward increasing the heat on the blade, and it might not even work.

Luckily, the miner didn't appear to be in a hurry. She supposed he did have a lot of time to kill.

"I'll give you a choice," the specter said. "Which sound do you think will be more pleasing? The gurgle of her blood as it floods out of her throat? Or the thud of her body as it hits the ground after I push her down the stairs? No, wait." The miner pressed the knife harder into her throat as he considered. Cara couldn't keep a whimper from escaping her lips. "I could cut her yellow throat, and *then* send her corpse down the steps. There you have it, boy. A third choice. Make up your mind quick, now. Or don't. I've waited only hundreds of years."

"You—you don't want to kill her," Zach said. His tone was conspiratorial as he added, "Trust me. She has so many opinions, and she never shuts up. And she judges you about *everything*. She'll annoy you to death—I mean, she'll make you wish you were really dead, so you wouldn't have to listen to another word out of her mouth. Is that how you want to spend eternity? Praying a ghost hunter will come and put you out of your misery?"

The specter was silent. And then he scoffed.

"You don't fool me, boy," he said, his voice low and scraping like the sound of a rattlesnake's scales against stone. "Tell me. Will you think she's so pretty when the flesh falls from her face? When her dark eyes rot in their sockets? When her shape fades away and she ain't nothin' but bone?"

Cara's body was an inferno.

"Sure, it's a treat when the coyotes come to feast on the corpse," the specter continued. "You can stay for that, watch if you want. I don't hold no grudges. Long as you put down that goddamned blade of yours. It won't stop me from doing *this*."

And he drew the knife across her throat—

—but it had gone liquid at the edges, soft as butter.

"How in the—?" muttered the specter, lifting the knife toward himself.

That was all the opening she needed. Cara pushed off the wall, pivoting to face the miner. His eyes narrowed, and he surged forward in a gust that smelled of something rotten, mold and putrefaction, aiming to wound her nonetheless.

She caught the blade in her hand. She loosed a slow exhale, her core burning.

Blazing orange as the sun, the metal melted.

Cara lowered her arm, breathing hard. The molten metal coursed over her fingers, dripping down like blood. When it hit the floor, it sizzled, burning straight through the wood.

"You," she said, despite her bruised windpipe, "should have been paying attention to *me*."

The miner stared at her in disbelief, clutching his useless handle. Then his eyes darted past her shoulder; whatever he saw there made him turn and flee through the wall. Zach was on his heels, disappearing through the panels.

Cara's legs gave out, and she sank to the ground.

For a couple minutes, all she did was gulp in air, shoulders heaving. Leftover smoke curled out from under her collar, from her sleeves. It hurt to swallow. She touched a hand to her throat—the skin had broken. Liquid metal and blood trickled down her neck; they both felt the same.

The scent of winter tore back into the room.

Zach. His eyes found her face, and his expression softened at once, the tension in his body melting away.

He fell to his knees beside her in the early-morning light. It seemed the Snake's venom kept him intangible even on Halloween, and her heart gave a strange shudder at how the light cut straight through him, almost cruel in how it pretended he was already gone.

He will fade away by tonight, a voice reminded her.

"Are you okay?" he asked.

She nodded. "I'm sorry," she said when she found her voice, the words tumbling in a rush. "You gave up something precious for me—a happy memory—and I thanked you by screaming in your face."

Zach shook his head. "No, *I'm* sorry. If I had protected you better when the white Snake showed up, you wouldn't have had to bite him. You wouldn't have swallowed his blood. It was my fault you were dying. And it's my fault those ghosts were able to get close enough to do this to you."

He couldn't touch her, not anymore, but he reached for her all the same.

She tilted her chin up to give him more access, holding herself still as his fingers ghosted over her jaw and trailed down her throat, as cool and light as frost. He made a soft, distraught sound in the back of his throat.

Cara said, "It's just a cut—"

"It's my fault."

With his hand on her neck, there was no way he couldn't feel how fast her pulse beat, frantic for no reason. He was only checking to make sure his ghost speaker was good to bring him back. If not for the fact that he needed her alive and well until then, he would not be

273

this close, making every nerve light up at his nearness. This touch was treacherous. This touch was temporary.

Tell that to her stupid heart.

"Careful, Coleson," she teased. "A girl might think you actually cared."

She shouldn't have been disappointed when he replied, "Can't have that," and pulled away.

Clearing his throat, he asked, "Where's Brittany?"

With a resounding crash, the ceiling caved in.

Brittany landed on the floor in a crouch, along with wood that had, up until two seconds ago, comprised part of the roof. Early-morning sunlight poked through, right before the hands and head of a miner dove through after her, his face contorted in rage.

"Above you—" Cara started to say, but Brittany was on her feet, twisting up to meet the descending ghost with a blade to his chest.

The man froze midair, and his own knife clattered to the floor as his form gaped open. His mouth twisted to spit out an ugly word, but he vanished before he could finish it. All that was left was a bit of ectoplasm dripping onto the floorboards, leaving an unappealing grease mark.

Brittany put her hands on her hips and sighed, shaking her braids free of dust that was a century and a half old. "That's definitely one of my least favorite parts. They have all the time in the world to get more creative, and what do they do with it? Insist on using the same old tired words."

Scooping her skull-embellished baseball cap off the floor, she jammed it back on her head and turned to face them. Numerous new rips marred the sleeves of her denim jacket.

She spotted the ghoststeel beside them and raised her eyebrows.

"Nice work, ghost talker."

"Oh—that wasn't me." Rising, Cara held the knife out. "That was Coleson."

Brittany side-eyed him as she turned over the weapon in her hands. "Didn't I tell you, 'Hands off my stuff'?"

On his feet as well, Zach held out his arms and grinned. "I didn't touch the blade."

Brittany nodded grudgingly. "Well, miracles happen. Maybe once she brings you back to life, you can apply to be a ghost hunter."

"It was an emergency," Zach said. "I should have been here."

Cara glanced at him. "Where were you, anyway?"

He rubbed the back of his neck. "I was, um, looking for this."

And he scooped something off the floor, where he must have dropped it, and held it out to her.

She took the cactus flower gingerly. It was dead—of course it was, he wouldn't have been able to touch it otherwise. Still, it was beautiful, its heart glowing gold, the color fanning out to a bright, burning orange for the petals, like she was holding a flame.

"Happy birthday," he said.

Her heart quickened. "You remembered?"

"I mean, it is Halloween. I'd have to be an even bigger idiot to not remember that." He shrugged, nonchalant, but hesitation flickered in his eyes. "You can throw it away if you want. I know it's just a stupid flower."

Cara hated her birthday, but his surprisingly endearing gift had made it the tiniest bit better. For some reason.

"You're wrong," she informed him. "It's not stupid, and I'm not throwing it away. *Especially* because you sound so sure that I will."

His eyebrows arched at the fierceness of her reply, but she didn't miss the tiny smile that flickered at the corners of his lips, like he was secretly pleased with her rebuttal.

"Shit, it's your birthday?" Brittany asked. "Why didn't you say something? Oh, man, I don't have a present!"

Cara laughed. "It's fine. I don't like to make a big deal out of it."

"You know what?" Brittany held out to Cara the knife Zach had used. "Take this."

"Are you serious?"

"As a grave." She pushed it into Cara's hands, along with a leather sheath. "This'll be your gift."

Cara slid the knife into its sheath, then looked back up at Brittany. The warmth in her chest swelled. A flower and a dagger. She hadn't expected this. "Thank you," she said.

It was the morning of the last day, shafts of sunlight arcing in through the holes in the walls and roof, the scent of rot fading from the air. The deadline loomed above her like an executioner's blade, but a small fire had flickered to life in her chest. Whatever her short-comings, Zach and Brittany had her back here, like Charlotte and Felicity did at home, and that was a gift all on its own.

TWENTY-SIX

The next threshold took them back to Autumn Falls.

Specifically, the town graveyard. Wrought iron gates barred their entrance. Beyond the gaps in the iron grew trees and vivid green grass, dusted with fallen leaves, color juxtaposed with the gray tombstones laid out in perfect rows.

It was autumn again. When Cara had left home, it had been snowing, the graves no doubt all shrouded in white. But here, ivy grew over tombstones, clinging in one final embrace. The trees were still losing their leaves, laying down their dead.

Not all the trees, though. Copses of cypress stood like sentinels to death, their refined, tapered bodies immortally green.

Cara took a step toward the gates, then stopped. She turned to look behind her at Zach and Brittany and gasped.

Nothing but empty white space loomed around them in all directions.

Besides Zach and Brittany, the only things in existence were the cemetery and the river, which flowed in the distance, a quiet blue line of mourning.

When she turned back to the gates, they swung open, creaking in the autumn wind.

Cara shivered; unease unfurled its dark wings inside her chest.

She twisted to meet Zach's questioning eyes.

"What?" Brittany said, looking between the two of them. "Something I'm missing?"

"This is the local graveyard back home in Autumn Falls," Cara said. "Or at least, it looks like it."

"Normally, there's other stuff around the graveyard," Zach added. "Like buildings and streets and the rest of town."

"According to the map . . ." Brittany made a clicking noise with her tongue. "This is the last threshold before the Snake."

Whether it was Autumn Falls or not, this place was the final obstacle they had to get through to reach the antidote. Cara's skin prickled—the last time the river had shown them something familiar, it had been the fog, using her memories of her mother and Laolao against her.

As soon as they'd entered the graveyard, a clang sounded behind them. Cara whirled around. The gates had swung shut. A gale—or some larger force—had pushed them closed.

Well, that was welcoming.

Something pattered onto her, a rapid succession of droplets. She tilted her eyes to the heavens.

Clouds the same color as the tombstones had encroached, and it had started to pour. She blinked against the water, squinting. No, it hadn't started raining when they'd entered—this was full-fledged, a storm that had already been underway for some time. It was like by crossing the gates they'd crossed a veil.

But she wasn't getting wet. Instead of falling on her, the rain fell *through* her—sinking into her skin and out the other side.

Like she was a ghost.

Inside her chest, the uneasiness increased and unfurled even more wings, her fear a murder of crows.

Cara had always hated graveyards.

She reached for Zach's hand, then came to her senses, snatching her hand back before he noticed. He was incorporeal, the cemetery apparent past his half-opaque form. She wouldn't be able to touch him anyway.

Brittany's ghost detector beeped.

They halted.

"This makes no sense," Brittany muttered. "It's telling me there are ghosts, but there isn't a single specter in sight."

Zach coughed.

"Yeah, no, I configured the ghost detector to ignore your ratings right after I met you. This says there are *new* ghosts." The device beeped a second time, then a third. Brittany smacked it on the side, but it beeped insistently. "Okay. What we're not gonna have is two specter ambushes in one day, because that's just embarrassing. I'll check this out, see where it beeps the most."

Brittany headed off into the trees.

In the distance, guarded by a single cypress, a group of mourners was gathered by a grave, dressed in black and bearing umbrellas above their heads. Men in suits lowered a bone-white casket into the ground. Cara couldn't make out any of their faces.

Zach strode forward but hissed in pain, a hand going to his side.

"What's wrong?" Cara tried to tug his hand away to see, but her fingers met air. "Coleson, *show me.*"

He lifted his hand to reveal a slice the length of her index finger glimmering below his ribs. A translucent white, it only appeared when she looked at it from a certain angle, like a colorless paper cut.

"No," she said, horror stealing her words. "No, you didn't—"

"I slipped when fighting the miners. It's okay, it's—"

"It's not okay." She wished she could grip his arm, get him to understand. "It hurts, doesn't it?"

Jaw clenched, he nodded.

"How are you even still here?"

"I guess the cut wasn't deep enough. Seriously, I'm fine—"

One mourner turned toward them, as if she could hear them. A flash of silver-blond hair.

"*Mom?*" Zach started forward.

"Coleson, no!"

If only he were still corporeal, so she could drag him to a stop. Instead, Cara was forced to chase after him, hissing his name.

"Coleson, stop! It's not real!"

He wheeled around so suddenly she had to dig her heels in to avoid running into him—or rather, through him. "You don't know that."

"It can't be. Remember the fog? All the things it showed us to try to lure us in? I have no idea what's going on here, but judging by everything the river's brought us so far, I'm going to take a wild guess and say that it's *probably* not what it seems."

It was a small gathering: Zach's mom, along with his dad and older sister and brother, judging by their appearances. A scattering of other people, perhaps cousins, aunts, and uncles, all with pale complexions and blond hair of varying shades and faces shadowed in grief. An elderly woman with hair the color of hoarfrost dabbed at her eyes with a silver handkerchief as the rest of the group tossed white roses into the grave.

No, it couldn't be real. For one thing, if this were really Zach's funeral, the entire town would have showed up. Teachers, classmates, mourners by the dozen.

Unless it was purposely a small funeral, by decree of Zach's parents.

"Plus, Laolao used her magic to hide your body, remember?" she said. "They wouldn't be able to find it. Whoever they're mourning—it's not you. And it's probably not *them*, either."

Who are they burying, then? whispered a small voice in her head.

"You don't need a body to have a funeral," Zach shot back. His shoulders tensed, like it was taking everything in him to stay in place right now. "They're my *family*, Tang. I can't see them and just not do anything about it."

"I know, but it's not them—"

"But what if it is?"

She stared up at him. His eyes were bright with unshed tears. They hollowed a pit in her stomach.

The voices floated closer. Behind Zach, half-visible through his form, the mourners had left the grave and were approaching.

She darted behind the nearest oak, but Zach refused to follow.

He turned and planted himself in their path. The mourners drew nearer, although most of them kept their eyes on the ground, silently grieving. His mom walked near the front, leaning heavily on his dad.

"Mom," he said, sounding for all the world like a lost little boy, but his mom didn't even look up.

She walked right through him.

Zach stood still as the rest of the procession passed, the others going straight through his form, too. A graveyard full of ghosts, traveling through each other like phantom ships in the night.

After the last mourner left, Zach seemed to come back to himself. He didn't look over his shoulder at them but strode toward the tombstone they'd left.

Cara chanced a glance back. One by one, the mourners glided through the gates and disappeared out of existence. She gritted her teeth but forced herself after Zach, catching up as he came to a stop in front of the silver-veined marble marker.

She'd known what would be on the gravestone, and yet, her heart stopped for a beat when she saw the inscription.

"*Zacharias Coleson*," read the name, freshly carved. "*Beloved Son and Brother*." Below were the dates of his birth and death.

Cara touched the gravestone, expecting air—but this was real, or felt like it, the marble cold as a corpse under her fingers and as solid. Goose bumps rose on her arms.

"We have to go, Zach. We're running out of time."

But Zach didn't move. Quietly he said, "They almost had a funeral for me when I was five."

Cara glanced sharply at him, but he was staring at the tombstone, hands shoved into the pockets of his hoodie. The rain poured down, falling through his shoulders, the storm and the silver of his translucent figure magnifying his ghostliness.

"Why would they do that?" she said slowly, not sure she wanted to hear the answer.

"Because I froze to death in a blizzard when I was five."

Shock stunned her into silence for a moment. He'd said it so casually, almost without emotion. "Coleson," she said softly. She'd thought she knew everything there was to know about him, but here was this tragedy materializing like an iceberg out of the mist.

Zach shrugged, eyes fixed on his gravestone. "I don't remember much. It was a freak snowstorm. Came out of nowhere. I was a dumb kid, and I got lost. My family didn't notice I was gone for hours. According to the medics, my heart stopped four times while they resuscitated me, but I was in a coma for a while after. It was a miracle I survived." He hesitated before he said *miracle*, almost imperceptibly, like he was quoting someone else. Like he didn't believe it himself.

"My parents didn't think I was going to make it, so they started planning. I overheard them when I woke up in the hospital. They were talking about what colors the flowers should be, but they hadn't made up their minds yet." He scooped up the bouquet of white roses they'd left on top of the grave. "Guess I no longer have to live in suspense."

It's not real, she wanted to say, but bit her tongue. Maybe it wasn't fully real, but that didn't mean it was fully *unreal*.

Zach began pulling at the petals, tugging them out one by one. They floated to the earth like snow. "I just can't seem to stop dying."

She lifted a hand to place on his shoulder—then pulled back, hugging her arms around herself. She couldn't quite decipher his expression, when last week she'd been confident she could read him like a book. Last week, she hadn't thought him capable of reading her. She'd been wrong on both counts.

His gaze was fixed on the petals, the repetitive ripping, but his eyes were somewhere far away.

"It was okay at first. Clear gray sky. The tiniest snowflakes. But they kept coming, and it was so, so cold." His brow pinched as if he were physically in pain from remembering. The petals continued falling. He tossed each bare stem to the ground. "I yelled for my family, but no one ever came. I watched the snow bury me alive. After a while, I didn't even mind the cold anymore. That's the worst part. The numbness, swallowing me whole. Slowly feeling myself become nothing." He looked up, locking eyes with hers. His irises flashed an intense ice-blue, sending a jolt through her stomach. "I can't go back there," Zach whispered, his fingers stilling. "I can't go back."

Cara blinked. "Hey, it's okay," she said. "You're not—"

"Don't let me go back, okay?" He shook his head. "*Please*, I can't. Not again. Don't let . . ."

He was begging now, and she didn't want him to. Not like this.

Now she knew how Zach must have felt when he saw her crying in the fog. Panicked, freaked out, and not sure what to do about the fact that the person you hated most was currently breaking down in front of you.

She took a step toward him. Zach looked like he might bolt, disappear through the gates into nothingness. His shoulders shook, his body so translucent that the emerald spikes of the cypress leaves showed through his chest.

Cara closed the gap between them, reaching a hand up to his face. Ghostly cold emanated from his skin, meeting the heat of her palm. He swallowed, his throat bobbing, but he didn't move.

He was an engine going cold on a winter road. He was glass shattered into a thousand beautiful shards. He was a tragic accident she couldn't look away from, no matter how hard she tried.

And it didn't feel right to look at him like this, when he was vulnerable, when he was fading, when he was *less*.

With a shiver, she realized the temperature had plummeted. The rain falling through them had turned into snow, as if the liminal space was reliving Zach's death along with him.

His voice was hoarse. "I've been living on borrowed time my whole life. It shouldn't scare me that it's running out, but every time I think of falling asleep in the snow, I—" He swallowed. "I can't go back," he repeated. "I can't, I can't, *I can't*—"

And then he froze and vanished.

The last rose, now nothing but thorns, succumbed to gravity and spiraled to its final resting place atop his grave.

"Coleson!" she screamed. *"Coleson!"*

Cara whirled. No, Zach hadn't suddenly teleported behind her like some great magic trick. She stepped back on her heels, spinning to look around. He wasn't by the cypresses, the iron fence, the section of gravestones so old wind had scored the names into amnesia.

He was simply gone.

The cut he'd gotten from the ghoststeel—had that been it? Or had it been the memory he'd given up for her? A ghost was all memory, only memory, and he'd already been fading before her eyes—

Or had they simply run out of time?

No. This couldn't be the end.

"Brittany!" she yelled. "Coleson disappeared, I need your help, where are you—?"

But the ghost hunter didn't appear, either.

They'd left her. They'd all left her.

Her breath came in bursts; her vision blurred. She stumbled, bracing herself against a cypress.

He was somewhere here. He had to be. And Brittany, too, just out of hearing range. She threw herself into a run, racing past row after row of tombstones until finally, shaking so badly she could no longer remain upright, she fell to her knees underneath the weeping willow at the lake's edge in the center of the graveyard.

This was wrong, wrong, wrong. Zach wasn't supposed to leave her.

Since agreeing to help him that day in the attic, Cara had known there was a large possibility that she might fail. That Zach might die for good. It would have been stupid not to have been prepared.

But maybe she *was* stupid, because she hadn't expected for it to feel like her heart was being torn out of her chest.

Cara didn't recognize the girl in the water staring back at her: dark eyes frantic and wild, face pale with fear, hair coming undone. Even if the rain striking the lake's surface hadn't fractured the image into myriad puzzle pieces, it would have been impossible to put them together into someone who was supposed to be her: calm and collected, not falling to pieces over *Zach*.

His name: already it hurt to think it.

"Tang?" said a confused voice behind her. "What are you doing? Why did you move?"

Her heart stopped.

The water wouldn't have shown his reflection. Cara could be hallucinating. Hearing voices in her head.

There was one way to tell for sure.

When she stood and turned around, Zach was there.

All the air left her lungs in a great shudder. She drew a breath, then another, relief moving through her like pain.

When Cara could finally speak, the relief had transmuted into anger.

"*You idiot*," she said, advancing on him. "Brittany told you not to touch her knives. You knew you could get hurt, and you did it anyway. I thought you'd disappeared forever! I thought you'd left m— I thought you'd left!"

"Whoa, slow down. Are you *mad* at me? What happened?"

"Of course I'm mad," she shot back. "You disappeared midsentence and scared the hell out of me. I just ran halfway across the graveyard looking for you, looking like a *fool*, when I shouldn't have bothered, because you're standing there perfectly okay—" Her voice caught, died, as she realized the meaning of what she'd said.

He was *okay*.

Her heart had yet to regain its composure; her heart still beat loud enough to match the raindrops drumming through her, snow no longer.

Cara pressed her lips together, folded her arms across her chest. "How do you feel?" she asked evenly.

Zach's expression had been shifting from confused to concerned to frustrated, but now it settled into a sardonic smile, the fractured version of him returning. "Like someone's been standing on my grave."

A wave of cold surged into the cemetery.

With it came shocks of emotion: desperation, misery, sorrow so strong she stumbled back.

"We're in trouble!" Brittany was running toward them, knife in one hand, ghost detector in the other, beeping like it had lost its tiny electronic mind. She reached them, panting, and swiveled to face the fence. "I found the ghosts. Actually, they found me."

Through the wrought iron, silver shapes crept their way, as many specters as there were raindrops.

TWENTY-SEVEN

Wails and moans reached her ears, a haunting melody magnified a thousandfold. This far away, the ghosts melting through the iron fence were as faceless as fog, their ethereal forms blending into one another. She couldn't tell if any had weapons—but ghosts didn't need weapons to kill, especially on Halloween. They could simply reach inside your chest, grab your heart, and *yank*.

"Can we fight them?" Zach asked.

"I can't believe I'm saying this, but there are too many ghosts to beat at once with brute force." Brittany spun her knives in her hands, eyes focused like a general preparing for war. "We need strategy to turn the numbers. And shelter."

Cara scanned the land—the lake, rows of tombstones, cypresses. Silver glinted in the corners of her vision. Ghosts getting closer. "The gates are shut. We can't outrun them. The only way out is to find a threshold."

But they didn't have time to search the entire graveyard. And there was no shelter that could hide them from beings who could phase through stone and wood like they were nothing.

But she could *make* one.

"I can construct a ghost-repelling barrier," Cara said, thinking out loud. Just like the one outside her house. She needed the materials:

bones, willow, a box of some kind, and most important, time. Her gaze flitted back to the lake, its surface restless with rain. "If memory serves, there's a small mausoleum on a hill beyond the lake." It would be the perfect place. A physical structure to serve as the foundation for the spell. "I'll set up the barrier there while Coleson searches for a threshold. And in that time, Brittany and I'll make a stand."

Hopefully not their *last*.

She turned to Brittany. "Got anything that'll slow down these spirits? And quickly?"

"I just might." Dumping her pack on the ground, Brittany riffled through it.

The ghosts were about two hundred feet away now, pouring from all directions, their individual features sharpening: a woman with hair in a beehive, a little girl with solemn eyes and a missing tooth, a man with a shiny bald head who clutched a briefcase. Eyes beseeching, arms reaching out.

If Cara were strong enough, she could compel them to leave this plane of existence. Her hand stretched out as if of its own accord—then moved to her throat, the bandage, and the cut underneath.

She'd already failed once this morning.

"Got it." Brittany popped open a brown leather case and palmed a black rectangular device about the size of a pack of cigarettes. Wire curled out of the top next to a red button.

Brittany pressed it.

Silver light radiated from the device in circles one after another. They passed through Cara like nothing, wind brushing over her face.

But when they swept through the first ghost, the specter clutched their head and screeched a sound like nails on a chalkboard before dropping to their knees.

"What *is* this?" Cara asked.

The ghost hunter's attention was focused on the spirits, all writhing and wailing in a state of agony. The circles came every few seconds, in steady intervals.

"A sort of ghost EMP. A last resort. It causes a ton of pain to the shades in its radius by disrupting the very particles of their ectoplasm, which isn't as humane as we try to be. And its radius is seven hundred and fifty meters, so we try not to use it in the city, where it can catch innocent spirits in its net."

The ghost EMP went silent, silver circles fading away.

"Okay, now we gotta set up the barrier." Brittany slid the EMP back into her bag. "After that blast, all of the spirits should be too wracked with pain to try attacking us. But the effects of the EMP aren't forever, and the higher-level ghosts overcome them first."

The mausoleum was small, cramped, and airless, perhaps ten by fifteen feet. Cara had half-heartedly hoped they might spot a threshold on the way, but of course it wasn't that easy.

She'd collected three twigs from the weeping willow. Brittany had supplied the box—an empty Nutri-Grain bar container—and bones.

"What kind do you need?" Brittany asked, searching through her pack as if Cara had asked for a stick of gum in class.

"Ideally, human, but—"

Brittany thrust three small bones at her.

Cara stared. "Where did you get—?"

"You don't want to know."

Now Cara bent on the floor, constructing the barrier. It took time, and her memory was weaker than she would have liked. She hadn't had to fully make a barrier since she was eight; she'd only had to replenish the one around her house. Brittany was pacing around the perimeter of the mausoleum, keeping an eye out, which did nothing for Cara's nerves.

She was almost done when a hand erupted from the ground and grabbed her ankle.

Cara gasped, dropping the bones with a clatter and jerking back. The fingers held on, emerging farther.

Unsheathing her knife, Cara swiped at the fingers with short, frantic strokes. They flopped to the ground as what must have been the body's other hand shot up, too, latching on to Cara's calf. Slowly, the spirit pulled itself out of the earth, stretching its stump toward Cara's face.

Its mouth gaped open. *"Hel—"*

"Brittany!" Cara screamed.

In a flash, the spirit was gone, and Brittany was standing over her, extending a hand to help her up.

"Thanks," Cara panted. She could still feel the imprint of dead fingers on her skin. "I slashed at it, but it didn't disappear."

"You gotta go for the heart. Anything else, the specter can survive without. Manifest again, regrowing limbs or heads."

"The heart?"

"Where the heart used to be," Brittany amended. "It's kinda like a shortcut. Stabbing its not-heart stabs the thing most important to the ghost, the thing keeping it on Earth. Severs its ties to this plane. How many blows it takes depends on the specter's willpower, though. Level five hundreds—spirits strong enough to touch humans when it's not Halloween—could resist. This was a weak four hundred. Which means the five hundreds have already recovered from the EMP, too—it's just a matter of time until they reach us."

Class As.

And without ghost-speaking abilities, this was how ghost hunters forced them to pass on. "It hurts them, doesn't it?"

Brittany regarded Cara, seeming to understand what she was getting at. "It has to. Nothing on Earth wants to leave. Everyone wants to stay at the party. Keep the fun going.

"But it helps me to think of it like not letting a drowning man drown you, too. These ghosts are dead. They just don't know it yet."

More hands were shooting through the ground now, grasping, searching. In the time it took for Cara to reach for her knife again, Brittany had amputated them all in one fell swoop of her blade. When the handless spirits continued to emerge, Brittany cursed, destroying them one after another in seconds.

Silver dissolved into air.

"I'm glad you're on our team," Cara said. "And that I'm not a ghost."

Brittany smiled. "Me too."

And then spirits began to melt through the walls of the mausoleum.

There was no time to finish the barrier now. She and Brittany shifted into fighting stances, back to back.

The effect of so many ghosts, jostling over each other, was dizzying. So many body parts blurring together. One specter's wide eye becoming another's. A nose overlaying a nose. Chests intersecting, not one beating heart between them.

Within minutes, Cara's arm ached, her shoulder already becoming stiff. Time blurred, the world narrowing to this tiny gray room. As soon as she took down one ghost, another took its place. The wave seemed endless. Not-heart after not-heart after not-heart, she dissolved spirits with her blade, until there were only a few left.

In a way, her mother might have been proud of her, taking down spirits in such a manner. Ghosts were no trouble when they were gone.

Fingers dug into her shoulder. A mouth at her ear. "*Help . . . us,*" Cara heard the specter whisper just as she dissipated it.

Help? Help how? And why?

A hand took her elbow, and she whirled, ghoststeel aimed for the spirit's heart. The spirit's other hand shot out to grab her wrist, stopping her.

Zach.

Cara stared at him, speechless, her breath frozen in her chest. She'd moved automatically to destroy him. She'd been so worried about him disappearing while she wasn't there, and here she'd almost—*she'd almost*—

"If you wanted me gone, Tang, you could have just said so." Zach's tone was teasing, but it had the opposite effect.

If he hadn't been strong enough to touch her, if he hadn't known her so well he could anticipate her every movement, then she would have killed him for good.

"Don't *joke* like that." She wrenched away from him and stalked to the box with the willow and bones. The wave of spirits had been taken care of, mostly thanks to Brittany, and Cara intended to put up the barrier before the next wave came.

Cara could feel Zach's confusion, but he didn't follow up. Instead, he said, standing behind her, "There's no threshold."

Cold stole over her.

"Then we're stuck here," she said, her words sinking with finality. Even if they managed to defeat the rest of the ghosts, there would be no way to the Snake afterward. "Unless defeating the ghosts reveals the threshold."

"What about compelling?" Zach said. "Can't you get them to leave? That was the last thing the miner said before I dispatched him. You tried to make them cross."

"Then you know it didn't work. I failed."

"Why didn't it work?"

Because I refused to learn ghost speaking from Laolao, and now I'm paying for it.

Her fingers moved over the bones, checking the pattern they were laid in. "Because their willpower was stronger than mine. I couldn't make them leave."

Zach laughed. The sound was steady and sunlit and real, a miracle in the gloom of the mausoleum.

"Your willpower was weaker than theirs? I don't believe that for a second. Tang, you could will a mountain to move if you wanted to."

If she wanted to.

The barrier shimmered into existence.

Cara stood, surveying it. She could already tell how weak it was, hasty and constructed from randomly found materials. It wouldn't last long.

And indeed, when the third wave of ghosts came, the spell caved in, invisible protection torn to shreds by the force of so many dead pressing against it. The barrier was normally unseen, but under such direct attack, it shimmered in the air like a heat patch, wavering under the assault. Tiny bits of it tattered away at once, like moths eating holes into a curtain, and the spirits forced their hands and then arms through it, widening the gaps.

Cara, Zach, and Brittany stood back to back against the wave as spirits poured into the small mausoleum.

No threshold. No way out. No way to defeat the ghosts.

Zach's hand in hers. She couldn't grip it, but still, it steadied her, and this time she was the one drawing strength from him.

"You can do this," he said, not a single drop of doubt in his voice.

He sounded so confident that, for a moment, she believed it herself.

What was there left to lose?

Cara closed her eyes. She drew a breath, stale air filling her lungs.

Go for the heart. She could do this—*if she wanted to.*

When she opened her eyes, the ghosts sharpened into focus. Everything else blurred. Marble ceiling into wall into floor. Inconsequential to the dead.

A small boy jostled to the front. When he grabbed for her, fingers sticky with candy eaten long ago, or perhaps blood, she grabbed on, too, leaning down to look him in his lightless eyes.

The hairs on the back of her neck, her arms, raised. Something thrumming inside her. A melody, like the one the Pied Piper played to lead all the children out of town.

When she reached for this spirit's heart—not with a knife, but with her mind—she felt what anchored him to this plane. He'd gotten lost long ago, and now he'd been wandering for centuries, looking for his mother. A scared little boy, wanting to go home.

"*It's time to go,*" she told him, her voice gentle and firm all at once, resonating as if from the depths of a limitless black cave. "*Your mother is not in this world but what's beyond.*"

And once she found what anchored him, she didn't need to sever him from this place; she needed to heal him until the pain no longer bound him.

He nodded, eyes squeezing shut. His straw-colored hair fluttered in the breeze like corn silk—and then he was fading, form disappearing as if with the wind. "I'll see Mama," he whispered, and then his whisper was gone, too.

The ghosts had quieted. One by one, they stepped forward, taking Cara's hands. She didn't have to fight them; she didn't need to. Their willpower twined with hers: a desire to leave.

And one by one, Cara helped them cross over.

The cemetery emptied, ghosts melting away like snow in spring, until there was one left, a young woman whose auburn hair spilled over the shoulders of her coffee-colored trench coat, a single bullet hole in her stomach.

"Thank you," she said, and went.

Then there was nothing but the rain, pouring down on the peaceful earth outside the mausoleum's entrance, and Cara, sinking to the ground as silently as a leaf drifting from a branch in autumn.

Her fingers touched something solid for the first time in what seemed like eternity—the marble floor. Adrenaline washed through her, and she closed her eyes, expecting exhaustion, but none came.

It seemed helping ghosts wasn't nearly as hard as fighting them. It had taken some energy, but it had also given her energy back. She felt calm in a way she hadn't in twelve years. As if putting these dead to rest had put something inside her at peace, too.

"Well, shit!" Brittany clapped Cara on the back, grinning. "Why'd you wait so long to pull out that trick, ghost talker?"

Cara glanced at Zach before looking back to Brittany. "Because before, I didn't know I could."

"I did." Zach knelt to meet her level, grinning at her. Pride shone in his eyes. "Told you no one can match you when it comes to willpower."

She let herself take him in. The effects of his ghoststeel wound appeared to be gone; the horror of seeing his own funeral, as well. His smile was open and unfettered, transforming his face like sunlight painting the walls of a tomb gold. She wanted to keep him like this. Preserve him like a photograph and never let him fade.

"No one can match me, huh?" She smirked. "Does that include you?"

His smile deepened. "Maybe I can," he conceded, "but I'd be hard-pressed."

The ground shifted.

It was not a rumble so much as a sigh, something settling back into place. Cara jerked to her feet in alarm, Zach automatically putting out a hand to steady her.

Outside the mausoleum, the graveyard was remaking itself.

Their hill sank and flattened out; in the distance, the land swelled as new hills hauled themselves into existence. The lake evaporated in an instant, grass rolling over newly dry land. The iron gates were gone, replaced by a crumbling stone wall that didn't look more than a few feet high. Trees bled into the blank space outside the graveyard grounds, a wild, thicketed forest. The closest gravestones had grown older, moss nestling itself more staunchly into the cracked markers.

"It's not raining anymore," Brittany said, and Cara realized the sensation of water falling through her skin had stopped.

And a few feet away, an abandoned church materialized, its weathered walls falling down, a threshold glowing in the entryway.

"That asshole river," Zach muttered. "Making us work for it."

Cara knew without looking that Zach's gravestone had disappeared—a grave that had never been his. This had never been the Autumn Falls cemetery. This was the resting place for a town whose name she did not know, and those had been its ghosts. To help the spirits of Autumn Falls, she'd have to return home.

She glanced at Zach.

But to help this one, there was one more place left to go.

TWENTY-EIGHT

The last threshold brought them to a veil of vines. Warm, humid air engulfed them like a breath from the rainforest itself, scented with loam and mineral-tinged water. Pink-throated flowers, faces dusted with pollen, blossomed across the emerald veil, which swayed with the breeze. Beyond, the river's rich voice beckoned.

"This is it," Brittany said, eyes charged with excitement, holding up the map. The icon for the Ouroboros glinted, outlined with gold. "This is where my gran stood. This is where we'll find the Snake."

Anxious thoughts crisscrossed Cara's mind and tightened around her ribs like vines, making it hard to breathe. She found herself looking at Zach for reassurance. For support. Because for better or for worse, they'd made this journey together and survived, and he'd been by her side the whole time.

She found him looking back at her, the glow of his ghost form turning the surroundings a little more haunted, a little more lovely.

The fire in her chest pulsed hotter, and the vines wrapped around her heart blackened and fell away.

"Ready?" Zach said.

Cara nodded. "It's time," she said to Zach and Brittany.

Together, they stepped through.

The rainforest opened up beneath their feet.

They stood on the edge of a rocky cliff. Just inches to their right rushed the river, so loud the force of its power rumbled through the stone under Cara's shoes. It spilled over the precipice into a waterfall that ended in a wide pool below, ringed with trees and vines. Mist unfurled from the surface, thin and ephemeral, and when it brushed across Cara's face, her heart skipped a beat as she recalled the fog. But this touch was gentle as a kiss, leaving only a sheen of water droplets behind.

Magic suffused the air. She could *feel* it on her skin, like silk, the same way she had in the meadow. This was a place of warmth, of light, of creation. Something primordial. It felt like they'd walked to the end of the world to get here, but at the same time, she had the sense she was standing where it had all begun.

And then there were the birds.

Swift, small, jewel-toned, sapphire and emerald and burning amber, ruby and russet, violet and amethyst. They dove, wheeled, clipped through the waterfall, darting out shining even brighter than before. Their wings sliced a constant susurrus through the dusk, a hum of high voices that never stopped, only rose and dipped like the creatures themselves. Their crystal tones, sharp and clear and sweet, created a kind of balanced cacophony, a bright orchestra of chaos.

To Cara's left, wide steps made of packed earth spiraled to the pool level, descending at a shallow incline.

Brittany grinned at Zach and Cara. "Race you there," she said.

"We didn't come here just to break an ankle!" Cara protested, but she was speaking to empty air. Zach and Brittany had already taken off.

Grumbling, she joined them at the water's edge a minute later, the shore's small chalky rocks crunching underfoot. Zach and Brittany were still arguing about who had won.

"My foot touched the bottom of the steps first."

"If you don't stop lying, Casper, I really will stab you with my ghoststeel."

Zach glanced at Cara, a smile touching his lips. "You'll protect me, right?"

She did a double take. She could no longer see through him—he was corporeal, looking almost alive again. Her heart clenched. *It must be the magic here.*

In a fit of impulsivity, she grabbed his hand and intertwined her fingers with his. "Nah," she said in answer to his question. "Brittany, feel free to take him out if he's getting too annoying."

It was worth it just to see his mouth fall open. Zach closed it, swallowed, then opened his mouth, but still nothing came out. He seemed to have forgotten how to speak.

Brittany's eyes went to their interlocked hands. She grinned and nodded knowingly, and Cara pretended not to see it.

Something splashed in the water.

The pool's surface glimmered like a mirror, not showing what was beneath. It could have been five feet deep or fifty. Except for the disturbance caused by the cascading waterfall, the rest of the pool was curiously calm, not a single ripple to be seen.

But just as the thought went through Cara's head, something flashed near the waterfall. Scales the color of midnight.

More and more ripples fanned out across the surface. Something was coming. Something large—and fast.

They all moved backward, giving the creature space. *A lot* of space.

Gradually, a serpent's diamond-shaped head emerged from the

water, and then its neck, and then its body, and then its body, *and then its body*. It was endless—too unfathomable to truly exist. At last, with a rasp of scales against stone, it slithered onto shore, gathering all of itself on land, glistening in sinewy coils the color of night. It gazed down at them with eyes that were startingly all white, save for a black slash of pupil in the center.

"Back again so soon?" it asked, voice as cool and fluid as the pool itself.

"Uh," Cara said, her practiced greeting disappearing completely from her mind. She had to crane her neck to meet the Snake's eyes. "We're not. Back, that is. I'm Cara Tang, a . . . ghost speaker."

The words—those simple two words that had defined her whole life but that she'd never felt ready to claim—hung in the air like smoke, expanding to fill the space and echoing all the more so after she'd closed her mouth. Even the birds seemed to be listening now, repeating the name to each other as they sang back and forth like a fascinating new melody.

Ghost speaker, ghost speaker, ghost speaker—

Zach gave her hand a reassuring squeeze, then smoothly picked up where she had left off. "I'm Zacharias Coleson." His voice was oiled with confidence and charm; he had shifted back into the Zach who talked to adults like he was their peer, who convinced teachers into letting him get away with breaking rules. The difference now was, Cara found his confidence reassuring rather than annoying. "And you must be the other Signet Snake. I guess you could say we've been dying to meet you."

Brittany stepped forward. She bowed her head, and when she spoke, every word was brimming with wonder. "I'm Brittany Livingston. My gran told me stories as a kid about how she found you once.

You gave her blood. You gave her—and the rest of the city—a new way to fight. To live. I've dreamed of meeting you ever since."

The Snake could show no expression on her face, but Cara had the faint sense she was merely humoring their silly little human ritual. When Brittany finished her introduction, the Snake did not speak at first but slithered forward. The great black serpent was relatively slender, as the other Snake had been—not something built to constrict but to lunge forward and bite. Still, she circled around and around them in ever-tightening coils until Cara felt dizzy turning her head to follow.

Finally, mist eddying around her belly, the Snake came to a stop mere inches from Cara's face. The slash of each Stygian pupil was as tall as an obelisk, and the whole of Cara's reflection stared back at her from the serpent's emotionless eyes. The Snake could have opened her mouth and swallowed her whole. Cara's blood rushed as the serpent's forked onyx tongue flickered out, tasting the air.

"Is it gonna turn into a person, too?" Zach muttered. Cara elbowed him.

Just when Cara's heart threatened to burst from sheer stress, the Snake spoke.

"I must have mistaken you for another human, then. My apologies—you have the same eyes."

Cara blinked. "Apology accepted," she replied, not knowing how else to respond.

The Snake receded a degree, gazing down at them. A sheen of water clung to her scales, which glimmered at times in the light but only in shades of black: raven and pitch, tar and ink.

"You have journeyed far to meet me, though you did not mean to. You have been exceedingly brave, though you did not wish to. And you have something to ask of me, something that would change your fates."

Cara shivered. The Snake's words carried the weight of centuries, of power unseen yet power still the same, secretly shifting the scales behind the scenes.

Cara glanced at Brittany, who gave her a nod.

"I've got a little more time to spare than you do," Brittany said. "You're up first."

But when Cara began to tell the story of why they were here for Zach's resurrection, the Snake stopped her.

"I know everything already. I've felt the vibration of every step of your journey, each small shift in the universe that you have created."

Zach and Cara looked at each other.

"Oh. So you already know why we've come," Cara said. "To ask you for the antivenom."

A wet membrane slid over the serpent's eyes. Pinpricks of light glinted in them like tiny stars.

"You have overcome trial after trial," she said, "and have been worthy enough to arrive." Her voice was rich as poisoned wine, aged in darkness and dripping with power. When she spoke, her words didn't simply reach Cara's ears but washed over her whole, thrumming through her head and body. "But what you seek is the last test of worthiness. Are you ready to receive the venom, ghost speaker?"

It seemed surreal that after this long journey, all they wanted was here. The black Snake's venom, antidote and antivenom to the white Snake's poison.

Cara opened her mouth, but Zach blurted, "Hold on. You're just giving it to us? You're not going to try to kill us or ask for something impossible like, I don't know, a giant egg made of gold or some shi—"

"Coleson," Cara hissed. "Shut up."

He turned to her. "I've heard my parents discussing art contracts with their lawyers. There's always a catch." Eyes on the Snake, he said, "Your companion *killed* me, so sorry if I'm a little distrustful."

The Snake didn't appear offended. Calmly she said, "Then you will find it reassuring to know that I am nothing like my other half. After all, that is the thesis of his and my existence. We were made to be opposites yet equals. Destruction and creation, life and death. Yin and yang. We maintain the balance of the world. Where he goes, decay follows. And I come after, reversing what he has ruined before time runs out." She slithered nearer to Zach, her forked tongue flickering out inches from his face. "And *you* have very little time left."

Cara drew a breath. "Could you tell us—?"

"One hour, forty-two minutes." The snake's tongue flickered in, out. "To be exact."

She, Brittany, and Zach exchanged worried glances. In less than two hours, Zach could be dead. For good.

"Now," said the Snake, "I will ask again. Are you ready to receive the venom, ghost speaker?"

"Yes, I am," Cara said, hoping the Snake couldn't smell her fear, and let go of Zach's hand to dig through her pack.

But the serpent laughed when she pulled out the vial, procured from the Library of Memories. Her expression barely changed, and yet laughter wound through the air like mist, intangible but unmistakable. "You won't need that," she said. "*You* are the vial."

"What?" said Zach before Cara could comprehend the serpent's words.

The Snake canted her head at him. "The ghost speaker doesn't inject the antivenom into your body. The ghost speaker receives the antivenom herself, and should she live, she will be able to harness the power imbued in my antivenom to bring something dead back to life."

"*Should she live?*" Zach repeated.

It made perfect sense, in an awful sort of way. The ghost speaker would be bitten by a Signet Snake to obtain the power to resurrect the ghost, who was a ghost because of a bite from the other Signet Snake.

That was the catch.

It didn't stop Cara's throat from closing up and the earth from suddenly feeling unstable beneath her. She gripped the vial so hard she thought it might break, her heart hammering in panic—but when she opened her palm, the glass had gone liquid, dripping to the shore.

Well, she didn't need it anyway.

Zach's hands clenched into fists, and he moved between her and the Snake. "It could *kill* her."

"The antivenom is the test and also the reward," the Snake replied, unblinking even as Zach tensed, anger drawing cords of muscle taut in his shoulders. "If she is worthy enough—if she is strong enough— she will live. A ghost speaker that cannot survive the antivenom would not be able to survive the subsequent act of resurrecting the dead."

If the Snake had hoped to pacify him, it had the opposite effect. "That's *bullshit*," Zach said in a dangerous voice, and took a step toward the serpent. Brittany put out an arm to stop him, but he shook her off.

Cara couldn't focus on him. Her heart was hammering in her chest. This was the moment, wasn't it? When she decided whether or not to prove her mother wrong. To embrace the magic in her veins. Every step on the quest had brought her here, introducing her to friends she never imagined, fire magic she didn't know she had, and defeating monsters she didn't think she'd be able to fight before. This was just the final step. What had been waiting for her all along, at the end of it all.

And anyway, she'd been judged and found unworthy by her mother her entire life, and it hadn't killed her. Whatever this antivenom did, it couldn't compare.

"I'll do it," Cara said. Her voice shook, but she said again, louder, "I'll do it."

Zach stopped arguing with the Snake and turned to her. She couldn't read his face. She'd known him all her life, and she didn't know what he'd say until he said, "That's not happening."

Fire sparked in her veins. "I'm sorry, I thought we were done with you telling me what to do."

He was shaking his head, not even listening to her. "We'll find some other way. I'm not letting you—"

"Find some other way? There is no other way, Coleson!" Cara stepped closer. "We spent an entire week trying to get here. We traveled all this way—during which I nearly *died*, in case you forgot—and now you want to just turn around and *give up*?"

He flinched like she'd slapped him.

"I haven't forgotten, and I never will," he said in a low voice. "What I'm saying is I can't let you risk your life for me again."

When she didn't say anything, he went on, "Listen, if this is about the money, I'll give it to you. The password to my account and everything."

The money. She'd just said she would risk *dying* for him—and he assumed it was because she was determined to get paid. That was what he thought of her. Something sharp twisted inside her chest.

Because it wasn't about the money, if it had ever been. She knew that now.

But she had to let him keep believing it so he didn't get close to the truth.

"You truly think that'll work?" Cara replied scathingly. "Transfers have time stamps. They'll find your body. They'll go through anything and everything related to you and your disappearance, and they'll see that, somehow, you managed to transfer a large amount of money after you died. Then they'll question me, and they'll seize the money, too. They'll blame me for your death. *It won't work.*" She folded her arms. "I have to let it bite me."

"But—"

"What's more, I made you a *promise*, Coleson," Cara continued. "I promised I'd help you. Do whatever is required as a ghost speaker. But now you're willing to die? Did you already forget how frightened you were of disappearing this morning? That's what's waiting for you if I don't do this! The only reason you're even corporeal right now is because of the magic here!"

And there was her fear again—the fear *she'd* felt when he vanished. The shock of it had been a physical blow to the chest.

All she knew was that she couldn't let that happen again.

Zach raked his hands through his hair. "Did you not hear the part where the Snake said you could *die*? Why doesn't that matter to you? Why are you so ready to risk your life for me?"

"Because—"

Because she loved him.

The realization came to her like light in a shadowed room, the shape of it revealing itself line by line, starlit and undeniable. Perhaps it had appeared a moment ago. Or perhaps it had been before her for some time, and her eyes had only just adjusted.

Somehow, somewhere along the way, the strings between them had sunk into her skin, and she'd gotten attached. He was threaded into the fiber of her being so intricately, so deeply, that to tear him out would be to tear out some vital piece of herself.

Deep down, she must have known it, like how she'd known the Snake's blood was slowly poisoning her. A love that lived in her veins, messed with her head and her heart.

Because I can't lose you.

But she couldn't tell him that. The truth thudded in her ears, sure as her own pulse, and she couldn't let him hear it. Not when he thought she was still doing this for the money. Not when the reason he tended her wounds, protected her, sacrificed for her, was because he needed her to raise him from the dead. Not when there were only two ways this could end: failure, which meant they both died for good, or success, which meant returning him to his own world, one of chandeliers and champagne, where there was no reason for them to hold hands or stay by each other's side.

Let him think her callous. Cold. Caring solely about getting what she was due.

As long as he was alive.

"Because of the money, of course," Cara replied. "You said so yourself. Don't mistake it for anything else—it's *strictly business.*"

Zach's face went tight.

It was their fight at the Library of Memories all over again, where she wasn't sure if she was winning, what winning even entailed.

But she was sure of what she didn't want to lose.

A hiss floated across the stony shore. "Your time runs short, ghost."

Cara moved closer to him, tilting her chin up calmly. "There's nothing for you to lose if I let the Snake bite me. Either we gain the key to bringing you back or—or it fails and you fade, but that's no different than how you are right now. So why are *you* so against something that might save you?"

Zach opened his mouth. "I—" He stopped, the muscles of his throat moving as he swallowed. "Because I—"

She hadn't known how much she'd been hoping to hear him say he cared about her until the words didn't come. A stupid thing to hope for. Chest going cold, she stepped back, watched him try again, hands gesturing at the air helplessly, and then she turned to the Snake.

Cara held out her wrist. "I'm ready."

"As you say, ghost speaker," the Snake replied. And she began to shrink, smaller and smaller until she was the size the first one had been, small enough to wrap herself around Cara's wrist and open her jaws to bite. Somewhere behind her, Brittany made a sound of awe.

"*Wait*," Zach said, and Cara looked back at him. In the light, his blue eyes were wild and filled with something she couldn't name. "Tang, I—"

The Snake sank her fangs through Cara's skin, and she screamed. Two points of pain burned through her from the punctures on her wrist, radiating outward until it overtook her whole body, until pain was the only thing she could feel. The world was rapidly shrinking, darkening, or maybe it was just the Snake returning to her former size, eclipsing the light. Maybe both.

Cara's knees buckled, and she fell. Someone caught her before she hit the ground—*Zach*, she thought.

Ice burned through her veins. She could feel the antivenom coursing through her blood, racing to her heart, her brain. The cries of the birds overhead faded out. Cara struggled to keep her eyes open—but even that seemed impossible. She parted her lips, fighting to speak.

"*Zach*," she said breathlessly.

His hand gripped hers. "I'm here," he said, and that was the last thing she was sure of before everything turned to fire.

TWENTY-NINE

She burned like a forest after a July lightning strike.

She burned like an oil spill too close to a spark.

She burned like a torch: down, down, down.

Cara didn't lose consciousness. Instead, she was *too* conscious. She could feel her blood moving through her body, each of her veins constricting and spasming as the antivenom tore through her system. Her pulse roared in her ears, blocking out all else. Gravity crushed her lungs; she gasped for breath; she feared she'd sink right through the ground, all the way to the Earth's core.

But the pain was worse than all that. The pain was worse than the wounds the fog had opened on her skin, worse than the miner's knife cutting into her throat, worse than the white Snake's venom. It lit up every single one of her nerves, white-hot pain that pressed against her lids and blinded her to color and movement and sound and anything that wasn't this all-encompassing hell.

She burned and burned and burned, until she simply blazed down to ash, and all her senses went silent, and the whiteness knifing through her vision turned black.

Dark and quiet.

She was grateful for this darkness. She could float here, away from a body she no longer needed. The universe did not care about her; she was inconsequential in the grand scheme of galaxies colliding and stars dying, and so it would let her go. There had been something important, something so urgent she'd come here to this vast, starless black sky that cradled her consciousness in a soothing embrace, but she'd forgotten what it was. She had forgotten who she was, too, but this did not alarm her. It did not matter. Nothing mattered. She was so tired, even with her eyes closed and pitch-black silence muffling her ears; she wanted to rest. She wanted to sleep forever.

But there was someone saying her name.

Or at least, what had been her name, when she'd had one. She was annoyed. Whoever this person was, annoyance seemed to be an emotion she'd frequently associated with them. They had no right to bother her, not when she was drifting in this dream space, so close to letting go. She could feel rather than hear each one of her last heartbeats, unsteady and slow and winking out like stars.

In the midst of all her darkness, the voice was a slice of light. A silver thread shining against the tapestry enfolding her, a lifeline she could hold. Despite herself, she strained toward it.

"Come back to me," the voice was begging, again and again and again. "Cara, *please*. I—I need you, okay? *Come back to me. Please.*"

And so she did.

Cara gasped for air. The burning in her chest eased, as if she hadn't been breathing, and every part of her ached with some deep, indescribable pain. She groaned.

"Oh, *thank God*," Zach's voice said. "Tang? Can you hear me?"

With great difficulty, she opened her eyes. Zach gazed down at her, deep creases drawn between his furrowed brows. Wordlessly, she lifted a hand, smoothed out the lines on his worried face. "I—" Her throat was hoarse from screaming. She swallowed, licked her lips, tried again. "I wish I couldn't."

He let out a sigh, his shoulders slumping. "I really hate you," he told her, and yeah, maybe Cara wasn't as good at reading him as she'd thought, but his fingers were intertwined with hers and he'd said it with a smile, so it was possible he didn't completely mean it.

"How—how long was I—?" Cara started to ask.

Brittany popped into her vision, pressing a button on a bulky black wristwatch. "Twenty-two minutes."

In the black space where she'd been, twenty-two minutes had been nothing.

"The longest twenty-two minutes of my life," Zach murmured.

Cara blinked up at him, furrowing her brow as she tried to remember what she'd just gone through. Hazy recollections of pain swirled in her mind, gauzy as smoke, slipping through her fingers when she tried to catch them.

But there was one thing she remembered.

"You said my first name," she whispered.

"You said mine first."

"No, I didn't," she insisted automatically, even as the memory of it solidified.

Zach bit his lip as he struggled to hold back a laugh. His fingers brushed across her skin, pushing a sweaty lock of hair from her face. But the only thing he said was, "Okay, Tang," so tenderly she could barely take it.

Brittany's voice cut in between them. "I'm glad you're all right, and I hate to interrupt y'all, but isn't the clock counting down? Zach's not alive yet."

Crap. Cara tried to sit up, and that was when her brain finally realized where she was: in Zach's arms. In his *lap*.

"Can you stand?" Zach asked.

When Cara nodded, he tightened his arms around her, then rose. He set her down, but as she slid out of his arms, he caught her hand once more, not letting her go completely. Warmth flooded from her chest to her fingertips.

His touch anchored her as the Snake, who had apparently been patiently waiting the entire time, slithered closer. "Congratulations, ghost speaker," she said. "How do you feel?"

Cara held up her arm where the snake had bit her. Color stuttered under her skin, a kaleidoscope of blue and scarlet and gold, snaking through her veins. As she watched, the hues blurred, flickered, and faded, leaving smooth tan skin, punctuated only by two pinpricks at the base of her right wrist.

She opened her mouth to answer, *In pain*, but then stopped. Sometime between waking up and now, that pain had ebbed away completely.

The more seconds passed, the better she felt, the antivenom bracing her from the inside out, sharpening her vision into high definition, ratcheting up the vividness of her surroundings. The birds glinted above, shouts of color almost too bright to look at.

She stretched out a hand and called her fire.

A flame leaped from her palm, stretching several feet into the air, the largest she'd made with that little effort. Beside her, Zach swore quietly, and Brittany whistled. Her fire burned an intense orange, a color pulled from the heart of the sun, heat fanning out like a lion's mane. With this, she'd have been able to melt the miner's knife in seconds, not minutes.

Cara met the Snake's eyes. "I feel great."

The Snake inclined her head. "The rest is up to you now, ghost speaker. But beware—just because you've survived the antivenom does not mean a resurrection is guaranteed. Or perhaps you will succeed in resurrecting him but you overdraw your power and your own heart gives out. Be wise."

"I will," Cara said. "Would you be able to give us a shortcut back home?"

Serpents couldn't smile, but Cara heard it in this one's voice. "That I can do."

The Snake's jaws gaped wide open, and Cara gasped. The whole universe was held in the great serpent's mouth, an inky galaxy swirling behind her fangs, planets and stars suspended in perpetual night. Then she bit down. Her fangs slashed through the air like it was gauze, something diaphanous, rending two ragged gaps hovering inches above the ground. Scenery shifted in the narrow tears of air—a portal to the ocean one moment; a desert landscape, the next.

"Whoa," said Zach. He strode up to one, reaching out a hand as if to stick it through, then seemed to think better of it.

"These will take you back home," the Snake said, and the gaps changed to show the Wildwoods, trees shrouded in snow. "I'll do the same for you," she told Brittany. "Once I grant your gift."

Zach surveyed the portals, hands on his hips. "Sure would have made things a lot easier if the first Snake had opened a portal to the antidote for us."

The Snake stiffened. "A thousand years ago, he could have, but he has lost that ability." Her tail thrashed. "Although I doubt he would have torn open space for your benefit even if he were able to. He enjoys being a stick lodged in the wheel of civilization, holding everything back. Or better yet, being the kerosene to set the whole wagon on fire.

He'd help build a city higher just to engineer a downfall all that more glorious. If he holds out a hand, it is to push you down and lift himself to where he wants to be. No, he would not have made it so easy to escape death as to rend a portal directly to the antidote for you."

Cara glanced down at the Ouroboros on her wrist before clamping a hand over it, as if by not seeing it, she wouldn't have to think about it. He'd given them passage to the liminal world, but only because she had bribed him and even then it had almost killed her. She wanted to believe that was the last of his impact, but the Creation Serpent's words rang in her head like a warning bell.

"Once, he was not this bad. If he destroyed, it was to maintain the balance, not to feed his own ego. The two of us worked in tandem, reminding humanity of the lines they walk between life and death. We were revered, written into history and lore. The humans—they turned us into the caduceus of Hermes. Do you know who that is?"

"The messenger god in Greek mythology," Brittany offered.

"Yes, hunter. He was the god of boundaries. As the only Olympian able to traverse the border between the living and the dead, he conducted souls of the deceased into the underworld. The Greeks gave him a caduceus: a staff with two snakes entwined around it, a symbol of polar elements in equilibrium. If it touched the dying, they would pass peacefully, but if it touched the dead, they were resurrected."

"All right, wait," said Zach. "I've had to believe a lot of wild stuff lately, but come on—you're not saying Greek gods are real?"

A laugh hissed out from the Snake. "Humans make up stories to comfort themselves about their fleeting lives, to pass the remainder of their mortality, to make sense of a world of chaos and fire. We did not come from myths. The myths came from *us*." She tilted her head toward the sky. In her glassy eyes, prismatic birds cut through mist.

"We used to choose which way the world spun. We used to influence kings and queens."

Zach, Cara, and Brittany exchanged looks.

"What changed?" Brittany said.

"The world shifted, and so did we." Her coils tightened, and she withdrew into herself, a defensive behavior. "He began involving himself with humankind to a degree that was unforgivable. When that black-hearted ghost speaker gave him that ring, he became even worse. While I—I have stayed here all these eons, waiting for travelers such as yourselves. For I have not forgotten what I was made for."

The ring the Destruction Ouroboros treasured so much—that had been from a ghost speaker? Cara wanted to stay and learn more, but they had to go. Still, she couldn't help asking. "And what was that?"

The Snake's eyes were as cold as stars. "For the end of the world."

A chill ran down Cara's spine.

"I hope to see you there," the Snake said. "Farewell for now, ghost speaker."

Cara bowed her head, to which the Snake inclined her head in return. "Thank you for all your help."

She turned to Brittany. "I guess this is where we say goodbye," Cara said. Finality thrummed in her bones, the ache of missing a friend before they'd even parted. "I'm glad you jumped on to our quest when you did," she said. "If you hadn't, well, Zach and I would definitely have been in trouble. You're a lifesaver. Literally."

Brittany grinned, holding out her arms. "Tell me about it," she said, and Cara hugged her fiercely.

When Cara stepped back, Brittany pressed something into her hand. A piece of paper.

"My contact info," Brittany explained, "in case you have a ghostie problem you need help with. Also"—she nodded at Zach—"I gotta know how this all turns out." She leaned in, whispering into Cara's ear: "I swear on my steel, if you let him get away after forcing me to third-wheel y'all for the past several days, I *will* show up at your house to personally kick your ass."

Cara's mouth dropped open. Jerking back, she darted a look at Zach to make sure he hadn't heard, then back at Brittany, who just grinned and held out her hand for a fist bump.

"Let's make our grandmothers proud," Brittany said.

Cara nodded, bumping fists. "Let's make our grandmothers proud," she echoed, believing the words for once.

"Come here, Casper," Brittany said, opening her arms.

When Brittany and Zach hugged, a hot, buzzing sensation ignited in Cara's gut, and when she realized it was jealousy, despite the fact that they were just saying goodbye, she knew she was in trouble.

Brittany whispered something in Zach's ear. He reddened and withdrew.

The ghost hunter grinned like the devil. "Off you go, kids," she said. "Cara, take care of that knife—it's a good one. Make sure you give it a name. And Casper, remember what I told you."

Zach coughed, the tips of his ears still crimson against the silver. "Yep," he said, his voice gruff.

What had Brittany told him? Cara shook off the question. The Snake was watching them, and time was ticking down.

"Stay safe," Cara said to Brittany, then turned to Zach. "I'll see you on the other side," she told him.

The rip in the universe churned invitingly. Wind blew loose strands of hair back from her face. Behind her, scales slithered across shore, and the Snake said to Brittany, "You have followed in your grandmother's steps. You seek the power to see the dead so that you may vanquish vengeful spirits who have lingered too long. And if I give what is of my flesh, you will help keep the balance between the living and the dead. Swear to me this is true."

"A blood oath?" Brittany didn't hesitate, scrambling for a container from her backpack. "I swear it—may I be true till the day I die."

Before Cara stepped through the portal, she chanced one look back.

The sight would stay with her for the rest of her life: the crystal-colored birds looping their chromatic song high in the sky above the Creation Ouroboros, leviathan-like body beautiful as myth, as she bent her great sable skull over the black glass bottle Brittany held aloft and, without a sound, began to weep tears of blood.

THIRTY

It was dusk in the woods, and it was snowing faintly. And Cara was alone.

Shouldn't Zach have been here by now? He had been right behind her. Had he messed it up somehow and ended up in an entirely different place? If anyone could mess it up, it would be Zach.

Cara allowed herself one second to close her eyes and take in a breath of the place she loved so much—then checked her watch.

4:22 p.m. Forty-nine minutes left.

She called up a flame, and a sudden wind shrieked through the branches. Boughs rattled, frenzied.

Cara bit back a gasp. A gust tore at her skin, making the fire waver. The trees almost seemed like they were leaning away from her.

From the flame in her hands.

She extinguished the fire and heard the forest exhale.

"It's okay, I won't hurt you." She placed a hand on the bark of the nearest oak. "You knew of my power, and you still let me in. Thank you."

Forty-seven minutes left. She spun, a smaller flame in hand, searching for Zach in the dark.

Just when she was convinced that he had indeed messed it up and was now halfway across the world, the woods shook, another portal ripped open the air, and Zach stepped into existence.

"Sorry," he said when he saw her face. "The Snake had one last thing to tell me."

Cara let out a breath. "You're cutting it close."

"I know," Zach replied, and then his expression grew serious. "She told me I need to step back into my body for you to start resurrecting, but once I do that, I'll be locked into oblivion. If you don't succeed . . . I won't know."

Zach seemed nervous. Like the stakes were finally hitting him. Without the magic from the Snake or Cara's amplification, Zach's form was so see-through the Wildwoods was visible through his translucent chest, his silver dimmed to gray, and she had to reassure herself that he was still there, that there was still time. But it hurt to look at him.

Instead, she nodded and turned to the clearing. Snowflakes floated from the heavens, one at a time, illuminated in shafts of dying golden light. To their left, the river—now a stream again—flowed into the small pool, and to their right stood the tree under which Zach's body lay hidden, surrounded by the analyx. The small red flowers had spread through the entire clearing, peeking out from the snow, so that when she and Zach walked toward the tree, it was like crossing a sea of blood.

Cara raised her arms to break the barrier, recalling those words Laolao had told her a week ago. A lifetime ago.

"Moqiu xianxian—moqiu zi hui." The barrier exploded in a circle of silver light, and when Cara blinked her eyes open, Zach's body was there.

Without a word, Zach stepped toward it.

"Wait." Her voice sounded so plaintive, almost pleading. She cleared her throat. "Not bothering to say goodbye, huh?"

"Why bother when I'll have to say hello right after?" His voice was steady save for the tiniest tremor.

"Zach," she said. A helpless laugh spilled from her lips. If she didn't laugh, then tears might spill out next. "That's not guaranteed. Remember what the Snake said—"

"I don't give a shit about what the Snake said." Zach held her eyes, and despite how faded he was, on the verge of oblivion, this was still him: arrogant and confident and irreverent. His voice softened, and this was him, too, when he said, "I don't need to when I've got you. You helped that hill-monster. You defeated the fog, something you couldn't even touch. And when I couldn't save you in that ghost town, you still came up with a way to save yourself. Something as small as death isn't going to stop you. I trust you, Cara."

She swallowed, looking at him. There was so much she wanted to say to him, so much that she didn't even know how to say. Nothing sounded right, and they were running out of time.

I can't lose you, she thought again. And again, she couldn't say it.

Her fingers trembled at her sides. She longed to touch his face, to hold him, one last time.

"When I found you here, you told me you'd haunt me for the rest of my life," she whispered. "Don't go back on your word. Even if I fail, don't go. Stay and haunt me."

What she was asking was impossible. They both knew it. If he had been felled by anything other than the Snake, he would have been a normal ghost, unfinished matters binding him to Earth, weighing down on him as heavy as gravity. Able to remain for eternity if he wanted. But as it was, he didn't have the choice to linger. Tonight, she would either resurrect him—or something would go wrong, and he would fade away forever.

Zach studied her, his eyes soft and shining. He drew close, one hand reaching out to trace her face, fingers trailing over her skin. His touch was the ice spreading over a lake in winter, the cold light of stars strewn across a night sky. All-encompassing.

A touch that was not a touch. A cold that melted away all too soon.

"If I could have stayed," he said, "I would have stayed for you."

A smile was the last thing he gave her before Zacharias Coleson sat down into his body and closed his eyes.

And then it was just her and a corpse she could barely look at, alone in the snow.

Thirty-nine minutes left. Cara needed both hands for this, not to mention all the energy she could get, which meant releasing her palmful of flame. But with her back to the setting sun, barely a glow on the horizon, she still needed to see. So, kneeling by the body's side, she touched a finger to the analyx like she was lighting a candle.

When it burned to the ground, another sprang up in its place, pushing itself out of the earth with a shudder, only to hiss as it caught fire. In this way, she had infinite fuel for her flame, at least until she brought him back. *Perfect.*

She placed a hand on Zach's chest, right over where his heart should have beat. With the barrier gone, snow drifted onto his body. The snowstorm was nowhere as strong as it had been earlier this week. Even the blizzard was fading.

Resurrecting meant anchoring another's life force to your own. Clearing her mind, Cara imagined a string connecting her to Zach. She could almost see it—that thread glowing red in the darkness, trailing from her heart to his. With it, she could pull his soul back into his body, pinning his consciousness into place.

She took a breath and pulled.

This, Laolao had told her, made the most sense as a method to bring back the dead. A person died when their soul left their body, possibly turning into a ghost. Here, the link between Zach's soul and body had been severed by the venom. With the antivenom of the other Signet Snake, Cara could pull Zach's ghost—what had been his soul—back into his body and tether them together again.

How will I know I've done it? Cara had asked the night they'd returned from putting up the shield around Zach's body in the Wildwoods.

Trust me, Laolao had replied. *You will.*

But as she tugged, a force seemed to tug back, yanking the thread out of her mental grasp. She'd gather energy, and it would be sucked away to some unseen place, like a black hole of magic. She was drawing a pail of water from a well, only to have all the water run out through a crack into the grass.

Her wrist burned; when she pushed back her sleeve, the Ouroboros mark seemed to twist in the afterglow of dusk, seething and hot.

Maybe I'm not trying hard enough.

She curled and uncurled her fingers and tried again. And again. And again. Her breaths came hard, and blasts of wind chilled her skin. The only reasons she hadn't been frozen yet were her fire power and the antivenom hot in her veins.

Next time she pulled, a pain ripped through her.

In tandem, the mark *blazed* on her skin, a miniature black sun imprinted on her flesh.

She cried out. It felt like the effort was drawing life out of her, instead of life back into Zach. She panted. Her ribs ached. Her bones were splinters through her body.

"How is that not enough?" she gasped. Pressing her hands to his chest, she sucked in a ragged breath and tugged once more.

She didn't know what had happened, but this time the thread stayed firmly in her grasp. The only thing was, now there was hardly any energy left in her limbs, like the pail had been mended, but it didn't matter, as only a little water lay at the bottom of the well.

The Snake's voice echoed in her head. *Perhaps you will succeed in resurrecting him but you overdraw your power and your own heart gives out. Be wise.*

To which she thought, in an echo of Zach's words, *I don't care.*

Every tug tore at the walls of her heart, pain radiating with each thrum of her pulse.

But Cara was nothing if not good at digging her heels in, especially when it came to Zacharias Coleson.

I trust you, Cara.

She paused and gasped a breath that was torn to the bone. And then she began again.

Cara tried to visualize the resurrection as she had her flame when she'd first learned how to control it. It was hard; her head spun. But she could see him so clearly in her mind, grinning, golden and whole and *alive*. Maybe she could make this real, if only she tried hard enough. She imagined him breathing, the steady rise and fall of his chest. She imagined him opening his eyes and looking up at her with that smirk of his. She imagined his voice filling the clearing as he said nothing but her name.

I made a promise, she thought. *And I'm not going to break it.*

She pulled and immediately cried out but gritted her teeth and tugged harder, determination coursing through her veins. This couldn't be where it all ended, on her knees by the body of the boy she loved.

She hadn't spent a week in the wilderness for nothing. She didn't have antivenom burning in her veins for nothing. She wasn't ripping apart her own soul for nothing.

The pain wrenched a cry from her lips.

God. It was as though she were being torn in two.

Something trickled from her nose past her mouth. She tasted iron. When she put a hand to her face, her fingers came away red. *Well*, she thought dully, *that can't be a good sign.*

Her insides were on fire. Her back was cold with sweat. Her exhales sent clouds of vapor into the air. And still, she didn't stop.

Zach couldn't just die on her. She needed to keep her promise. She needed to bring him back.

She needed *him*.

At that, she felt the bond latch into place, the knowing feeling of *home* settling into her bones. Her end of the thread no longer tore into her heart, but was a part of it, a connection held tight and sure. When she reached for it, she could sense it leading from her heart to his, shining in the dark.

She let out a breath, folding her hands in her lap.

The fading light found Zach, as it always did, illuminating the angles of his face—his brow, his cheekbones, his mouth. Head tilted back. Hair wet with snow: a golden crown dusted with diamonds.

He looked like a new god, waiting to wake.

"So wake," she whispered.

Her hair had come loose from its ponytail, hanging around her face. Cara brushed strands back and checked her watch.

5:14 p.m. Fifty-two minutes had passed.

Cara swallowed. Slowly, she reached for him, wanting to know but at the same time *not* wanting to know. Her fingers brushed the side of his neck. She forced herself to hold them there, to stay still, to breathe.

Nothing.

Time had run out.

He was gone.

THIRTY-ONE

"*No,*" she whispered, refusing to believe it. She pressed her forehead against his and closed her eyes. Her back ached, and her thighs cramped from kneeling for so long, and despite her fire magic, her fingers tremored with cold, as if her marrow were made of frost. All her energy was gone, sunk into the endeavor of resurrecting him, and now her inner fire burned low, not enough to keep her warm. She was shaking.

"Open your eyes," she said. "Please, Zach. Just open your eyes."

But when she opened her own, he was still dead.

"No," she repeated. "We've come so far. We fought monsters. We got the antivenom. You can't be—*you can't be . . .*" Her throat closed up, and she choked on her words. "Just open your eyes, Zach," she begged again, like he could hear her. "You can't be gone. I—*I need you.*"

She leaned back, reached for the thread again, desperate.

Cara tugged at the bond, but there was no response. No answering thrum, no sign of life.

It was over.

She'd failed.

All the fight went out of her. She threw herself onto his chest—his still, unmoving body—and closed her eyes. No tears slipped down her face. She had nothing left in her to cry. Instead, a yawning, black pit opened up inside her, starless, merciless, threatening to swallow her whole. She'd started to care about him—as stupid as that was— and now it was tearing her apart. There was no fire inside her, no ghost in front of her. She was only a girl alone in the woods after sundown, her bones bound together with nothing but grief.

Cara didn't know how much time had passed before she made herself move. Shadows suffused the clearing. A headache pounded at her temples, her mouth was dry like she'd never drunk a drop of liquid in her life, and numbness had hollowed her out, soot where her heart had once burned. She stared at Zach's lifeless form.

The analyx continued to flicker around him, like candles at a vigil. The fire had melted the snow away. She glared at the flowers. How dare they still live while he didn't?

With a wild cry, Cara tore at the nearest patch, ripping them out of the earth. For a moment, nothing happened, their bodies strewn motionless across the ground.

And then new ones unfolded in their place.

Cara ripped these up. When more came, she ripped those up, too. She pulled up analyx by the handful, growing more and more frenzied as the blossoms welled back up like blood. With every new blossom, the hole inside her opened deeper and deeper, spilling something vital. In mindless fury, she reached and tore, reached and tore, until there was a pile of flowers at her feet. Enough to shroud a corpse.

And still, the flowers grew back.

She paused, chest heaving, nails stained with dirt, fingers wet with melted snow. Even the ones she'd torn up were still alive, their petals vibrant, the bright red mocking her. Nothing she did mattered. No matter how hard she tried.

What had been the point of all this? What had been the point of ghost speaking? What had been the point of breaking her promise to her mom, the point of leaving home? What had been the point of fighting off monsters and finding the antivenom and getting attached to him, if it all led to *this*?

"I'll burn you to ash," Cara warned the flowers, voice breaking. "I'll raze you down to the roots."

Yes, that had been the problem. She hadn't gotten rid of the roots, too.

Cara tried to stand. Exhaustion roared through her; her vision whited out, and she fell. Her knees slammed onto the ground, but she hardly felt the pain. Bracing her hand against the tree trunk, she raised herself back up. She stared down at the flowers, swaying, but she remained on her feet.

She clenched her fists, digging inside for a spark. By sheer will, her fire burned, a pale gold, paper-thin flame, transparent as a ghost against the dark.

That was when she noticed a few flowers were burning down—and nothing came back.

One by one, the analyx wilted, folding in on themselves. Their bodies tilted toward the earth, bloodred petals blackening down to the roots and creating a garden of dust and ash.

Her fire faltered. She froze, hands hanging empty at her sides.

Not taking her eyes off Zach's face, Cara sank to her knees in front of his body. Hope twisted inside her: a terrible, feral thing made of longing. She held her breath, her chest tightening with each heartbeat he didn't move—

But then a groan escaped his lips, and his eyes fluttered open.

All the breath left her lungs. She had only enough to whisper,

"*Zach.*"

A smile curved his mouth as he looked up at her. A smile soft and sweet, like taffy on the tongue. A smile for which she'd burn bridges. Forge new alliances. Sink ships.

A smile for which she'd bring back the dead.

When he spoke, his voice was low, and rough with disuse. "Hey, Tang."

There was a heartbeat, and then he added, with that familiar smirk of his: "Took you long enough—"

What little air he'd managed to inhale flew right back out as she flung her arms around his neck.

His arms came up to hug her back, wrapping her in a tight embrace. They stayed like that for some time, holding each other, her face buried in his shoulder.

Relief was such a violent thing. How else could she feel both empty and full? She was both the wildfire and the flowers growing back. She was the knife and the exit wound, surprised to find herself not bleeding. She was a girl, and she was a ghost speaker, and she'd brought him back to life.

Eventually, Cara pulled back but only slightly, keeping her arms looped around his neck. Her face heated as she realized that somehow, she'd ended up between his hips, the inside of his thighs grazing the outside of hers. Zach's hands had slid down to her waist, and there they rested, like it was the most natural thing in the world.

"I knew you'd do it." He gazed up at her, his smile only having grown, and God—wasn't her heart supposed to stop hurting now? His face wore the same soft expression of wonder he'd had when she was practicing her fire—like he was watching magic, a miracle, but he wasn't looking at the flame in her hand.

He was looking at her.

Zach's brow creased.

"You're bleeding," he said quietly.

Once more, she registered the feeling of warm blood running from her nose. "I'm okay," Cara said, but he was already reaching for her.

Gently, Zach wiped the blood away, his thumb brushing over her lips.

She wanted to kiss him so bad it hurt. But she couldn't stand the thought of that expression in his eyes—one that could almost be called fondness—turning into shock and disgust. He was alive again, but he still wasn't hers.

Instead of reaching for him, Cara reached for her bag. She dug around before taking out the LaCroix.

At the sight, Zach threw his head back and laughed. And maybe she was delirious from exhaustion and sleep deprivation, but in that moment, she could have lived on that sound forever. She had no need for food or drink or sleep, not when she had this. Not when she had the sound of his laughter, joyful and alive, filling up her head, her chest, her very soul.

Cara knocked her water bottle against his can of LaCroix, and they drank.

THIRTY-TWO

When Cara felt strong enough to try standing, she braced a hand against the tree trunk and painstakingly got to her feet. Every single muscle in her body complained, but she ignored them, holding out her hand. Zach took it, and she pulled him up, not without effort.

Once vertical, Zach wavered. "Whoa," he said, and tilted into her. Flinging her hands up, she caught him.

He was so close she could see the subtle coloration of his eyes—lighter blue around his pupils, then deepening in hue at the edges of his irises.

"Sorry," Zach murmured, grin sheepish. Cara could get used to the sound of him apologizing. "Not quite used to gravity again yet."

Zach startled when her hand brushed his throat but held still as Cara found his pulse. It surged when her fingers landed on his skin, life unmistakable, beating faster in answer to her touch. For a heartbeat, electric blue flickered through his veins like neon lighting up signs on a cold night: *alive, alive, alive.*

She closed her eyes and listened.

Opening her eyes, she made to pull away, but Zach caught her hand, turning it over and tracing a thumb over the two pinpricks on her wrist. Goose bumps rose on her skin. "They're just like the ones on my ankle," he said. He looked up, grinning. "Hey, we match."

And then he bent his head and brushed his lips over her wrist, where the Snake had sunk its fangs. She bit back a gasp. Could he see he was unraveling her without even meaning to? Her blood ached in her veins.

"Before we go home," Zach began, voice tentative, "I've got to tell you something."

Hope rippled within her, growing until her body could barely contain it and budding teeth that would pierce her heart.

"I should have said this earlier, but I didn't know how. I was scared, and I didn't think there would be a point to it if I ended up dying. I didn't want to ruin the time we had left together." He looked down, then back at her. "But you brought me back, which means I can't avoid it any longer. I know I mean nothing to you, and you only saved me for the money, and you'll go back to hating me before the sun comes up.

"But here it is anyway. I told you what I saw in the fog. That was a lie. It was only you. It has *always* been only you."

She couldn't breathe.

Tenderly, he took hold of a loose strand of hair, tracing it with his slender fingers down to the end. "And I know you think I'm an idiot and I don't notice anything, and for the most part, you're probably right, like you always are. But Cara, I could draw you from memory. Your hair—it looks black, but it turns reddish in the sun, and it glows like fire. Your eyes, too: when they catch the light, they're like living embers, and when you throw that glare at me, sometimes I forget how to speak. You're stubborn and brave and smart, and I'd be dead without you by my side. When I had none, you were my pulse. You manage to get under my skin like no one else, and I never want to be rid of you, because all the chaos in me falls silent at your touch." He drew a breath. "You—you make me real."

He looked down, drawing a single circle over her snakebite with his thumb, then carefully dropped her hand.

"Go ahead, break my heart. I don't mind. You're a flame I would happily let burn me alive."

Zach.

So easy to say with clenched teeth, with a snarl showing canines. The start, a dagger between the lips. A smile on a knife's edge.

And the close of his name, that sharp -*ch*: it was a shot in the dark. The ricochet of a bullet. The end of heartbreak at the beginning of the throat.

"Zach," she said.

He smiled at her, but it was wistful, resigned. "Have I told you that I love the way you say my name?"

She grabbed his hoodie, dragged him down to her level, and kissed him.

It took her a second to realize he wasn't kissing back.

Cara pulled away. "I'm sorry," she whispered, not able to look at him. She'd misinterpreted, somehow, or it had been a trick. "I shouldn't have—"

Then his mouth met hers, and the clearing faded away.

Her eyes fluttered closed. Zach's lips were cool against her own, dry but soft. His arms circled around her waist, holding her tight to him. He smelled like winter—crushed pine needles, skin bared to the cold.

Zach kissed her like he was still a ghost, and this was what would resurrect him, if he had any say about it. He kissed her like he had decided, after a week of being dead, that he didn't care for air anymore. He kissed her like he needed nothing else to live but her, only *her.*

Cara traced a hand over his jaw, and he made a sound in the back of his throat that sent fire racing through her belly. A delicious heat curled through every part of her, from her fingers down to her toes, warming her to the core. She forgot what it was like to ever be cold. She forgot her name. She forgot everything except for what it was like to be kissing him—there was just this, a kiss that would keep her going until the end of the world.

She pushed him gently toward the oak until his back hit the trunk. Right now, she wasn't sure who was holding up whom. If not for the oak, they might simply sink to the earth, among the autumn leaves and dust from disappeared flowers.

Zach's hands had found their way to her waist, slipping under the hem of her shirt. His fingers were cold, courtesy of him recently being a ghost, but they moved expertly up her back, sending welcome shivers through her stomach that were quickly consumed by heat, ever rising. Light bloomed behind her eyelids, brighter than any breaking of dawn.

This was how she knew it was real. Because when the fog had touched her, her mind had gone blank. But when *he* touched her, her mind went wild with color, tinting each and every thought in the hue of desire.

She reached up and threaded her fingers through his hair, reveling in the gold in her hands. It was as soft as she'd dreamed. Hungrily, she deepened the kiss, tugging him closer and closer until she was certain even their atoms were touching, forming a bond nothing could break.

Zach groaned. "*Cara*," he murmured, his voice low, somehow both soft and rough at the same time. He uttered her name so quietly, so *reverently*—as if it were a prayer, as if it were something precious.

Boldly, she bit his lower lip, taking it between her teeth, and was pleased to hear him hiss a swear into her mouth.

He pulled his mouth away from her, but it was only to trail tiny kisses down her jaw, then throat, in retribution. Her skin must have been covered in sweat and dirt, but he didn't seem to care. When he reached the bandage covering the cut the miner's knife had given her, he paused, then planted the lightest kiss possible. She clutched his broad shoulders, the muscles of his back hard under her hands, and tried to stay upright.

Then his lips were back on hers, locking her in a kiss until, at last, the need for air was too much to ignore.

Reluctantly, they broke apart. She pressed her forehead to his, both of them gasping for breath. Their exhales spilled white clouds of air.

"I may," Zach panted, chest rising and falling quickly, "have been wrong about how much you hate me."

Cara laughed. "You do have a tendency to be wrong."

Zach drew back a little, keeping his arms around her. "I'm sorry for freezing up," he said. "I just couldn't believe it. I thought I'd started dreaming."

"Do you usually dream about me?" she teased, in an echo of his words from the meadow.

She wasn't prepared for him to admit, "Yes. All the time."

Cara stared at him, a blush blazing across her already heated cheeks. Damn him, *he* was supposed to be the flustered one, not her.

"I thought you didn't care about me," she confessed. "That you only cared about keeping me safe so I could resurrect you."

Pain flickered over his face. "You thought that?" She nodded, and he drew her close, eyes anguished. "Every time you were in danger, I thought about calling the whole thing off. It would have killed me if you died. Not just because you wouldn't be able to bring me back, but because it would have been my fault. My failure to protect you. Your cuts, your scars—you got those because of me."

"It was my choice," she reminded him. Cara put a hand to his face, fixing him with a steady look to make sure he got it. She felt him leaning into her touch, waiting for her to continue. "My choice to help you, my choice to bleed." She swallowed, gathering her words. "I didn't want to lose you."

Zach blinked, eyes going wide. After a moment, he asked, "So it really wasn't about the money?"

Cara shook her head, passing her thumb over his cheekbone.

He considered this for a moment. "Do you still want that money?"

At that, she gave him a smirk. "What do you think?"

He laughed, leaning down to brush his lips across her collarbone. "I think," he murmured into her skin, "you're incredible."

Frissons of pleasure rippled through her body. She wanted this moment to never end, to stay here in this clearing forever, holding him in her arms, alive and *hers*.

But night was coming, and they'd have to go home eventually. The river whispered from behind, a hush of sound.

"What are we going to tell everyone?" she asked. "They'll wonder why we're not fighting anymore."

"We'll figure it out," Zach assured her, confident as ever. "What they think doesn't matter. In the end, you're my ghost speaker, and I'm your ghost."

"*Was*," she couldn't resist correcting.

Zach rolled his eyes, like she knew he would. But instead of replying with something sarcastic, he lifted her hand and pressed a kiss against her knuckles, as a knight would swear fealty to his lady. "Dead or alive," he promised, "I am yours."

Mine. She kind of liked the sound of that.

The thread in her heart thrummed.

His brow furrowed, and he put a hand to his chest. "Do you feel that?" he said. "A string or something connecting us. Resonating."

"I had to anchor your life force to mine to raise you. I guess it stayed." A thought crossed her mind, and Cara ducked her head, smiling to herself.

"What is it?" he asked, tipping up her chin with his hand, bringing her eyes to his.

When she told him about the red string of fate, how it connected lovers meant to be together, a smile like sunlight spread over his face, and he dipped her into a kiss, soft and slow and sweet.

Then a dog barked.

Zach and Cara jerked apart at the sound. She turned to see a golden blur of fur barrel at her seconds before it bowled her over.

Blaze's fluffy face filled her vision. On her back on the ground, Cara laughed, hugging her dog. "Hi, boy. Did you miss me, buddy? Did you miss me?" Blaze danced around her in a jingle of dog tags, making happy little snorts. Every time she tried to get up, he'd fling himself on her again, poking his nose in her face, so she waited, petting his thick, golden fur. "I missed you, too," she told him, which set off another round of exuberant tail-wagging and face-licking.

Eventually, Blaze calmed down enough to allow her to sit up. When she did, she blinked in confusion at what she saw—who she saw.

"Mom? Laolao? What are you guys doing here?" Her gaze slipped between the two of them. "Can you—can you see each other?"

Her mother and grandmother walked toward them from the edge of the clearing, Blaze's leash hanging from Laolao's ghostly hand.

Then Cara realized who she was with. What she looked like. She shot to her feet, smoothing down her hair, throwing it up in the fastest ponytail ever in an attempt to hide the mess Zach had made of it. Her lips felt hot and swollen from all his kisses; she pressed her hand to her mouth, trying to cover it, then let it drop to her side. It was useless.

"We came to find you because the seven days are up," Laolao explained. Cara's mom hung back as Laolao enfolded Cara in a chilly hug. "We thought you were in trouble because you hadn't come back yet." Laolao glanced at Zach, her eyes twinkling behind her glasses. "But now I see that you do not need our help."

Oh, God. Cara had made it all the way through the liminal world and back, only to die of embarrassment a mile from home.

Zach nudged Cara. "Is your grandma there? I can't see her."

"Mr. Mortmanger's glasses," Cara remembered. "Put them on."

How did Zach manage to look hot in anything, even the storekeeper's spectacles? With glasses perched on his nose, he looked like he actually studied, which shot her attraction to him sky-high.

Your mom and grandma are right there, Cara told herself. *You are not allowed to make out with him. Even though you really want to.*

"I am glad you are safe and alive, xiaogui," Laolao said. She smiled at Zach. "Both of you."

"I have so much to tell you," Cara started, the words spilling out of her mouth. "I met a ghost hunter whose grandma walked through the liminal world before. I used my powers to help ghosts pass over! And we found the Signet Snake. Both of them, actually."

Laolao had been beaming this whole time, but now her eyebrows rose. "Two snakes?"

"Yes! Turns out, the antidote to the first Snake's venom is the venom of the second." Cara bit her lip. Something in her grand-mother's face was a little strained. Maybe all this reminded Laolao of how she'd failed to save her friend those years ago, not knowing what the antidote was. "The white Snake can change into a human, which was really weird. He had a ring that let him do it, and the black Snake said that a ghost speaker gave it to him. Have you ever heard of something like that?"

Laolao laughed. For some reason, it sounded a little nervous. Apprehensive. "Sounds like there is much to discuss," she answered. "But for now . . . you should say hello to your mother."

Laolao turned away from Cara to Zach, and she watched as her grandmother clasped his hands in hers, Blaze circling excitedly around them, tail whipping so fast against Zach's legs it had to hurt. Cara heard Zach thanking Laolao for all her help, but their conver-sation faded out as Cara's mom, who had been silent the whole time, walked up to her.

It was the moment Cara had been dreading.

Wrinkles framed her mom's eyes, ones Cara couldn't remember seeing before. Her mom looked older, more tired, and Cara's heart waterlogged with regret. *She'd* done that to her mom.

"I'm sorry," Cara said truthfully, and braced for the consequences.

But instead of scolding and shouting, her mom pulled her into a hug.

Cara froze in shock. She couldn't remember the last time her mom had hugged her. Hesitantly, Cara embraced her. Practical in all aspects, her mom wore no perfume, seeing no sense in fragrance for the sake of fragrance. She smelled like unscented Eucerin mois-turizer, the only lotion Cara had ever seen her use. She smelled like home.

When her mom pulled away, she said, "I am the one who's sorry."

Cara stared at her. Her mom didn't hug her. Her mom didn't apologize. Was Cara hallucinating? Was she dead?

"I don't like the way we parted," her mom continued. "I . . ." She sighed. "I shouldn't have treated you in that manner. It was wrong of me, and I hurt you. I realize that now, after talking to Laolao."

"I hurt you, too," Cara said, her throat closing up. "I disobeyed you." She'd been the most disrespectful daughter in the world.

"But it's my job as a mother not to hurt you. I'm supposed to give you a better life." Her mom shook her head, regret deepening the lines on her face, the wrinkles Cara had helped give her. "My life is not your life. I cannot force you to live it." She hesitated. "Xiaogui."

Little ghost.

That was all Cara had ever wanted to hear. She tucked her head into her mom's shoulder, burying her sniffles. Cara's mom rubbed her back soothingly.

"How are you able to see Laolao again?" Cara asked when she'd recovered enough to do so. "What happened?"

Her mom nodded thoughtfully, looking into the distance as she remembered. "When my mother came back to the house and found your note, she demanded we speak, growing more and more insistent by the day. She left messages everywhere. She flung open doors and slammed them closed, often in the middle of the night. One morning, she even put our couch on top of the roof, which was hard to explain to the neighbors." Her mom gave a little laugh, glancing over to where Zach and Laolao were still talking. "I had ignored her for so many years, and I was adamant I would ignore her for more, but this time it was different. You were gone, and I think we were both scared of what might happen to you, that you might not return. I began to regret what I said to you, and I feared that if you did return, you and I would never speak again, the same way my mother and I didn't. But after so long living in the same house and not talking, she and I came together for a common purpose. For you. We communicated by writing on pieces of paper. And when I woke up this morning, I saw her." Her mom's eyes glistened; she dashed the tears away quickly, pretending they hadn't been there.

Emotion welled in Cara's throat. What had it been like for her mom to see Laolao for the first time since her death? And her first ghost in who knew how long?

The wounds that had distanced her mom and Laolao may not have healed, but they'd scarred over enough to build a bridge that would hold a space for reconciliation, that would bear the weight of them speaking again after ages of silence.

It was what Cara had always wanted: her mom and Laolao talking again. She hadn't realized until now that it wasn't up to her to bridge the distance. It had been something only they could decide to do, and at last, they had.

That was when Cara's mom noticed the dressings on her throat and hands.

"What happened? Do you need to go to the hospital?" Alarm fluttered in her voice.

"No, I'm good, it's okay," Cara said quickly. "Just some minor injuries."

Cara's mom examined her. She nodded, looking unsatisfied but appearing willing to believe her. She squeezed Cara's hands. "I'm glad you're not dead, so I will ground you only for the next six weeks."

Cara's mouth fell open. *The next six weeks?*

"Did you think I would be so grateful you were alive I would let you off with no consequences? Remember, I told you I would double your punishment if you got into trouble with that boy. Six weeks at home. No friends, no movies, no meeting up to 'study.' You under-stand me?"

Cara swallowed a sigh. "Yes."

Her mom smiled grimly. "And now I must talk to that boy."

Uh-oh.

Across the clearing, Zach looked up as Cara's mom turned in his direction. She advanced, and he backed up instantly, almost tripping over a tree root in his haste.

Cara had to bite the inside of her cheek to keep from laughing. Her mom was a petite five-foot-two in comparison to Zach's six-foot-two, but Zach looked scared for his life.

"What is your relationship to my daughter?" she demanded in English.

"I, uh," he said intelligently, his usual charm around adults seem-ingly gone. He cleared his throat. "I'm Zach Cole—"

"I know who you are," she snapped. "I *asked*, 'what is your rela-tionship to my daughter?' Do you have good intentions? What are your plans for life?" Cara's mom paused. "Have you had sex? Did you get her pregnant?"

Oh. My. God.

"Um, I—" Zach's face had gone bright red. He sent Cara a deer-in-the-headlights look. *Help me*, he mouthed.

Laolao stepped up to the plate. She placed a hand on Cara's mom's shoulder. "Ah, let him be. The poor boy just came back from the dead, after all. You can interrogate him later. For now, we should go home. Zacharias and Cara need to sleep after the ordeal they have had."

Cara's mom stared at Zach for several long seconds, during which

Zach appeared not to be breathing. Finally, Cara's mom sighed. "Yes, let's go home." Turning to Cara, she said, "I'll make you something while you rest. And I'll cut you an apple. I know you forgot to eat healthy when you were running around."

Home. Sleep. Food. Talking to her mom and Laolao when she woke. Texting Charlotte and Felicity that she was back. Figuring out when she could next see Zach again. There were many things she had to do, but these were the most important. These seemed like a good start to getting herself back on track after this week. Building blocks for the kind of life she wanted to live in Autumn Falls.

Cara knelt, calling Blaze over so she could hook the leash back on his collar. Standing up, she held her hand out to Zach, who took it, a grateful smile on his lips. With Zach and Blaze on either side and Laolao and her mom behind her, the Wildwoods surrounding her like a hug, Cara made her way home.

THIRTY-THREE

ONE WEEK LATER

"Ah, Fall Festival. An event celebrating the season of autumn held in Autumn Falls—what could be more picturesque? Apparently, keg stands," Felicity said in a deadpan, concluding her tour guide narration of the scene.

Cara stood with Felicity and Charlotte off to the side of the Falls lookout point, watching Ian Donegal slip a flask from his pocket. For a second, the metal caught the dying light and glinted a familiar silver, making her heartbeat quicken.

No ghosts here, she reminded herself. *Just teens illegally drinking—perfectly normal.*

And even if there had been ghosts, it wouldn't have been a problem. She knew now that ignoring your problems wouldn't make them go away, that there were better ways to deal with them, and she had what it took to solve her troubles.

In fact, Monday morning, Cara had arrived at school early on a mission. She'd looked all over, eyes peeled for silver. Five minutes before homeroom, she'd finally found Mr. Toole mumbling to himself in the library, a place she'd never seen him in before.

When she gathered her courage and approached him, he didn't seem surprised she could see him, only mildly disgruntled she'd interrupted his cleaning. He'd leaned on his broom, surveying her from under his bushy black brows as she asked if he would like to pass over.

"So, you're the ghost speaker everyone's been looking for." He'd squinted at her. "Why are you asking if I want to pass over? Am I not doing a good enough job keeping this place clean?"

"You are, sir," she'd reassured him. "Which is why you deserve to be rewarded for all your hard work. You've spent so many years taking care of others. Let me do the same for you."

Silence had settled in the library, thicker than dust. She had felt the hard knot where his heart would have been, a sense of duty and service that had kept him coming back day after day.

But finally, he'd nodded. "That would be nice," he said. And with her hand on his arm and a whisper in the hush of the shelves, Mr. Toole crossed over.

Cara stood there for a moment, breathing in the scent of floor polish and lemon-scented cleaner that still hung in the air, closing her eyes as peace settled inside her—and then the bell for homeroom had rung.

Now Saturday slipped below the horizon, and she was here with her friends. Originally, Cara's mom had ungrounded her only for her birthday, but Cara had managed to persuade her mom to unground her for tonight, too—she hadn't exactly been able to celebrate her birthday on Halloween, after all.

"Hey, we're back." Ben jogged up to them, Thomas Yeung and Kameron Sinclair in tow. "Sorry for the wait. There was a line for the spiced apple cider."

"It's okay," Charlotte chirped with a sweet smile, setting aside the notebook she'd been sketching in to accept a red Solo cup from Thomas. "We weren't bored or anything."

Felicity and Cara grinned. From anyone else, that would have sounded sarcastic, but Charlotte had genuinely meant it.

"Oh, yeah?" Ben handed Cara's cup to her, then took a sip of his own. "What were you guys doing?"

"People-watching," Felicity replied. A powder-blue backpack was slung over her shoulder, and her fingers kept inching toward it whenever the party seemed to lose her interest. Cara knew from experience the backpack stored a book and at least one backup. "You know, I'd bet that flask that Ian has not so secretly in his coat is one hundred percent vodka."

Kameron squinted. "How can you tell?"

Across the clearing, Ian shook the flask and yelled, "*VODKA!*" His buddies whooped.

"That," Felicity said dryly.

All around the lookout point, their classmates chatted and danced in the growing dark. Groups of friends lounged on the logs around the crackling bonfire in the center of the party, some toasting s'mores. People dropped slips of paper into the fire, scribed with the names of crushes they wanted to have like them back. That was the tradition, after all. With the magic of the bonfire, your crush might be yours in a year. Some lucky people for whom the bonfire had already worked its magic were sneaking off hand in hand to go make out in the woods. The smells of burnt sugar, intoxication, and woodsmoke rose into the heavy dusk air. After the sun set, the air itself became a more tangible thing, the twilight a velvet curtain to hide behind. The famous Autumn Falls was a roar just out of sight, the river speeding past the edge of the party and careening drunkenly over the rocks.

"You there?" Charlotte said, waving a hand in front of Cara's face. "You look a little distracted."

"Hmm? Oh, yeah. Just thinking about all the homework I missed."

While she'd been gone, Principal Olan had seen fit to declare two snow days. With the weather, the teachers had extended deadlines. Mr. Ursan had given them the weekend to finish up their projects, with a remark to turn them in by Monday at 8 a.m. on the dot or "fear his wrath." Still, Cara had a lot of ground to cover.

But that wasn't why she'd been distracted all night.

Cara felt for the thread in her chest. She hadn't gotten the chance to talk to Zach in person all week, but they'd been secretly texting. They'd discovered that with the string, they could tell where the other person was. Not a precise location or a specific measurement of distance but rather if they were far or close.

And she knew Zach was somewhere in the woods, coming to her.

The thread trembled, and her pulse leaped like a deer from a forest fire.

Across the clearing, Zach—shoulders limned by shadow, not silver—met her eyes.

Upon seeing her, his face broke into a wide grin. She felt her lips automatically curve into an answering smile. Fighting back the urge to run to him, she acted casual, watching Zach out of the corner of her eye.

Zach, too, forced the smile from his face with visible effort, transforming his features into a mask of anger instead. Gaze locked on her still, he strode through the crowd. His voice rang through the air, slicing through the smoke and liquor.

"Hey, Tang!"

To everyone else, Zach sounded pissed off as hell, but to her, the undercurrent of fondness that ran through his words was as clear as water.

Felicity groaned, physically burying her face in her book. "What did you do this time, Cara?"

"I knew this peace was too good to last," Charlotte said sadly.

Heads turned as Zach made his way to her, a ship carving a path through the sea. Voices whispered excitedly, anticipating the inevitable explosion.

He stopped inches away. A tiny smile flickered on his lips, one only she could see.

"You know," he began, "I've got a problem with you."

Cara crossed her arms. "And what are you going to do about it?"

His smile widened. "This."

And in front of everyone, he leaned down and kissed her.

The party hushed.

Then, as people started to register what they were seeing, whistles and whoops came from the crowd. Charlotte gasped. Felicity dropped something with a thud.

"What," said Felicity, "the *fuck*?"

Cara kissed him back, running her fingers through his hair. The gentle pressure of his hands at her waist pulled something taut in her core, made her ache with an ardent kind of hunger. The whole world was here in his arms; no one else existed.

Before they could get too into it, she broke away, grinning at the disappointed noise Zach made. They'd done it like this for a reason, and now it was fulfilled. Better to rip off the Band-Aid all at once.

His breath brushed her ear. "I missed you," he whispered.

Damn him and his beautiful mouth. Resolve crumbling, she reached for him—

"Ahem."

Cara turned to face Charlotte and Felicity, who was holding her now dirt-stained book with her arms crossed.

"Got any more secrets you'd like to share with the class?"

As a matter of fact, I do.

Cara smiled. "Noon tomorrow. Meet me at the tree house, and I'll tell you everything." She'd have to sneak out of the house, but that was inconsequential.

"Fine." Felicity sniffed. "But I'm only forgiving you because of how much money I'm going to make tonight."

A beat passed. Then Cara put it together.

"You bet on Zach and me?" she sputtered.

"She's had it going since fifth grade," Charlotte piped up.

"I can't believe you guys." Cara shook her head, but she was smiling, even as Felicity dragged Charlotte off to help her "collect."

Zach looped his arms around her neck from behind, pressing his body into hers. "Let's break up to mess with her," he suggested.

Cara laughed, reaching up to take hold of his arms. "Nice try, Coleson." She tilted her head back into his chest, fire blossoming through her when she met his eyes. "You can't get rid of me that easily."

"That's what I thought," he murmured, and brought his mouth down to hers.

A chime sounded from her pocket—the sound she'd assigned to Brittany's text messages. Upon arriving home, she'd updated Brittany with the results of their quest, and Brittany had done likewise. The ghost hunter had returned with the blood, and now with new weapons forged, her gran's legacy hadn't been lost but furthermore secured. Everything was A1. Aside from Brittany's mom grounding her for the foreseeable future. But her family *definitely* took her seriously now.

Brittany: Have you named the knife yet

No, Cara hadn't named the knife yet. It was currently buried in a drawer of clothes, along with the hill-beast acorn and the flower Zach had given her.

"Let's take a picture for Brittany," Cara told him. She'd wanted to tell Charlotte and Felicity about her and Zach first, as they'd had to deal with her and Zach fighting for way longer. But now they were Autumn Falls official, they could share the good news with Brittany, too.

Zach was all too happy to oblige, pressing a kiss into her cheek as she screwed up her face and pretended that she wasn't enjoying it.

She sent the photo to Brittany.

Cara: Here's something better

Two seconds later:

Brittany: THAT'S WHAT I'M TALKING ABOUT

Brittany: FINALLY

Brittany: HALLELUJAH A MIRACLE HAS COME

Zach checked his phone. "We got very different messages," he observed, and showed Cara his screen.

Brittany: Casper if you fuck this up I WILL hunt you down.

Congrats!

"Yo, Zachy boy!" A guy ambled up, red Solo cup clutched in one hand. He was on Zach's swim team—Tucker something. Lank brown hair, fish-belly white skin, cloudy blue eyes.

Zach stiffened, repositioning himself so his body blocked Cara's.

"Congrats, man," Tucker said. "Looks like you finally tapped that sweet Asian a—"

Fury roared through Cara's body. She stepped forward, but Zach got there first.

He clenched his hand around Tucker's arm in a vice grip, shoving

Tucker's cup back into his chest and spilling beer down his shirt. Tucker stumbled back, oily hair falling into his eyes.

"My bad," Zach said pleasantly, towering over Tucker, who tried to wrench free fruitlessly. Zach's hold didn't loosen one bit. His voice was low as he suggested, "Why don't you go and clean yourself up?"

Nostrils flared, Tucker's eyes jerked from Zach to Cara back to Zach. Lips pressed so tight together they were a white line, he nodded.

Zach let him go, and Tucker scurried off, tail tucked between his legs.

Turning to her, Zach wrapped an arm around her waist. "Sorry you had to hear that," he murmured, his voice gentle again. "You okay?"

Nodding, Cara nestled into his chest, her heart rate heightened but beginning to calm, mind still clawing for what to say in the wake of the disbelieving, white-hot anger such ugly words had sparked. It had happened so fast. What should she have done? What *could* she have done? Maybe she should have punched Tucker. But there was no doubt who would have been punished in that scenario. Still, she said, "I could have taken him."

"I know." Zach dropped a kiss on the top of her head, soft as snow. "But I didn't want you to have to."

They were back in Autumn Falls. Yet the real world had its own kind of monsters.

Cara hadn't realized until now that she could trust Zach to help her fight these ones, too.

She sighed, looking up at him. His gold hair was gilded in the scattered firelight, his blue eyes bright even in the shadows of dusk. Despite the drop in temperature, Zach wore only a tightly fitted, dark gray, short-sleeved T-shirt and jeans.

"Aren't you cold?" she said.

"That's what I wanted to talk to you about tonight, actually." Zach glanced around. "Can we go somewhere more private?"

Cara raised her eyebrows but nodded. Felicity and Charlotte weren't back yet, so they wouldn't notice her sneaking off into the trees.

Fingers threaded through hers, he led her deeper into the Wildwoods. The carcasses of beer cans and crumpled cardboard cases littered the ground. They passed one enthralled couple after another tangled in each other's arms under the branches.

Finally, Zach stopped, looking around to make sure no one was nearby. Her curiosity had risen; whatever he wanted to tell her, he clearly thought it was important.

"Before I show you, you gotta promise you won't tell anyone."

"I won't."

Slowly, Zach stretched out his arm, palm faceup. For a moment, nothing happened.

But then she saw it—tiny specks of white. Snowflakes, appearing in the air like stars in the gathering darkness. Hovering above Zach's hand—and nowhere else.

The string between them was quivering.

Inside the tangled forest of her ribs, her heart was a wildfire. Snapshots played across her mind, one after the other, like slides on a projection screen in a darkened room of memory. His jaw, cheekbones, lashes, clear as light and tragic in a meadow of extinction. Him leaning into her touch, vulnerable, no pulse under her fingertips in a graveyard of dead hearts. His eyes, unguarded and looking at her in a way she couldn't begin to describe, chest rising and falling as he gasped for breath.

A week of magic.

And now here they were again, back to the beginning at the end—a snake swallowing its own tail.

Cara drew a breath. She met his eyes.

"Snow," she said. "But . . . how?"

"When I got back home last week, it started to snow inside my room. I freaked out when I realized the snow was coming from *me*—I might have gotten stuck to my frozen doorknob for a good twenty minutes."

She laughed, holding out her hand to catch one of his snowflakes.

"I can make snow, ice, call up freezing wind . . . and I don't get cold. Not anymore. I've been dying to tell you, but I wanted to do it in person, so I waited." He looked at her. "To see what you would think."

Cara took his hand, tugging him to her. "Well, first, I think I understand why it snowed when you became a ghost. Maybe this power was frozen inside of you, and when you died, it unlocked it somehow."

"That makes a lot of sense." He kissed her. "See, this is what I keep you around for."

She shook her head, fighting the stupid smile she could feel coming on.

"We're fire and ice," Zach said in a ridiculously pleased tone, and the smile won.

In a way, it fit perfectly. Opposites but of the same nature. Both elements.

"Your family," she said. "Have you told them yet?"

"No." He glanced away. "Still trying to work out how to. Or if I should at all."

Zach had snuck back into his house after he'd awoken in the

Wildwoods. She knew he'd casually asked Luke to tell his parents he'd been there all week, if they asked, that is. Luke had shrugged and agreed. It hadn't been necessary, after all. Zach's parents assumed their younger son had been at home the week they were gone. Cara knew him well enough now to know that it bothered Zach more that his parents *hadn't* asked about his whereabouts than if they had.

"It's okay." Cara took his face in her hands, bringing him back to her. Just like he'd told her, she said, "We'll figure it out together."

"Together," Zach repeated. A grin curved his mouth.

In the dark of dusk, snow falling around them, she fisted her hands in the fabric of his shirt and pulled him to her, pressing her lips to that grin, eliciting a sound of agreement from the back of his throat. His pulse sped against her skin, their shared thread shivering.

And inside her heart, the fire rose to life.

EPILOGUE

In a quiet town called Autumn Falls, in the liminal light between day and night, a dead man comes back to life.

Six feet deep in the ground of the town graveyard, his heart beats for the first time in fifty years, muffled by earth but unmistakable. Reverberating like a dissonant chord, the pulse travels through the November dusk, rippling outward through the graveyard's wrought iron gates through the quaint narrow streets, over oaks autumn-bare, and past buildings—schools, stores, homes—filled with the living who have no clue what's happening.

Oh, but the dead do.

Death this loud draws ghosts. The promise of rot, the hiss of broken breath between teeth, the resounding ring of a heart that should not beat. The world folding and creating something so terrible nobody can look away, not even the dead. This man is alive once more in the starkest, darkest sense of the word, but his pulse is a death knell. With it comes a shift in the wind, a foreboding note of cold. When they feel it, every ghost in Autumn Falls knows that something is wrong. And they shiver, because although there are hardly any things in this world that spirits fear, this man is every single one of them.

In a forgotten corner of the cemetery, ghosts begin to gather in wait, blanketing the dying grass like a mercury spill. The older ones hang back; the younger ones, who were born less than fifty years ago and have only heard stories of what this man was like alive, press forward, daring each other to get closer to the tombstone and the body buried beneath it.

A girl with a heart defect, forever eight years old, squints at the name on the grave marker stained brownish-black and mottled with lichen and moss. No one has ever come to keep his tombstone pristine. No one has ever laid roses on his grave. "*Ambrose,*" she reads in a voice clear and high as a bell.

And the earth shudders.

A hand breaks free of the dirt. Then a second, fingers flexing and finding purchase on the disturbed ground. Like this, Ambrose pulls himself free. It isn't easy to dig yourself out of your own grave, but Ambrose makes it look effortless, clambering up and out as smoothly as a cicada, quietly biding its time underground and waiting for the right conditions to come back.

Ambrose looks surprisingly good for being dead half a century. He cuts an imposing figure against the fallen, decaying leaves with his dark hair and tall frame, dressed all in black. His eyes are an odd blue—the hue of a drowned corpse, cold and devoid of life. Untouched by sun, his skin is pale and bloodless. Crepuscular shadows carve his cheekbones into hollows. A curious circular symbol marks the underside of his right wrist: a snake eating its own tail, seeming to writhe in the gloaming.

He brushes a speck of dirt off his suit, immaculate as though he were put to rest in it the day before. As idly as if he were checking his watch for the time, he reaches for a close-by cypress, ceaselessly green among all the skeleton trees.

When his fingers make contact, the cypress blackens and crumbles into dust.

Ambrose's skin looks a little tighter now, fitting better and brighter around his skull. He casts his drowned-man's eyes on the specters: his subjects, his soldiers, though they don't know it yet. The promise of revenge feels good: like fresh air through resurrected lungs. When he speaks, his voice is silky smooth. Predatorial. The movement of a shark through lightless waters.

"Finally," he says, and smiles.

ACKNOWLEDGMENTS

Thank you to my agent, Paige Terlip, who saw something in Zach and Cara that even I didn't at the time. Your whip-smart savviness and kind, thoughtful comments make for the best combination that I could have asked for. Thank you for cheering me on even when my writer's block and imposter's syndrome made working on my book seem impossible. I don't know how I got so lucky, but I'm so grateful that we found each other.

Thank you to my editor, Alice Jerman, whose warmth and enthusiasm make every call a delight! From the moment we talked, we just clicked. Every author should be so blessed to have an editor like you. I am so glad we're on the same page about romance and that you fell in love with Zach and Cara and pushed me to even higher standards. Thank you for getting my book and all the weird things I put in it, liminal spaces and all.

Thank you to my team at HarperCollins: Clare Vaughn, Catherine Lee, Alison Donalty, Jon Howard, Gweneth Morton, Lisa Calcasola, and Vanessa Nuttry. This book would not be possible without all of your hard work. Thank you also to the cover artist Hillary D. Wilson for creating such a gorgeous and vivid cover. And thank you to the sensitivity readers—any misstep is on my part, not theirs.

Thank you to Sandra Proudman and Shannon Thompson for

taking a chance on this book and being my Pitch Wars mentors and basically changing the course of my publishing journey. I seriously don't know where I would be right now if it weren't for Team Snicker-snee. Your feedback was invaluable and transformative. You are the reason why the ending of this book isn't 100x sadder, and for that, I'm sure readers will thank you, haha. So excited to cheer for us and for where our words will go in the future! And shout-out to Pitch Wars for being such a force in the writing community that shepherded countless writers, including my friends and me, to agents and book deals but also gave us the vital tools to revise and pitch our stories. RIP.

Thank you to Allison Liu, my best friend, who has read multiple versions of this book and been excited about them all. I am still so proud that this book made you cry at work, haha. Your undying love for Zach and Cara fuels me. I am so lucky to know such an amazing human and writer in real life—you're one in a billion and I can't wait for your wonderful words to take publishing by storm someday soon. Here's to a lifetime of cracking jokes/screaming/cheering in Google Docs comments!

Thank you to Chloe Gong, who is brilliant, talented, and one of the funniest people I know. Your clever wit and sharp insight make me treasure every single one of our conversations. I so appreciate always being able to go to you to talk about publishing and books.

Thank you to Christina Li, who is the light of my life and one of the sweetest writer friends I have. Your pragmatic and intelligent comments make our Zoom/FaceTime calls the best. I still cackle when I recall your boyfriend calling you out for simping over Zach on main. Your smile is literally sunshine. My gratitude to you for sensitivity reading.

Thank you to Rhea Basu and Alina Khawaja, who rooted so hard for this book and for Zach and Cara. I will never forget your excitement and the comments you left while reading (especially the Club Penguin picture you dropped directly into the document, Rhea). Thanks for being so on board for hot ghost boys.

Thank you to Chelsea Abdullah and Kyla Zhao (fellow PW mentee!), who read this book for fun but also wrote the kindest blurbs for sub! Your enthusiasm for my characters and story meant/mean the world.

Thank you to E. M. Anderson and Ann Zhao, who proofread this book like lickety-split for sub. Typos will never stand a chance against the two of you. (Also thank you for the wonderful comments you left as well, hehe!)

To lovely writing friends who I am so glad to know: Kamilah Cole, Sara Hashem, Ann Liang. Your text messages and screaming reactions give me life.

Thank you to my sister. You're really annoying. But you're also the reason why everyone who knows you knows about my book (because again, you're really annoying). I kid, I kid. I can hear you saying right now that "that's not funny," so moving on to the praise: thank you for being such a fierce supporter of this book. Seriously, it's heartwarming. You are so smart and driven that I'm certain you can conquer anything you put your mind to. I am quite sure that by the time you're done, the penguins in Antarctica will know about my book deal. And yes, I know that you're doing this partly so I'll buy you lots of bubble tea, but still. You're the best sister in the world (and also my only sister).

Thank you to my mom and dad, who nurtured and supported my love for reading and writing since I was a child. Who sent me to young writers programs and conferences. Who accompanied me to book events and festivals. Dad, you read me bedtime stories when I was a kid. You took me to libraries, where I lost myself in the stacks of books for hours. Mom, thank you for helping with the Chinese in *If I Have to Be Haunted* and telling me ghost stories when I asked. I am also quite sure that everyone who knows you knows about my book, so good luck to anyone who doesn't want to hear about it. I'm a storyteller because of you two.